Nightlight

(Book One of 'The Three' series)

Nicola Thomas

Copyright © 2023 Nicola Thomas

All rights reserved

The characters and events portrayed in this book are fictitious. Any similarity to real persons, living or dead, is coincidental and not intended by the author.

No part of this book may be reproduced, or stored in a retrieval system, or transmitted in any form or by any means, electronic, mechanical, photocopying, recording, or otherwise, without express written permission of the publisher.

Cover design by: Nicola Thomas using Canva

Acknowledgements

The author wishes to pass on her sincere thanks to all of the creators – writers, musicians, designers, artists, casts and crews – of all the amazing books, television shows, albums, comics, graphic novels; anything and everything that has helped inspire her and has been explicitly or implicitly referenced within this work.

All inaccuracies regarding geography are mostly intentional, and most word choices are quite deliberate.

She would also like to thank her family and friends (including the cats and dogs and rabbit).

And a massive thank you to everyone reading this.

To
My Nan

NIGHTLIGHT

Chapter 1

Even though Alice Andrews had been working at the Library for a couple of months now, she made an effort to truly look at the building at least once a week. Every time she did, it was like she noticed something new, some small change that enhanced its beautiful and somehow terrifying majesty, and she could only wonder at how much time and effort had gone into constructing such an impressive building. Indeed, it seemed almost impossible that such a building could exist in the real world; there was a power and otherworldliness to it that struck her as belonging to a fictional landscape where great magics, dragons and knights of an honourable realm would reside.

The Library of New York was several stories high and took up an entire block of its own. It was comprised of a huge planetary dome flanked by a triangle of towers, with a myriad of stained-glass murals depicting scenes of the continuing battle between Good and Evil; Light and Dark; from St George and the dragon, to Heracles and the Stymphalian birds, to unnamed figures in angelic and demonic forms. It was an imposing and impressive building that commanded the utmost respect.

Though few could attest to it, the Library had not always looked like this. The appearances of all six Libraries had shifted and changed over the courses of centuries and millennia, taking forms that would keep their contents safe, preserving life and artefacts of great cultural and supernatural significance. Although much of their origins and purpose had long been forgotten, there were certain scholars and entities that worked to preserve all that the Library in question stood for.

Although everything above ground maintained the appearance of a typically prestigious college library – with almost all such floors accessible to the general public – everything below was carefully guarded. Supernatural entities were granted free access to the first two sub-levels; special clearance allowed up to sub-level 4; beyond that, only the Guardians, Head Librarian and those with special dispensation were allowed to tread the hallowed halls of the Library's hidden vaults.

The foyer was equally impressive, albeit far more modern with several stands of paper maps and cultural leaflets, as well as several interactive tablets, to guide visitors to temporary displays or the correct section for the books they were after. There were a few self-service check-out machines, but as Alice had discovered on her first day, most people preferred to check books out at the front desk and it always lifted her spirits to hear that dull thump of rubber and ink against paper.

She strode quickly across the polished, marble floors and ducked through one of the few modern, heavy fire doors, and hung up her coat and bag on the allocated peg. She flicked on the kettle, made a cup of tea and sat down at the help desk, ignoring the pull of the OTS and its currently forbidden contents.

A brief smile crossed her lips as she thought about the handsome stranger she had noticed in the subway, a smile that was quickly replaced by a sad sigh and a puzzled frown, as she also remembered the disconcerting sensation she had felt before their eyes had momentarily met. She sighed again and mentally shook herself, forcing herself to concentrate on the tasks she was paid to do, little knowing that her isolation from the supernatural world was coming to an end from which there would be no return.

Chapter 2

Located on the ground floor, the Occult Testimonies Section (also known as the OTS) was one of the few rooms on the ground floor that was almost permanently locked. It was also one of the few rooms of supernatural texts that could be accessed by ungifted mortals, assuming they had – as any supernatural needed to have – permission from the Head Librarian. Despite being a witch herself, Alice had never been inside the OTS and had only ever seen the section opened once in her brief spell at the Library. Even then, the individual (whom she thought was also a witch) had been accompanied by Dr Anthonys himself and he had stayed inside with them until they had finished. She had asked once about going in, after noticing that the door was unlocked, but Julius had said no, and she had not enquired again.

The others had all looked fairly uncomfortable when she had asked them about it; Laura and Kate had told her that the OTS was haunted as whispering voices had told them to leave. Ethyl Jenkins and Clara Smith would cross themselves and say that "nothing good would come of that room". Stephen and Rupert said it was "weird and creepy".

On the day that Sam Harvelle-Walker come to the front desk with a special note of admittance to the OTS, Alice had once again been wondering what exactly was inside. Although she had not been using her magic any more frequently, she had felt a surge in supernatural energy, and was wondering if the OTS might have some answers. For the moment, she had a newsletter to proofread and database software to update that hopefully would not break the entire system. She also needed to wipe down and examine the returned books for waylaid and forgotten "bookmarks" before they could be placed back onto the shelves. She scanned the area around the front desk to ensure there was no one after her attention, and although her eyes lingered briefly on the stranger in the doorway, she returned to her tasks expecting no immediate interruptions.

The stranger, however, was paying much more attention to Alice.

"So that's Endora's granddaughter? Don't seem like much, does she?" said the old woman critically, frowning at Alice's lack of bearing and timid appearance. Even though she had lacked the arrogance normally displayed by her kind, Endora Price had still carried herself with the bearing of a true Witch, commanding the attention and respect of a room simply by entering it. To see a Price being barely visible was bordering on the unnatural.

Sam sighed and rolled his eyes. His great-grandmother had been rather too present of late. Especially for someone who had been dead for over fifty years. "I thought we'd decided there would be no talking in public?"

"The Library don't count and you know it."

"Well, I wish it did," muttered Sam, flinching slightly as the old woman clipped him round the back of the head. He looked at the Witch at the front desk, her supernatural energy flickering beneath the surface of a reasonably relaxed aura. She seemed to be in her own little world, clearly happy where she was. It was an unusual treat to see, not that he had seen anyone look unhappy working in the Library unless, perhaps, they had just been inside the OTS.

"Why's she working here? Bet she don't need to work with all that money her name brings."

"I thought Endora was your friend?" said Sam, making sure no one was paying any attention to him. He was fed up of people looking at him as though he was a crazy homeless man. Technically, he did not have a home, but he had his VW

Camper, and he was Psychic, not crazy, and such distinctions mattered.

"She was," Gisella Harvelle admitted, begrudgingly.

"And she looked out for me as best she could," Sam reminded her.

"I know. But it ain't natural seeing a Witch like that. And a Price... tut," Gisella observed disapprovingly.

"Not all of us follow the traditional routes of our gifts," said Sam, watching the spectacled brunette swivelling around in the large black office chair. Admittedly, it was rare to see a Witch with the potential of his or her powers so carefully concealed; Witches were rarely known for their modesty. He liked her.

"Don't be getting any ideas," said Gisella with a stern look. She was all too aware of her great-grandson's penchant for the ladies. She supposed it wasn't his fault, given that too many of his ancestral line had been promiscuous and wild during their lives, herself (begrudgingly) included. "She ain't right for you. And she's got darkness on her."

"Will you please go now?" Sam said, with an exasperated sigh.

"Fine. Still don't know why you think we need the books. Ain't nothing we ain't dealt with before."

Sam let out a growl-like sigh and the old woman glared at him before vanishing from his sight. He took a deep breath and gave a small, wry shake of his head. Much as he loved her, his great grandmother's Sight was not as flexible as it used to be – she saw only glimpses of absolutes rather than considering context and final outcomes. Yes, there was a darkness around Alice Andrews, but there was a lot more to her than that alone. He brushed his clothes, trying to rid himself of any visible untidiness and checked the faint reflection in the glass door. He was fairly confident he looked good, but it did not hurt to make sure.

"Excuse me?" Sam said, loudly but politely, as he

approached the desk.

"Good afternoon, how may I help you?" asked Alice brightly, turning around from the books she was moving from the returned pile to the appropriate trolleys.

"I need a babysitter," he said, returning the bright smile. The man in front of her made her think of a drummer in a metal band, with his scruffy confident demeanour, the jewellery and leather bands on his wrist. He had kind brown eyes and a wicked grin, and a kind of roguish appeal, even if he had the air of someone who was always on the move. He looked like he was in his mid-thirties. Something about him suggested that he was not yet a father; he certainly did not look harassed enough to have children. *If he needs a babysitter, it's probably to keep him out of trouble*, she thought with a smile.

"Why a babysitter?" she asked, one eyebrow raised, her curiosity piqued.

"I need to go into the OTS, and that usually requires a babysitter, although I think you guys prefer the term, "supervising librarian". I have got my permission slip." He slid a piece of paper across the desk, and after a cursory glance, she nodded and handed it back.

"We can do that. But, yeah, I don't think babysitter is the right word, given we're all way past the high-school age such a term suggests," Alice said, mentally face palming at her rambling.

"Some definitely more than others," said Sam mischievously, and Alice tried to try look disapprovingly, as their eyes met upon a shared glance over at Ethyl Jenkins, a sixty-something widow with shrewd green eyes, ash-blonde hair and a decidedly school-marm-ish demeanour. Mrs Jenkins looked at them, and as her eyes narrowed behind her large, dark-rimmed glasses, Sam and Alice looked at one other like guilty school children.

"If you could just give me a moment, Mr Harvelle-Walker...." Alice said, using her extremely polite voice.

"Dear gods, call me Sam," he interrupted, looking

horrified. He felt too young to be in that territory; it was bad enough when some of the street kids yelled 'Hey Mister' at him.

"I shall see if there is anyone around to supervise you in the OTS," Alice finished.

"Can't you do it?" asked Sam, deciding he would prefer Alice's company to that of Stuart or Julius. He would definitely prefer it to being watched suspiciously by Ethyl Jenkins, who was not overly fond of him for various reasons, only some of which were justified.

"I don't think so," Alice said. "Above my pay-grade," she whispered, conspiratorially. "Besides, only Dr Anthonys and Julius can open it, so I'll have to find one of them."

"I'd appreciate that, Miss Andrews. I'll just wait here," he said, leaning against one the marble columns, nonchalantly flicking through a movie magazine that he picked up off the periodicals display. Mrs Jenkins was giving him the evil eye, even as Sam cheerfully called over a "Hello Ethyl, how's things?".

Alice shot him a curious look as she left the desk, wondering how it was that he knew her surname; she was quite sure it was not on display anywhere. She walked briskly up the red carpeted stairs to Dr Anthony's office and knocked on the door. There was no reply, and Alice remembered that he was attending a seminar regarding 'inter-library lending, preparing for student influxes and signs of mental distress during mid-terms'. She would have to see if she could find Julius, wherever he might be.

"Stuart is not here today."

"Jeepers, Ju," said Alice, jumping in surprise, turning to face the man that had suddenly appeared behind her. It never failed to amaze her how a man of his size and stature could be so stealthy. "Where did you come from?"

"How precise would you like me to be?" Julius asked, slightly flustered, his dark face wrinkled with confusion.

"Er, doesn't matter," Alice replied, smiling gently. *Like the drink, only not spelled the same.* Some days, he really did make her think of John Coffey from *The Green Mile*. "It's just an expression people say when someone seems to appear out of thin air."

"Surely the air is always thin?" said Julius, the consternation on his face deepening.

Alice frowned slightly, wondering how best to explain that one. She decided not to go down that particular rabbit hole. "Don't worry about it Ju, it's just another expression. Anyway, there's a Sam Harvelle-Walker here to use the OTS. I was looking for Dr Anthonys for the key and to supervise; I'd forgotten he's not in today."

Julius looked down at the young Witch carefully. He could see that she was being affected by the spike in supernatural energies, but there was nothing that suggested anything had changed within her own powers. They were still buried deep, protected and hidden from most prying eyes and thieves, and Julius was convinced that Alice would not attempt to play with forces that she did not understand. He would also make sure that Sam behaved himself.

"You can use my key," said Julius, after a moment's consideration.

"I thought I wasn't supposed to go in there?" said Alice, trying to hide the slight glimmer of excitement.

"You will be okay. The others do not like the room, so they will not volunteer to do this task. I am dealing with something in the basement, so we must see how you do. Do not touch any of the books without gloves, and remain at the desk. In the light. As soon as Sam leaves, put the books away and lock up again. No lingering," Julius said, his tone even more solemn than normal. He took out a large collection of keys from the pocket of his grey slacks, and took off a slight, ornate key, which he then placed into Alice's hand.

"Okay," said Alice, looking at the key in the middle of her palm. There was a strange prickling sensation radiating from the strange iron key – it was cold, blackened with age, and adorned with a pentacle shaped bow. She picked it up by the stem feeling strangely drawn to the idea of looking at the Library through the holes of the bow, but she kept her eyes on Julius.

"Perhaps you should use these whilst handling the key," said Julius, unlocking Stuart's office and returning with a pair of latex gloves. "No food or drink in there. Promise me."

"I promise," said Alice, slightly bewildered, snapping on the gloves. When Julius reluctantly passed the key back, the prickling seemed to stop, or at least, was severely muted. "Should I lock the door whilst we're in there?"

"No," said Julius, sharply. "That would not be wise. I will post security outside."

"Okay," said Alice, suddenly feeling apprehensive. "Do you want to explain why I need to take all these measures?"

"Yes, but I must not."

"Okay," said Alice. She was intrigued and slightly concerned, but she could see that Julius was genuinely uncomfortable, and she wondered what or why it was he could not speak to her. She wondered if she should just ask if he knew that she was a witch. It would be a relief to talk to an actual person about it, especially given what she seemed aware of things that her co-workers were not. Or he might think she was mad. She was beginning to think it might not matter either one way, rather than trying to deal with everything on her own. Before she could say anything more, Julius dismissed her.

"You may accompany Sam to the OTS," he said, quietly.

"Okay," said Alice, walking back to the front desk with a mixture of relief and disappointment. She smiled as she approached Sam. He was handsome and a little taller than her, which were always attractive qualities, not that she could really imagine him being interested in her. "Looks like I'm babysitting you after all."

"Pay-rise?" Sam asked.

"Hmm, let's hope," she said with a returning grin.

"Nice gloves," he commented, noticing her blue hands.

"Yeah..." said Alice, looking at the latex on her fingers as she unlocked the OTS door. "I'm not sure if I'm supposed to get you a pair or not. I thought maybe it was to prevent oil transfer or something, but I'm not even supposed to touch the key." She hoped Sam would not notice quite how strange a sentence that must have been.

Sam looked at her carefully and the key she was holding up between her fingers. He could not tell how it was effecting her, but he could certainly sense the power of the object and the ghosts trapped within its grasp. It was certainly not an object he would be able to handle without severe headaches, and he was grateful that Stuart and Julius would keep it away from him. "I can wear some if it'll make you feel better, but I haven't needed to on my previous visits."

"You come here a lot?" asked Alice, glancing at him as she pushed open the door. Admittedly, she had not been there long, but she felt that she would have noticed him.

"Only if I have an unusual problem, which does seem to be a little more regularly of late," Sam replied, rubbing his temple. No matter how hard he tried to prepare for entering the OTS, it was always a little worse than he expected. He pushed the voices clamouring for attention and the energies of restless books to one side, and focused on the woman in front of him. He was relieved that a Witch would be in the OTS with him. Not only was it good to have the distraction of an attractive woman but the general integrity of her character was like a light in the darkness."If the books can't help, Stuart or Julius usually can."

"Sorry that you're stuck with me then," said Alice, her face creasing with worry as she shut the door behind them. She looked around the small, musty room and wondered if the rumours of its haunted nature were true after all. "I'm not as well-versed as they are. Do you know which texts you are after?"

"Yeah, although no alphabet or Dewey decimal system here; Stuart has a different system for Occult texts. Mainly because they have different... requirements. Hence, you contact him about your problem and he sends you back the permission slip and the numbers of the books he thinks will be of best use, which are... 487, 1089 and 6743f," he said, reading off the slip retrieved from his pocket.

"Okay," said Alice. "I'll be as quick as I can, but it's the first time I've been in here." She ducked under the bar and opened up the special storage cabinet of occult tomes. It had a strange smell of mustiness, burning and decaying flesh, and although she knew there was nothing in there – that nothing had been in there since the last time it was accessed – it felt like something was lurking within. *Maybe it's the books*, she thought, trying to make a joke of it, only to realise it was not an amusing or comforting thought. She used a finger to help scan the irrelevant numbers, choosing not to physically touch the spines.

"Really?" asked Sam, with some surprise.

"Yup. I'm not convinced Julius wants me to be in here now, he seems concerned for some reason," Alice said, surprised that she let the truth fall so easily from her lips; it was not something she would ever have said to Laura or Kate and she had known them for months. "You are scarily easy to talk to," said Alice, eventually identifying the necessary texts. She pulled one out all the way and the others just a little so that she might go back to each book; Julius' demand for cautiousness was infectious.

"I get that sometimes," Sam said, nonchalantly leaning against the librarian's desk. "It used to be handy when I was a musician – making sure we actually got paid for gigs in some of the backwater bars and the like. Calming down the men of the women my bandmates should not have slept with."

"How many times did you have to do it for yourself? I hear drummers are very popular," she teased, placing the last of the three on the desk. She placed them side by side, not allowing them to touch.

"Well, that's an interesting read, and I'm offended Miss

Andrews," he replied with a grin that let her know he was not. He piled the books on top of one another without a second thought.

"Because you weren't the drummer?" she asked sceptically.

Sam laughed, his long lean fingers suddenly tapping out a quick paradiddle on the side of the desk. "No, I was the drummer. But I did not sleep with anyone's other half, probably because I'm better at reading people and hopefully have a few more scruples."

"Ooo, scruples. I like," said Alice, nodding approvingly as she made a note in her head. "Sorry, I like words. Sometimes it sparks in my mind when people use ones that are not regularly circulated."

"Fair enough," said Sam with some amusement, but without mockery. His brown eyes twinkled charmingly at her. Alice felt like she could talk to Sam for hours, but she also had the feeling that he had more pressing concerns. "Well, good luck finding your answers," said Alice, reluctantly turning the conversation to an end.

"Thanks," replied Sam, with an apologetic smile. He did not particularly want to end the conversation either. Unfortunately, he was not at the Library to help her, but because the spirit he was going to be dealing with was proving immune to his usual suggestions.

Sam spent the day flicking through the books, scribbling the occasional note, and consulting some kind of dictionary that he would pull out of the faded khaki backpack by his feet. Alice looked up occasionally, but remained at the desk, re-reading Stephen King's *It*. She had hundreds of new books that she should probably read instead, but lately, she had been feeling a need for the familiar. As she read about the monster and its stalkings, using the fears of each Loser to manifest itself, she glanced uncomfortably over her shoulder and wondered if she should have picked a *Discworld* novel instead. She shook her head and gently cursed her overactive imagination, reminding herself that she was there to watch over Sam and help out if she could. If there was anything lurking in the dusty crevices of the locked cupboards, it would have to wait.

Chapter 3

For the next six days, Sam continued to present his note and Alice donned the blue gloves to let him into the room and access the books. Although she did not get the sense that she was in danger whilst inside the OTS, she could feel that there were some strong forces within the locked cabinets that would certainly take advantage of careless individuals if the chance presented itself.

Despite the fact that one of the silent guards now stood outside the OTS each day – presumably at Julius' request – Alice was still not quite sure that they were real, as no one else appeared to interact with them. The guards' appearances were quite uniform and ordinary, but there was at least one seemingly male guard that she had begun to recognise. On the second day of seeing him sit there, Alice had introduced herself and he had replied with the single word "Austin". She then tried talking to the others, but they would just blink wordlessly at her. Logic suggested that if they were hallucinations, then all would have offered a name or none would have, but it was a far from perfect solution to her concerns.

Whilst Alice could admit that the OTS was a little spooky, she did not understand why the others detested it so. It was quiet and poky, smelling of oak and lead, and bathed in low, artificial light. There were no windows and the left hand wall had been adapted to make three small reading cubicles with iron studded desks and green-headed lamps, whilst the back wall housed shelves of newer books on Witchcraft,

Ideology and other recent thoughts and explorations into the occult. There was a growing pile of journals relating to possession and demonic activity, and some periodicals focusing on aberrant behaviours in Nature. She had to admit that her curiosity was piqued, but Alice took her promises seriously, so she left what she could, alone.

However, on the seventh day, Alice felt that she had to re-evaluate the conditions of that promise. Sam had rushed out, seemingly as if he had found a solution, but Alice had been unconvinced. Maybe it was a Witch thing, but somehow she knew Sam needed more help than the Library could provide. She sighed unhappily; she wanted to honour her word to Julius, but she was concerned about Sam. She was aware that she was already stretching it by lingering, but she had concluded that her promise was made regarding food and drink, and she was just having a hard time moving with speed.

"I can't see you, but I'm pretty sure you're there and that you came in with Sam. I don't know for sure that I can, but if you would give me some idea what he's dealing with, then I can at least try to help him."

Nothing happened, and after a few moments, she chided herself for thinking that there was some guardian spirit watching over him. Alice looked at the book still in a dilemma, but the more she thought about it, the more it seemed wrong not to try and help. She sighed again and sat down in Sam's vacant chair. Before she could touch it, the book in front of her suddenly slammed shut. One to her left flipped open, and the pages rustled and flicked, until the movement finally stopped.

Her blue hands reached over and carefully looked at the open book. Like the other three, it was an old leather tome, filled with brittle, yellowed pages, written in what was probably Latin. Alice was never particular sure about the languages used in occult texts. Although she could not speak anything other than English, bad English and American, (with the rudiments of high-school French and German somewhere in the recesses of her brain), if the text was about the genuine supernatural and witchcraft, then she could read it. It was like having an automatic translator – no matter what the language was, the words would shift into English after a short while.

Although she had refrained from looking too closely at any of the books, she knew that Sam had been investigating ancient spirits, powerful magics and demonic presences. Even with the gloves, these tomes – and this one in particular – gave off an energy that left a bitter aftertaste of evil that stuck to her gloves like an ashy residue.

Using a wooden lollipop stick, Alice scanned the words quickly, having to summon more willpower than she knew she had, not to read every single word. She was certainly interested, but reading carefully was definitely breaking her promise. There was also the fact that occasionally whilst concentrating, Alice knew she had a tendency to mutter aloud, and that was likely to be very dangerous as a Witch in a room full of occult texts – even the least capable of practitioners knew that you never spoke Latin in front of supernatural books.

From what she could tell, Alice deduced that Sam was dealing with a particularly malevolent poltergeist, possibly a Baa'll, that was more dangerous for having absorbed demonic energy as it had passed through the Veil. Whilst Alice was unsure with how much stock to place in the notions of Heaven and Hell, or Angels and Demons, she was sure that there were different planes of existence and that sometimes, the fabric separating them became slightly worn or frayed, allowing things to slip through. She frowned and carefully locked each book away again before she turned her attention back to the spirit, unable to properly concentrate on the Baa'll until she had asked it something.

"Why didn't you just tell him?" Alice asked, placing a pen and a piece of paper at the other side of the librarian's desk. She knew Sam was not a witch, but she did not believe it was because *she* was a witch that the spirit could communicate to her.

She watched, reading upside down as the pen wrote in carefully formed block capital letters.

HE AIN'T LISTNING PROPERLY

"Why not Swayze the book like you did for me?" said Alice, forgetting that not everyone would get the *Ghost* or *Supernatural* reference.

WON'T LET ME. WE HAVE AN UNDERSTANING

"Figures," Alice muttered, more to herself than whoever she was talking to.

MEN

Alice smirked. "I know, right? Thank you," she said, taking back the pen and the paper.
She quickly exited the room, locked the door and absent-mindedly thanked Austin for standing guard, trying to remember if she had all the necessary ingredients for a banishment at home. As a precaution, she popped into a New Age Wiccan shop that was down one of the side streets near the station to stock up on unprocessed wax and sage. She had a quick look at the other goods, but it was mainly incense, scarves and holistic aids. The witch at the till gave her a strange look, and Alice felt slightly uncomfortable as she placed her items on the counter.

"Cleansing a rather large house," she lied, quietly.

"Me and this other powerful Witch I know do cleansings. We don't charge much," the witch said, looking down at her with unveiled contempt. The till was elevated; the witch sitting on a high stool behind it, painting her nails in a bored fashion. Given the level of customer service, Alice was unsurprised the shop was otherwise empty.
I, Alice silently corrected in her head *This powerful Witch and I*. She also bit her tongue regarding her own assessment of the

witch's talents. "Thanks, but I'm pretty sure I can handle it."

"Well, best take this just in case it goes wrong," said the witch, pushing a business card across the counter. "It can be really frustrating for the spirits if amateurs mess these things up."

Alice took the card, thinking it should at least get recycled – *it would certainly be good for compost given the amount of bullshit it proclaims* – and noticed the silver, the calf's leather and a slightly shimmering black crystal on the shelves behind the custodian. Given the price tag next to it, the witch running the shop had no idea that it was an extremely rich and potent lump of tourmaline.

"I'll also take the silver, leather and that... black rock, please," said Alice, playing up to the witch's low opinion of her.

"Black onyx is no good for a cleansing," said the witch looking at her in disgust and pity.

Very true, but that's not black onyx that you are seriously overcharging for, and I don't want it for the cleansing per se. "I know, I have a friend that needs a confidence boost," Alice lied again.

"Sure, "a friend"," the witch said mockingly with a smirk. She added the items to the total and handed them to Alice to put in her bag.

Alice fought the urge to turn the bottled blonde into a toad. She had no idea if it was actually possible – she had not encountered such a spell so far – but she almost felt willing to make the exception and try; after all, spells had to start somewhere. Luckily for the witch, Alice was too unconfident and too polite, so she merely handed over the money, said "Thanks" and hurried home.

Alice had never been much of a practitioner when it came to magic – most of what she did just seemed to happen, such as the auto-translate and the occasional freak weather incident – but she did have a basic understanding and her grandmother's craft-book. Having been discouraged from using her powers and also threatened by nuns at boarding school, Alice had consequently decided not to use her powers all the time and rarely used for her own gain. She did not know if she had the ability to help Sam with his problem, especially as she could not be certain that he was dealing with an empowered poltergeist, but magic was in her blood, and she felt compelled to try and help if it was at all possible.

She prepared several types of candles, several smudging sticks of sage, and a special jar of white salt, along with the phonetic translations of several incantations and a specially crafted protection pendant. Writing it out had been the worst part; it was unnatural to her to increase the size of her writing and print each word carefully, but she had been made painfully aware that her natural script was slightly illegible and that could certainly cause problems when it came to using spells. Alice was pretty certain that she had done it all correctly, but she double-checked with her grandmother's craft book just in case. Then, she put the contents into a black gift-bag, and first thing in the morning, left it by the sign-in/out book. If Sam came back and requested the same books, he would see the bag when he signed out; if he did not, then she was ready if she ever came across anyone else dealing with a poltergeist.

Chapter 4

There was a strange little ping and Lady Jane pushed her spent lovers to one side. Whilst she was very aware of where she was and the company she currently had littering the apartment, she was momentarily confused by the High Magic alert. She climbed over the body of one of the males beside her, ignoring his look of disappointment and anger as she shook off his attempt to embrace her.

"Come on, mi'lady," he said mockingly with a smirk.

Lady Jane picked up the dagger from one of her discarded stiletto boots and held it against his throat, watching as genuine fear crossed the large, muscular man's face. There was nothing in her cold, dead eyes that suggested that she would not use it. Rather, the amusement lurking there practically begged him to give her a reason.

"You should probably wake your friends and clear out. I'm not in the mood for company."

"Yeah, sure," he said, unable to hold her stare.

She pushed herself off the bed and walked naked across the open-plan penthouse. Only two rooms were walled off and separated by doors. One was the huge, luxurious bathroom, and the other was one that mere mortals never set eyes upon, unless she was planning on slaughtering them. She closed the runed African Blackwood door and smiled, basking in the comfort of blood and black magic. The five strangers would be gone by the time she reopened it, or she would use them to replenish her pantry.

There were three tables in her reliquary. The central one

was a dark alter, adorned with skulls, bones and body parts, black candles and an exquisite chalice filled with blood. The second, to her left, had been laid with a darkly woven cloth, imbued with dark magic that naturally enhanced her own particular skill set.

It was where she carefully cleaned, maintained and made her weapons, adapting them as necessary for her prey. Jars of silver nitrate, dead man's blood, deadly nightshade, digitalis, wormwort, wolf's bane, cardelium extract and several other varieties of poison and neurotoxins lined the shelves alongside cages of rats, mice, small birds and toads. There was also a jar of spiders, although Lady Jane had some reservations about their presence; there was a magic to spiders that she did not entirely trust.

It was the third table to which she turned her attention. The back wall was covered with photographs, maps and notes; lists of seemingly innocuous details and a map with several circles and brightly coloured lines. There were locks of hair and fur, a stolen scarf and several inaccurate building blueprints.

She was not expecting the ping to mean much; chances were that it was another failed attempt of Coven acolytes trying to complete spells from the Book of the First or some other ancient rite, but one of the reasons she was the best, was that she took nothing for granted.

There was a small fridge situated between tables one and three, and she shook one of the jars of blood as she lifted it, swirling it roughly to disturb any sediments or congealing viscera, given that she had not been particularly choosy about where the blood was obtained so long as it was fresh at the time. She poured it over the dark quartz crystal ball and waited for either the image to appear inside or a small grey wisp to make its mark on the map. The ball remained inscrutable as it spat out the tiny wisp. It danced across the streets before landing confidently in a rather unexpected place. Annoyingly, even the wisp could not pinpoint the exact location, but it was in the vicinity of where Lady Jane knew the Witch resided.

"Well, well, well," murmured Lady Jane with a begrudging admiration. "Turns out our nerdy little squib is not such a squib after all."

She turned to the dark alter and sliced open her palm with an intricately, runed blade. She squeezed her blood into the stagnant pool already in the ornate goblet, waiting for it to simmer and scream. Her master would be most pleased with this news.

Chapter 5

The door to the Head Librarian's second office was open, and Sam was hit by the emanating waves of warmth and the smell of herbs. After the stress of the past two weeks, it was a welcomingly familiar experience. Luckily, the sense of coming home was stronger than any other memory that might be triggered by the scent of sage; a smell that he was regularly exposed to as an added line of defence against any spirits that might be interested in more than just passing on a message.

"Hey Doc," said Sam, knocking on the door frame. He waited until Dr Anthonys had acknowledged his presence before entering. He glanced around the room, glad that it only seemed to change with the addition of more books and papers.

"Sam," said Stuart Anthonys with a smile of relief, looking up from the yellowed pages of a large and ancient leather bound book. He put down the magnifying glass and motioned for his visitor to sit down in one of the chairs on the opposite side of his large oak desk. He returned his spectacles to his nose, and smiled again, observing that Sam was no worse for wear after his three-day excursion. "Come on in; we've been worried about you. Did you get it sorted? I was concerned that those books weren't going to help."

"They didn't really. Maybe before, but not this time. Luckily, someone left me this." Sam held up a black gift-bag before handing over an unsigned card.

"Interesting," Stuart said, looking at the carefully printed blue ink before returning the card. "Who is it from?"

"Come on Doc," said Sam with a grin. "I don't think you

need to be clairvoyant to work that out."

Sam was a genuine Psychic. He could not predict the winning lottery numbers, given that the future was largely unwritten and shifting, but he could get glimpses. He could certainly see into the pasts of items and people if they were inclined to share, and he could also know a lot more about a person than they might ever tell another living soul from the briefest of encounters. Sam could also communicate with spirits and ghosts, assuming they felt like talking. Or in the case of some, like his great-grandmother, if he felt like listening.

"Alice Andrews."

Sam nodded. He then took an amulet from around his neck and showed it to the Librarian.

"This was in the bag?" Stuart said with some surprise, taking the proffered trinket and turning it over in his hand. He lifted his glasses onto his forehead and examined the necklace carefully. He had never seen such an amulet before, and certainly not one in such pristine condition. Anything similar that he had come across was tarnished with age, having been handed down through generations from a time when the world was younger and a Witch's magic was far stronger. In these modern times, it was rare to find a truly powerful Witch and even rarer to find one that had undertaken the years of study and practice needed to hone his, her or their 'Craft to the levels of High Magic.

He picked up the magnifying glass and looked at the charm more carefully. It was made from silver and black tourmaline, which demonstrated that the maker knew the best materials for protection against spirits, evil beings, curses and potentially even dark magic. The intricacy of the design was what truly made the amulet extraordinary. Like any artistic practice, there were nuances that made a universal symbol personal, and this triquetra had some beautifully intricate flourishes that appeared to depict runes and leaves. It was undoubtedly a rare example of High Magic, and as such, a very generous gift to bestow upon a relative stranger.

"It was handmade within the past week," said Sam.

"No," Stuart said, looking up in surprise, unable to believe that the young woman upstairs could be capable of such magic. In fact, as none of the Witches that had come into the Library had taken any notice of her, he had been wondering if Julius had overestimated Miss Andrews' powers.

"Oh, it was," Sam assured him. "I wouldn't normally touch something like this because they're usually weighted with ghosts and lingering horrors."

There was a pause, and the Librarian pursed his lips doubtfully. He knew that Sam was very gifted and that even the weakest of Psychics would avoid touching an artefact like the pendant for fear of the nightmares they would experience – reliving the echo of past terrors and pains that such an amulet would have been used to protect against. All the same, it was hard to believe that it had been made so recently and by one so inexperienced. He did what any uncomfortable individual would do, and changed the direction of the conversation. "Have you said anything to her?" he asked, returning the charm to Sam and his glasses to his nose.

"Not yet. I wish I had more time to talk to her, to be honest. We're still going to be good friends though."

"I hope that's all," said Stuart with a slight frown. Sam had already caused a couple of temporary assistants to leave after breaking their hearts. It was one of the reasons why Ethyl complained about Sam, not least because one of those temps had been her grand-niece.

"She is not interested in me as anything other than a friend. She has her eye on someone else," Sam said calmly. "Although, that's not to say I wouldn't if she offered."

Stuart rolled his eyes and chose to ignore Sam's teasing. "But she gave you the bag?"

"No. She left it at the front desk," said Sam, tying the amulet back around his neck, where it blended in with the metal-inspired jewellery and family trinkets.

"I don't remember anything being left at the front desk

for you," said Stuart. It was admittedly rare that he spent much time in the public sector of the Library, but a gift bag like that would raise questions.

"Because it was left for *me;* no one else could see it."

"That's not possible," Stuart said dismissively.

"She left a conditional spell on the bag; I didn't see it when I came in, but I could when I left. Can't say I wasn't surprised," said Sam, unable to keep the admiration out of his voice. He pulled one leg up across the other, and absent-mindedly began drumming on the black denim, just above the top of his heavy, black boots.

"That's very troubling," said Stuart, frowning. Such deceptions were not supposed to happen in the Library.

"Not really," Sam assured him. "I think even if the Guardians didn't detect it – which is definitely something – the Library would have stepped in if there was anything to worry about. Or Julius. What's troubling, is that she has no idea."

"What do you mean?" Stuart asked sharply, staring at Sam intently.

"She has no idea about any of it. Subconsciously, she accepts it all, but she doesn't know. About the Library, the Guardians, supernaturals... Any of it. She barely knows anything beyond the fact that she's a witch, and she certainly has no clue just how powerful a Witch she is, let alone what she could be." Sam shrugged. "I know the Library isn't supposed to interfere or pick sides, but as far as her powers and the supernatural world is concerned, I think it's far better for us all if she can stay here and learn from you."

"You like her," Stuart said, unable to agree with Sam's assessment. He felt sure that Sam was exaggerating about Alice's lack of knowledge. After all, if she had made the pendant, she had to have had some extremely good teachers to have learned such a design and probably a historically powerful bloodline.

"So do you. And Julius. And the Library. We all feel like she's one of the good ones, and I don't think that will change if she has the right people around her."

"Are we the right people for her?" Stuart queried.

"I might not be." Sam grinned. "But she likes it here and being comfortable is important for her. I don't think she would fit in anywhere else, even if a coven did decide to pick her up now."

"She doesn't have a coven?"

"You really haven't spoken to her about her being a Witch?" asked Sam with some surprise, his face creasing with concern.

"Julius implied that it would be meddling to mention it before she brought it up herself, and you know…"

"…we're not allowed to meddle," Sam finished in a mocking, sing-song tone, rolling his eyes.

"Rules are rules," Stuart said, sharply with a disapproving glare.

"They're stupid rules and you know it. They're probably Church rules, not Library rules, and if they're from the Fallen, well, you already know how many problems that would throw up!" Sam knew that it was futile to push the point – it was a conversation they had had many times before over the course of their friendship – but it nonetheless irritated him. He let his annoyance out with a sigh and a slightly exasperated throw of his hands. "Whatever. You or Julius need to talk to her, because she currently thinks she's hallucinating the Guardians, and the books talking to her, and goodness knows what else, poor kid."

Stuart looked at him, still unconvinced. Sam shrugged and stood up to leave – you could lead a horse to water but you could not make it drink.

"You should go and have a word with her," said Stuart, still mulling over this new information regarding the witch, or Witch, upstairs. He stood up and briefly shook Sam's hand, not wanting to trigger Sam's Sight. "She's been worried about you. As were we all."

"I planned to and as I said, she's a sweet kid," said Sam, adding after a moment's thought "Even though we're probably about the same age." He paused for a moment. "Talk to Alice, okay? The sooner, the better. By the way, can I call you Ju like she does?" he asked, eyes twinkling as he turned to Julius, who had suddenly appeared in the doorway.

"No." The large black man remained completely impassive.

"OK." Sam laughed. "See you soon, Doc. Gotta go down south for a while. Take care."

"One day, you're going to have to stop running, Sam," said Stuart, with a rueful shake of his salt-and-peppered head.

"One day," Sam agreed, giving him a wry smile before closing the door.

Stuart shook his head again, and turned his attention to the man everyone assumed was his next-in-command. "Julius."

"Stuart." Julius sat down in the chair that Sam had just vacated.

"Why didn't you tell me about the bag?"

"I wanted to see if anyone would report it. They did not." Julius' deep, calm, rumbling voice did not betray any emotional inflection.

"You don't find that troubling?" Stuart asked, beginning to pace. It was not an easy task to accomplish, given that there were far too many papers and books on the floor. It was also unlikely that the motions would have the impact of underlining his concerns, given that Julius did not recognise many non-verbal cues.

"No."

"You do not think it is a concern that we have a Witch capable of High Magic, up in the library?" Stuart pressed, looking at Julius with great consternation.

"No."

Blood from a stone, Stuart Anthonys thought, shaking his head and pinching the bridge of his nose. *Blood from a stone*. Strictly speaking, Julius was far more important than he was, but there were occasions where he felt that as the Head Librarian he should be in-charge. "No one in the service of the Library is supposed to meddle. This seems awfully close to meddling."

"It isn't," said Julius. "All we did was give her a place to work."

"Hmm." The Head Librarian frowned sternly, unconvinced. He fixed Julius with a probing look. "Why *did* you bring her here?"

"It was the right thing to do," Julius replied without hesitation, and Stuart knew there was nothing more Julius would say on the subject.

***

Alice was supposed to be putting the returned books onto the shelves now that her lunch break was over, but she was worried about Sam. The library was still quiet; Mrs Jenkins and Laura had yet to return to the front desk, so she sat down at one of the computers. *Permission or forgiveness?* She mused silently, staring at the monitor and the empty password box that opened when she pulled up the personal contact information file. One hand pulled worriedly at her lip, the other hovered over the mouse.

"Neither," a Brooklyn-accented male voice said.
She looked up, startled, and then smiled as she looked up at Sam. "I am so glad you're OK... not dead at least," she said, a great deal of relief in her voice.
Sam grinned. Strictly speaking, he knew Alice would worry about him, but he did occasionally get things wrong. "Definitely not dead, definitely OK now," said Sam, with some seriousness.

"I didn't realise your situation was so bad," said Alice, with a concerned frown.

"Neither did I. That little kit you left me genuinely saved some lives. So, I needed to say 'thank you'... and reassure you in case you were worried."
Alice felt slightly embarrassed; she was not good at accepting

compliments or believing that anything she could do would make a difference. "You looked like you needed help and I just hoped that I knew enough that it could be of use. I'm just glad it was." She held out her hand. "I'm Alice, Alice Andrews, by the way. I know we saw each other every day for a week, but I don't feel like we've been properly introduced, so..."

Sam smiled, and interrupted her. "Sam Harvelle-Walker. If you ever need a Psychic or a friend, you now have me."

An electric shock passed through them as their hands touched. Sam tried to hide a sudden stab of pain and concern as he was hit with the sudden certainty that the Darkness was growing and it was very interested in Alice and those that knew, and would know, her. It was not a proper vision – those played out like short films, usually filled with detail and lasting several minutes, rendering him completely unconscious – but it was definitely some kind of warning. He tried to simply smile back at the beaming Witch in front of him. Luckily, it appeared that Alice had not noticed his twinge of discomfort, or if she had, had assumed it was due to the electrical current.

"Sorry. That seems to happen when I find a genuine friend," said Alice, pleased, moving more books onto her trolley. "Could be a coincidence, but I like the idea that it's a sign of a true friendship formed. Never really had too many of those."

"You'll find them," Sam said, feigning more brightness than he currently felt. He paused for a moment, his brain quickly going over all that it had just seen. "And you could always try online dating," he added casually.

"Online dating? You think?" she said, eye-brow raised and lips curled sceptically.

Sam smiled cryptically and shrugged his broad shoulders in a way that suggested it was *definitely* worth a shot.

"OK, maybe I will," said Alice, not entirely convinced.

"If you end up getting married because of this, I want an invite."

"That seems a tad unlikely, but of course." She laughed,

and scribbled down her name, number and address on a piece of paper, and exchanged it for his business card. "Psychic?" she questioned with a raised eyebrow.

"It's a family business," Sam said. He could not help but grin at the scepticism in her eyes.

"Well, I guess if I'm going to take dating advice from someone, it might as well be a psychic." Alice shrugged, and smiled. "Try and drop in if you get back to the city before my wedding."

"And here's me thinking you were a Witch, not a Psychic."

Alice looked startled, her brown eyes filling with fear, as she furtively looked around to see if anyone had heard him. She wheeled out the trolley and stood next him, looking around again, before whispering "You know I'm a Witch?"

"Of course," said Sam, kindly. "I'm a Psychic. And you definitely shouldn't worry so much. You know on some level that there's a lot more than just humans and Witches, otherwise you wouldn't have made this for me." He pulled out the amulet. "I swear to you, being a Witch is just a small part of this weird and crazy world, and as long as you trust who you're talking to, you can stop feeling like you're going insane. Cross my heart." Sam sighed. "I'm sorry that I have to leave town so quickly, but I have a friend that needs my help."

"I understand. Message me or something so I know you're... not dead at least?" she asked, silently correcting that to who.

"I promise," he said, drawing a cross over his heart. "Thanks again, Alice." He gave her a quick hug; the visions tended not to appear when there was little to no skin-to-skin contact. "And no, you are not hallucinating the Guardians; Austin is real."

Alice shot him another look of surprise and relief and watched him leave, feeling sad that the first real friend she had made since moving to America was going out of state. She gave him a final wave as he raised a hand at the door, and she glumly returned to work. She was pretty sure that she would see him again though. She pushed the trolley up the ramps to the second floor, and began to replenish the crime section, too deep in thought to hear the approaching footsteps.

"Alice?" said Laura, cautiously.

Kate, Laura and Alice were all in their early to mid-thirties, however, Laura and Kate had been working at the library for several years, alongside Ethyl Jenkins and Rupert Travers, after getting degrees in Library Sciences. Kate was a slightly serious, but very bubbly, homebody type of woman; Laura was a likeable, free-spirit, who was very passionate about supporting different causes. Whatever Laura's current project was, her hair was now bright purple.

Given the slightly tentative tone, Alice was pretty sure that Laura had not sought her out for a casual chat whilst they worked. "Yes?"

"Dr Anthonys wants to see you in his office."

Ah balls. "OK, I'll just er, move this trolley." She waited until she could see Laura was back at the front desk, before heading towards the little dip of stairs leading from the second floor of library books and the second floor office.

"Not that one," said Julius, appearing from seemingly nowhere.

"Ye gods Ju!" Alice gasped, giving a head-shake of disbelief, concurrently amazed that she had refrained from swearing. *How on earth does a man that big move without a sound?* "You'll give someone a heart attack one day if you keep sneaking up on people like that."

"I will work on making sure that does not happen," Julius said in his deep, comforting voice. He began to lead her towards the Head Librarian's other office.

"Right. So, where are we going?" There had been rumours of another office and although it was clearly one of the more plausible stories circulating between the library staff, it was – up until now at least – just a story.

"Sub-level 4."

"How many sub-levels are there?" she asked, almost running to keep up with him. With the second office becoming a reality, Alice really hoped the orang-utan existed too.

"A lot."

Julius was as mysterious as the day she had bumped into him. He had reinforced her first impressions; he was a genuine gentle giant, extremely intelligent, but seemingly clueless about human nature and somewhat lacking in conversational skills. He was tall and muscular, and Alice reckoned he was in his fifties, since he looked older than her, but not as old as Dr Anthonys, who she knew was in his early sixties. Still, on the rare occasions where she really saw Julius' eyes, she felt like he was older than the world itself. Regardless, Alice liked, respected and admired him, and she was grateful that he had gotten her into the library, even if it ended up being for so short a time.

"Julius?" she ventured, timidly.

"Yes?" Julius replied, looking down at her.

"I just wanted to say thank you for all of this, and if I'm fired, I'm sorry if I've disappointed you."

"You haven't," he said simply, before leaving her outside of the Head Librarian office in the dimly lit halls of sub-level 4.

She stared after him in surprise and shook her head in mild disbelief. It probably should not, but there were still times when Julius' behaviour baffled her. "Hmm, reassuring, not," she muttered as Julius moved out of earshot. Did that mean she was not getting fired, or that Julius just was not disappointed in her if she was to be fired? She rolled her eyes and cursed herself for overthinking.

Alice pushed up her glasses, took a deep breath and tried to prepare herself for the worst. She knocked at the wooden door with its ornate, bronze 'Head Librarian' placard, and only entered after hearing the customary "Come in".

Chapter 6

The Witch and the Head Librarian had spent very little time together. There had been the brief, slightly awkward interview that had taken place after Julius' insistence and although some basic opinions had been formed, very little knowledge had arisen in the following months.

Stuart's impression of Alice had been that there was something vaguely familiar about her features, and that despite the definite suggestion of magic about her, she was not a particularly powerful witch. He had assumed that this lack of power was the reason she had not used the name of her coven to demand a position in the Library.

She was almost stereotypically English with her quiet reservation, politeness and penchant for tea; she spoke with a distinctly educated Queen's English that the Americans often associated with the likes of Hugh Grant and Helen Mirren, which often reminded him of his previous life in London. She answered all of his questions with consideration and intelligence, and he had felt no great reservations about taking her on in a temporary capacity. She had proven to be a hard-worker, enthusiastic and popular with the visitors, but no greater endorsement of her acceptance was than that of the Library itself. It had embraced her – quirks, magic and all – in a manner that Stuart had rarely seen, choosing to subtly help her more than it had with any other Novice, Trainee, volunteer, staff member or visitor.

From the other side of the very plain and lacklustre desk, Alice had felt that Dr Anthonys was a good man, weighted down with a sorrow and responsibility that seemed to be beyond his years. He was a good-looking older gentleman with a large, honest face and she had been unsurprised to notice more than a few female visitors of varying ages giving him more than a second glance. He was intelligent, slightly uptight and stuffy, but also seemed to genuinely listen to and care for his staff. She had been taken aback by how sparse and impersonal the office had been – no photographs, no pictures, no strange curios or mementoes – just a tidy little desk, filing cabinet, three chairs, a plain wall clock and a rubber plant.

Very early on, Alice had observed that Dr Anthonys spent very little time in the office, although he was always there whenever visitors were expected. It was therefore unsurprising to hear that the others had theories and stories of secret offices and hidden alcoves, along with rumours of underground passages, buried treasures, ghosts, goblins and cursed artefacts. She supposed as a Witch, she should take some of those stories more seriously, but her life seemed so separate from the world of magic, that she approached it all with the healthy scepticism of someone that wanted to believe, but did not have the faith to do so. All evidence considered, a second office seemed practically guaranteed.

It was a sizeable room, but more like a well-loved library in a country estate than an office. There were hundreds of papers stacked into gravity defying piles in front of shelves that housed hundreds of books and occult paraphernalia, that ranged from a raven perched on a skull, to talismans, tapestries and herbs. There was a large, open fireplace; two big armchairs with an ornate table set between them, and a more practical swivel chair behind the large oak desk, that was cluttered with a couple of lamps, a basic PC and a further hundred papers, some writing implements and a lot of books. It was warm and comforting, smelling of oak, sage, lavender and old books. As offices went, it was definitely the kind that Alice could aspire to. It was also far more in-keeping with her view of the Library and Dr Anthonys than the one upstairs.

"Miss Andrews." Stuart stood up and motioned to the comfortable chair that Sam and Julius had recently been sat in.

Alice felt that Dr Anthonys' tone and gaze were not quite so comforting. "Sir," she replied, trying not to stare at the random little things that were trying to catch her eye as she crossed the pentacle-patterned rug and sat stiffly in the padded leather chair. She could have sworn the raven wanted to tell her something, but she refused to go down that route again.

"I, well… Are you happy working here, Miss Andrews?" he asked awkwardly, not entirely sure how to broach the subject of the amulet, as he sat behind the overburdened desk. Despite all the clutter, there were few personal items beyond the mug, pens and the magnifying glass; only the backs of two photograph frames that peeked up behind a pile of papers suggested that he might have a life beyond the library.

"Very much so," Alice said, slightly puzzled. "Er, why? Have there been complaints?"

"Oh no, not at all. You've been doing a marvellous job. But er, there are certain rules that are important to the neutrality and integrity of the Library… That is to say," he said, noticing Alice's ever-growing expression of bewilderment "It is not the Library's policy to "meddle" in the affairs of others."

"Is this about Sam?" she asked after a moment.

"Yes," Dr Anthonys confirmed, his grey eyes fixed firmly upon her face, watching as the colour rose indignantly in her cheeks.

Alice swallowed hard, and tried to hold his gaze as she spoke. "The actions were entirely my own; not the Library's. I saw someone that appeared to need help. I made an educated guess, believed I was in a position that might provide some aid, and so I tried. To help. It happened to help, it might not have, but I had to try…" She could tell she was waffling and fell silent, not quite knowing why she felt so defensive in the first place.

"Why?"

"Why?" repeated Alice, looking puzzled. "Well, because it's the right thing to do. Surely anyone…"

"No, Miss Andrews, not "anyone would have" at all," Stuart said, interrupting sharply. "Most in fact, would not. Especially one that was in the employ of a Library where there are strict rules."

"Well, I'm sorry if my actions are an affront to the library or the Library, but I'm not sorry that I tried to help Sam, and if it happened again, I would do exactly the same thing," Alice said, feeling defiant and slightly proud of herself. For a moment, Alice held her head up high as she looked the Head Librarian in the eye, before returning to her natural inclination of looking at the floor. She thought about continuing her argument with the fact that she had never been told such a stupid rule, but decided she had probably said enough. Particularly if the expression on Dr Anthonys' face was anything to go by.

Stuart let out a long breath, looked down at his papers for a moment and then back to the Witch nervously sitting across from him. He was not entirely sure that he was making the right decision, but he could feel a barely perceptible presence guiding him. "I'm promoting to you to novice Librarian. You will receive a small pay increase, and you now have access down to sub-level 6 until such time as the Library seems fit to increase or revoke your clearance."

"Pardon?" Alice said, looking up in surprise.

"You are being promoted, not fired as you perhaps feared. You will learn a lot of very interesting things over the course of your new position, and frankly, very few who are not born into this way of life have what it takes to progress past the public floors. I believe this position will not only be of great benefit to the Library, but to you as well."

"Oh," she said, still slightly stunned. "Thank you."

"Before you return to your duties, Miss… May I call you Alice? And you don't need to keep calling me sir, although I appreciate the show of respect."

"Of course."

"Just a couple of things, you are a witch, are you not? A

born witch, I mean?" the Head Librarian asked, watching her reactions carefully.

"Yes," said Alice, trying to hide her surprise. She had not realised that Dr Anthonys was aware that there were individuals who were born with witchcraft in their blood, and those that acquired skill from practising such traditions as Wicca. She certainly had not realised that it was obvious to him that she was a witch. She supposed she should have known though, given the nature of the OTS and its visitors. And the Guardians, although she was still coming to terms with the fact that they were not just in her head. All the same, it was a relief.

"I take it you've noticed the books, and that we seem to have two kinds of people working here?"

"I believe so," Alice replied with a touch of uncertainty. She supposed he meant that maybe not everyone could see the Guardians, which would explain why no one else tried to speak to them, now that she knew they were real.

"I'm sure you can imagine why that is, given your nature and the fact that there is the library that anyone can access and the Library which most can not. You are in rather a unique position of having a foot in both worlds. I trust you can keep the two separate."

"Yes, sir." Alice said, although she was not entirely sure she understood everything he was saying. Her face scrunched up with thought, Alice got up to leave. She was at the doorway, when he called out to her.

"Oh, one last thing," Dr Anthonys said, waiting until she was facing him again before continuing. "Why did you not sign your name in the card you left for Sam? He showed it to me before he went to see you."

"I didn't think it mattered," Alice said simply, holding on to the door frame.

"You're a curious creature, Alice Andrews," Dr Anthonys said, looking at her appraisingly, before taking off his spectacles and peering down at the text on the desk through his silver-handled magnifying glass. "Keep up the good work."

Chapter 7

Even with the subway journey, walk and a quick call into the shop for milk, Alice's head was still reeling with disbelief as she entered her apartment. She turned off her iPod, hung her coat on by the door (along with the black woollen hat, gloves and matching scarf), took off her ankle boots and filled the kettle, before heading to the airing cupboard.

"Sam's okay," she told Onion, lifting him off the fleece-blanket she had placed on top of the towels. She was always amazed that he actually used it instead of the towels, but she could not deny that he might simply move onto it when he heard her entering the flat. Onion liked to play dumb when it suited him, but she was well aware of how intelligent he truly was.

"Sam?" the cat asked, yawning as she carried him to the kitchen bar.

"The guy I made the Poltergeist-Be-Gone bag for. He came in today – said it worked." She put Onion on a stool and he stretched, refraining from putting his claws into the padded leather when he caught Alice's warning look.

"Why wouldn't it?" asked Onion. "You can be a competent Witch when you want to use your powers." Onion's voice was like that of a very reserved, well-bred, middle-aged Englishman, and at times like these, he reminded her of Alan Rickman's Professor Snape addressing Harry Potter – decidedly sardonic and more than slightly arrogant. In regards to his actual pedigree, she had no clues, but despite his meagre age and unproven birthright, he expected to be treated like royalty;

he was a cat after all.

"It's not that I don't want to use them; I just don't think I should use them all the time," she said, sitting down on the stool next to his.

"I would," he said, wistfully, a wicked glint in his yellowy green eyes.

"Yes, but that's because you're a narcissistic psychopath, dear kitten," Alice replied, stroking his head with absolute affection, before blowing into the tea and taking a very careful sip. "Anyway, I apparently need to make an online dating profile, as it was strongly suggested to me by a psychic."

"A psychic or a Psychic?"

She was not quite sure what he meant, so she pulled the card from her jeans pocket and put it in front of him to read.

"Oh," said Onion, impressed. He recognised the Harvelle-Walker name – they were a lineage of Psychics of great renown and with a reputation; not all of which was good. They were, however, considered to be some of the best readers of people, places and objects, in the world. Also, naive and unassuming as Alice was, Onion knew she had decent instincts and would not have helped out someone to the extent she had, if she did not like him in some way. "That'd be the latter then. And he's the guy you helped?"

"Yes." Alice rarely questioned Onion on how he knew things or why he did not explain more of the supernatural to her; she just accepted it, in much the same way as she accepted the fact that she could speak to some cats but not all of them spoke back. She sometimes had the impression that like Julius, Onion was not allowed to say as much as he wanted to.

"Well, as advice goes, I believe this is a reliable source," said Onion. "And, I can help with your profile."

"Nope," Alice laughed, walking over to the PC, firing it up and typing 'online dating' into the search engine. She did not know why, but she opted for the third site down, and signed up for a free account. She quickly filled out the form with basic information and the bare-bones of a profile, still feeling sceptical and suspicious. It was hard to know what to say when she knew she was really quite boring, keeping mostly to herself and immersing herself in the invented worlds of authors and film makers. She did not have many photographs of herself, and didn't particularly like the ones she had, but eventually she settled on one that summed her up best. "The only one who would be even less helpful in this scenario, would be Kathie."

"You don't trust your best friend?" Onion questioned, slightly surprised. He jumped up onto her lap, partly because he felt like being comforting but mostly because he was nosy.

"Not with an online dating profile. Kathie would either big me up beyond all recognition or suggest crazy things, and almost certainly encourage the wrong sort of guy, either as a joke or as some unsuitable experiment to help me find out what I really want." She clicked on a button that said 'singles in your area'. "Like that one" she said, pointing to a guy that looked like an old B-movie's idea of a Mexican bandit, "Or that one," pointing to a man that gave off a decidedly serial killer vibe. "Or him..." she said slowly, bringing up the profile page of the third photo to catch her eye.

"What's wrong with "Robert"?" Onion asked, looking at a photograph that appeared to be of a fairly normal, good-looking young man. To be honest, Onion thought that "Robert" looked a lot like someone Alice would go for, and apparently liked video games, movies, books and pizza, all things that Alice also liked.

"Possibly nothing," she said, with a slight shrug, trying not to show any of the spiralling emotions she was feeling. "But he's not gonna go for someone like me. Even if that's really the guy behind the profile, he's more likely to go for someone like ... her" she said, bringing up the picture of a blonde with too much make-up in a faux Yoga outfit. "Which I say because I'm pretty sure I've seen him in a coffee shop with a woman like that."

"Yes, I can see that being a drawback of being in the

area," Onion commented, watching her closely through sideway glances. He wondered if this "Robert" was Mr Platform Nine. Although she had never really spoken to him about the mystery man she felt an inexplicable connection to, he had overhead her talking to Kathie and occasionally heard her scolding herself to "just forget about him".

"I think he works near the library; or at least not so far away, because I'm sure I've seen him queuing at that weird little coffee cart on the corner and I can't imagine anyone thinks the goods there are so exceptional it's worth going out of their way for..." Her words trailed off as she got lost in her thoughts. Then she sighed sadly, shook her head decisively and stood up. "This is a stupid idea." She turned off the monitor. "Let's get some food." She lifted Onion from her lap, set him on the floor and shuffled into the kitchen, large empty mug in tow.

Onion waited until he was sure that Alice would not be able to see him. Then he jumped up onto the chair, onto the desk and rubbed his head up against the monitor, knowing that he was more than capable of turning the screen on and off again. He was aware that it was risky, but he could also see that there was something about this guy for Alice. He nosed at the Naga mouse until the cursor was over the 'willing to meet for dinner' option, and used his paw to click the left button. Then he turned the monitor off and sauntered innocently into the kitchen to be fed.

***

Alice had never quite managed to stop thinking about that guy – Robert – if one accepted it as a genuine profile. The guy from platform nine that she had never expected to see again, but had actually caught sight of several times since. Tall, handsome; the kind of features that the word 'chiselled' would apply to. He had sandy-blonde hair, blue eyes and an amazing smile, and he always appeared well-dressed and well-groomed.

Sometimes, it seemed as if they would nod to one another or give small smiles of acknowledgement; once she thought he had smiled at her in a grocery store and her heart had skipped a beat. He had had a bit of stubble going that day, and she thought he looked sexy in a slightly scruffy, rogue-ish way. She had smiled back shyly, and had thought about maybe waving, something that might serve as an invitation for him to try talking to her, since she could not really be sure a guy like that would actually be smiling at a slightly chubby, four-eyed, plain brunette in an oversized top, leggings and mid-calf brown boots. Unfortunately for Alice, the bobble-headed skank in front of her in the queue went over and put her grubby claws into him, and she had turned away in abject mortification and disappointment, because obviously he had been smiling at the blonde.

Then there had been that one time when she thought she would burst into flames because he had lightly grabbed her arm...

They had both been in the new bakery-slash-coffee shop. She had been in a world of her own, one earphone in, listening to some rock music, whilst the other rested against her chest so that one ear was open for the call on her takeaway pumpkin-spiced mocha latte and trying not to faint from anxiety. It had been a gentle gesture, but his touch had made her feel like she was burning up with nerves and anticipation.

"Sorry. Didn't mean to make you jump. You left this on the counter," he said, handing over her copy of *Dracula* that she was reading for the umpteenth time. It was a pleasant voice – warm, masculine, American, no-discernible state or district accent that she could recognise – it seemed to fit his appearance. He was taller than her by a few inches, and just like that moment in the subway, something about him made her feel safe. The blue long-sleeved top he was wearing seemed to make his eyes even bluer.

"Oh. Thank you," she said, slightly stunned and very

surprised, having been convinced that she had put the book into her bag long before she had reached the counter.

"It's one of my favourites too," he had said with a grin, before apologising and returning to his seat opposite another, blonde, bobble-headed skanky-ho, who probably only saw how the blue top accentuated his chest and not his amazing eyes. In all honesty, Alice could not have said if it was the same woman as from the grocery store or not, and was fully prepared to admit she could have been perfectly pleasant, even though that was just code for 'but I'm pretty sure she's a bobble-headed skanky-ho'. Not to mention, who would go out in so few clothes on in the middle of winter, other than skanky tramps? *Still, what did it matter anyway...* She sighed, and returned to the present.

It was the eyes. It was always about the eyes for her, and there was definitely something about his. That shade of blue, the optimistic twinkle, kindness, intelligence... well, at least that was what she thought she could see in those brief moments of seeing him. There was, she was forced to admit, something about him.

Considering she had been staring at the same page of *The Night Watch* for the best part of an hour, Alice decided to look at the dating site again. She switched the monitor back on and his photograph sprang back up. She looked at it for a moment, then shut her eyes and mentally scolded herself. *You are definitely now bordering on stalker-y.* She clicked on the mail icon and scanned through the several message headers, the expected nonsense from creepers, players, charmers, 'that one guy'... and one that said "Dinner Invite". From Robert.

"Damnit cat!" Alice seethed, mortified. She looked around, but Onion was nowhere to be seen. She let out a deep breath and turned her attention back to the monitor. It felt like she was at that part in a horror movie where you do not want to watch, but can not look away. She was practically wincing, half of her head covered by a hand as she read the message through one open eye.

"Hey Alice,
It's nice to put a name to the face I keep seeing around. I hope it's you or I'm gonna feel pretty stupid when you meet me for dinner tomorrow. At 7. At the Leaky Cauldron?
Hope to meet you properly tomorrow,
Robert"

The panic attack hit hard, and she sat down in the walk-in wardrobe for a moment trying to get her breath and sanity back. She sat there, in the warmth and darkness, trying to make some kind of coherent thought, even if it was just *'ohmigod, ohmigod, ohmigod'* a million times over. At least they were words, and she tried to just visualise writing out the words until the panic had subsided. She took one last deep breath and returned to the computer.

"Hi Robert,
I thought maybe I recognised you too.
Looking forward to dinner,
Alice"

She hit send and immediately shut the computer down, afraid that if she thought about it too much, she would message him to cancel.

Chapter 8

"Yes!" exclaimed Robert Evans, unable to hide his excitement.

Given his housemate's bedroom door was already wide open, Clive Goodwin simply wandered in, Knicks mug in-hand."What's the…" He peered over Robert's shoulder at the computer screen, scanning the message on the dating website. "Oh, is that the girl you've been trying to stalk?" he asked. "Well, she has nice eyes, at least."

The photograph of the woman in question showed a pair of big brown eyes, framed by black glasses and unruly dark brown hair; the rest of her face was obscured by a huge drinks mug. There really was not much to go on, certainly not enough for Clive to see what his housemate was so excited about.

"I'm not sure even you'd have the energy to keep up with someone who drinks that much coffee," Clive added.

"She drinks tea," Robert corrected him.
Clive gave him a look.

"It's not stalking. I heard her talking to herself when we were both in that coffee-shop over on Third. And she's English, so if Rahul was anything to go by, they practically need that stuff in order to live."

"Kinda sounds like stalking," said Clive, with a grin. "Although, in fairness to your kind, it is a common MO."

"I notice things about her. I can't help it. I feel a connection to her, that I can't even begin to explain, even though I'm pretty sure she's a Witch," Robert replied, ignoring Clive's little dig at his species.

Robert was a Vampire. Mostly. Technically, he was not a proper Vampire until his thirty-ninth birthday, when he would inexplicable die and rise again, but he was a vampire. A Fledgling or a vampire without the capital letter, but as his parents were Vampires and their parents were Vampires, he was definitely a Vampire. Or would be. He rarely drank blood – for the most part, he ate like a human being – but occasionally, he needed haemoglobin supplements. He had fangs, although they only appeared when he needed to drink blood or when he lost control of his emotions, which was not often as he was generally pretty laid back. The fangs were accompanied by red eyes, talon-like fingernails and ice-cold skin, alongside his ever-present superhuman speed and strength. He had a sharp mind and lightning fast reflexes, a heightened sense of smell, the ability to see auras, unnaturally good hearing and a reflection. He was not adverse to silver or garlic, and as long as it was not a really hot and sunny day, he was perfectly capable of walking out and about during daylight, much like being extremely pale or ginger. He could only be killed by decapitation or a stake through the heart, and although he had been discouraged from making any significant attachments to mortals, Robert had nonetheless found himself drawn to a woman barely glimpsed in the subway several weeks ago.

Most supernaturals had an ability to see auras, so he was used to noticing the occasional splash of vibrant colours in crowded places, but he had never experienced anything like hers. Her aura that day, had been like a lighthouse in the darkest storm. The colours within it had been muted, but the brilliance of it had been blinding. Given how bright "Alice" was, it would have been easy to track her down, but it was not something he had ever approved of when others did it. He knew some of his brethren thought it was romantic, and goodness knew that was how a lot of the literature tried to portray it, but to him, it was just creepy.

"Oh," said Clive, knowingly. Maybe even disapprovingly. Robert refused to rise to the bait. "She's not like that."

"Look, I'm just reminding you that it's well known that female Witches only use Vampires for sex. Sometimes magic. But mostly sex."

"I'm telling you, she's different."

Clive remained sceptical, but could tell that Robert was strangely touchy about "Alice". It was unusual, since Robert's opinion of Witches was the fairly typical one, but obviously, he truly believed this girl was different. Clive also internally conceded that it was unfair to judge someone neither of them had really met. "Well, I guess she doesn't seem to have that arrogant glint in her eye. And she's using a dating website, which considering that Witches think everything should fall at their feet in adoration if they want it, goes against type. Presumably, you'll find out…?"

"Tomorrow," said Robert, leaning back in his chair. "We're having dinner tomorrow, because if I give her too much time to think about it, she won't come."

"You sure you're not stalking her?" teased Clive. "Seems like you know a little too much considering you've met her, very briefly, once?"

"We've smiled at each other twice as well," said Robert, realising as soon as the words left his mouth, that he was in no way helping his case. He twisted slightly to look at his room mate. "Look, you're a cop. You trust your instincts right?"

"Yes. And I agree that sometimes, you can tell a lot from a brief encounter. Just be careful, okay. If it turns out she is your typical Witch, don't be too upset when it turns out to be as meaningless as your last six dates."

"Gee thanks, I was so afraid you might sugar coat it," said Robert with a dry laugh. Admittedly, his last few dates had gone nowhere – they could have gone as far as the bedroom, but in truth, he had been less than committed to begin with – too busy thinking about her.

"Why are you even on a dating website?" asked Clive, interrupting Robert's thoughts. "It's not like you ever have a problem attracting women."

"Work forfeit," Robert replied. "And I don't attract women – I seem to attract airheads. Besides, I've tried twice to ask this girl out and each time it's gone wrong."

"You mean you've had a bubble-blonde with practically no clothes and massive breasts on your arm?" Clive teased, taking a sip of his coffee.

"Kinda," Robert said, pulling a face at the memories of the grocery store and the coffee shop. "Every time I've almost had the chance to talk to her, these women, who clearly overestimate their allure, hang off me like I'm some fuckwit that only dates the most superficial and vacant women possible. Which is another reason why I can't let her think about it too long, as she might start thinking she's 'not my type' when she is way more my type than women like this." By coincidence, he pulled up the same female profile that Alice had shown Onion. Mandi who loved dogs, dancing and had multiple photographs that accentuated her cleavage to great effect.

"Must be dreadful," Clive said, rolling his brown eyes before admiring the breasts on the profile picture. He grinned as Robert clicked the picture away with a disapproving glare and shake of his head. "I'd hate to have beautiful women throwing themselves at me too."

"They're not really though," said Robert, trying not to stare at Alice's photo. He liked the look of her eyes. "Beautiful, I mean, because it's all surface. You wouldn't want a relationship with them. At best, you might get some OK sex out of it, but that'd be it."

"I think your standards are too high. It's probably great sex, and quite honestly, that'd do me."

"Well, I'll send the next bubble your way then. Assuming she's a Zombie too."

"Please do," said Clive at once.

"...Although, that said, you could scratch one of them, and then after their first meal they'd already have more brains than they'd had previously."

"Wow. Harsh much?" said Clive, slightly ashamed of himself for laughing at the comment. He looked more closely at "Alice's" profile page since Robert had brought it up again. "So why her?"

"Don't know yet; there's just something about her. Hopefully, I'll find out – if it's really her and she really wants to meet for dinner. But in the meantime, I could set up a profile for you. You could ask "Mandi with an i" out for organic tofu."

"Gods no. You, my friend, will most likely go out for dinner and meet this girl, and if nothing else, probably get a great evening of sex out of it." Clive ignored the slight narrowing of Robert's eyes. "I, however, would choose to meet with this bubble of yours, and find out it's actually Mr 40-year-old-Cheeto-beard or Ms. twenty-years-older-than-in-the-photo-and-can't-stop-talking-about-her-ex."

"Pretty sure that's what my workmates are hoping for," said Robert, with a wry shake of his head. "Hence them adding the caveat of having to meet someone for dinner and not just have them laughing hysterically at some of the messages from interested parties."

"If they're that amusing, you should share," said Clive, thinking he probably needed more laughter in his life. "Anyway, I should get some sleep. I've got the early shift tomorrow, and will no doubt have to deal with more alcoholic homeless guys rambling about how 'something big' is 'hanging in the balance' and 'beware the prophecy'."

"Doesn't sound vague at all,"said Robert, closing down the dating site tab, and briefly scanning the Amazon best-seller lists.

"Right?" said Clive, pulling a 'the-shit-I-deal-with' face. "And there seems to be more of it going about. You've not heard anything, have you?"

"No," said Robert "but at the moment, I don't have a lot going on with supernaturals right now."

"Still avoiding your old haunts then?"

"Yes. Not just because of Ariana, but mainly because

The Crypt got new management and now it's filled with those weird groupies that give themselves up to be drained. It's still owned by actual Vampires, but that is not a scene I want in on."

"Fair enough. Can kinda see why your lot would cash in on it though," said Clive, thinking that Vampires really did not need any more "good press". Zombies, on the other hand, needed a serious overhaul in the PR department.

"It's still tacky," said Robert "and wrong."

"The Were are just as bad, right?" said Clive.

"Kinda. There's definitely some kind of Furry scene out there, and I suppose it would be stupid of them not to take advantage. Although again, it seems morally ambiguous or something. It's more complicated with the Were though; I mean,... nope, don't really want to finish that thought," said Robert, grimacing and giving a shudder of disgust. Much as he respected other people's choices, it did not mean he had to approve of them. "Oh," he said, brightening slightly. "On a potentially less sketchy note, my old college room-mate tells me they have a Zombie speak-easy, so maybe you should take a trip to Seattle. See if you can't find yourself a nice Zombie girlfriend there."

"Maybe," said Clive, thoughtfully. "Anyway, I'm turning in. Try to keep shouting to a minimum, and if I don't see you beforehand, good luck with your date."

"Thanks. Hope no one vomits on your shoes," Robert replied with a grin.

Clive rolled his eyes, shook his head and closed the door behind him.

Robert chuckled and decided to run about in *Destiny 2* for a little while before heading to his own bed. Contrary to popular belief, Vampires quite often slept at night, especially the ones that were not quite immortal yet.

Chapter 9

Although Stuart could not hear the books in the same way that the Guardians and Alice could hear them, he was nonetheless attuned to the general energy of the Library, and something had unsettled it. It was nothing evil, there was nothing malicious about it, but there was definitely some kind of disturbance. He frowned, and quickly left his public office to see what was causing the commotion.

"'Morning Dr Anthonys," said Alice brightly, crossing the foyer.

"You're early," he said, slightly distracted in trying to find the source.

"I'm always early," replied Alice, wrapping the earphones around her iPod and putting them in her bag. "The books seem chatty today."

It took a moment, and then he realised what was causing the furore.

"Okay, I stand corrected. I am sorry that I doubted you, Julius and Sam," he muttered to the Library. He was surprised by the Library's actions, since it would normally keep anything that would cause such disturbances from entering. He turned his attention back to the Witch. "Miss And,… Alice, I'm sorry, but I think you need to leave."

"What have I done?" she asked, confused. Alice had felt lighter walking into the Library, since she no longer had to worry that she might lose her job. Before leaving the previous day, they had renegotiated her contract for a raise and full-time position, whilst agreeing that she would receive additional training in order to oversee some of the paranormal aspects of the Library's collection. Somehow, she felt that her relationship with Dr Anthonys had become more friendly and less formal as a result.

At the same time, she was feeling extremely nervous about her date. She was not quite sure if she wanted the person she was meeting for dinner to actually be "Robert" or not. If it was not him, then it was easy; she was used to disappointment. If it was him, then there was the risk of him deciding that she was not pretty enough, or smart enough, a rejection that she would feel was justified and to be expected; but as unlikely as it was, it could be him and he might fall for her too and somehow the idea that she might actually be deemed worthy of his love, was almost more terrifying than the rejection. But no one wanted to hear such thoughts, so Alice locked it inside her head with the rest of her low self-esteem and depression. *Did I actually take my pill before I left?* she wondered, trying to visualise the foil tabs of antidepressants.

"Nothing as yet, but the books seem flustered, and you seem to be – how do I put this? – a mess. Not physically," he assured her quickly as her face creased with worry, and her hands began trying to squash her hair down "but mentally and emotionally, it seems. Is something wrong?" Dr Anthonys asked, gently.

"I have a date," said Alice, slightly embarrassed.

"And that's a bad thing?" Stuart asked with some surprise.

"Not sure yet. I am very nervous though."

"Well, it's making the books nervous too, and I can't have you starting your new duties in this state. It's exactly the sort of energy some of books would feed upon. If I may say so, you don't seem to be very in control of your powers."

"What powers?" Alice laughed, looking bemused. Stuart looked at her, startled to see that she was not joking. "I think we may need to invest in some extra training before you go back down in the sub-levels," he said. "I had hoped you could at least watch the Library's procedure for unpacking strong magical tomes today, but I see now that would be a very bad idea." Concerned etched itself in the slight wrinkles of his face, as he tried to decide which task was more important. "I think I should stay with the book, but..." He looked decidedly unhappy as he weighed up the time and preparations in place against the unfettered magic in the woman below. "At least drink some tea. I'll get Julius to provide you with some Xaliren; it might help to keep you calm and put a curb on your magic."

"Like a binding?" asked Alice, thinking that sounded a bit extreme. Still, if it would help her to stay calm, maybe it did not matter. "Thank you," she said, as Julius appeared from behind a bookcase, handed her a small tin and immediately disappeared again; she had mostly given up with trying to work out how he always seemed to be in the right place at the right moment.

"Nothing as powerful as that," Stuart assured her. "Clearly, your gifts are connected to your emotions, either because you're untrained or because you're an empath of sorts. It's hard to be sure at this juncture, but if you're more relaxed, then your magic should be more settled too. However, I don't feel that I can allow such energy in the Library, given that the book arriving today is not known for behaving itself."

"OK." Alice hesitated, not particularly relishing the thought of an entire day left to her own devices and trying not to obsessively worry over her impending date. "Isn't there something I could do? Run an errand of some sort, anything?" Stuart looked at the young, panicked face that was silently begging for some kind of distraction. He frowned, trying to remember what it was that Ethyl had brought up in the last meeting. "Julius says you're into photography," he said, waiting for all the dots to connect.

"I am an enthusiastic amateur," she said with a smile. *Ah yes, that was it.* "Well, Ethyl has arranged for a local neighbourhood exhibition of some sort to be placed in one of the study halls. A history of the boroughs, or some such... I'll be honest, I should really pay more attention to the everyday goings on, or delegate it to someone else to handle. Perhaps you could take some photographs we could display?"

"Sure," said Alice, relieved to have anything to keep her occupied. She thought about a few places that might exemplify the heritage of the city, as well as more modern day markers. It might even help give her the boost she needed to explore a little further afield. "That could be fun actually."

"I'm sorry; it's not quite what you were hoping for..."

"No, it's great," she said, suddenly enthused by the task. "Thank you. It means a lot. And thank you for the tea. I will have a cup when I get back to my apartment."

"Alice?" He said, pausing until she looked up at him expectantly, suddenly hit by memories that had been partially buried for a long time. "You seem like a lovely young woman, and I sincerely doubt that you need to worry so much about your date."

"I appreciate that," she said, with an unconvinced smile. "I'll make a start on that project."

***

Alice attempted to drink the herbal tea and made a sandwich to help endure the strangely bland yet bitter taste. She scribbled down some notes, deciding that she would shoot in colour and then convert them to black and white afterwards. She also decided to try and concentrate on taking photos in or around the park, seeing as that would put a bit more distance between her and the Library. She did not quite understand what risk she could possibly pose, but if Dr Anthonys felt it was best, she could live with the side project. Empty swings could always make a powerful image, and although Alice often avoided photographing people, she could hardly do this project and not include some crowds. The city was as much its people as it was the sports teams, skyscrapers and food.

It was freezing, but there was still beauty to be found in the watery sunlight and the frosted surfaces of plants and statues. She knew not all, if any, of her shots would suit Mrs Jenkins' vision, but she felt that New York and winter were fairly commonly associated, probably because of the Pogues or *Home Alone 2*. She had not photographed many people, but as she neared a small coffee cart, she thought there was something stirring about the image of steaming drinks and breath hanging in front of each person in a shivering queue. Then, as she began to focus more on the scene she was photographing, she realised that "Robert" was in the queue.

All at once, her nerves and anxiety flooded back despite the camera, and it only got worse when he seemed to look at her. She probably looked like a stalker, sneaking around trying to surreptitiously photograph him for the shrine in her basement, just another image amongst a tableau of other unwitting victims, encapsulated in a red heart and eyes blacked out with marker... If it was him, he was definitely not going to show up at the 'Cauldron now.

She tried to retreat backwards into the park, collided with a woman carrying a lot of boxes, and ended up falling on her arse in a puddle of murky water and dead leaves. She apologised to the lady profusely, helped to pick up all the boxes and tried to hurry off into a hell-mouth, whilst looking for another exit. It had not been the finest five minutes of the day.

She put her mud-laden gloves into a carrier bag, and sighed. There was little she could do about her trousers and coat bar dejectedly head home and hope that she could get clean before her contamination worries got out of hand. Given that the sun was already beginning to set, Alice decided she might as well spend the next couple of hours doing laundry, standing in the shower and staring at the wardrobe wondering what she should wear on a half-blind date.

Chapter 10

Whilst the Leaky Cauldron on the corner of Maple and 31st, had been around for over fifty years prior to the release of what had become one of the most popular book and film franchises of all time, it had nonetheless taken advantage of the association, adding some flourishes to what had already been unusual décor. It had incorporated a more rustic look of exposed brickwork and open fireplaces, with plenty of broomsticks, scarves and other memorabilia upon the walls, as well as boasting a selection of unusual drinks – ranging from Hobgoblin ales to Butter beers and Gillywater based concoctions, as well as blood-based beverages for a slightly more select clientele. The menus were equally diverse, catering for vegans and vegetarians, to omnivores, carnivores and Zombies. Of course, the normal people that wandered in were amused and would occasionally try to order things from a not entirely suitable menu, and the staff would generally make appropriate substitutions. It was unsurprisingly a popular spot for the pop-culturally savvy and supernaturals, and therefore seemed to Robert to be the natural choice for a first meeting.

  He was stood outside of the big wooden doors, not quite in the doorway, but still beneath the awning of the giant 'The Leaky Cauldron' sign that was still adorned with the vestiges of the festive season. It looked like a clear night, but the weather had been very temperamental of late, and although he did not feel the change in temperatures as most others would, he was not especially fond of being stuck in cold, wet clothes. There were a lot of people entering and exiting the establishment – some hoping to get a hot meal, others just to enjoy the warmth of alcohol and companionship as the new year continued in typically freezing fashion.

The Leaky Cauldron's popularity did give Robert some minor concerns. No one had come out and said that it was forbidden for Vampires and Witches to have meaningful relationships, but they had certainly given him that impression. Robert did not know why, given there were no objections to either race using the other for sexual flings, and when he had queried it, no one seemed to have a definite answer. It generally was not an issue since both species held the other in relative contempt, but he did wonder how much talk his date with Alice was going to generate. Especially if it went well.

He was positive that Alice was different, but he had made a plan in case she was just another stereotypical Witch. Even if he got the impression that she was arrogant, contemptuous and rude from the minute she stepped out of the taxi, he was going to try and enjoy a meal out. If her personality was not too abrasive, then he would not object to them spending the night together if that was what she wanted to do; whatever she proved to be like, he was determined to make an effort because he knew he would not get her out of system if he did not.

He could tell that she was near now – the air seemed strangely charged around her and there was a strange glow coming from one of the bright yellow cabs turning at the lights. Robert wondered if her aura was as blinding to all the other supernaturals or whether it was just because he was attracted to her.

He stepped closer to the curb as the taxi pulled up and after a moment, a very nervous brunette practically fell into his arms. Leaping colours swirled and changed around her, and Robert tried to concentrate on using human sight rather than the supernatural one. He threw all his plans out of the window; if there was ever a moment of 'love at first sight', this was it, and Robert knew that this was an encounter that was going to end in happily ever after or heartbreak.

"I'm not actually stalking you," she blurted out in a mildly defiant tone, maintaining her balance by grabbing the top of the taxi door. She moved aside as the couple wanting to take the now-vacant cab glared at her. Robert took her arm again as she steadied herself and moved her artfully out of the way, before letting her go.

"Hi, I'm Robert. I didn't think you were, but I'll keep an eye out now, I guess," Robert replied, his eyes twinkling as he grinned at her. Her big brown eyes glanced at him shyly from behind thick glasses, the slight tinge of green and black make-up accentuating their beauty. She was not wearing a lot of cosmetics, and the only scent he could catch was the slight perfume of lavender and shampoo. She was wearing brown boots, thick black leggings; the rest of her outfit was underneath the aubergine duffel coat, red scarf and matching bobble-hat and gloves.

Alice felt heat radiating from her cheeks, despite the chill she felt through her winter garb. Her nerves were not helped by the fact that Robert was indeed the guy from platform nine and that he was as handsome, confident and charismatic as she had imagined. (Yes, there had been the brief encounters too, but she had still been concerned that her imagination had since distorted the actual image). "Sorry. Hadn't planned on saying that out loud. Er, hi, I'm Alice. Nice to properly meet you."

"And you. I can finally stop calling you Dracula girl," he teased. "I guess you don't remember..." he trailed off, as he noticed her startled glance.

"I remember," she said, quickly. *There are not enough faces or palms to get me through this night*, she thought, mentally face-palming. She knew she should say something like 'oh, I didn't think you'd remember that, especially as you were with a bobble-headed skanky ho' although probably without the last bit, but she just stood there, completely silent and beginning to panic.

"We have a table upstairs," Robert gently suggested. "Unless you'd rather just stand here. I don't mind, but we are kinda in the way. And you look cold." He wanted to reach out and hold her, to use his gifts to keep her warm and help take the edge of what appeared to be crippling anxiety, but he was not entirely sure if that would help her relax or cause her to run. He was surprised that she was not using any magic to help herself; he had certainly seen more than a few Witches using their powers to keep themselves unencumbered by layers.

"Upstairs will be fine," Alice finally managed to say. She thanked him quietly as he held the door open for her and paused for a moment, so that she could follow him to the correct table, especially as she did not know what name the table was booked under. She supposed it was pretty obvious which one was theirs, since it was the only one with candles, flowers and a small 'reserved' sign, but one could never really assume such things.

He held the shoulders of her coat as she self-consciously shed her outerwear and she quietly thanked him again as he placed it on the back of the chair he held out for her. Once he seemed convinced that she was settled, he removed his dark blue cashmere coat and took the seat opposite.

Robert was slightly surprised that she was wearing a simple black-and-purple striped jumper dress. It was a nice dress and suited her perfectly, giving her some curves without being overly clinging or revealing, but again, the decision to dress for comfort and practicality was unusual – both for prestige and wealth hungry Witches, and the women he usually ended up on dates with. The only jewellery she wore was a silver and amber treble clef pendant that hung around her slender, lightly tanned throat. He tried to distract himself from the pounding blood vessels, reminding himself that he did not drink blood yet and that he wanted to get to know the woman in front of him; not rip her throat out.

"The flowers are for you. I hope they're ones that you

like," Robert said "Although I suppose I should have checked that you're not allergic to them. Or if you have any allergies in general. Or dietary requirements. At least if you're vegan, they have a menu for that here." *Nice*, he thought as he mentally face-palmed *Very smooth.*

"They're beautiful, thank you," Alice murmured quietly, glad to have the distraction of looking at the bouquet. It was a simple and elegant arrangement of red roses and white gerberas, fleshed out with sprigs of white gyp and deep green ferns. She smiled at him briefly, before glancing away. The nerves in her stomach seemed to somersault when she caught a glimpse of his blue eyes, to the point where she was worried that she was going to throw up over his expensive looking black shoes. She had no idea if they actually were expensive given that she had little to no interest in shoes, but they certainly went well with the black jeans and open-collared pale blue shirt he was wearing.

They smiled awkwardly at one another as Robert passed her a menu. Several times, they both opened their mouths to speak and found themselves unable to make any words come out.

Alice wanted to hide under the table. Part of it was the anxiety; part of it was that she thought maybe if she could not see his eyes, she might be able to talk to him. The fact that he seemed to have gone quiet made her wonder if he had realised what a mistake it had been to ask her to dinner, which made her even more worried about talking in case she said something so stupid, he would leave before even eating anything. She was also a bit stunned by the menu – apparently gastropubs in the States, or New York at least, were a bit more akin to fine dining than she was used to back home in England.

Robert was finding it hard to talk for similar reasons. He had never known a Witch to be so shy and quiet, and he was slightly thrown by the fact that she seemed to be very down-to-earth and not particularly "magical". It was like she had put her powers in some kind of standby mode, because within the blinding light of her aura, amidst all the waves of panic and worry, there was a great power that could only been seen if one was really looking. He was concerned that she was embarrassed to be seen with a Vampire, and trying to hide her true nature. It was not the way he wanted someone to feel about being with him and it further compounded his concerns regarding whether this was going to be something that needed to be kept secret.

Their respective worries were forced to halt as the tall, red haired waitress appeared at their table.

"Hi. I'm Jennifer. I'll be your server for the evening. Are you ready to order? Would you like some drinks whilst you take a few more minutes to decide on food?" The words sounded innocuous enough, but Alice felt like there was something off about the woman's tone.

"Just a diet coke for me please," Alice said quietly, feeling slightly intimidated by the commanding and striking appearance of Jennifer. There was a beauty and elegance to the waitress that the slightly drab uniform could not mar, and the confidence with which she carried herself made Alice feel even uglier by comparison.

"I'll have the same, thank you," said Robert. "I'm ready to order if you are?" he said, looking over at Alice.

"Er, I'll have the lamb burger with twice cooked chips please," said Alice, picking slightly wildly from the mid-range of the menu. "Medium-well please," she added. A few places had started cooking burgers only to medium and it was too pink for her. She supposed that must be some sort of culinary faux pas, given that Robert and the waitress looked at her with some surprise.

"Black Angus porterhouse, medium, with the red wine jus and a side of chips, please," Robert ordered. His surprise was that Alice had ordered actual food instead of a salad.

"Would you like the house red with that, sir?" asked Jennifer. She was surprised by Alice's order, both in terms of her being a Witch and in terms of a first date. She too was more than familiar with women trying to be something they were not by ordering dishes that were not what they would choose if dining with friends; in terms of being a Witch, she was surprised that Alice had not demanded the most expensive things off the menu or something ridiculous that they did not serve.

He glanced over at Alice.

"Oh, please don't feel like you can't have a drink on my account," Alice said at once, feeling flustered.

"Just a glass then, please," Robert replied, given that it would be slightly criminal not to have a good wine with a good steak.

"Do you want any more sides with that? Any starters?"

"No thank you," said Alice.

Robert shook his head and Jennifer departed, shooting a curious look at Alice as she left.

***

After the drinks were placed in front of them, Robert tried starting with a topic he hoped would help her relax and open-up a little.

"So, you're a photographer…?" he asked, casually. He had seen her a couple of times carrying a large DSLR camera and she had always seemed pretty intent and engaged with whatever it was she focused on.

Alice wanted to say that it was a hobby rather than a profession, but the sentence did not make it out of her mouth in quite the way she intended. "Not really," she said.

"Oh, I just thought I'd seen you out with a camera," he said, slightly puzzled.

"You probably did." *Palm. Face.* Silence. Panic. *Shit, he did see me.* "I was just…"

"Stalking me?" he finished, gently teasing her.

"No, I work at the Library. We're going to have an

exhibition and I was asked to take some photos, I guess to use as backdrops or something," she replied, somewhat stiffly. *Dear gods, it's like I don't know how conversation works any more.* "What do you do?"

Robert looked at her for a moment and then said quite calmly and seriously, "If it helps, I don't collect women's ears in a bucket."

Alice blinked at him, her eyes slightly wide before her head tilted slightly and creased with suspicion. It took a moment for all the pieces to click, but then the unsure smile gave way to a genuine laugh, and suddenly, a different person was sitting in front of him.

"How often has that been reassuring to, well, anyone?" she asked, smiling.

"First time it's been a success," said Robert, returning the broad smile and internally breathing a sigh of relief. "Usually it seems to have the opposite effect. People get very nervous about their ears all of sudden."

"Maybe it's the specificity of *'women's* ears'," Alice suggested. "They probably think you're lying or that you collect men's ears."

"I really don't. I tend to go for the eyes." He winked, grinning as she laughed. "And you have very nice eyes."

Alice's smile grew and a blush coloured her cheeks as she looked away shyly for a moment. She was not used to compliments and being English, was slightly uncomfortable about accepting them. "I'm not sure what that says about me that a conversation about collecting ears is an ice breaker," she said, trying to off-set the compliment with self-deprecation.

"I'm just glad you've watched *Coupling*," said Robert, noticing that the tension was leaving her shoulders, and he felt a glimmer of satisfaction that she was becoming more at ease.

"It was, is, a good show. I'm surprised you've seen it though, being American and all."

"I had an English room-mate in college. I'll be honest, I didn't have a plan B if you hadn't seen it; guess I was prepared for you to actually run. Although I'd have been disappointed," he added.

"Sorry," Alice said, looking apologetic. "I just get very anxious sometimes. Usually, I'm the one saying things like that, accidentally more often than not, mind, and people have no idea what I'm talking about and then I panic even more. As in I reference a lot of different things; I'm not quite at Jeff standards of talking absolute rubbish about collecting body parts or losing them or whatever. My mind just flits a lot and I seem to sponge up random movie and TV lines."

"I think that could be fun, trying to guess what you're referencing if my own sponge-brain can't immediately make the connection."

Alice smiled, liking the sound of that. "Can we maybe try again, please?" she asked shyly, and he nodded. "Alice Andrews, nice to meet you." She held out her hand.

"Robert Evans," he said, taking her hand. A shower of small, red sparks flittered like a mini-firework between them. Despite the electricity and brief flames, he did not let go. "I think that's the first time I've actually seen an electric shock."

"Me too," Alice said quietly. Her gaze kept slipping away shyly, but she was smiling. Although it was not the most comfortable of positions, Alice was quite happy to keep her hand in his. There was something warm and comforting about his touch that made her feel safe, although the anticipation of his touch moving elsewhere made her skin burn and her heart race. She sighed and withdrew her hand, needing to go and wash her hands before eating. It was not as severe as Obsessive Compulsive Disorder, but it was certainly something that sent her into a mild panic if she did not do it. "Sorry. Please excuse me a moment."

"Of course," said Robert, at least ninety percent certain that she would not try to escape out of the restroom windows. As soon as Alice was out of sight, Jennifer returned to the table and frowned at him. He looked at her expectantly, slightly surprised that he was already garnering disapproval for wanting to know Alice Andrews better.

"You are aware that she is a Witch, aren't you, Robert?" Jennifer Harper asked. Her own experiences with Witches had never been particularly pleasant; despite the fact that she was an extremely wealthy and successful Vampire, she had still found certain avenues barred by the influence of certain Covens. "It's not obvious, but she definitely is one of them."

"I know," Robert said, carefully. He took a sip of the diet soda and wondered when he had last been on date where it had been the drink of choice. Usually, his dates wanted to pick the most expensive wine on the list, either assuming or knowing that he had a lot of money. Whilst this rarely bothered him since he was partial to a fine vintage, he was sometimes irked since the wealth was his family's and he actually lived out a fairly modest lifestyle through his own means.

"She's not cast some kind of spell on you, has she?" Jennifer had had experience of a few Witches attempting to bewitch Vampires in similar ways to abhorrent people who used "date rape" drugs. Although she doubted that a potential squib could influence a member of the Vampire royal family (certainly the closest thing Vampires had to one at least), it was worth checking.

"No," Robert replied patiently. *Not in that sense at least*, he added silently.

Jennifer let out a huff and shook her head; she knew she had no right to question a Vampire of his status, but Robert was still a fledgling and she knew him well enough to have concerns. "They're bad news. You shouldn't be associating with their sort. No offence, but particularly given who you are and that you are rather attractive for a man, surely you can do better? I mean, she doesn't exactly scream 'great in the sack' either, although I admit, there is something kinda cute about her."

"I appreciate the concern, but whatever happens between me and her is none of your business," Robert said, politely and firmly.

"But..."

"I don't care," Robert interrupted. "I like her. Just because she has the ability to use magic, doesn't automatically make her a bad person or an unfit mate for a Vampire, should it come to that."

"Fine," said Jennifer with a shrug of resignation. "Just don't be surprised when it all goes horribly wrong or if the Elders decide to say something."

"It's none of their business either," said Robert, crossly. "If my great-grandfather wants to make an issue of it, he can bring it up, but telling me not to date a Witch simply because she is a Witch is hypocritical nonsense."

They both glanced towards the restroom doors, knowing that Alice would be returning momentarily. Jennifer let out another exasperated noise before composing herself and greeting another couple that had wandered up into the restaurant.

"Sorry I took so long. I made the mistake of checking my phone and had to... return a call," Alice said, smiling as she sat back down. She felt that saying 'I had to leave a message for my cat' was not first date material.

"No problem. You made it back before the food," Robert said.

"Only just." Alice smiled and murmured her thanks to Jennifer as the pretentiously plated food was placed in front of her. She understood that dining out was supposed to be an experience but at the same time, she failed to see why food had to be delivered on a piece of slate rather than an ordinary plate. It looked and smelled delicious, and the portion size was very generous. As she thought about how best to eat her burger, she wished she had ordered a steak; on the other hand, if this was going to last, he was going to see her make an utter mess of eating something at some point, and in all honesty, who really looked that elegant eating in any case? She cut the fluffy brioche bun with its large spiced lamb patty and salad in half and sprinkled a tiny amount of salt on the chips.

She noticed him watching her, a slightly bemused smile

on his lips. Internally, she said *fuck it*, and took a bite of her burger, unable to stop her eyes from glancing over to see his expression.

"What is it?" she asked, after finishing her mouthful, trying not to sound as panicked as she was beginning to feel.

"Nothing really," said Robert, smiling. "It's just I have never known a girl to be so normal on a first date."

"I guess we women have a tendency to try and pretend we're not just slightly better looking variants of men," Alice mused cheerfully. "However, I caught the news earlier about some sportsperson retiring at thirty-six and the newscasters made it sound like he or she was ancient. So, given that I'm practically at death's door, I should probably be myself." She took a sip of her drink. "And I panic ordered."

Robert laughed before his expression turned to one of concern. "Is it okay though? You can order something else if you don't like it?"

"Oh, no. It's delicious," said Alice at once, and meaning it. "If I can't finish it, I'm definitely taking it home for Oni-, er my lunch tomorrow."

He wondered what she had been about to say, but he did not press, especially since he could see her face twitching with whatever dialogue was going on inside her head. *She's adorable*, he thought knowing that it was not a sentiment to say aloud. He had found that as a rule, women did not like to be called adorable or cute when they were trying to project an entirely different image.

As they continued to eat, the conversation between them flowed easily between all manner of subjects from their jobs and their thoughts on the city, to England, favourite foods and films. Everything except the facts that Alice was a Witch and Robert was a Vampire. It did not seem like Alice was particularly bothered about their differences, and Robert was beginning to wonder why it was that her powers were so muted if she was not trying to hide them from the rest of the world. She did not seem to have any issue with any of the other supernaturals in the 'Cauldron, smiling politely to everyone that looked over and she only seemed to flinch at his touch because there seemed to be too much electricity between them; every time his fingers brushed against hers, sparks literally flew.

Robert tried to steer the conversation towards the topic by asking about her favourite book, and of course, she had excitedly chattered about why she loved Bram Stoker's Gothic work and how she had happened to be carrying the copy he had returned to her.

"So, do you really like *Dracula*?" she asked, remembering that he had said he did.

"Yes. I mean, it's got a lot about Vampires wrong, but it's entertaining and clearly influenced a lot of other writers since. Bit of a poor show killing off the main character, and a Vampire at that, but it's a good read. Easier and more interesting than a lot of the literature from that time."

"Dracula should not have tried to come between Mina and Jonathan; you should never try to come between people in love. That's just my read though," Alice said, shrugging.

"So you don't think all Vampires are evil and need to be destroyed?" he asked in a light tone.

"Only the sparkly ones," Alice said with a grin, as she took a sip of her drink. "I reckon vampires would be like everything else in the world – there'd be good ones and bad ones. I think only Angels and Demons are born or created Good and Evil. I don't know, it's not like I know any," she said, with another careless shrug.

Robert tried to hide his surprise, suddenly realising that she genuinely did not know he was a Vampire. Given that she was a Witch (and he was quite sure of the capital letter now that he had met her properly), he had assumed she would have known. He reached out across the table and took the hand that was nervously twirling a glass, into his. It was the first time he had intentionally reached for her since they had shaken hands and he felt his own sense of anticipation and nerves, as he felt the suddenly rushing blood beneath her skin.

"Well, you know one now." He was about to tell her, when there was a sudden crash of thunder, causing the sentence to die on his lips. The lights went out and everyone looked towards the window as a blinding streak of lightning split the sky. Just as suddenly, the power came back on and everything plugged in sprang back into life with unexpected volume and brightness. An unusual song blared through the speakers; one that Alice clearly recognised, as her eyes lit up. He watched as she was lost in listening to it, her expression slightly glazed with a kind of love, understanding and something decidedly erotic. For a few moments, he was stunned. She did not seem like that kind of girl, and the sudden idea that she was, began to cause some discomfort.

She tutted and pulled a face as it was switched back to the less intrusive middle of the road pop music. "Aww, I love that song."

"What was it?" Robert managed to ask, also disappointed by the music change, but slightly relieved. It was never a great situation when such things happened and certainly not with someone who did not appear to be overtly sexual. He tried to get his mind out of the bedroom and focused on the way her eyes lit up as she began to talk about music.

"'*Silent Voice*' by Shaman's Harvest," Alice said at once. "Very into them at the moment and I particularly love that track. Also a big fan of Brigade, Adelita's Way, Shinedown, The Black Moods, Red Sun Rising; and older stuff like AC/DC, Nirvana, UFO, Blue Oyster Cult, Journey, etcetera. I'm a rock chick at heart. I like other stuff too, but mostly rock." The sudden disruptions had caused the bubble they had been in to disperse; time and other real world applications were beginning to intrude. "It really is getting kind of late now, isn't it?" Alice said, seemingly with some reluctance, glancing out of the window at the black sky and quiet roads, although since the sky seemed to go black by 4pm, that was not really an indicator of the time.

"We could probably still get dessert, if you fancied anything?" said Robert, also wanting the evening to continue.

"On or off the menu?" she teased with a wicked grin, that was quickly replaced with an expression of mortification, her face turning bright red as she realised what she had said.

He wanted to laugh so much, because she was surprising and adorably sweet, and he was more than willing to go for either option. A small smile played on his lips, as he watched her look away from him. He refrained from teasing her about her question.

"Sorry, please excuse me for a moment," Alice said, quickly getting up and knocking over her empty glass at the same time. She quickly righted it and tried not to run into the ladies room.

Robert chuckled as he watched her duck into the restrooms, and could not help but think he was quite possibly the luckiest guy in the whole world right now. He looked at his watch and realised she was right. In fact, they had been there for five hours without noticing how quickly the time had ticked away. He sighed, indicated for the cheque and was in the middle of settling the bill when she returned.

"You could have at least waited for me to offer," Alice said with a wry grin, as Jennifer walked away with a slight shake of her head.

"I hope you know that there is no way I would let you pay for dinner," said Robert. "I just realised that you were right, and it is late, and for some daft reason, I suggested meeting in the middle of the week, when we both have work in the morning, probably. Well, I unfortunately do."

"Yeah," said Alice. "Me too." She bit her lip and looked thoughtful for a minute, a gesture he was beginning to recognise as her steeling herself to say or do something she was not sure she should. Her gaze flickered momentarily to the table, before she looked up at him, her eyes big and beautiful above her glasses. "We still have to eat tomorrow though, right?" she said, pushing the glasses back up her nose.

He grinned. "Definitely. Do you fancy anything in particular?"

"I guess it's been a while since I've been out for Chinese food," she said, shrugging.

"Er, I know a place that does the most amazing crispy shredded beef and kung-po chicken, and the chow mien is outstanding. But it's take-out, so I get if you wouldn't be comfortable coming to my place, although my house-mate could play chaperone, if you did want to try the food and not be alone with me?" *Ohmigod, weird much*, he thought, instantly regretting that the only place he could think of was his local take-out.

"That sounds good," Alice said, smiling. "You have already assured me you won't take my ears, after all."

Robert smiled back, letting out a silent sigh of relief as he helped her with her coat. "Can I give you a ride home?" he asked, as she turned back to face him.

"If you're sure it's not out of your way," she said, annoyed with herself for not just saying 'yes, please'.

"Doesn't matter if it is," he said. "It's no trouble, and it's better than you waiting on a taxi or an uber or however it was you were planning on getting home."

Alice smiled, feeling relieved and grateful. "Thanks, I'd appreciate that then."

They drove to her place in a silence that was only interrupted by the sat-nav giving directions. It was not the awkward silence of earlier, but a mostly comfortable silence that was underpinned by the nervousness of *how are we ending this night?*

"Thank you," Alice said, as they pulled up outside the terraced brownstones. "And thank you for dinner. And these beautiful flowers. I had an amazing time."

"Me too," said Robert. "I'm looking forward to tomorrow. Not the tidying up, but definitely dinner. Would you like me to pick you up straight from work, or …?"

"Sure, that's fine," Alice said, immediately. Picking one outfit a day was more than enough hassle. "I'm not one for costume changes, if I'm honest, so apologies if it looks like I've made no effort whatsoever."

"I'm sure you look beautiful whatever you're wearing." She put her hand up to brush her fringe out of her eyes again, but before she could, he reached over and did it for her. His hand lingered against her face as he leaned in towards her. "Goodnight, Alice Andrews," he said, before kissing her gently. For some reason, she looked slightly surprised but she was definitely pleased.

"Goodnight, Robert Evans," Alice whispered, unable to find her voice. She so desperately wished she could just be *that* girl, the kind of girl that felt confident enough to just sleep with any guy with whom there was an equal attraction, but she was not. She opened the car door. "See you at five thirty." He waited until the door of her building closed behind her before turning the car around and heading back to his own home.

Chapter 11

The books were still a little more animated than usual, but at least it was not quite to the same degree as the previous day.

"You've made your point," Stuart muttered at the Library in mild annoyance. "Now if you wouldn't mind..." An invisible shroud descended, setting the books back to normal. He walked down the stairs and greeted the Witch as she emerged from the staff rooms. "Alice."

"Good morning, Dr Anthonys," Alice said, with a smile.

"You could just call me Stuart," he replied, looking bemused. He inclined his head slightly, indicating that she should follow him.

"I'm not sure I could," Alice said, uncertainly. She had always struggled with addressing teachers with anything other than formal address; talking to her lecturers at university had been a cause of great discomfort. "May I call you Dr A instead?"

"If you'd rather," Stuart said, looking at her in amusement. He had come across this with other English Novices in the past, but at least Alice was trying to be flexible and he supposed it was not a million miles away from Sam calling him 'Doc'.

SS1E17 had once been a small lecture theatre, in a time when the sub-levels had been more open and there had been a little more camaraderie between the supernaturals. In recent years, it had become a default storage space for old furniture and exhibition pieces, but with Julius' and the janitorial staff's help, Stuart had once again turned it into a classroom.

The old gas taps still worked, and he noted Alice's nostalgic smile as she automatically attached the rubber hose of an old Bunsen burner and slid into one of the workspaces.

"I suppose we should start at the beginning. I presume you are aware of the Three?"

Alice thought for a moment. "The fairytale about the first Were, Vampire and Witch?" she suggested, adding as she caught the look of concerned surprise on his face "I guess not."

"Well, you're right about it concerning the Were, the Witch and the Vampire," Stuart said. "It's just that it's not a fairytale and although they are considered the first of the modern day supernaturals, they were not strictly speaking the first of each 'species'."

"Oh. So, there are actually Were and Vampires, as well as Witches?"

"And Psychics, Zombies, Familiars, Angels, Demons, ghosts and all manner of other creatures usually often attributed to be figments of an overactive imagination."

"Oh."

"You really don't know this?" asked Stuart, looking at her carefully, searching her face for some sign that she was joking with him.

"No," said Alice, trying to ignore the little voice telling her how ridiculous and stupid she was for not knowing; if there were witches and familiars and magic, why wouldn't there be all the other things? That said, planets existed but there was still no proof of life on them. "I vaguely remember stories about the Three from when I was little, but I got sent away to boarding school aged seven and all talk of magic stopped. Apart from a few weird things happening to me and doing the odd little bit of magic, I guess I just kinda forgot about it."

"What happened when you were seven?" asked Stuart.

"I don't really know," said Alice, with a shrug. "All I did was make an amulet. You know, like the one I made Sam."

"You made that amulet when you were seven?" Stuart

said with a look of alarm that Alice missed as she mournfully played with the flame on the burner.

"Well, sorta. I mean, I made one when I was seven for my mom. My grandmother was trying to make one and said 'do what I do', so I did. The one I made for Sam, I made like, the day before I gave it to him."

"What book is it from? I've never seen such a design."

"An old one. Was kinda noisy now that I think about it, but I don't recall ever knowing what it was called or the name of the amulet," said Alice, thinking carefully. She could see the whole thing so clearly in her mind's eye – could see the dark ink on yellowed pages, the words shimmering and twisting under her gaze, carefully enunciating the words that Nanny Price told her to repeat, as her small fingers carefully coaxed the materials into a shape a little more perfected than the one her grandmother was making. "I just copied my grandmother and remembered it. I kinda figured that's how Witches got their magic – from absorbing spells – like software updates or something."

"So you're saying you can look at a spell once and you're able to replicate it at will?"

"Yes," she looked at him carefully, again noting the surprise in his eyes. "Is that not how it works for most Witches?"

"I have never heard of any Witch being able to do that," said Stuart, thinking that it would certainly be a boast that many would make if they could. "Would you be able to demonstrate by making an amulet for me, please?" he asked. He was fully prepared for her to tell him that she would not and that a Witch's craft was personal and not for the eyes of mere humans, even ones working in the Library; it was the response he was used to.

"Sure. I need some silver, blessed black calf leather, a piece of black tourmaline, some vanilla, ginger and a sprig of sage. Please."

She picked up the silver and began rubbing it in her hands with the sage, vanilla and ginger, gradually twisting and forming it into a triquetra. Then she used the tourmaline to draw some tiny and intricate symbols along each of the arches. Once all the symbols were drawn, she fused the stone into the centre and threaded it onto the leather thong. She closed her eyes and clasped the pendant between her palms again for a moment before saying "Blessed be," and placing it on the desk.

"Could I go and get a cup of tea, please?" Alice asked, suddenly feeling tired and slightly mopey. She had been too happy to get much sleep, although Onion had been far more interested in her leftovers than hearing about how well things had gone with Robert.

"I'm sure Julius will bring some any moment now," Stuart said absently, looking at the pendant carefully, completely stunned not only by the piece itself, but by the seeming ease with which it had been made.

Alice sighed and nodded thoughtfully. "He does always seem to know when people need tea. My nan was like that too. She didn't quite have the whole appearing out of nowhere trick though."

As if on cue, there was a knock and the door opened without waiting for a reply. Alice looked over at Julius and gave him a tired smile; Stuart merely gave him a very brief nod of acknowledgement before his attention returned to the amulet.

"This tea is because you like it; this one you need to drink to help replenish your energy," Julius said, placing a small tray on the table, pointing to a large mug of English breakfast tea and a small, china teacup of an orange-y brown liquid with bits of flora floating in it. There was also a cinnamon bun with a generous topping of frosting and extra cinnamon.

"Thanks Ju," she said, looking into the herbal tea. She pulled a face at the mere thought of drinking it and the grimace deepened as she drank it. "Urgh. Why do they all taste like twig water?" she asked looking up. Even though Alice had not been expecting an answer, it was still somewhat disappointing that no one was paying attention. Julius had already disappeared and Dr Anthonys was still examining the amulet in amazement. She let out a mildly frustrated breath and shook her head. She began to pull the bun apart, shrugging to herself since she had no idea why her mentor was so fascinated by a simple protection charm.

"This is astonishing," Stuart said, finally looking up. "I've never seen an example of High Magic in this day and age."

"High Magic?"

"The highest tier of magic. All things considered," he continued "I only gave Sam's a cursory glance, but I wouldn't be surprised if this was from the Book of the First. Given what this is supposed to be able to protect the wearer from, it could certainly pre-date the Three."

Alice looked at him, hoping that it was the sudden exertion that was making her feel quite so stupid. "Wait, sorry. Are you saying this isn't some simple protection charm that all Witches can make?"

"Good grief no," Stuart replied, looking aghast at the suggestion. "This is a form of magic talisman from the beginnings of the supernatural lineages, when magic was stronger, more potent, and Witches had greater need of protection from Demons and spirits and other creatures generally associated with Darkness and Hell."

"Oh," said Alice. "I guess I figured that since I could make it, it must be pretty simple and commonplace."

"I confess, I do not know every Witch in the world, but I do not know of any living Witches that could make an amulet of this magnitude. I think they would be lucky if they could make even a crude imitation of it, even with years of study under the tutelage of some of the world's most highly respected magical teachers."

"So there is a Hogwarts?" said Alice, with a teasing smile, still not quite able to believe that her abilities were in a far greater league than she had ever imagined.

"No. There are, if I recall correctly, twelve supernatural

learning institutions, not including the Libraries, three of which are exclusively for Witches," adding as he caught Alice's mischievous look "over the age of twenty-one."

"So they don't go there to learn about different kinds of magic and controlling their powers and all the weird and wonderful stuff in the world then?" She had to admit, she was feeling ever-so-slightly mollified by the fact that she had not missed out on Witch school after all.

"No. It's mainly for those wishing to push their craft further than the expected limits and to learn more about the magic of bygone times. Part of it is preservation of old secrets and the sanctity of artefacts belonging to the original Witch; some might come to the Library and use that knowledge to care for the Three as a result." Stuart continued. "Even those Witches would be hard to pressed to recall even the simplest of magics from a High Magic book. They certainly would not be able to make something like this from memory." He held up the pendant, still unable to hide his amazement. "May I keep this, please?" Again, he was fully prepared for Alice to say no.

"Of course," Alice said, not entirely sure why he was asking. "It'll work better for you than it would anyone else. It will work for other people if you need it to, but it'll be more effective for you. Although I hope you won't need to use it."

She really was a surprising individual and Stuart had to admit that it was very hard not to like her. He could not help but think that her seclusion from the magical world had worked out, if not entirely in her favour, certainly in that of the rest of the supernatural world. One could only imagine the misery she could have caused under the tutelage of a Witch like Alcina Wesker or Damian Ashford, two Witches that embodied and embraced the arrogant and ugly habits that had turned the rest of the supernatural communities against the former champions of magic.

He gave a small cough and tried to clear his throat. "Well, I suppose we can safely conclude that your powers are substantial to say the least. Truly remarkable," he murmured under his breath. "But, to return to the basics... The Three exist. Although they were not the first of their kinds, the Were, the Vampire and the Witch possessed powers unlike any of their kind before or since. They formed the first ruling council of supernatural affairs, they were champions of the mortal world, dedicated to keeping humans safe from the monsters in the dark. As time went on, the need for the Three dwindled in the wake of science and changes in belief that seemed to diminish the influence of those beyond the Veil. We don't know quite know how or why, but rather than die they went into a state of stasis, and there are dedicated supernaturals who care for them."

"And for the most part, Were, Witches and Vampires are as you have probably read about. The Were Turn on the day before, after and of the Full Moon – mostly into pack predators like wolves or coyotes, but not exclusively. Vampires drink blood, although rarely to the point of causing death, and Witches can do magic. There are also Angels and Demons, ghosts and spirits, and other entities that are generally not supposed to be on earth. They exist on another plane; in another dimension so to speak, beyond what is commonly referred to as The Veil."

"How fragile is The Veil?" asked Alice, suddenly feeling a gnawing concern growing in the pit of her stomach.

"It's not fragile at all. It's extremely strong, but since no one truly understands how it works or who made it, like anything that has existed for such lengths of time and dealing with constant pressure, there are parts that are slightly weaker than others. But it's holding."

"And if it broke?"

"Then we would be witness to an Apocalypse. The End Times. Certainly the end of the world as we know it." He caught the look on her face. "I shouldn't worry too much about it. It's highly unlikely to happen in our lifetimes, if at all."

"It's still possible though," said Alice, with some consternation. She shrugged, adding "Although the way the world's going at the moment, human beings will probably bring about a form of End Times on their own." *And it would probably serve us right.*

"Probably not today though," said Stuart with firm reassurance.

"No, probably not," Alice said, trying to think about better things and the fact that 'today' still held the promise of a second date with Robert. Unfortunately, something about Demons and the Veil was beginning to eat at her.

Stuart noticed. "Perhaps we should move onto some practical magic. We can discuss the Veil at another time. Truly, it is not going anywhere. Your powers, on the other hand, will not come under your control unless we start working on that. I suggest that we start with simple spells, such as glamour spells, and progress to see how advanced a spell-caster you are. Perhaps by gauging how powerful you are, we can try to understand a little about how you can make your magic work for you consciously, and then we can work on reining in the unconscious effects."

"That sounds potentially more involving at least," Alice said, with a slightly wicked glint in her eyes. "Winguarrrrrrrdium LeviOhhhhsa," she said, sweeping her hands in a down and upwards motion.

He closed his eyes, pinched the bridge of his nose and counted to ten. *Of course, you could go off people.* "Perhaps after lunch, and not fictional spells from Harry Potter."

"You mean to say that I can't make things float?" asked Alice, slyly; levitating items was one of the few pieces of magic that she found extremely useful.

"I mean to say that you won't achieve it by saying the words from Harry Potter. If J. K. Rowling is a Witch, I doubt she would be so irresponsible as to place actual spells in a mass-consumer product."

***

Lady Jane looked up from her knives as the High Magic alert went off again. This time it landed squarely on the Library.

"That is interesting," she mused. It had a been a good few years since there had been any magic conducted on Library grounds, and probably centuries since there was High Magic. The seeming ease with which Alice Andrews was doing it certainly illuminated her master's interest in her, but that the Library should be so accepting of it was a note for concern, although she doubted that her master would agree.

Chapter 12

Dr Anthonys was relieved that Alice seemed much brighter after her lunch break, and although she had voiced concerns about being completely useless as a witch, she was actually very accomplished and a very quick study. A lot of the practical magic she could do seemed to be known intrinsically, but she did not necessarily know the correct names and combinations. For instance, if he asked her to make a Zarkandor seal, she would look at him blankly; if he told her what it was used for (trapping ghosts), and if she had created one before, then she could do it again without any reminder of the ingredients or method. It did not seem to matter what the spell was or what it needed, if the components were there, she could make it and it would work. If she said the words, the right result would occur, assuming the spell itself had been written correctly.

There had not been many incidents, but there were a few. One had been down to a slight mispronunciation; another to the illegibility of one of the words. In one instance, the spell that was supposedly a "cure" for arachnophobia certainly seemed to have been recorded incorrectly; Alice spoke the words and spiders began pouring from the ceiling.

"Well, they got that wrong, unless they were actually aiming for some form of immersion therapy" she said, covering up what she could. She did not want any of the spiders getting trapped or drowning or spoiling her tea. She did not necessarily like spiders, per se, but she certainly did not like to wish them harm. She muttered an 'undoing' spell, and said "Sorry, you can go home now," and the spiders disappeared.

But she lacked control. Unless she was concentrating, she could not say the spells without them happening. The number of times the green practice apple had run off, having been turned into some kind of living form just because she had attempted to sound out a transformation spell, was astounding. The fox kit had been rather cute; the cobra less so.

Admittedly, neither of them could quite work out why anyone would want to turn one thing into another, ("Seriously, why would you want to turn something into a toad? - they could both understand wanting to turn some*one* into one – And why a kettle? Why not just get a toad and then you have both, instead of either or?") but at least it was not dangerous magic; it was easy to see the results and it tended to keep her from daydreaming too often. Stuart had also been expecting the effects of such glamour spells to be relatively brief, since it had been his experience that most Witches could not maintain the effect for more than a couple of hours at best. Taking that into account alongside Alice's lack of experience, he had been surprised when the practice fruit continued to look like an owl, several hours later and whilst she had been practising other spells.

Alice looked at it, waved her hand and muttered 'reditus forma', and the tawny owl visage disappeared to reveal the Empire apple it really was.

"Remarkable," Stuart said. "Now if we can just get you to exercise more control, you will be quite the Witch. Spells should not work simply because you say the words; there should be intent and effort behind it. Julius wants to try and teach you some meditation techniques – I personally think I would have more luck trying to get this Barbinda to work." He tapped at a spell in an ancient tome, that was proving to be far harder to perform than it should have been.

Alice stuck her tongue out childishly at the suggestion that she would be a bad at meditation, mainly because she knew he was right. Her mind was always racing away, thinking of a hundred different things...and now Robert, and occasionally a hundred different things they could do. She smirked and then mentally shook herself, trying to focus on the spell in question. She concentrated for a moment, looking at the ingredients, calculating in her head and frowned at the result.

"That will never work for you," Alice finally concluded, looking at the Head Librarian. His brow furrowed and she quickly explained. "Basically, it's wrong. *I* could probably follow that exactly and get it to work if I *really* put some intent behind it, cos I'm a Witch, and an awesome one at that, apparently; but it won't work for you or anyone else who doesn't naturally possess a great deal of power. Challenging as some magic is supposed to be, this would take more force than is... right." She bit her lip and tilted her head. "I can tweak it for you, if you want," she offered, uncertainly. "All things considered, as the Head Librarian, I can see how a binding potion for negative books would be useful. Maybe I could check that book more thoroughly for you tomorrow or something?"

"That would be much appreciated and probably quite invaluable," said Stuart, gathering up his own things and putting the pointer and marker pens beside the now cleared white board.

"Indeed," she said, grabbing a wooden ice lolly stick to flick through a few of the pages and pulling faces at some of the other spells. "Who gives the Head Librarian a book that is essentially '100 Useful Spells for Librarians' with incorrectly written spells in it? Seems weird, but I suppose it happens, people writing down the wrong amounts or people calling things by different names." She checked the clock on her phone. 17:17. *Robert would be here soon.* Alice tried to stop herself from smiling and failed.

"Go," Stuart said, shooing her off with mock exasperation. He did not know whether it was genes, the certain level of naivety or the way some of her emotions seemed to be so freely displayed, but there was something that made Alice seem a lot younger than she actually was. A brief, painful memory stabbed at his heart and it was his turn to force himself to concentrate on the present, as he unconsciously rubbed at his side.

"Thank you for all of this," Alice said, smiling gratefully at him. She had genuinely had fun as well as learning a lot. "I know I can be trying at times, but this has been brilliant."

"You're welcome," said Stuart, somewhat surprised to admit that he had missed mentoring potential new Librarians. He supposed it might be time to put out feelers for new recruits; if he was going to teach one Novice he might as well attempt to teach seven. "It's been quite educational for me to see a Witch working on her craft. The few that come in tend not to chat; they collect what they came in for and you don't see them until the next time they need something. And of course, unless they ask you directly, you never know what they want or if it ever works."

"Well, if I can explain it, I will try to," Alice said, grabbing her bag. "See you tomorrow," she said, practically flying out of the room.

Dr Anthonys watched as the solar system hanging from the ceiling, slowly ground to halt. For the past hour it had been moving with all of the known planets moving at the correct relative speed and orbit. He had figured it was one of those that she would not have been able to explain.

Chapter 13

"Hey," Alice said, running down the steps of the library, throwing her arms around the neck of the handsome man leaning against a black Honda Accord, that had its hazard lights flashing. She drew back slightly, wondering if she was being overly familiar for a second date, but Robert did not seem to mind. In fact, she thought that maybe he looked slightly pleased; he certainly did not look embarrassed, which was a relief.

"Hey," Robert said, kissing her cheek. "You didn't forget or decide you suddenly have to emigrate back to London then?"

"I'm not from London," Alice laughed, rolling her eyes. There was a tendency for the Americans she had met to immediately ask if she was from the capital city and if she knew the Queen, whom, of course, she did not. "Wrong city, but right country at least. I mean, I hope you don't think London's a country because it isn't."

"I know. English college room-mate, remember?" he said with a grin, opening the car door for her.

"Well, you never know. And to be fair, it's so tempting to troll with these kinda things, especially as there was this one guy I met who asked if England was in London. Like, seriously asked it; I probably just politely corrected him, but seriously, mind-blown that anyone could think that..." She trailed off, realising that she was rambling again and that Robert was looking at her in bemusement. She let out a deep breath and buckled her seat belt. "I was a little worried you might not show up, that maybe you'd had a better offer," she said, settling into the passenger seat.

"I'm not sure there could be a better offer," he said, shooting her another smile. "Beautiful girl, Chinese food, a selection of movies or games – at the moment, the only thing that could be better is knowing for sure whether my housemate plans on sticking around or not."

"I'm like, 95% sure I trust you," Alice teased. Now that she was fairly sure that he liked her, she felt incredibly comfortable around him. For a short while, she had wondered if she was being desperate, needy, weird or crazy for agreeing to go to his house the day after meeting him, but she really did like Chinese takeaway food and him.

"And I'm, like, 95% sure I'm going to need the chaperone."
She laughed before her face grew mildly grave. "Are you a Vampire?"
Robert unconsciously froze and did not look over at her. "Yes."

"Okay," said Alice, with a shrug. "You should probably know I'm a Witch, although I suppose you probably know already."

"I suspected. It's not entirely obvious though,"

"I suppose you think I'm kinda stupid, not knowing last night."

"I was surprised, but at no point have I ever thought of you as being stupid." He glanced over at her. "I am curious as to how you're so sure now."

"I spent the day doing Potions and Defence Against the Dark Arts," Alice replied with a laugh that deepened with Robert's 'not-quite-sure-whether to believe that' look. "The Head Librarian is teaching me things that I guess most supernaturals just grow up knowing. I guess my parents had their reasons for that." She paused for a moment. "Is it a problem? I hear Witches aren't particularly well liked."

"Not to me. Witch or not, you're the most interesting and beautiful woman I've met in a really long time."

"Thanks," she said, smiling and blushing as she pushed her glasses up shyly.

***

They pulled up alongside a nice little house that was fairly identical to all the other little houses on the street. It was a world removed from all the skyscrapers and concrete, and Alice felt like it had been a lifetime since she had seen front gardens and driveways.

"Not quite what you were expecting, is it?" said Robert, with a grin.

"No, not really," said Alice, looking at the blue house with navy highlights and white trim. It had a porch with a swing chair and a real-life white picket fence. "I guess I thought you'd have some kind of tricked out bachelor pad in the heart of the city."

"Not on my salary," Robert laughed. "When I was younger, I did admittedly live in a tricked-out bachelor pad that belonged to my cousin, Jack, but I guess I'm still too human to not feel like I'd outgrown that kind of lifestyle."

"Hmmm," said Alice.
Robert looked at her carefully. He was finding her unusually hard to read.

"Looks like your front garden needs some TLC," said Alice, noting the piles of dead leaves, the uneven grass and the borders of dead plants as they walked up the short crazy-paved path.

"Front garden?"

"Yes," said Alice slightly snippily, before she stuck her tongue out at him. "The garden at the front of the house. Just 'coz you'd call it, I dunno, a yard, I suppose?"

"I suppose," said Robert with a smile, opening the brown, wooden door with frosted glass panes. "Honey, I'm home," he called, making sure he could be heard over the music. He squeezed Alice's hand reassuringly and closed the front door behind them, before leading her into the front room.

"Alice, Clive. Clive, Alice," said Robert, his right hand unconsciously indicating between them as his housemate came down the stairs.

Clive was a little shorter than Robert and had a slighter build. He had an oval-ish face; big dark brown eyes framed by long, thick dark eyelashes; and short, cropped black hair. Although Robert had already told her that Clive was in his thirties like they were, Alice felt like he was older. She supposed it was the air of authoritative confidence that carrying a badge and a gun gave to the really good cops, as well as the all black outfit.

"Nice to meet you," said Alice, holding out a hand and smiling uncertainly, trying not to bite her lip. He seemed to pause for a moment, his soft brown eyes studying her curiously for a moment, before extending his coffee-coloured hand.

"Pleasure's mine," said Clive, shaking her hand politely. He winced at the sudden stab of static electricity, noticing that Alice seemed mildly pleased and amused. "You're like, already, my favourite girl he's ever bought here. He's actually tidied up and there's suddenly food and drink in the fridge."

"How can you shame me like this in front of new people?" Robert asked. "That hurts me, like here." He put a hand over his heart. "Do you mind giving me a few minutes?" he asked, turning to Alice. "Stressful day."

"Sure, no problem," said Alice. Unusually, she already felt comfortable despite being in another new environment and meeting another new person. She watched as he bounded up the stairs and smiled awkwardly at Robert's housemate.

"Would you like a drink?" asked Clive.

"Just a diet coke or something, please?" Alice replied.

"Coming right up." He disappeared into the kitchen and Alice started to look around the living room.

It was a comfortable, airy room, without a lot of clutter. A few extension cords filled with different plugs, but otherwise, it was remarkably tidy. Two large sofas, one of which was directly opposite a 65" 4K Ultra HD TV, and her eyes swept across the room, looking for all of the speakers, of which there were several to go with 9.1 DTS home cinema system. There was also a projector and blackout curtains, as well as a number of consoles and controllers. She was a little jealous.

The wall behind the sofa was pretty much just shelving for movies and games; she was a little disappointed by the lack of books, but then she figured maybe Clive was not a reader. Or possibly, neither of them liked to share their books, which was understandable. There were a couple of tables, clearly positioned for beverage and snack resting, as well as the expected assortment of remote controls and the Chinese take-out menu.

"Thank you," Alice said, perching on the edge of the sofa as Clive brought over her drink. She was not sure if she might be in someone's spot, given that the cushions were slightly more worn on the settee facing the television, than the one on a diagonal to it. She frowned unable to stop the jealous niggle eating at her.

"Spit it out," said Clive, noticing her expression.
She looked at him, seeing only gentle curiosity in his expression. *Definitely the face for a good cop*, she thought *unlike the Twelfth Doctor*. "I really don't want to be asking this, but exactly how many girls are we talking here?" She coloured slightly.

Clive laughed. "Sorry, that's on me. Not many. He doesn't really bring anyone round unless they're pretty important. He's genuinely not a new girl every night kinda guy."
She tried to cover up her relief and pleasure. "What about you?"

"What about me?" echoed Clive, grinning.
"Are you the 'new girl every night' kinda guy?" she

teased, thinking Clive seemed far too nice to be like that.

"I wish," Clive answered. Not that he wanted to be a man-whore, but the occasional one-night stand or brief fling would be a welcome change to the painstaking task of finding a Zombie female. Much like the Were, Zombies had to be careful around humans as it was far too easy for them to pass on their gift/condition/curse (delete as appropriate). Whilst the Were condition could only be passed on through deep biting or deep clawing in either form, the Zombie condition could be passed on through the simple exchange of bodily fluids. It was not so virulent that it could be caught from a sneeze, but certainly kissing and sex were out of the question.

Other negatives included ageing as normal, wounds and breaks took a long time to heal, and unless one wanted to turn into a shambling, decomposing wreck, one had to ingest human brains on a fairly regular basis. On the plus side, he was extremely hard to kill, which was useful since Clive had wanted to be a detective ever since he had been a small kid and certain criminals were far too trigger-happy.

"Unfortunately," Clive continued "Being a Zombie makes that a lot harder than it is for Vampires."

"Not just a bite thing then?" Alice asked.

"No. It's a bit more *iZombie* than *Dawn of the Dead*. No visions though," he added, foreseeing the question as she clearly understood the references.

"Shame. I imagine that would make your job a little easier."

"Speaking of which, should I be reminding people they probably shouldn't go into strangers' houses?"

Alice coloured slightly. "Well, he doesn't feel like a stranger. And I'm probably more than capable of taking care of myself."

"I might be more worried about him than you," said Clive with a grin.

"Afraid that I'm the Wicked Witch of the East?"

"I was."

"But not now?"

"Not now."

"Good," she said, smiling. "Really not one for evil intentions."

"It's reassuring to know that I am unlikely to return and find his head in the freezer."

"As long as you maintain that it is a possibility," Alice said, getting up and studying the movie shelves.

"Well, I am aware of most of his bad habits, so sure, it's always a possibility," Clive said with a grin, looking at his housemate as came down the stairs.

"Seriously? It only took 10minutes for you two to start a murder plot?" Robert asked as he made his way into the kitchen.

Clive just grinned and grabbed his things from the side bowl.

"Don't get into too much trouble whilst I'm gone," Clive said, putting on his jacket and opening the front door. "Oh, and Alice?"

"Clive?" she replied, turning her head to look at him and smiling quizzically.

"Be gentle with him. He's more fragile than he looks."

"Dude, I don't even know what you're trying to do to me at this point," Robert said, lounging against the kitchen door frame. "This is like, beyond shaming. Go, begone."

"I'm gone," Clive said, nodding his farewell to Alice.

"'Night," she said. "I like him," she added, turning to Robert as the front door closed.

"Should I be jealous?" Robert teased, coming to stand beside her.

"Not with your eyes," she said, a slight swoon to her tone as she looked at his ocean blue irises. She pulled a face of irritated embarrassment. "Said that out loud, didn't I?"

"Yup," he said, looking pleased. Smug, but in a cute roguish way. He looked at the movies in her hands. "Those are your choices?"

"They are," Alice replied, seriously.

"Like for real? Not just cos you think this is what I might

be into," Robert asked, raising one eyebrow sceptically.

"As I said yesterday, I'm too old to be bothering with that shit any more." Alice laughed. "I can't really decide, so these for a few of the ones I felt like I could watch right now. *Alien*, *Aliens*, *Silence of the Lambs*, *Seven*, *Captain America* or *Star Wars*, the original trilogy. *Rogue One* also acceptable. Or *Firefly*; I assume you have that somewhere, but you said movie."

Robert smiled. "I want to say *Star Wars*, for the sheer fact that I kinda want to make you stay the entire night to watch them all. But again, work night, so, I guess *Alien*?"

"OK," Alice said, promptly putting the other movies back in their allotted places. "I gotta ask, what's with this?" She swept her hand along the middle shelf. "I mean, it's fine I guess, but er, I wouldn't really pick anything off it." She took a second look. "Well, maybe *Miss Congeniality* and *Fever Pitch*. And I do like *Ever After*. And I don't think *Stardust* should be there."

"That would be the ex shelf," he said, moving to stand behind her. The middle shelf was a collection of what would generally be described as "chick flicks", either left by old girlfriends or bought in the belief that they would appeal to certain girls. "Not really my thing."

"No wonder it didn't work out," she said, turning to face him. *Dear gods, those eyes.* "*Dirty Dancing*? *Love Actually*? *The Notebook*? Stab my eyes with a lightsaber." He was so close, she felt like she could not breathe. Part of her wanted him to back up just a little so that she could maybe think again; most of her wanted to get closer.

"You are just full of surprises," Robert said, with a slight shake of the head and a crooked smile.

"How so?" asked Alice, looking up at him, bemused. She felt like the air around them was pressing against her. Her gaze kept darting to the floor, unable to keep looking at his eyes and lips. She felt like she was burning up.

"Okay, I know it's a silly thing to say, but you kinda look like you might be more into the romantic stuff."

"I am a romantic at heart, I just for some reason don't

enjoy soppy, love films. I'm okay with the fairy tales, but I'd rather stuff blow up and aliens burst out of chests... Which sounds like such an appealing quality now that I say it aloud," she said. She laughed, feeling slightly more normal. She looked at him quizzically. "Is that terrible of me?"

"No," he said, grinning.

The next song suddenly blared out a hundred times louder than the last, making her jump. It was slight, but it was enough that her body brushed lightly against his, and he decided that she had to be going as crazy as he was. He kissed her. It started off as innocently and gently as their goodbye kiss the previous night, but as she began to kiss back with more and more passion, it lasted longer and longer. He sat down on the sofa, pulling her down with him, so that she was straddling him. He kissed her again, could feel her blood racing, and when she pulled lightly on his bottom lip with her teeth, he felt his eyes turning red and his teeth lengthening. He had to stop, internally admonishing his Vampire side for wanting to get carried away.

"I love your music," he said, momentarily breaking away to let her catch her breath, recognising the song from the night before.

"Really?" she asked, her voice slightly ragged, as though she had forgotten that breathing was necessary.

"I've no idea," he admitted. "I haven't really been listening. I do love what it does to you, though."

"It's good music," said Alice with a bright smile, her eyes sparkling. "Well, I like it at least. And it does make me feel strangely sexy and confident and beautiful, even if I have to close my eyes to imagine it to be true."

"You are definitely sexy and beautiful, and when you believe it, you do get even hotter. And you should believe it, cos I think you are incredibly sexy and beautiful." He stared intently at her for a moment. "May I?"

"As long as you're not preparing to take them for your eye bucket," she said, as he slowly removed her glasses. "It's fine though, I can barely see anything at the moment in any case."

"They're too beautiful to go in a bucket," he said, staring at the dark flecks in her brown eyes. Her pupils were large and dark, making her look young and innocent, but there was a glint that tried to suggest she was anything but.

"You do seem to know all the right things to say to a girl," she said with a smile, before closing her eyes and kissing him again.

He helped her pull off her hoodie, and she pulled off his jumper. "I like this top," she said absently, as she revealed the long-sleeved blue shirt that she recognised from the coffee-shop. She timidly ran her fingers across his chest, and he honestly could not remember wanting a woman as badly as he wanted her right now. His fingers brushed against a ticklish spot on her side, and she gasped, flinching in a movement that seemed to invite him to play with her breasts. His hands slid up the inside of her top, and he paused for a moment, giving her the chance to stop him, but she did not. His thumbs caressed the cups of her bra, and she moaned, her back arching slightly, her head tilting back, hair falling away to expose her neck. He kissed a trail down from her lips and along her throat, the tip of his tongue reaching out to taste the slight saltiness of her skin. He could feel the blood pounding with her desire and uncertainty, so close that he could almost taste it. He could feel his canines beginning to extend again. *It would be so easy...*

The fire alarm went off, and the spell was broken. He put his demon back in its box, grateful that she had not noticed, and feeling somewhat concerned at how easily it seemed to be escaping.

"Erm, wow," she said. She was still sitting on him, looking slightly dazed. She reached for her glasses and slid off his lap onto the empty sofa seat beside him.

"Yeah... I should really turn that off." He felt a little dazed himself; he was unused to feeling such a powerful urge to drink blood.

"Is something burning?" she asked, sniffing the air tentatively.

"Wasn't cooking anything. Must be the batteries going or something. One minute." He went into the kitchen and pressed the red button in the middle of the smoke detector. He had no idea when they had last changed the batteries, if at all, and as he thought about how close he had come to biting Alice's neck, he supposed the timing was fortuitous. "Would you like another drink?"

"No thank you. I still have quite a bit left," she called back from the other room.

He got himself a beer from the fridge and retrieved a small bottle of thick red liquid from the back of the top shelf. He used the stopper to place three drops of coppery B-negative onto his tongue and hoped it would be enough to quiet the demon for the rest of the evening. The last thing he wanted was to scare Alice off by becoming an uncontrollable bloodsucker.

Robert was not surprised when he returned from the kitchen to see her looking at the take-out menu he had left on the table earlier. Of course he was a little disappointed, but he understood.

"Sorry," Alice said, looking up at him with a rueful smile.

"Don't be. It's fine," Robert said, sitting next to her.

"I want to. I just can't. Not just yet."
He kissed her softly and quickly. "It's fine. Whenever you're ready."

"Thank you."

"So, dinner and a movie?" he suggested, picking up the remote and turning on the TV.

"Sounds good."

***

After they had finished eating, Alice curled up next to him on the sofa with the familiarity of a long-term lover, and Robert loved how it all felt so easy already. Apart from when they started kissing. Then it all felt new and exciting.

"I'm going to change the batteries," Robert said, after the fifth time, suspecting that the cause was not entirely natural.

"OK," Alice said, looking flustered as she straightened her clothing again.

Robert ducked into the kitchen and took the batteries out of the fire alarm, and returned to the sofa without a word.

For a little while, they continued to watch the movie, until the shy, furtive looks at one another turned into kissing again. Part of him wanted to just lose himself in the attraction, but he could not help being extremely curious as to whether the fire alarm was somehow Alice's doing. He was conscious of not being too assertive, but he had to push a little to be sure. Alice had slowly ended up with her head on the arm of the sofa, and now he was practically laying on top of her as he kissed her, his hands moving up along her legs. *Just an experiment*, he reminded himself, *unless she wants to…*

The fire alarm went off again. *That's infuriating*, he thought, sighing, *but incredibly sweet.*

"Damn thing must be broken," he said, climbing off of her and going through the charade of sorting out the appliance; he had a feeling that she would be even more embarrassed if he told her she was making it go off. "Still, I suppose it's getting late and you have a cat to see to?" he called from the kitchen.

"Yeah…" Alice agreed, reluctantly. She looked at her phone for the time. It was getting late. "I don't think he'd mind much if I stayed out all night, if he could open the packets on his own." She stood up, hastily pulling on her hoodie and gathering the rest of her things before she could change her mind.

"I don't want you to go," Robert said, as he grabbed his car keys. "In case you were thinking I'm trying to get rid of you." He pulled her close.

"And I don't really want to go," she said, allowing herself to melt into another kiss. "But you're right, I do need to."

"How about Saturday then?"

"Yes. I would love that."

Chapter 14

"I hate working Saturdays," said Bruce, sitting down at a desk filled with books, manuscripts, a computer and a phone. There was a holder full of pens and a lot of different coloured highlighters and sticky notes. It was not too dissimilar to the cubicle desks of his workmates, although most of them had tried to personalise it at least in some small way. With the exception of Robert, everyone had a photograph or two tacked up of being on holiday with their respective partners, calendars, sports flags or whatever else helped them to get through the more tedious days. If Robert had anything personal around, it was locked within his desk drawer.

"Like you actually have better things to do," said Jeff, leaning back in his chair. "Doesn't Christopher work like every weekend under the sun?"

"Yeah, but it gives me chance to watch all the stuff he's not into. Sports mostly," Bruce replied. "Or go play some pick-up with a few guys in the building. And he usually pops home for lunch. If he can."

"I'm okay with it," said Patrick, scrolling through his e-mails. "Beats listening to Sally go on about how we need new curtains, which I'm quite sure we don't. I mean, as long as they don't let the light in, surely they're fine?"

"Urgh, hope she doesn't mention that to Susan. If I end up looking at fabric samples, I'm blaming you," said Jeff, picking up a yellow highlighter and flicking through another manuscript.

"Anyone want anything from the machine?" asked

Bruce, getting up again.

"Already?" Jeff asked, incredulously. "Fuck knows how you're not the size of a house with the crap you eat." He rolled his eyes as Bruce merely shrugged and looked at him for an answer. "Too early for me."

"Nope," said Patrick, shaking his head. "Sally's on at me to diet, and that woman can tell when I cheat. And I want to get a breakfast burrito at lunch."

"Where's Rob?"

"Matt's office. Phone, I think."

"Eh, he never eats anything in here anyway," said Bruce, glancing over to the office before walking off to the snack machine in the communal rest area.

The third floor was empty bar the four of them, although the building was far from empty. There was security downstairs, and various skeleton crews for each department at Achronus Publishings, just in case there were any printing issues or problems with distributors or heaven forbid, complaints from writers or their agents.

"Hot blonde is in too," said Bruce, sitting back down.

"When you say that, do you mean the woman that the rest of the office is calling "Hot Blonde", or are you talking about some different person?"

"The one you chauvinist pigs call "Hot Blonde"," said Bruce. He thought about throwing the frickles at Patrick, but if Patrick was dieting, he might actually eat them instead of throwing them back. "The women in the office call her something else entirely, when not using her actual name. Also, I don't generally find blondes hot, unless tall, dark blonde and handsome over there decides to switch sides," he teased in a loud voice, as Robert exited the office.

"Luckily, I am confident enough in my sexuality not to be concerned by this harassment," said Robert, stealing a frickle. He pulled a face. "How can you eat a whole packet of those things?"

"Easily," said Bruce grinning, tipping the packet into his

mouth as the others shook their heads despairingly, making various noises and faces of disgust.

"Well, I hope you've got some mints, 'cos we have a meeting on six after lunch," said Robert.

"Oh?" Bruce managed to mumble over the crunch of a mouthful of food.

"Yeah, that's all I know. They want our team up on six at 2pm."

"Maybe you'll actually notice Hot Blonde this time then," said Patrick.

"Who?" asked Robert, not able to picture any females in the building that they might consider to be hot and blonde.

"Like they know her name. Jane something. You know the sixth floor rarely bothers with us shmucks on the third, although that woman clearly wants to get her red lacquered nails into you," said Bruce.

"No idea who you're on about," said Robert, picking up a stack of manuscripts from Bruce's desk and taking them over to his own. He grabbed a highlighter and started scanning through the first of the submitted novels.

"She started about a month ago or something. We were in the lift with her once and she was definitely flirting with you," said Patrick, incredulously. He lifted his hands from his keyboard, his face etched with disbelief.

Robert raised his gaze but continued to look blank. He blinked at them quizzically and returned to his speed-reading.

"I'd love to be you for a day," said Jeff, wistfully. "I've never known what it's like to have so many beautiful women throw themselves at me, that I barely notice when a hot chick in the office is after me. Or..." continued Jeff, thoughtfully. "Maybe I have switched sides, after my dinner date with the dude off the dating website."

As per the forfeit provisos, Robert had shown Jeff the message from Alice agreeing to dinner, but that had been the extent of it. As far as Robert was concerned, he only had to provide proof that he had messaged someone for a date and that said person had agreed to it; he had not felt the need to show off her profile or go into details of their dinner after the fact.

"She's not a dude," said Robert, patiently. He dragged his highlighter across an incredibly long and awkward sentence.

"Figures that if it was a woman, you'd sleep with her on the first date," said Patrick.

"Low opinion of me much?" asked Robert, shaking his head in disbelief. Every time he thought his colleagues could not reach a further misogynistic or chauvinistic low, they found new depths. What was slightly more annoying, was the fact that they were only this bad when it came to his love-life.

"No, very high one actually. Totally expect you to seal the deal first time," said Patrick, raising his hand and grinning as he nodded his head in a smug fashion. "Up top playa!"

"I am amazed any of you are married," said Robert, decidedly disappointed in himself for being amused. He did not high-five his co-worker though. "No, we didn't sleep together."

"So she could be a..." Jeff started.

"She is not a dude," Robert interrupted, rolling his eyes, trying to focus on the manuscript before him, even though he already knew it was going in the rejected pile.

"Is she a troll?" asked Patrick, sympathetically. His green eyes twinkled and he grinned broadly.

"No!" said Robert, beginning to lose patience, even though he knew they were joking. "She's beautiful, smart, funny... She's special, okay and we'll move at her pace. So if you could please drop it now, that would be awesome."

Jeff began to open his mouth and Bruce punched him in the arm, shaking his head as he did so. "Shut it," Bruce hissed quietly at him. Bruce then turned back to Robert. "You're seeing her again then?" he asked, with genuine interest.

"Yeah, supposed to be taking her to Martinelli's this evening."

"Oh, so you do plan on..." Jeff trailed off as Bruce and

Robert glared warningly at him. "Taking her out for a nice dinner then?" Jeff amended. Given that Martinelli's was a quaint Italian bistro, filled with cliches and candles, it was generally considered in the office (mostly by the men) as the place to take a date when one wanted to push the relationship towards sex.

"Yeah," said Robert, continuing to watch the others carefully. One more false move and he would be done with talking about his personal life. "She's more into horror movies and thriller books, than chick flicks and romance novels, but I think she'd still like stereotypical romantic gestures – like candlelit dinners and flowers. Is that flower stand on 21st still there?"

"Think so," said Jeff, cautiously. "I only remember to look when I'm in trouble."

"And then you'll probably need to upgrade to jewellery and shoes and handbags in order to gain forgiveness," Patrick muttered, dismally.

"Not sure about that yet," said Robert, bemused. "As in, not sure that's what she's into, as well as not sure we're quite into that territory yet. This is only our third date. The flowers are because I want to buy her flowers."

"Mm hmm," murmured Patrick, exchanging a knowing look with Jeff. Just because you did not know you had done something wrong, did not mean that 'she' agreed.

"Three dates in four days?" calculated Bruce. "That seems like a lot."

"Does it?" asked Robert. "Maybe. I don't know. Like I said, she's special. And I love being around her. Anyway, can we seriously now not talk about women, and either get on with some work or talk about the horrendous season the Patriots are having?"

"Indeed. What's next on the wager calendar?" asked Jeff.

"Not sure, but I think it's my turn to choose the forfeit. I'm thinking bungee-jumping or sky-diving or waving a 'Best Season ever!' banner at a Knicks game."

***

The two o'clock meeting, from a business standpoint, went well; on a personal front, Robert felt it was a nightmare. The fact that it had gone well enough that they had decided to move the meeting up another floor to include the big-wigs and the author, meant that not only did he have to change into his suit and tie, but he had to call Alice twice to apologise for being late and pushing back dinner. The third time he called her, he said that he understood if she would rather just cancel, but Alice had said they could get dinner at the 'Cauldron, if he wanted, and that she would meet him there.

If the fact that it had impeded his dinner plans was not enough, Robert had hoped that he was not going to be needed on *The Devil Possesses* project any more. Originally, he had wanted to stay on the project until the novel was released, but after all the rumours about changes in the author and a ridiculous number of impending amendments, he had gotten the feeling that he was better off trying to find something new.

But for some reason, Damien Houseman, author of *The Devil Possesses*, had requested Robert and his team be put back on the project for the book's launch.

Houseman was present at the second meeting and Robert had almost not recognised him. Clearly, something major had happened in Houseman's life over the past few months. The Houseman Robert had met several months ago, would never have wanted a big launch, but this one was excited to push a huge event, one that would essentially cash-in on the recent successes of TV shows like *The Exorcist*. Given the show's renewal, and the continuing popularity of horror films in the cinema, the book was now going to be launched in late August, to coincide with Fall scheduling. Apparently, the big-wigs and Houseman now wanted to hire out a house in the Hamptons, and thought a lavish party that would feed into the idea of demonic alliances leading to power and wealth was the way to go.

Robert did not know how or why so much effort was being put into *The Devil Possesses*. Admittedly, the original draft he had seen felt different, new and worth being pushed for greatness, but if the changes were true, then it had become another generic horror novel. Still, Robert was not in a position to make the decisions, nor did he want to be, so he smiled and nodded and agreed to talk to Human Resources and Public Relations on Monday to start the ball rolling on invites to various well-known authors, actors and politicians, as well as the proof reading and the more usual tropes of releasing a new book.

He was relieved when they finally got out of the office and he cursed as he looked at his watch.

"You okay?" asked Bruce, looking up from the text message he was writing.

"Yeah, just annoyed. We really weren't needed. All they did was ruin everyone's dinner plans," said Robert, crossly.

"Sorry about that," said Bruce, even though they both knew it was not his fault. "So, is dinner cancelled or has the venue changed?"

"Changed. Why?" said Robert, looking up from the phone screen. "And why are you grinning like that?"

"Well, I figure changed means she's equally into you, which is a good thing," said Bruce.

"You think?" Robert questioned, a slight smile tugging at his lips.

"Yes. And ignore the posturing from the other two, because no date is waiting three hours if all they're interested in is sex."

"Christopher is really rubbing off on you, isn't he?"
Bruce gave a small smile. His relationship was not quite so long in the tooth that he had reached Patrick and Jeff's levels of cynicism when talking about it. Admittedly, he did not have the same brightness that Robert had, but there was enough that when talking about his better half, a little pride crept into

his voice. "A little. He does make me think a lot more, even though he tries to leave a lot of the psychology at work. He's far too good for me."

"Will he enjoy going to a big party?" Robert asked, smiling. He had met Christopher a few times and thought he was one of the few genuine, everyday heroes. A nice guy working with underprivileged and abused children, who always maintained an air of positivity and a voice of reason. Robert also got the impression that Christopher, much like Susan and Sally, would not turn down the chance to dress up and experience the extravagance of the excessively rich for a night.

"Will he ever!" said Bruce with a grin. "Will Alice? Assuming you're still with her by then." He had to add the caveat, just in case. Although Robert was never one to kiss-and-tell, he would normally give them a bit more than he had done regarding Alice, and that alone made Bruce think that maybe Robert had finally found the right person.

"I'd like to hope so," said Robert, smiling. He shook his head and smiled as he pictured how Alice's face would scrunch up with scepticism and disappointment at the idea of having to wear a formal dress, associate with a form of the elite and endure fancy foods and wines. "And no, I'm fairly confident that it's probably one of her worst nightmares. She'd go though, if I can't get out of it."

"Well, I hope you can't, especially if we don't get to meet her beforehand," said Bruce.

"Or him," joked Jeff.

Robert rolled his eyes as the others laughed and shook his head. He drowned out their noise and sent a text to Alice, apologising again and letting her know that he was finally on his way.

Chapter 15

On the off-chance that there was a table free, Robert called up Martinelli's again, having already spoken to the owners to cancel his original reservation. He still wanted to take Alice to the quaint little Italian bistro on 21st and Crescent, and give her the cliché experience of drippy candles, roses and violins, but there was nothing doing. He momentarily gave Rizzoli's a thought, but given that it was on the other side of town and Alice was probably already starving, he sighed and resigned himself to the fact that he would have to settle for taking her to a much less romantic dinner at the Leaky Cauldron.

Alice was waiting in the foyer, her large winter coat folded over her arms, nervously looking around, and Robert felt bad for adding to her anxiety by being even later than expected.

Robert walked hurriedly towards her and kissed her cheek. "Sorry about all this. For mucking you about and then being late. I also owe you a massive bouquet of flowers. Although, since I was hoping to buy you some flowers anyway, I guess I owe you two." He loosened the scarf and took off his coat.

"No worries. I understand," Alice said, deciding not to mention that it had been agony waiting for him, wondering if he was actually going to show or whether he had realised that he should probably be with someone far more confident and beautiful than she was. "I feel under-dressed," she said, looking at his attire.

"I feel overdressed." He sighed, rubbing the back of his

head briefly. "Work stuff. One of the books we're releasing soon is tipped for "big things", so we get called into a meeting to discuss one thing, which somehow leads to a last-minute meeting with our big-bosses and the author, which of course, means that I, and a couple of colleagues, have to do a last-minute costume change. Luckily, we all tend to keep a spare suit for just such occasions."

"Surely that's a good thing? A 'big thing' book, not necessarily the costume change," said Alice, stealing shy glances at him. She had always had a thing about good looking guys in nice suits. She thought maybe it was the "James Bond effect" - the unconscious association of an elegant suit and a handsome man, with danger, lust and excitement.

"I guess. I don't like the book much myself, so I guess I was hoping I was done with it," said Robert. He had liked its original iteration; not the one up for release. Everything about Damian Houseman and *The Devil Possesses* seemed to have become twisted and unpleasant since he signed the writer. "It's not for a while yet, but I guess if you come with me, the launch won't be so bad."

"You look very handsome though," she said, admiring the way the impeccably tailored suit seemed to make accentuate his physique and although it was a shade of blue that bordered on being black, it was enough to made his eyes stand out even more.

"Thanks. You look amazing," he said.

"Thank you."

Robert paused a moment, let out a breath and stopped to really looked at her. "I'm sorry. Seriously, though, you really do look amazing, I mean, screw work, I am here with a gorgeous woman that I haven't even kissed yet." He kissed her shyly smiling lips. "Better already," he said with a smile. The green eye-shadow really brought out her eyes, and the neckline of her knee-length blue dress was far more daring than anything she had worn previously, even if she was still wearing ankle boots and leggings. And the fact that she seemed to be so happy when they kissed, made her all the more beautiful. Robert kissed her again, his free hand skimming over the side of her thigh and up to her waist. *Not leggings*, he realised, suddenly feeling quite hot and bothered. Luckily, someone opened the door and as the bitter winter wind brushed the back of his neck, he used it as an excuse to stop himself doing anything too crazy too soon. "We should go sit. We're in the way again."

They walked upstairs and took the table at the window where they had sat for their first date.

"Are you okay?" Robert asked, looking at her. She was looking as anxious as she had on that first night, perhaps even more so.

"Mmm-hmmm," said Alice

He watched as she took a large sip of her wine and tried not to pull a face at the taste. He smiled and chuckled internally, once again thinking that she really was adorable at times.

"Are you sure? You seem a little on edge."

"I'm just... over-thinking things," she said, swirling her drink a little, watching the liquid and occasionally glancing up at him with a small smile.

"Definitely don't do that. You'll have a lot more fun if you don't," Robert said, reaching out to take her hand and watching as a little cascade of red sparks flew.

"Easier said than done," she replied ruefully, although her eyes did brighten momentarily. Her shoulders dropped and she sighed. "You should know, I have depression and sometimes it gets really bad and I am awful to be around," she blurted out.

He held her hand a little tighter before she could pull it away. "I appreciate you telling me that, but if you're trying to scare me off, you'll have to do better than that."

Alice smiled gratefully at him, and straightened up a little. "Okay then, what about the fact that I might be the most powerful Witch in the world?"

"It's impressive," said Robert, shrugging and leaning

back in his chair, keeping her hand in his, his eyes twinkling with good humour. "But, er, still not scary enough, sorry."

"I have a talking cat who is extremely hard to please," Alice added.

Robert momentarily let the act drop. "You have a Familiar?" he asked, noting the pride and love that always appeared in her eyes when she mentioned her cat. "Cool. I've always wanted to meet one."

"Seriously though, if he doesn't let you pass, I don't think I'm supposed to see you any more," Alice said, with a little bit of worry and sadness in her eyes.

"I'll be on my best behaviour around him," Robert promised, even though he had a feeling that whatever it was that the cat would judge him on, was something far deeper than manners. He could understand Alice's concern though – he certainly did not like the idea of not seeing her again.

Alice sat back and looked at him, biting her lip as she looked at him with some scepticism. "You're really not phased by any of this, are you?"

"No," he said, smiling at her. "I'm not."

"Would you like to meet my cat?" she asked, her eyes large as she bit the inside of her lip and looked at him.

"Sure. After all, you've met my house-mate."

***

They pulled up alongside a street of Brownstone apartments, and Alice was beginning to feel even more flustered. Her stomach felt full of butterflies, and her skin felt like it was on fire. For various reasons, Alice had never been one to bring a guy home and even though she wanted Robert, she still felt slightly hesitant.

"Are you sure about this?" Robert asked, taking her hand again as he brought the car to a stop outside of her building. "We really don't need to rush anything."

She smiled and looked at him, trying not to stare too deeply into his eyes. "I'm sure." She got out of the car and waited on the steps of her building, just admiring the clear night sky for a moment, whilst her body start to flame informing her that Robert was now stood next to her. Given that the night-time temperature was supposed to be minus2, it felt a lot milder. "I like the stars," she said shrugging, as she stared at the twinkling lights in the clear velvet black skies. Not being a naturally forceful or forward person, she blushed and bit her lip shyly, before looking into his deep blue eyes. "OK, this might sound a little silly…"

He stopped the rest of her words with a firm and passionate kiss, and Alice felt like she was melting into him. She almost could not feel the sudden, cool rain soaking into her clothes, and with her eyes closed and brain swimming, she certainly did not care that her carefully styled hair would be ruined. It was harder to ignore the hailstones though.

Bloody winter weather. She reluctantly broke away and fumbled to open the front door. She undid her coat and tried to dry her glasses on her dress. It was a far from perfect job, but it helped enough to see that the skies were still clear and the hail was only on her building's front steps. Alice shot a sheepish glance at Robert.

"It's a little weird, I guess," Robert said, laughing softly as he pushed a lock of his wet hair to the left. "Not as noisy as the fire alarm though."

Alice's cheeks turned red. "It's kinda new to me too," she confessed, trying to wring out as much water as possible onto the welcome mat in the porch. She shook her head in slight disbelief and wry amusement at the slowly dissipating, extremely localised precipitation. "Sorry," she said as she led the way up to her top floor apartment.

"It's a good way to get a guy out of his clothes," he teased, loosening the black tie and undoing the top button of his shirt.

She froze with her keys in the door, slightly mortified

and blushing furiously. She knew he was joking; she just found the idea of kissing in the rain romantic (and it had been amazing, even if she had just wanted to kiss under the stars for a bit), but she could not deny it; as she turned to look at him, noticing how the white shirt was now clinging to his finely toned torso, that it was not only incredibly sexy, but did provide a legitimate reason for him to take his clothes off.

"I'll get you a towel," Alice squeaked, immediately giving herself a mental face-palm. She coughed discreetly, trying to clear her throat and regain some dignity. "You should hang your jacket on the fire-guard. There's tea and coffee in the kitchen if you want some, to like, warm up or something," she called as she ducked into the airing cupboard. She pulled out two large, warm white towels, tried to collect herself and headed back to the living room. She paused for a moment, watching as her black cat brushed himself up against Robert's leg and allowed Robert to stroke his head. "That's Onion," Alice said, putting the towels on the sofa and taking Robert's other hand. "You can make friends with him in the morning."

Chapter 16

Alice tiptoed out of the room, and leant against the kitchen counter as the kettle boiled. She jumped slightly as Onion stuck his cold nose on her ankle.

"Sorry puddin'," she said picking him up for a quick hug. She walked over to a cupboard, pulled out some Felix and emptied the pouch into Onion's breakfast bowl. He sniffed it and promptly turned his nose up at it. He jumped up next to her, and she rolled her eyes, knowing that he would eat it later when she was not around. Feeling too happy and ever so slightly guilty for somewhat neglecting the cat, she did not shoo him off the counter.

"You look happy," he said, rubbing up against her.

"I am," she said simply. "He's, well, he's amazing." She looked in the cupboard for a so-called "normal-sized" mug, as well as retrieving one of her own normal-sized mugs. The difference was that Alice's held roughly 20oz, whilst the other held 10oz. She hoped that the coffee was going to be okay; she had pretty much just pulled a fancy looking packet off the supermarket shelf and was hoping for the best since she did not drink it herself.

"He's a Vampire," said Onion carefully, watching her closely. He was not sure how the others were going to react to this; although he had not been told he was specifically to keep Alice away from Vampires, Onion had a feeling this was not going to be welcome news. However, Onion had done his duty; he had judged Robert and found his heart worthy of his mistress; and he had never seen Alice this as happy.

"I know. He also has blue eyes. What's your point?"

"No point. Just saying." Onion purred as she gently rubbed his ears and stroked under his chin. "He does pass, regardless of what he is."

"Not quite sure what I'd have done if he hadn't," Alice said, quietly. Although the electric shocks and Onion's duty rarely differed, she still felt reassured when people passed Onion's judgement – if he allowed her guests to stroke him, they passed; if he hissed and his tail poofed up, she started plans for removing them from her sphere, since experience had taught her to ignore him at her heart's peril. She picked up the cat again, and kissed the air just above his head, before putting him back on the floor. "I will see you later." She picked up her tea and the coffee for Robert and felt like she was floating back to the bedroom.

"That shirt looks good on you," Robert said, pushing himself up so that he was sitting against the pillow.

"It looked good on you too," she said, smiling shyly.

"I think you should wear it all the time. I'm honestly not sure I've ever seen anything as hot as you in my white shirt, with black stockings."

She blushed, and Robert thought that it only made her look more beautiful. She shook her head, but she decided to take the compliment without arguing. It was not the easiest thing in the world for her, but Alice felt that if anyone could make her believe she was beautiful, it was Robert.

"You also look taller than yesterday," he said.

"Really? I don't know… why…" She dropped the mugs, as she stopped floating the minute she caught sight of herself levitating in the mirror.

Robert caught them both, and steadied her all in a split-second. He placed the drinks on the bedside cabinet and turned back to her. "Are you OK?"

"Yes. I've just never done that before either," she said. Both of his hands were on her waist now, and she had one hand on a strong and steady arm. She trailed the fingers of her other hand lightly over his shoulders and down his torso, her eyes remaining on his. As she skimmed the top of his trouser waistband, she heard his sharp intake of breath and felt amazed that she could have that kind of effect on a man like him. She bit her lip, deciding that for now at least, she was just going to do what she felt like doing.

"Were you leaving?" she asked softly, slightly stunned by how attractive she found him, standing there only in smart trousers. Something about the lack of socks and shirt just made it incredibly sexy.

"No," Robert said, not moving, staring back into her beautiful brown eyes. Dark, mysterious eyes that seemed so full of contradictions. It seemed like he could stare into them and always find something new and unexpected. "Just didn't want to startle your cat. Besides you have my shirt."

"I'm sure he's gone out now though." She undid the button and pulled down his zipper, her eyes still locked to his. "If you wanted to stay in here."

"Oh, I definitely want to do that," he said, kissing her and pulling her back onto the bed.

***

"So, about the whole vampire thing....?" Alice asked, cautiously. She was genuinely interested to know how much of the fictional mythology measured up to the reality.

"Hmm?" Robert replied, quizzically raising an eyebrow.

"What's it actually like?" She turned onto her front and propped herself up on her elbows to look at him. He looked roguishly handsome, with one hand under his ruffled head, exuding a quiet air of confidence. He entwined the other into hers.

"Well, it used to be that a small sect of Vampires were big on seducing virgins and turning beautiful woman, but it was never really like that for the species as a whole. In the beginning, Vampires were far more demonic and would rip peoples' throats out to satiate their need and want for blood. After the Three, a balance developed between the human-side and the demon that craves blood. Over the centuries, Vampires have evolved to survive without killing. Most Vampires eat normal food, but supplement that with "energy feeding" and blood. In terms of the energy, it's kinda like we absorb strong emotions, sometimes unintentionally, but it never usually hurts anyone, although I suppose if one fed to excess, then it might." He paused for a moment; Alice was staring at him with large, fascinated eyes. He inwardly smiled, knowing that if he was to tell any of his kind that a Witch had asked to know more about how Vampires lived, they would laugh and call him crazy. He had a feeling even Clive would find it hard to believe. She nodded her head and he continued.

"In terms of blood, most Vampires only need a small vial two or three times a month. Sometimes we do just crave blood, kinda like you might inexplicably crave ice cream, but we generally don't drink much even then. We might need to consume more if we're injured, to speed up healing, but it varies.

We're okay with sunlight; we just can't deal with very strong sunlight for long periods of time. All Vampires have supernatural strength and speed, heightened senses, and can live indefinitely, as far as I know. It's not that much different from being human – just some added dietary requirements and it all goes on a bit."

"Could you turn me into a Vampire?" she asked, curious.

"If you wanted me to. That would require me biting you and you drinking my blood. Not sure if you would feed like I can or whether you'd always need to drink blood. Although, to be fair, I'm not strictly a real Vampire yet. Not until next year, so that might change. Or I could give up my immortality by visiting The Three, which I guess they kinda use to keep themselves going. And some Vampires do do that; either because they can't or won't turn someone they love, or just get tired of the existence."

She gave him a sideways glance. "You mentioned unintentional feeding..."

"Yes. And yes, sorry," Robert said, kissing the hand he was holding. "You've seen *Stardust*, right?"

"Of course. One of the few occasions where I love the film as much as the book, despite the differences," Alice said. "Have to admit, I do like the song in that."

Robert grinned, amused by her rapidly jumping mind. "Well, at the moment, you're kinda like Yvaine, shining on the boat. When human emotions are that strong, it's like being a solar panel – you just kind of absorb it. I don't know how many other Vampires will unintentionally or intentionally try to feed on you whilst you're shining like this, but I swear I'll never let any of them hurt you."

"I'm not worried," Alice said earnestly. "Besides, you're the reason these things are happening." Her voice dropped to a whisper. "I've never felt like this before."

"Me neither."

"I'm in love with you," she said, pushing herself up to clearly see his face, slightly worried that making such declarations were going to make him leave.

"I'm in love with you too," he replied simply, leaning over to kiss her.

***

After a third session of activity followed by a brief sleep, Alice awoke and stretched sleepily. She felt Robert's eyes on her and she turned over to face him, seeing a rather fuzzy version of his features. She lifted her eyebrows questioningly as she smiled. Her heart swelled, knowing that he was still there and that it was all real.

"So what about the whole Witch thing?" asked Robert, reaching out to touch a strand of her long dark hair.

"What about it?" asked Alice, the light in her eyes dying slightly.

"Well," said Robert "Is there anything *I* should know about?"

Alice's smile faded as she shrugged uncomfortably. "To be perfectly honest, I'm not sure. As far as I know, the majority of my family and ancestors are, were, Witches. I was born a Witch and I've always been able to do magic, although mostly I don't." She proceeded to tell him what she had told Dr Anthonys, whilst watching as her fingers traced patterns across his finely toned chest, unable to look in his eyes. She just felt so useless and stupid. She sighed. "I don't have a coven; I don't dance naked and consort with Satan; I have no desire to turn children into mice; cats sometimes talk back to me, and I am still learning to control the, I don't know, side-effects of having powers. Apparently stuff floats when I'm very emotional. Or the weather changes," she muttered, sheepishly. "I really am still learning and discovering what it might mean to be a Witch. And much as I disparagingly joke about being powerful, I actually am. It's not a boast, it just is. I don't feel like it comes from a bad place or anything, it's just a bit overwhelming and I can't always control it. And Onion talks, sometimes. I think he can open doors too, but not cat food, for some reason. But I don't think that has anything to do with me."

"I'm pretty sure Onion is a Familiar, and he can talk to whomever he wants to. Don't know about the other cats though," said Robert, smiling gently. He took hold of her hand and kissed it. "What's bothering you?" He waited silently, listening to the changes in her breath as she worked out how best to say what was on her mind.

She closed her eyes and bit her lip. "Do I scare you?"

"Scare me?" echoed Robert, unable to stop a laugh from escaping. It was too adorable an idea. "Sorry, but no. Not in a million years," he replied firmly.

"Well gee thanks," said Alice, feeling remarkably relieved and slightly insulted. "Is this because you're a big bad vampire or something?"

Robert laughed again. It was a deep sound, comforting and

genuine and devoid of malice."No, it's not," he replied, kissing her softly. "It's because you seem like a good person – honest, kind, trying to do your best. And I love you."

"I love you too. But how can you be sure?" said Alice, not quite able to believe such nice things about herself.

"Sometimes you just know things, don't you think?" he said, smiling at her.

"Yeah, I guess I do," she said, smiling back at him as she looked into his eyes. *Such amazing eyes, blue like oceans and just as deep and dangerous.*

"Good. Well, I guess I should shower and then we should get some… dinner," Robert said, picking up his watch from the side of the bed. It was already six in the evening.

"I guess," said Alice, with a little reluctance. She was hungry, but she also did not want to break the little bubble spending the day in bed with him had created. She kissed his cheek and rolled off the bed. "Gimme a sec to find you a towel, and then you can join me."

Chapter 17

Lady Jane kicked off the impractical red high heels and quickly shed the conservative blouse and skirt that was the expected attire of her day-to-day job. She did her best to make the drab human attire look sexy and enticing, but there was only so much she could do without becoming obscene, and that would be altogether the wrong attention to garner. She merely needed to look good enough to get those in charge eating out of her perfectly manicured nails for as long as her current charade was necessary. She took out the pins holding up her ashen blonde hair and allowed it to fall down her back, the ends brushing teasingly against her pale, porcelain skin.

She strode into the reliquary and was not surprised to find that there had been no more attempts at High Magic, after those two pings in January. Part of her still believed that Alice Andrews had merely been lucky with those little forays into the deeper arts, and given the reports she had been getting from The Vault, it was unsurprising that the Covens were giving 'The Book of the First' a wide berth. Of course, Miss Andrews was far too busy falling in love to concern herself with magic.

Lady Jane wondered how much sway the prophecy had in shaping the lives of the Witches and Vampires; certainly there was no way that such a mouse of a Witch could have attracted such a stunning specimen of a Vampire without its influence. She supposed it was a good thing that Robert Evans had thus far resisted her considerable charms – for the prophecy's and her master's sakes – but she had to admit that she found his utter lack of interest irksome to the extreme.

To her displeasure, Lady Jane had given him more chances than she would normally allow or need. He was too much of a nice guy for her to normally take any interest in and not yet a true Vampire, but she imagined that the depths of his nature would still give him the strength, the stamina and the tools to make it cruel. And if he did not, than at least she would have taken something from that annoying little goody-two-shoes English woman. Her frustrations were further compounded by the fact that despite not enticing him into her own bed, some strange magic obscured her from being able to watch him with the Witch. She did not suppose it would be anything exciting – lots of kissing and tenderness and missionary no doubt – but still, the voyeurism was usually something of a perk, as well as an insight. Sex sometimes brought out an honesty in peoples' natures that they normally kept hidden. Hellgods knew, there had to be some kink to make that little Witch interesting.

The reliquary began to hum and Lady Jane's mood immediately lifted. There was only one being in the realms that had the ability to make that happen and she immediately opened the door, sinking to her knees as she waited for him to appear.

"My beautiful pet," Lord Sargeraxs said with a curious smile, using borrowed hands to lift her bowed head to meet his gaze.

"My Lord," Lady Jane answered, rising to her feet. She supposed that she should at least be grateful that her recent reports of the Witch had caused her master to venture – in part – into the mortal realm. Rumour was that Lord Sargeraxs had been keeping an eye on Alice Andrews since the day of her birth, but it was only since she had developed a relationship with the Vampire, that the demon had deemed her potential worthy of personal scrutiny.

Sargeraxs frowned as he looked down at the male body, cursing its lack of control and patience. "Attend to me, my precious. Then we shall discuss business as intended."

Chapter 18

"Hello?" Alice said, slightly groggy as she answered her phone. Alice was not a morning person. Although she was up and moving, she had not yet finished her tea, which meant she was currently less than human. Even as she drank it, she still felt like she would drift off again if she kept her eyes shut for more than a minute. She rubbed the sleep from her eyes and tried to focus.

"Happy birthday, darling."

"Thanks Mom," Alice said carefully. "Thank you for the card and gifts too."

"You're welcome. Sorry it wasn't anything more personal, but we weren't sure what you might have picked up since the move."

"How's things? You and Dad okay?" Alice asked politely. Gillian Andrews (nee Price) and Terrance Andrews had been married for just over thirty-seven years. They were both born to powerful Witches, and although Endora Price had married a human, her lineage and her reputation remained indisputably high regard. Endora Price had been the reigning Supreme from the remarkably young age of twenty-one, and had held that highest of honours, alongside her position on the High Council, until her death. Alice supposed it was a good thing that her maternal grandparents and great-grandparents were no longer around, given that Alice was probably going to be the one to break the prestigious Price bloodline. Her father had an older brother who had married into another witching family, and they had three daughters and a son, who were also married with children. Alice had only just found someone she could imagine spending her life with, and she was not sure whether children would be possible even if she was to change her mind and decide that she wanted any.

"We're both fine. Are you? Do you have any plans?"

"I'm okay. Robert's taking me out for dinner, I think. He hasn't actually told me his plan yet," she sad, unable to stop smiling. She really had to work on the whole sappy smiling thing, although she did like the fact that despite the depression telling her that she did not deserve to be, Robert made her happy.

"Who's Robert? Have you finally met a nice Witch to settle down with?" Gillian asked, unable to keep the note of excitement out of her voice.

"Er, I would definitely like to spend the rest of my life with him," said Alice. She figured she could bite half of the proverbial bullet. "He's not a witch though."

"Oh well, never mind," her mother said, slightly disappointed. "Your grandmother married a human and they were very happy together. As long it's not one of the others."

"Mom!"

"I'm sorry, but life is just easier if they aren't."

Alice sighed. "Surely it wouldn't be that awful if I was dating, I don't know, say, a Vampire?"

"Of course it would!" her mother said, at once with a note of panic. "We sent you away so you couldn't date one."

"You what?" Alice spluttered angrily, nearly choking on a mouthful of tea.

"This is definitely not a conversation I wanted to be having on your birthday," Gillian replied with an uncomfortable tone.

"I can imagine," said Alice, wide-awake now. "But we are *so* having it. So why exactly did you send me away?"

There was a sigh of resignation from the other end of the line. "We were told that we should keep you away from vampires and your friend Edd was all glittery."

Amusement overwhelmed her anger, as Alice literally face-palmed. To think that Witches might actually consider *Twilight* to be true lore... It was a good thing she had not been drinking – she definitely would have spat that all over the counter from laughing. She tried to keep the giggles at bay. "Vampires don't sparkle, Mom. That's just not a thing. Robert thinks maybe a Were came up with it. I think maybe a Zombie."

"Oh," her mom said, a tinge of embarrassment to her tone.

Alice scratched her right eyebrow. "So, you sent me to New York because you thought Edd was a vampire, not because he's gay?"

"Of course. Plenty of gay Witches about, after all."

"Oh, of course," said Alice, slightly flabbergasted. *That was a good word too, flabbergasted. Definitely underused.* "Well, who said I should stay away from Vampires?"

"Your grandmother," Gillian Andrews said, quietly.

"Seriously? Why?"

"We don't know honey, we just tried to keep you away from all of it, for your own good. I don't know what it was, from the very first moment she knew we were having a girl, she was very concerned. She loved you dearly, please don't doubt that, but she was very worried about you and Vampires. More so when you copied that amulet she was trying to make."

"But I just did what she told me to do," Alice protested, weakly. Given what she had learned about the amulet since she had started studying in the Library, she supposed she understood a little better now why it had caused concern. It did not lessen the pain felt by a seven-year old Witch though.

"I'm sure she did, darling, but she didn't expect you to be able to do it. I still can't make one of those amulets, even now. And I have tried; I'm not sure anyone in our coven can," she added. "Even your grandmother struggled with that design and she had studied at Miss Robichaux's and Miss Cackle's, not to mention having years of practice. No one was expecting a seven year old to do High Magic. I think it scared her slightly, although for you, not of you. Never of you."

"Oh," said Alice, trying to wrap her head around these revelations.

"It'll be fine," Gillian continued. "I can't imagine you'd really come across any vampires anyway. They tend to be quite arrogant and shockingly wealthy, and well, they don't like to mix with Witches from what I've heard."

Alice was quiet for a moment, really not sure how to respond. "Erm, well, okay. I'm sorry Mom, but I have to go. I have to get ready for work."

"Oh, of course. Well, I hope you have a lovely evening and enjoy your day. And I look forward to hearing more about this Robert person. Talk to you soon. Love you."

"Love you too. And love to Dad. 'Bye," said Alice, putting down the phone and looking at it, not quite sure how to process the knowledge that it was actually frowned upon for her to be with a Vampire when she was very much in love with one.

She closed her eyes, screwed up her face, and shook her head as she let out a long breath. *I so can't wait for Robert to meet my parents*, she thought despondently. She shuffled into the shower and went through the motions, just feeling detached from herself, and certainly no longer in the mood to try and celebrate anything.

"Happy Birthday," Onion said.

"It's a birthday at least," said Alice gloomily, setting out his food. "Sorry, thank you. Mom was on the phone – she kinda harshed out my happy because I'm not supposed to hang around Vampires."

Onion gave her a look and not just because of the information.

"Season 7 *Supernatural*," Alice said with a shrug. "You know what I'm like when I watch these things. Anyway, I will be back after work. Your breakfast is down, the biscuits are available if you want them and the cat flap is unlocked, so try to behave. And much as I appreciate the gifts, it's truly okay if you don't get me one this year."

She zipped up her boots, wrapped a scarf around her neck, put on a black, cat-eared beanie, the aubergine duffel coat and slung her bag across her right shoulder. "See you later," she said, rubbing his ears before leaving.

***

Although she had not told anyone that it was her birthday, Laura had greeted her with a cake decorated like Captain America's shield. As a group, they had bought her some bright flowers and an Amazon voucher, and Alice had needed a moment to hide in a corner to cry a little. The depression usually had her so convinced that she was worthless and undeserving of kindness, that she was often overwhelmed when people were nice to her.

She smiled and thanked them, but she could not stop thinking about why her grandmother had thought that she should be kept away from Vampires. She had to believe there was a genuinely good reason for it; it was heartbreaking to consider that her family were just stereotypically supernatural-racist. Of course, if there was a good reason for her not to be with a Vampire, then how was she going to handle that? She did not know if she could break up with Robert; her heart felt heavy and sick just contemplating the idea.

Alice left work at the end of the day, still unable to ignore the niggle at the back of her mind, and began wondering if she was just looking for an excuse to self-sabotage the relationship. Maybe it would be less painful if she broke things off with him before he got the chance to find someone better – like an exotic Countess that was beautiful, sophisticated and a connoisseur of AB-negative served in the proper glassware.

Nothing seemed to be shifting the dark cloud that was wrapping its insidious tentacles around her heart and mind. She cried a little in the shower, listening to a playlist of melancholy songs, and unconsciously dressed in her darkest, most comfortable but slightly unflattering clothing. She felt broken and lost, and even Robert's presence could not shift it.

Robert had planned an amazing birthday evening for her. He had taken her to the botanical gardens, where he laid out a blanket and set out an elegant picnic of fancy-looking simple foods. It had made her laugh a little, as he had made little cards giving each dish a fancy name with a simple description in brackets; Robert kept trying to take her to a fancy Michelin star restaurant and she was happiest with something familiar, like a burger bar or The 'Cauldron.

She had tried to act as if everything was fine. She was pretty sure he was not fooled, but since she was still trying to work it all out, she did not want to talk about it and he did not press. He had made a playlist on his phone of some of her favourite songs and he held her underneath a clear skylight so that they could stare up at the night sky without Alice freezing to death. Alice had never felt so special and loved before and that almost made everything worse. The black fog continued to pull her in, making her subdued and unable to break free of the doubts and worries that were no longer just limited to her depression.

"Do you want me to stay?" Robert had asked, after walking her up to her apartment.

"No thank you," Alice had replied, quietly. "Sorry. Thank you for going to so much effort, it really was a wonderful idea. My head's just in a really bad place."

Robert had looked concerned, but left it at that. "Okay, but call me if you need me?"

"Of course," Alice had said, slightly untruthfully.
They shared a brief kiss and after he had gone, Alice had simply changed clothes, brushed her teeth and hidden under the covers.

Chapter 19

It had been about two months since the incident with Sam and she was still learning new things everyday. Julius had told her that sub-level 7 had the rarest of ancient legible texts; below that, the floors were mostly filled with artefacts that needed special casings and bindings; the kind of weapons and trinkets that posed more threat to those that would touch them, than of atmosphere or human oils perhaps spoiling their quality. Understandably, Alice was not allowed to go down that far, but the Library rarely let her past sub-level 1 unless she had a meeting in Dr Anthony's office. She had tried once – purely to see if she could – but found that the lift did not work, doors did not open and there were invisible barriers blocking her way. She had apologised to the Library and gone back to her duties.

Alice felt a deep connection to the Library and the books within. She had always loved books and treated them all with an equal amount of respect, unless she really did not like them, in which case she was ever so slightly less respectful. She would put the books back carefully into their places, took care to wipe down smudged or dusty covers. She even found herself apologising to them if she had to use them in the photocopier. Of course, the first time that she had sensed the rustling of pages and a low hum of energy emanating from the shelves, she had thought she was going mad. It made sense to her that they would, especially when gathered as they were in the Library, but she was surprised that she would be included in it. Alice felt that the reasons were a little clearer as her studies progressed; the books were like anything else – if you treated them with respect, you were treated with equal measure.

Magic aside, Alice loved the quiet, order and general cleanliness. She loved the smell of books, tea, coffee and table-polish; loved the low-lighting from the dimmed chandeliers and the green-headed reading lamps; loved the different textures of the dust jackets and covers, and of the marble and mahogany. It was a place of calm and comfort; somewhere she could be alone and not feel lonely. If she felt chatty, she would sit at one of the front desks, helping visitors find their way around, or to aid them in their knowledge quests either by pointing them to the relevant sections or bringing up resources from other areas, such as old newspapers, microfiche and videos. If she felt like it was too much to be around other people, she would just organise the books, or start cataloguing the latest editions, or archiving some of the old ones.

As a result of her promotion, Alice now spent five days at the Library; three for normal library duties and the other two for witch studies, or sub-level 1 cataloguing. Occasionally, she worked the odd Saturday as well, usually when tasked with a slightly larger witchcraft undertaking, but that happened far less frequently since meeting Robert.

In regards to her lessons, Alice was unsure how much progress she was actually making regarding the emotional control of her powers, but she had a better grasp on them as a whole. She could read charms without them having immediate effect and the weather seemed to be less temperamental unless she was particularly overwhelmed by an emotion. Sometimes, she wondered if she would ever be able to fully control it or if one day, she would just go completely mad and be at the mercy of her supernatural desires.

She knew that the power was a part of her; and not in a purely figurative sense. It was in her blood and it was as important to her survival as her head and her heart. It just sometimes felt too big. She wondered if that was why supernaturals could tell each other apart from humans, that their otherness was just a bit too much for their physical forms, and it leaked out slightly, like low-level radiation.

Although Alice and Stuart were supposed to be making a more coherent catalogue of the books that had moved themselves throughout various rooms in Sub-level 1, they both had a tendency to go off task. Given that they were dealing with texts that had been written numerous years in the past, with loose pages, missing covers and no synopses on the back, they were forced to look at the texts themselves to determine what they were actually about. For two bookworms, each with his and her own particular interest in the supernatural, it was incredibly slow going. Stuart seemed to be preoccupied with finding information about binding books, Witches and hauntings; Alice was after more information about Demons and Angels. Ideally, she wanted something that was at least grounded in some truth and experience, but it was proving elusive.

"Angels and Demons and the Veil," Alice wondered aloud, wondering if saying the words would somehow cause the right book to appear. It did not. The book in front of her was concerned about Demons breaking through and very speculative as to whether the Angels would help out mortals if they did. However, it read more like a doomsday manifesto as opposed to a text one could trust.

"What about them?" asked Stuart, looking up from the text he was studying.

Alice did not expect the Head Librarian to have the answers in this instance, but she figured he was at least someone to bounce her own speculations off. "Can they be detected? You know, in a similar way to how those connected to the supernatural seem to consciously or unconsciously recognise other supernaturals?"

"I'm not sure, to be honest. I think it would be much harder, since they are more powerful, but then again, they manifest in very different ways. I imagine if you were particularly in-tune with your environment, you could probably detect a change that could haven been caused by a slight rift in the Veil. Unfortunately, not much is known about any of them."

"How much *is* known?" Alice pressed. "It just seems like the books are concerned with listing a whole bunch of types of Demon. Wraiths, Retzgils, Ardinas, Lamia and a whole bunch of others that I daren't even try to pronounce. There's not really a lot about them and definitely not a lot about fighting them. Is there something that has more than this?"

"I don't know, Alice. I've never really thought too much about Demons if I'm honest; there's too much evil in this world, for me to worry about sources beyond the Veil. What little I remember from Creation texts at the British Library, is essentially what anyone might tell you, if they happened to believe in Angels and Demons." He took a sip of water and looked over at Alice. She was staring at him intently. "Legend has it that before the Earth passed into the hands of mortal men, it belonged to Gods, Titans, Angels and Demons. It was chaotic and savage; a time of constant war for dominion. The Gods eventually destroyed the Titans and after some time ruling on earth, chose to retreat into some higher realm. Angels and Demons continued to live on Earth, having reached some kind of uneasy truce, but once the various evolutions of the six forms came into being, war erupted again. The Gods decided to create the Veil, and forced the Demons and Angels to leave."

"Okay," said Alice, mainly just to show she was still listening and interested.

"These realms supposedly reflected the dominant qualities of the two beings; Demons being cruel, destructive, greedy, angry and lustful created what we would call Hell; the Angels as protectors and creators, seeking to nurture life and find joy within it, created Heaven. The Angels were content to allow the time of Mortals to pass without much concern; the Demons were – are – not, given that cruelty brings no pleasure if it's not being inflicted upon those who would oppose it. So

Demons try to get through the Veil or manipulate and coerce others into breaching or destroying it; and a few Angels, the Fallen, believed that it is not a fair fight for Mortals to face Demons alone, so they are on Earth, supposedly, to help us."

"Hmm," said Alice, slightly disappointed.

Stuart noticed. "There are a few reasons for why we don't know much more than that," he explained. "One, there's not been a lot of activity from either side in the last couple of centuries. Two, most of the individuals interested in the Veil are not interested in it for the sake of scientific knowledge or understanding; they want something from the other side. Thirdly, whilst much may have been written when the threat was more imminent and recent, rather than ancient history, should any of those texts still exist, they are most likely transcribed in languages that you or I, even with magic, would be unable to decipher."

Alice wondered if that would actually hold true, the babel fish in her head did seem to work on any text pertaining to the supernatural, so in theory, she might be able to read whatever dead language they might come across. She was already finding that particular gift useful with some of the books they had gone through; if she could not read them, they were currently in the wrong section. However, she was also aware that if they did have any such books, they would be far deeper than she was allowed to go, and quite possibly too volatile for her slightly wayward powers.

"But what about detecting a Demon or an Angel? We know there are one or two about, so don't we have anything that might help us – me – recognise one?" Alice insisted. "Surely if we found one, we could ask them about the Veil? Or waterboard them," she added after a beat.

Stuart looked at her, bemused. "I really don't know of any detection spells, but, in theory, if we were to find any, we could ask. Chances are if we were to find a demon, they would not be particularly helpful. They inevitably give themselves away – whether that's from the human host fighting back or from the human body being unable to contain forces it was not designed to deal with – but for the most part, Demons do not want to be discovered; they do not want to run the risk of being sent back. They are renowned liars, and would most likely manipulate any one wanting to know about the Veil, into lifting a corner or allowing the demon to pass through."

She supposed that made sense. "And the Fallen?"

"And the Fallen are not supposed to talk about it and they generally do not let mortals know of them. Hence, you could be stood next to one and never know it, if they did not wish you to." Stuart pursed his lips and let out a deep breath, trying to keep his personal opinion of the Fallen's methods out of the discussion. "The Veil is strong and healthy, and while it remains so, the Fallen will not discuss it with mortals until such time as they deem it necessary. The Fallen are here to protect, but much like the Library, or rather, the Library when it was conceived (since I'm quite sure it is no longer as neutral as it once was), they are not allowed to interfere. Only in the event of a large tear, when the demonic threat is perceived to be greater than the mortal realm can deal with, will the Fallen intervene."

"That sounds kinda lousy," said Alice. "Wouldn't it be better to teach people like you and me how to mend the Veil or something?"

"I have expressed similar sentiments, but sadly, that is not for us to decide."

"Do Angels need to possess hosts in order to pass through as well?" Alice asked.

"No. They fall, quite literally through it, and can not pass back. Not until they are destroyed in some manner. They exhibit a relatively human appearance, but they do not age as we do; they do not get sick; they do not die; I believe they have some minor premonition abilities, extraordinary strength and resolve; and wings."

"Really? Wings?" said Alice, interested and theoretically impressed.

"So I've been told. I have yet to see with my own eyes."

"Is that possible? Would we be able to look upon them like that?"

"The Fallen are not in their truest forms. That is probably beyond the range of human senses and comprehension. I do not know if their true voices would cause one's head to explode or if their true form would render one blind, but it is possible, I suppose."

Alice smiled and nodded her head in approval at the *Dogma* and *Supernatural* references.

"I don't spend all of my time working. And I do have Netflix," Stuart said, with a wry grin.

Alice laughed. "Well, that's good to know. It's supposedly unhealthy to be obsessive about stuff."

"What's bought up the concern about the Veil and the creatures beyond?" asked Stuart, regarding her furrowing brow and continuing disappointment.

"It's that book I'm working on for you," she replied, shrugging. "The '100 Useful Spells'?"

He nodded. "Julius won't let me have it back."

"Nor should he," said Alice, firmly. "I'm convinced there's something hinky about that thing. Obviously, I've not gone that far into it, and I'm trying not to skip too far ahead, just in case I come across something I can't handle. Which I realise shouldn't really be a worry if these are spells for non-witches to perform, but... Erm, yeah, it's the book, and the fact there's one or two spells in there that I have come across that pertain to demons and they're not very effective. I honestly don't understand how I know this, but I certainly wouldn't want to entrust my life to those spells working."

"Well, much as I might think you may be overreacting a little, I believe you should trust your instincts. You're an exceptional natural Witch, and if your gut says something's wrong, you should trust it. I wish I could give you more reassurances about the Veil and the unlikelihood of Demons passing through," Stuart said, looking at her in concern.

"I'm sure it's nothing," said Alice, with a smile that did not quite reach her eyes.

Chapter 20

Although it was not an allocated "Witch" day, if it was quiet, Alice would spend Friday afternoons working on the '100 Useful Spells for Librarians'. If the book had an official title, it had been lost to the ages, along with the cover and several other pages.

No one knew where it had come from and as one of the older texts in the collection, it was not in any of the known systems. The parchment itself and the ink that had been used were quite unremarkable, and from those characteristics, general estimates put the book's age as somewhere within the time of the Three. Other than her own feelings, there was nothing to suggest the book was remarkable in any way and certainly nothing to suggest it held sinister intent.

Dr. Anthonys had assured her that the book was safe, that all books of similar ilk were subject to a litany of stringent and arduous checks by several skilled Librarians, all of whom had been specially trained to look for texts that seemed innocent but could harbour something dangerous. Even Julius had declared that the book itself was fundamentally acceptable. There were plenty of books buried deep within the catacombs of the six Libraries that were abhorrently evil, but he had assured her there was nothing for her to be concerned about regarding this particular volume.

"Not even, shall we say, a spell that could only be triggered by specific parameters?" she had asked, a couple of days after looking at the book properly for the first time.

"No. Not even a spell like the one you put on the bag for

Sam Harvelle-Walker."

"You saw that," Alice said, looking sheepish.

"The Library and I see everything," said Julius in his characteristic monotone.

"But you left it there?"

"Yes."

"I thought you weren't allowed to meddle," said Alice, teasingly.

"We are not," said Julius. "But we can sometimes leave things be, if we are sure that they are doing the right thing."

"How can you ever be sure of that?" asked Alice, slightly troubled by the theology of such an answer.

"I have Faith," Julius replied, simply.

Alice thought about that for a moment, and wondered if she had any Faith. She was not sure, but she trusted certain individuals and she was pretty confident in her instincts.

"And you're positive this book is "OK"?" she asked, a minute later.

"Yes."

"Do you know where it came from? Who wrote it? Anything like that?" she questioned. It was not that she did not trust Julius, but she could not shake the feeling that there was something suspicious about the tome.

"I do not." Julius was not often one for questions. "Why does this book concern you so?" he asked, the slightest of worried furrows upon his brow.

"I can't explain it exactly," Alice replied, shrugging. "I don't really think there's anything wrong with the book itself, per se, but, well, a lot of the spells are wrong."

"People make mistakes."

"Yes, and that might be all it is, but I feel like, I don't know. I feel like it's deliberate. I feel like someone left this around so that people would, I don't know, feel safer." She paused, sighed, and tried to see if she could explain it better. "Like, say there was a tiny chink in a wall and someone thought, 'oh well, that's OK, I've got some poly-filler if it gets worse', and it does get worse, and they go to use the poly-filler, and find out that what they really have is a bag of icing and now it's too late to stop the wall collapsing.'"

"That is quite the analogy."

"I think it works though."

"You believe this book to be... icing?"

"Yes. I don't even entirely know how I know some of this stuff, but I know when the spells in here are wrong. And some of it is insidiously subtle, as though it could be a simple translator or transcription error. Things like 10 wormwort instead of 1, or 3 blackcurrants instead of blackberries."

"But we have used some of these spells, quite regularly in fact."

"Yes, which is what concerns me. Spells like this, and this, and even this one, work as they are," she said pointing to various pages in the book. "But they're like, surface spells. Up against something, I don't know, big, it would be like a single air-plane shooting at King Kong." That was a bad analogy considering her audience. "My point is, the big spells won't work. But the little ones are designed so that you think they will.."

"I believe I see what you mean," said Julius.

For some reason, that was not enough for Alice. If the seriousness of what she believed was not being taken on-board by Julius, she needed to make it clearer. She tried again. "OK, ignore the 'why would you want to do that and how comes you constantly have access to a toad' aspect of this example, and try to go with me here."

Julius nodded.

"Say you pick up a book about transformation. You skim through the book, making note of one or two things you think might be good to make one day, like turning a toad into a car or a motorcycle. For whatever reason, you're not used to magic, so you don't want to go straight to that spell, and besides, you don't need the car yet nor do you have the space. So you try one of the spells at the front. You turn the toad into a mouse, and then into a cat. Cool, you think, this works. You then try another spell but that one doesn't work. You look at it closely and think that maybe you pronounced a word wrong, so you try saying it slightly differently, and then you get the dog you were expecting. So you kinda think that any other errors you come across are your fault, rather than it being a deliberate mistake."

She took a sip of tea, and checked that Julius was following.

He nodded again, and she continued.

"One day, you see a good deal on a car. You're tempted, but you think, I still don't really need one, and besides, Stuart is giving me a lift later on, and if needs be, I still know the words to that spell, so I can turn a toad into a car. Life continues on, the words are still in your head, but you don't need it, so you kind of forget about it. You certainly don't think about testing it or practising it. Then you get to that day when you really really need a car. Like, maybe your best friend is going to die if you do not have a car right that second. So you try to turn that toad into a car. You made the mouse, the cat and the dog, but no matter what you do, how you try to say it, that toad will not turn into a car. And the reason it won't turn into a car, is because you weren't given the right words. That book you read, had no intention of giving you the ability to turn that toad into a car, but it damn well wanted you to believe you could."

She could see from Julius' eyes that she had finally managed to convey what she had been struggling with ever since Dr Anthonys had shown her the Barbinda spell. She sighed and shrugged, the depression and low self-esteem suddenly throwing doubts into her convictions. She bit her lip and forced herself to continue. "I know I'm not a Guardian or really authorised to make the call, but I think this book should be locked up until I've finished correcting it, because…well, if we return to the toad and the dying friend for a moment." Alice took a deep breath. "Right, so, you try to turn the toad into a car. It doesn't work, you're desperate, and you can remember the words for turning the toad into a motorcycle.

It's not preferred, because a motorcycle is not as appropriate as a car would be, but it would get you and your friend to a hospital quicker than walking. So you say the words, and the toad becomes a man-eating monster that kills you both and wanders off down the road, killing and destroying and maiming everything in its path until someone stops it."

"I will put a lock on that book with immediate effect," said Julius.

Her shoulders dropped with the release of a great weight and Alice let out a sigh of relief. "Thank you. And thank goodness you guys have been helping with my powers... I dread to think what could have happened." Certainly something far worse than animated teapots, flashing lights and purple squirrels. "You need not worry. As you requested, this is practically the safest room in the entire Library – usually wards and security of this magnitude are reserved for sub-level 7 and beyond."

"Good. I don't think there's anything in there that conjures beasties, but I'd definitely rather be safe than sorry," said Alice.

***

Regardless of her personal feelings towards the book, Alice was almost certain that they were not sufficient grounds to have the book destroyed, and so she had started to make a new copy for Librarians and others to use. Julius and Dr Anthonys had supplied her with parchment and inks that would not absorb traces of her powers, and she had managed to devise a kind of 'preview' spell that would show the effects of the things written down, so that she could not accidentally do what the original writer had intended.

Although she had yet to find a spell that in actuality would conjure a rampaging beastie of some sort, several spells in connection with demons, would do nothing at all; one that was supposed to bind a demon's spirit to its corporeal form, would actually grant it the ability to move from host to host with astonishing ease, whilst another that was supposed to allow the casual spell-caster temporary spectral sight, actually blinded them from detecting supernatural activity of any kind. Still, she tried to stave off her potentially paranoid preparations by prioritising those spells that had more immediate applications to life in the Library.

The first spell she had fixed was the one Dr Anthonys had been trying to use – a Barbinda for negative books, which meant that whilst the negative energy would remain (possibly important for the posterity of the text) that energy could not be used by the object or others around it. The problem had been that the amounts of each ingredient were out by some small measure, and Alice had painstakingly practised the potion until it was as near perfect as possible. After that, she had started working on the spells in order, finding that at least as far as the first twenty spells were concerned, fifteen were useable (but most could be improved), two did not work at all and three could be made to work with some effort. Logically, she knew that it was hardly proof that the book was created with sinister intent, but it did not reassure her either.

Chapter 21

"Alice Andrews, Witch, novice Librarian and lover of Vampires," a familiar voice said in a hushed tone.

"Just the one Vampire," Alice said, grinning broadly as she looked up from her typing. She moved round to the front of the desk and threw her arms around him. "Sam! It is so good to see you. How are you?"

He hugged her back, surprised by the affectionate welcome. Although they had exchanged a few messages, he had not realised that he meant that much to Alice. "Next time, give me a heads up on the hugging. I want to selfie that shit and make everyone jealous."

Alice laughed. "Eejit," she said affectionately, colouring slightly. Then she frowned. "Is something wrong? I feel like you turning up here means someone's in trouble." The look she gave him suggested that "someone" was code for "you".

"Not this time," said Sam, smiling and realising that Alice meant a lot to him too. "Cross my heart," he added, drawing said object over his heart. "Just here to grab lunch with my favourite Witch. If she can be spared?" he said raising his voice as he looked up to the second floor landing. "Doc. Julius." He waved a hand.

"Hello Sam," said Julius.

"If she wants to have lunch with you, she is free to go. There is nothing pressing regarding this afternoon's session," Stuart said.

"Wicked. Let me grab my stuff," said Alice. "Not that I don't love my study sessions, of course." She lowered her voice.

"You should probably go talk to them – I think Dr A has a soft spot for you."

Sam nodded thoughtfully. "I think it's because he likes collecting waifs and strays. He has six rescue dogs in the Library's secret garden."

"No way," said Alice in disbelief. Dr Anthonys seemed too neat a person to have dogs, although she did have to admit she did not understand his systems with books and papers in his office, if indeed there was one. The secret garden seemed less surprising, other than the fact that she would have hoped the Library might have gently pushed her in its general direction, given that she was quite fond of plants.

"I swear," said Sam seriously, his eyes wide. "Scout's honour," he added, hoping he was doing the right salute as he held down his pinky and thumb.

"I want to believe you, but I find it super hard to make that compute," said Alice, slightly sceptical. "And I definitely don't believe you were ever a Scout."

Sam smirked. "Well, fair enough, I wasn't. Accept it or don't, but I am not lying to you. I actually find it hard to lie to you," said Sam, rubbing the back of his neck with something of a grimace. "It's very uncomfortable." Having spent most of his life on the road, (firstly with his parents, then with the band and now, because he was not sure how else to live) and spending more time than he would have liked lying and grafting to keep himself out of the hospital, coming across someone to whom he told the absolute truth to, was a little disconcerting.

"Well, go say hi properly, I need to rearrange some plans." She disappeared into the staff room, and Sam wandered up to where Julius and Stuart were watching.

"So, how's things?" asked Sam, cheerfully.

"Quite well, thank you. How are you Sam?" Stuart asked, cautiously pleased as always to see the Psychic.

"Can't complain," Sam replied, brightly. "Just taking a me day."

"Is everything okay?"

"Yup. Just checking in on my friends, nothing more than that." Maybe it was a mid-life crisis or getting older in general, but Sam felt the need to be around his friends more often, particularly since his growing abilities had caused him to sever ties with the band.

"Why? What have you heard?" Stuart asked quickly.

"And this is why Psychics have no friends; you can never just drop in without them thinking something bad's gonna happen. At least Alice thinks it's because *I'm* in trouble," said Sam, shaking his head with a wry grin. "Nothing out of the ordinary; just the usual chatter. The big, the balance and beware the prophecy."

"Prophecy?"

Sam shrugged. "There's always at least one," he said, masterfully hiding the flinch at his carelessness. He thought about it for a moment and stole a quick glance at Julius. The Fallen said and did nothing.

There was something about Sam's casualness that did not entirely convince the Head Librarian. "Well, I suppose there has been some chatter about a Witch, a Vampire and the Veil, but it all seems more like idle gossip than a prophecy," said Stuart. "I suppose that given Alice's powers, maybe I should have a more thorough look."

"Oh, so you've noticed that she is actually a Witch then?" Sam teased.

Stuart shot Sam a warning look, but could not hide a smile. "Yes. But you have to admit that even now, she hides it well."

"That she does," said Sam. He could tell that Alice was more powerful – or at least more confident with her powers – but she was still hiding it. He was not sure whether it was intentional or not, but as even his great grandmother had observed, it was just as hard to tell that Alice was a Witch as it had been before. "She is thriving here though, isn't she?"

"Oh yes, marvellously," said Stuart, with a hint of pride in his voice. "The Library is very fond of her, she gets on quite well with everyone, and she has a lot of enthusiasm for even the most mundane of library tasks."

"Well, make sure you let her know. And not in that weird, backhanded way you English people have. Just tell her she's awesome."

"Are you sure there's nothing we should be concerned about?" Stuart asked again, glancing at Sam curiously with a sideways glance.

"There's nothing I'm aware of. This is just general concern about a friend. If I'd ever had a sister, I think I'd feel about her the way I feel towards Alice," said Sam, thoughtfully. "Maybe you should let her meet the dogs. Still just the six?"

"Just the six, and Alice is a cat person."
Sam laughed. "Pfft. I think you're afraid of letting her see you as a person." Sam sighed and looked serious for a moment. He knew he was hardly one to be talking, but all the same, some things needed to be said. "Not all of the running away we do is physical," he said.

Stuart rubbed his temple wearily and unconsciously touched his left side. "You're probably right."

"I usually am," said Sam, with a grin. "I was right about her, wasn't I?" He added as Alice walked out of the staff room and waved up at them.

"Good to go," she called up.
Sam shook hands with Julius and Stuart, and was hit by a small glimmer of the Head Librarian talking to a beautiful, intelligent woman in an expensive, tailored black dress in front of a Monet. "You should probably go to that cheese and wine evening, Doc," he said, walking down the stairs.

***

"So, did online dating work out?" asked Sam, as they exited the Library.
Alice stuck out her tongue, and beamed. "You know full well that it did."

"You look a lot happier than last time. And more confident," Sam observed.

"I am. I guess. Well, definitely happier, not sure about confidence," she said, smiling broadly as she always did when thinking or talking about Robert, even by proxy. "But again, pretty sure you know that already."

Sam grinned. "True, but most people tend to freak out when you tell them how they're feeling. Not that it isn't completely obvious just from looking at you. It's also more of a habit than anything else. I'm sure Robert must be like that, even though he knows he can be himself around you?"

"Yeah, I guess so." She paused for a moment and then lightly punched him in the arm.

"Hey, what was that for?" asked Sam in surprise, rubbing at the site of a slight throbbing.

"If you couldn't've told me he was a Vampire, you could have at least warned me that the entire supernatural world would be gossiping if I happened to date a non-Witch supernatural!"

"Ah, yeah, that. Sorry," Sam said, looking and sounding apologetic.

For some reason, Alice did not quite believe it. "Hmm," she said sceptically.

"Anyway, I'm starving," said Sam, changing the subject. He did not want to admit to Alice that the gossip about her choice of partners was nothing compared to the attention that was heading her way. "Know any good pie shops around here?"

"By which you mean, like a pastry pie or pizza pie?" asked Alice, looking at him with a hint of confusion, wondering if she was making it up that some New Yorkers referred to pizza as pie.

"Pizza."

"Don't know why I said that to be honest. It's not like I know a good pie or a good pizza place," Alice replied. "I haven't really explored that much to be honest and much like Chinese, it's something we've mostly ordered in."

"That's okay," said Sam reassuringly, giving her shoulders a quick squeeze. "Assuming it's still there, I know a place."

***

Mario ushered Sam and Alice into a small red leather booth at the back of the restaurant. Alice had never been in a restaurant that so resembled a scene from a movie about the Italian-American mafia. Red leather booths, white table cloths, black and white photographs of people with Mario and his father and occasionally, mother; there were candles in old wine bottles, tiled flooring and a long wooden bar. It was filled with locals, the accents running the gamut of the Five Boroughs and their respective heritages, and Alice almost felt nervous about talking in case her English accent garnered more interest than she wanted.

Mario had greeted Sam like an old friend, with a huge hug and a kiss upon each cheek; he looked like he was going to do the same to Alice, but she supposed the look of abject discomfort stopped him, so he merely gave her a big smile. She sat down and looked at the menu, whilst leaving Sam to catch up with old acquaintances for a few minutes. A waitress ('Candice' according to the badge on her striped shirt) took her order with a suspicious look and returned momentarily with a jug of water, a beer and a diet coke.

"Thank you," said Alice, inwardly rolling her eyes as the woman glared at her before flouncing off.

For a moment, Alice wondered why she was being treated with barely veiled hostility, but as she watched, it was obvious that the woman was interested in Sam. She supposed it would become clear that she was not Sam's date, but until that point, she would have to endure. Sam sat down opposite her, and a few moments later, Mario put a little tea-light candle on the table.

"More romantic," he said. "Few minutes for pizza. Not

long."

Alice smiled and thanked him.

"Not on a date, Mario, she's a friend," said Sam, patiently.

"He's a good man. Needs a good woman. You forgive him," Mario said, ignoring him.

"I'll think about it," Alice said, her eyes twinkling.

"What are you playing at?" asked Sam, when Mario had moved out of earshot again.

"Can't you read my mind and find out?" teased Alice, unfolding a napkin and laying it on her lap.

"Maybe, but I don't like doing it, especially to friends," Sam said seriously, frowning at her. "Besides, although I could focus my gift, if you want to call it that, on a specific thought, that's not really how it works."

Alice smiled to reassure him that she had been joking, before laughing at herself. "Just delusions of grandeur," Alice explained. "Felt a little homesick, so I watched an episode of *Sherlock*, so now I fancy myself as a detective-come-psychologist."

"Okay," said Sam, curious. "So how does this play into you letting Mario think you're my girlfriend?"

"Honestly, Mario will realise it soon enough, although I think he genuinely hopes I'll be a good influence on you. Besides, it's more for the drama queen waitress' benefit, if you're wanting a date, given you were checking her out."

"I did no such thing," interrupted Sam, indignantly. They both knew that was not true.

Alice merely smirked and shook her head. "Anyway, she likes the idea of stealing you off me, and if she thinks she is the cause of a row between us, that will make you all the more attractive to her. You know, if that's what you want, 'coz not to be judge-y, but she's not girlfriend material."

"I don't know how to answer that right now," said Sam, bemused. He tried to think of how many waitresses he had actually taken home from Mario's. *Too many*, he admitted to himself.

"Okay then," said Alice, with a laugh. "This explaining how clever I am is so much fun by the way. No wonder Sherlock is so addicted to it."

"And how long will this delusion last?" asked Sam, taking a long swig of his beer. He was amused by how much fun Alice appeared to be having. At the moment, the Witch in front of him seemed a far cry from the shy, courteous librarian of only a few months previous.

"Not long," said Alice, shrugging as she sipped her own drink. "I'm not naturally inclined to notice things, so I'll forget before long. And if I do notice things, I'll forget to apply it logically. I do it all the time, watch something and aspire to emulate it somehow."

"Well, I hope you watch something less influencing the next time we meet."

She laughed. "I'll try. I'm very particular about trying to remain extraordinarily English though."

"Can't see you losing that," said Sam. "Besides, the Doc has been here forever and he is still very obviously English."

Alice smiled warmly as Mario brought over the pizzas, he smiled back at her and gave Sam a warning look, before leaving again.

"Well, I have to say Ms. Holmes, it does look like your deductions are correct," said Sam, grabbing a quarter of his pizza, and folding it up. "It's the proper way to eat pizza," said Sam, as Alice looked at him dubiously.

"I'm thinking I might just cut my slices into manageable ones," said Alice, using the knife and fork to tear each quarter into three. "This is a ridiculously big pizza for one person. Even for four."

"How long have you been in New York?" asked Sam with teasing incredulity, his mouth still full.

"Gross," said Alice, trying to find somewhere else to look. "Clearly not long enough," she answered, taking a small bite of her own pizza. Her eyes widened; everything about that bite seemed perfect. The mozzarella cheese to rich tomato sauce ratio, alongside the topping to dough factors... "Oh. Mi. God! This is like the best pizza ever. I have to bring Robert here. Or turn him into a toad for two hours for holding out on me."

"You're gonna bring another guy to my spot?" asked Sam, miming a dagger to his heart.

"Of course," said Alice, matter-of-factly. "Besides, I don't think you're in New York long enough for it to be your spot, so now it's mine."

"Yeah, you're definitely not that nice," said Sam with a smile.

Alice finished her mouthful of pizza and stuck her tongue out. "You want me to help you get a girl or not?"

"I guess. It's been a while," said Sam, grinning suggestively.

"Public service – you... overshare," said Alice, feeling ever so slightly disturbed. Kathie and Robert were the only ones that she could just about stomach discussing sex with. "Girls never want to know about that stuff."

"I'll try to remember that," said Sam.

Alice looked at him suspiciously, not entirely sure he was joking. "You really don't think that should just be common sense? Would you really want to know anything about my sex life?"

"Maybe not," said Sam, laughing. "Although, it's obvious when *you* last had sex."

Alice went bright red. "Don't even..., just no," said Alice, shaking her head, face etched with disgust at the thought of talking about her bedroom activities. She shuddered, and returned her attention to the pizza.

Sam laughed. "So, when's the wedding?"

Alice did not think it was possible to blush any harder than she had been, but she had a feeling that she had managed it. "Don't encourage me," she begged. "We've not even moved in with one another yet, so I definitely should not be imagining fairytale weddings. I mean, he might put the forks in the dishwasher the wrong way round or squeeze the toothpaste from the middle."

Sam nearly spat out his drink from the laughter. "Boring, but sensible, I suppose," said Sam, coughing on the hastily swallowed swig. "God, how did I end up with a sensible friend?"

"I'm hardly the only one. You surround yourself with sensible people so that don't have to be the sensible one."

"Maybe I just like who I like?" returned Sam, not entirely convinced Alice was wrong.

"That too," said Alice with a grin. She cut up another slice of pizza, sadly beginning to feel a little full already. "Okay, can I slap you when we have this fake argument, 'coz I've kinda always wanted to do that, please? Not to you particularly, but as a general thing." Her eyes lit up hopefully as she widened them, trying to emulate a puppy-dog look.

"I swear, quiet girls are the worst," said Sam wryly, unable to keep the amusement out of his eyes.

"And you need to box up the rest of my pizza. If I find you've stolen a slice, we're no longer friends."

"I'm not sure a hook-up is worth this," said Sam, leaning over to try and take a slice off her plate. She batted his hand away from the three-quarters she had left and scowled, before noticing the amulet that had slipped out of the neck of his white t-shirt.

"Hey, you're still wearing it," she said with a smile.
Sam fingered the pendant and looked down at it for a moment. "Of course. It's the most powerful protection amulet I own, could ever own probably," said Sam seriously, as he smiled at her gratefully. "It's hard for Psychics to own amulets like this, as they're usually too, for lack of a better word, haunted. Besides, it's not often I get gifts."

"Don't run off so often then," said Alice. "Plenty of people like you. And you could always try having a girlfriend for a change, albeit, not her." She surreptitiously nodded her head towards Candice.

"You really aren't eating any more of that?" said Sam,

looking at her pizza sadly.

"I think I'm like ninety percent tea, so there's not a lot of room left for food. I have a grazing style of nutritional intake. Believe me, I def-finitely want to eat this, I just can't," she said, looking at it with an equal amount of dismay.

"I'll make sure it gets boxed. All of it," he said, drawing a cross over his heart.

Alice smiled, and gave him a look of mock warning. "Thank you. Right, I'm going to use the rest room, I expect she'll flirt with you while I'm gone."

"Okay Sherlock. See you in a few."

Alice schooched across the booth and ducked into the bathroom. She decided to actually use the facilities since she was there, but waited a moment to peer through the crack of the door, just to see if she was right. Since there was definitely no reason for the waitress to be bending over quite like that in front of anyone, she presumed she was correct. She gave herself a little moment of smugness, and immediately straightened herself up and tried to look stern, angry and jealous. She momentarily considered pretending that it was Robert and not Sam who was being flirted with, but was slightly afraid of what she was capable of if that was the situation. As the waitress was now practically sitting in Sam's lap, she frowned and stormed over to the table. Sam had not answered the question so she decided he would have said yes.

"What the hell do you think you're doing?!"

Candice gave her a look that tried to suggest nothing was going on, but was failing to keep her own smugness at bay. Still, clearly Alice's stare was enough to keep her from saying anything as she quickly vacated the vicinity of their booth.

"How could you? And on my birthday!" said Alice, firmly slapping Sam, angrily grabbing her stuff and storming out of the restaurant. She kept a tissue to her face, hoping it looked like she was crying and not about to burst out laughing. She walked down to the park and sat by the fountain, waiting for Sam to find her. She found an English penny in her pocket, made a wish and tossed it into the water, lazily swinging a foot against the smooth, stone base.

"So, did it work?" Alice asked, as a dark-haired man with a pizza box half-heartedly jogged towards her.

"Exactly as you predicted. She put her number on a napkin, tucked in the side of the box." He rubbed his face gently. "I think you enjoyed that a little too much."

"Skank," Alice muttered. "She's the kind of woman that gives the rest of us a bad name," she said as way of explanation, as Sam shot her a look of amusement, shock and curiosity. "Hand over the pizza," she said, taking hold of the box and smiling.

"Mario said to tell you that I'm lucky to have you as you're a good friend," said Sam, reluctantly letting go of the box being pulled from his hands.

"Can't argue with that," said Alice. She suddenly felt really tempted to eat more pizza, but she knew she would regret it if she did. She looked at the box almost longingly, the glimmer in her eyes fading slightly. She was never very good at asking important things in case she could not deal with the answers.

"Indeed not. Anyway, spit it out, Andrews," said Sam, smiling. "I don't need to be psychic to see something's on your mind."

She stuck her tongue out. "Don't rush me. You know what I'm like and where I'm from. The English have very strict protocols for asking important questions, which generally involve a lot of sighing and internal arguing."

"I've noticed, although the Doc is not as bad as you."

"Okay, well, I've been looking up various bits of literature on the Three, most of which is very unscientific and disorganised. You'd have thought someone would have written some kind of Lexicon or something."

"It's probably lower down. Although if you asked nicely, Julius or the Doc could probably get it for you."

"Oh," said Alice, feeling stupid. "Yeah, I should probably

do that. Maybe next Tuesday then. Anyway, I came across something that said spirits could sometimes enter the bodies of Psychics."

"It's rare, but yeah, it can happen. Usually the spirit has to be invited in, but occasionally, if you get a very powerful spirit and a relatively weak Psychic, then you can get hijacked." Sam paused, thinking about the young girl that had hijacked him because he could not speak Russian well enough. "Or if you have a very determined spirit that thinks you're doing an awful job of getting their message across." Given the look of pain, grief and anger in her parents' eyes, Sam had not asked what the little girl had told them; it had certainly not been anything good.

"Has it ever happened to you?" asked Alice.

"Once or twice," Sam replied. "If it's easier for the spirit to communicate directly, I let them borrow my body, but sometimes the spirit gets impatient with how I choose to relay their message and I get jumped before I can offer."

"It's not like demonic possession though, right?" Alice said.

Sam looked surprised. "No. Not at all. Demonic possession is about taking control of a human host body, displacing the host soul and allowing the demon access to the mortal realm. Demons don't care about the soul they're trying to consume. To be fair, spirits don't always care too much for you either, but they just want to move on. Even with hijacking, it's about the message; they definitely don't want my ugly shell. It makes you feel cold and disjointed and sort of, crowded. It's not a great feeling and slightly worse if you're not prepared for having another soul with you, but a demonic possession would definitely be a million times worse."

"Is there any way of allowing non-dead spirits to enter a non-dead host?"

"Like astral projection?"

"No, not really. More like dream walking I guess," Alice said with a shrug.

"I've heard it's used by shamans and different indigenous cultures, but it's not something I've tried. If you need someone read though, I can help you out."

"No, no. I don't want to go visiting anyone's dreams," Alice reassured him quickly. "And thanks, 'coz I would go to you if I was really concerned about a person's intent. I guess, I was thinking maybe, you know, if someone slipped into a coma or some sort of catatonic state caused by otherworldly means. Then you could potentially go into their minds and help them out, possibly."

"What on earth have you been reading?" asked Sam, genuinely curious now.

"Yeah, I guess it's silly. Sorry," Alice apologised.

"No, if something's bothering you, trust your instincts." Alice shrugged. "It's just the book I'm working on for the Library. Every time I come across something weird in it, I try to think how to combat it, you know, if someone uses the spell before I've fixed it."

"And you found one that puts people into comas?"

"Well, no, but…"

"It's fine. Don't worry about it," Sam said, throwing his arm reassuringly around her. "Well, I can ask around. And I can drop off any particular herbs I find out about next time I visit, although African dream root is the obvious one."

"Thanks. I'd appreciate that," Alice said, gratefully. "So where you off to next?"

"Boston. A friend of my grandfather works at a cemetery and is concerned. Thinks the ghosts are upset about something and wants someone to have a word."

"Hmm, fair enough," said Alice, not really sure what else to say. "Oh, that reminds me, you should listen to your guardian angel a bit more.'"

"Huh?" asked Sam, giving her a look of confusion.

"The spirit that sorta hangs around you," Alice said, smiling as she raised her eyebrow questioningly, not entirely sure if she was intruding on some kind of secret. "She said you weren't paying attention when she tried to help you identify the Baa'll."

"Ah," said Sam, understanding bright in his eyes as his grin returned. "That'd be my great-grandma. And it wasn't deliberate. There are a lot of voices in the OTS. Honestly, it was probably better for me that she told you. The solutions I knew of weren't good enough and the stuff I was trying from the books didn't help either."

"Well, if you have to go in there again, I'll tell the others to keep quiet. I might not be able to see or hear them in the same way you can, but I have ways and means and I'll... put them on a time-out or something." Alice frowned, looking down at the water, its surface too rippled and dark to see a clear reflection. Regardless, she pulled a despairing face at herself, knowing that she was quite possibly the least threatening-sounding thing in the park at that moment.

Sam laughed and hugged her shoulders reassuringly, glad that he could not see anything more than a human was supposed to as he did so; it was no easy feat when next to a supernatural of Alice's power. He was quite sure that once she had found the right words, any potential threat would be suitably terrifying coming from an Alice that truly meant it.

"You want to come back to mine to freshen up?" Alice asked, as they started walking back towards the Library.

"Are you suggesting I smell?" asked Sam, pulling at his t-shirt and giving it a sniff. It did not seem so bad to him; maybe a little lived in, but nothing horrendous. Musky at worst.

"No," said Alice, with a laugh "just thought you might like the chance to use a good shower with all the little luxuries that your average flea-ridden motel does not have. If the gatekeeper lets you pass, then you may use the guest bathroom, which I don't think has been used by any guests," said Alice, after a moment's thought. "Can't really see Onion having a problem with you."

"Your Familiar." It had been a long time since he had been around a guardian Familiar. Sam had to admit that he was intrigued; and a hot shower and clean towels was also a luxury he had not experienced in a long while.

"My cat, although he obviously does not like anyone to think that. I am clearly just there to open tins," said Alice, affectionately. "He seemed impressed with the name when I showed him your card."

Sam balked slightly. "Did he mention anything else?" he asked, trying to sound casual. There were few things that made Sam uncomfortable, but his family and events in their recent history, did.

"About you? No. Why should he?" Alice said with a confused laugh, looking at him bemused.

"Let's just say, although the Harvelle-Walkers are a prestigious line of Psychics, we don't have the most sparkling rep." Sam really did not want to go into the specifics of what his parents and other ancestors had done, especially when he was enjoying the novelty of having a real friend; Julius was far too aloof and immovable, and there was always going to be a slight barrier with Stuart.

"Ah," said Alice, deciding not to push. Instead, she placed a comforting hand on his arm and gave him a sympathetic smile. "Eh. I still like you."
Sam grinned. "Thanks. I like you too. Definitely the best female friend I have ever had."

Alice gave him a sceptical look. "I get the feeling I am the only female friend you've had."

"What can I say? Most ladies find me irresistible," said Sam, flashing her his most charming of smiles.

"Eh," said Alice, shrugging. "You're not ugly, I guess," she teased, grinning.

"Gee thanks," said Sam, looking unimpressed. "Last time I take you to an awesome food place."

"You know other awesome food places?" Alice asked, interested. Given how right he had been about the pizza at Mario's, Alice would happily try out other eateries on his recommendation.

"I know where to get the best everything in this city," Sam replied, solemnly. "I even figure that I know the best person to make me some citronella and sage candles." He smiled at her hopefully.

"Who might that be then?" Alice asked innocently. "Maybe he or she could make me some too, although odd combination, isn't it?"

Sam pulled a face of wry annoyance. "The cemetery's on the river. Even at night the mozzies try to bite the fuck out of me."

Alice's face screwed up with concentration as she nodded sympathetically given that if there were any biting bugs around, they seemed to enjoy snacking on her. She was trying to visualise her magic cupboard and saw a big space where the sage was usually kept. There was not a lot of wax left either.

"Ah balls," she said, her shoulders slumping.

"What?" asked Sam, concerned and amused. He had rarely heard Stuart swear and there was something about the English accent that made their cursing all the more unexpected.

"I'll need to buy more wax and sage and citronella, and the easiest place to get it from is near the station. And they don't like me in there."

"Oh?" said Sam. If it was the shop he thought it was, he would be surprised if they remembered her from one visit to another. Every time he went in there, Charisma, the witch that usually worked on the counter, flirted with him without ever realising that she had done so on several previous occasions.

"I suppose, technically, I may have swindled them slightly. But to be fair, she was a total bitch," Alice said, briefly telling him about the tourmaline incident.

Sam laughed. "Serves them right. And their mistake, so you should definitely not feel guilty about it."

"I think that's the problem," said Alice, looking slightly abashed. "I don't feel guilty about it."

"Well, it'll be fine. I think it'll be remarkably easy for you to get them to treat you with a bit more respect, if that's what you what," said Sam, looking carefully at the sign above the shop. Within the arching and sweeping flourishes of 'Modern Magicks' expensive lettering, were symbols for the witches coven. It was a fairly common practice for Witch businesses to incorporate the mark of their coven into logos or signage, since much like celebrity endorsements, it could provide added prestige to an establishment. Any member of The Crown of the Pale Moon certainly did not miss a chance to show off their allegiance, and Modern Magicks was no different.

Alice was slightly surprised when she opened the door and the bottled-blonde failed to say anything, merely giving her a look of disgust and a withering smirk as she took in the pizza box and eyed Alice's figure. Then her pale-blue eyes turned to Sam and she flashed him a brilliant smile.

Sam smiled politely back. "I'll hold that for you," he said, reaching for the box.

"Thanks," Alice said, giving him a grateful smile, trying to ignore the imaginary daggers being thrown at her head. "I'll just be a minute." She picked up a wicker basket and walked to the back of the shop, glad that she would not have to witness another woman fawning over Sam. She supposed she could see that Sam was an attractive guy, but the fact that these women were doing it in front of her, when she could have been his girlfriend, appalled her.

She picked up some candles, rolling them in her hands to test the quality of the wax. Infusing already shaped candles was tricker than forming them from scratch, but it took less time. She sniffed at several small bottles of sage and citronella oils until she found ones with the most potent scents and after a moment's thought, threw in a couple of jars of crushed minerals.

"What? Her? You can't be serious?" Blonde woman said, her voice loud with disbelief.

Alice frowned and tried not to worry about it. She knew she should not care what that bitch thought, but such an exclamation hardly instilled confidence. She loitered by the incense sticks and scarves for a moment longer, liking one that was dark blue and embroidered with rose gold stars, but reluctant to buy it given the staff.

"Just these please," Alice said, walking over to where the witch and Sam were talking and laying the items out on the counter.

"Would you like a bag for those?" the witch asked politely, as she rang up the items.

"Er, no thank you," said Alice, after a moment, not entirely able to hide her surprise or suspicion. "I've got a bag I can use." She moved her purse into her pocket, shifted the keys, lip balm, tissues, mints, iPod and notebook and eventually came out with a black canvas bag. She did not remember putting this particular shopper in her handbag but she recognised it as a bag that her grandmother had used.

"That's $115 after coven discount, of course," the witch continued.

"Oh, thanks," said Alice carefully, handing over the bundle of notes and accepting the change, shooting questioning glances at Sam who merely stood quietly to one side.

"Here's one of our cards, in case we can help you with anything else," said the witch. "Have a nice day."

"You too," said Alice automatically, still trying not to shake her head in bewilderment. As soon as they were outside and Sam handed back the intact pizza box, Alice demanded an explanation. "Okay, what the hell was that about? Did you tell her I was your sister or something?"

Sam laughed. "I wouldn't do that to you. She was flirting in a painfully earnest way, and let's face it, you do not need to be dealing with the fallout of my philandering."

"Ooh, nice," said Alice, nodding approvingly to the use of the word; not so much to the fact that it was applicable.

"I make an effort for you," said Sam. "I just told her you knew Endora Price."

"Why would you mention my grandmother?" Alice asked with a bemused laugh.

"I think that's for someone else to go into," said Sam, thinking that it would probably raise more questions than he had the answers for. "But I didn't tell her how you knew her, just that you did. Anyway, you see that symbol on your bag?"

"Yeah?"

"That's the insignia for a coven called The Crown of the Pale Moon. It's kind of a big deal. If you look closely at that shop sign," he said, pointing to Modern Magicks "particularly within the big flourishes of some of the letters, you can see little symbols that if you put them all together, would form..."

"...the same symbol as on my bag," finished Alice, looking interested. "Do all Witches do that?"

"Not all. Ones in the Pale Moon usually do though."

"I think I had an e-mail from them," Alice said, thoughtfully. It reminded her that she needed to get better privacy protection; magic or not, these covens should not have found her, let alone her e-mail address.

"Wouldn't surprise me," said Sam. "You're going to be a very sought after Witch."

Alice looked at him sceptically. "If you say so, Casanova. Anyway, let's grab your van and go to mine. I'll make candles while you shower. You should probably do some laundry while you're at it."

"Are you sure you're not suggesting I smell?" said Sam.

Chapter 22

Mondays, Wednesdays and Fridays were normal library duties, whilst Tuesdays and Thursday mornings focused on how best to deal with the supernatural texts, both in terms of maintenance, cataloguing and transferring. Tuesday afternoons, Alice got to play with magic; Thursday afternoons, Julius tried to teach her how to meditate.

There was a space on the third floor, that was well-lit and got the afternoon sun. It was quiet and warm, nestled away in a forgotten corner, and Julius had emptied it of all furniture, bar two chairs and a desk. He would place a large, beautifully carved jade oil burner in the middle of the desk, alongside a glass vase of fresh flowers (usually gerberas or daisies or something from a similar family), a jug of water, a single glass and a CD player.

The first attempt at meditating had been less than successful. The room had been practically empty that time, apart from the two cushions Alice and Julius were to sit on. They had sat down, legs crossed, arms resting on the thighs, palms upwards, which was known as the Sukhasana in yoga.

Julius told her to try and focus on an image in her mind, like the flame of a candle, and to try and empty her mind of everything else. So, of course, Alice's brain filled up with the most random thoughts possible, and she began spiralling into a madness inducing loop that made her bored and frustrated. Julius tried to get her to calm her mind by focusing on saying 'sa ta na ma' whilst consecutively touching each finger against her thumb, but in her annoyance, she just kept trying to go faster and faster, enraging herself that her fingers could not keep up with the sounds. Then she felt thirsty, and so could not stop thinking about a cup of tea and it was all too much like sitting in a two-hour long exam, waiting for everyone else to finish when you had already answered all the questions.

Alice tried to do as Julius asked, tried to relax and clear her mind, but it really was not happening. Even when she could get herself to focus on one thing, it was not really just one thing but more like multiple narratives involving one person. They persevered for an hour, until there was a knock at the door, whereupon Dr Anthonys told them that the kettle had been making a dubious run for it.

The following week, Julius had ensured that Alice had been properly fed and watered before attempting the meditation, and he also brought in the desk and chairs. Upon finding out that lavender was Alice's favourite scent (as no one had yet managed to bottle the scent of home baking); that she found the sound of water, soothing; and that she considered bright oranges, reds and deep yellows to be comforting, Julius had added the other accoutrements to the desk.

Instead of telling her to clear her mind, Julius told her to concentrate on her breathing and on trying to hear the raindrops. Although Alice did not achieve a clear mind, she did at least manage to be quite calm, still and relaxed for a couple of hours, which everyone had to agree was a marked success in comparison to the previous week.

In the successive weeks, Julius had sent her on what Alice could only consider to be 'ridiculous errands', tasks that had left her frustrated and stressed and wanting to hide in the nearest cupboard. Of course, she had quickly figured out what he was trying to do, and was getting at least a little better at taking a deep breath and calming down before things started flying or before the weather took a sudden turn. It still felt as though she could not properly meditate, even when she tried to just focus on the rain and the sensation of her breathing, and unfortunately, she did not feel as though today was going to be any more successful.

She waited to see where Julius was going to settle and took her own seat on the floor twisting herself into the Sukhasana, since she still was not flexible enough for a full Lotus. Julius had seated himself at the desk and Alice pulled a small face of annoyance. Sometimes he would meditate next to her; other times, it seemed like he was studying her. Today, was clearly a study day and Alice felt that it was just another irritation to add to her fractious mood.

She took in a deep breath of lavender-scented air through her nose and slowly let the breath out of her mouth, trying to release her fidgety mood with it. She covered her yawning mouth, let out a couple of sighs and tried to crack her neck before trying to settle once more.

She relaxed her shoulders, took deep breaths in and out, and closed her eyes, trying to concentrate on the distant sound of raindrops. Five minutes of mindfulness would be a good start, and she tried to remind herself to think of things in manageable chunks rather than as an insurmountable whole.

"Alice."

Alice opened one eye and glanced around suspiciously. She knew there was no one in the room other than herself and Julius, but the voice certainly had not been the deep, monotonous thunder of her companion. She gave herself a little shake, dismissing the sound as a trick in the pipes or some other creak or groan that her overactive imagination had turned into a gremlin speaking her name. She closed the eye and started again.

"Alice."

Alice frowned and opened her eyes. "Can you hear that?" she asked, momentarily forgetting who she was talking to. She looked at Julius' furrowed brow and asked the question more explicitly. "I mean, can you hear something saying 'Alice'? Or anything other than the raindrops for that matter?"

"I can not," said Julius, looking at her with a slightly stern expression. He knew Alice always tried to meditate properly, but there were times when she seemed less than committed and prone to find reasons not to continue. He was not entirely sure whether this was one of those times, given that Alice seemed particularly restless.

"Hmm. Okay. Sorry." She straightened her back, closed her eyes and began to focus on her breathing again, relaxing into the scent of lavender and the soothing patter of the rain.

"Allllliiissssssssss." It was low, raspy and sinister. It was like a horror movie cliché voice, but it was worse than just a noise; it was like she could feel it somehow.

She flinched and her eyes flew open. It had been louder that time, felt nearer, felt… wrong.

"Ju?"

"Yes, Alice?" Julius replied. He did not express exasperation if indeed he truly felt it, but there was a tiny inflect in his voice that Alice and Sam could often pick up on, even if no one else did.

She hesitated for a moment, wondering if she was perhaps just imagining things. "Are you saying my name, like to try and teach me to not get distracted or something?" Alice knew that if she could ask the right question, Julius would not lie to her. If that was what he was doing that was fine – and by the manner in which he seemed to work, he would not think about hearing the words he was speaking – but Alice did not like feeling as though she was going mad.

"I am not," said Julius, looking at her in concern. "Are you okay?"

"I'm sure it's nothing," Alice replied, giving her self a mental shake, her eyes slightly downcast, as doubt wrinkled up her face. She smiled wanly at Julius, took a deep breath and started again.

In. Out. In. Out. In. Out. In…

"Allllllllliiiiiiiiiiisssssssssss." The voice started again, and Alice tried to push it away.

… Out. In. Out. I hear only raindrops, I hear only raindrops, I hear…

"Don't ignore me Allllllliiiiiissssssssssss." The voice was beginning to sound annoyed.

In. Out. In. Out. Leave me the fuck alone. In. Out. Clearly you are a manifestation of my depression and you can leave me the fuck alone. I've done mindfulness; you can piss off ...

"Come to the window Alice," the voice ordered.

Alice winced, opening her eyes and reluctantly looked at the window. There was only the slightly fogged windows with a few drops of condensation running down.

"Come to the window Alice. Come out and play," the voice ordered again.

Go away. She took a deep breath and started again, trying to ignore Julius' concerned stare. It was not the depression talking nor was it anyone inside the Library. Whatever it was, she could deal with it herself.

"Alllllllissssssssssss." The voice sounded more frustrated now. "Come to the window. I know you'd rather do that than your stupid meditation."

Alice ignored the fact that the voice was right. *In. Out. In. Out. I hear only raindrops...*

"Come to the window now!" the voice demanded.

Leave me alone. Alice unconsciously began rocking back and forth.

"Come to the window."

I will not. Who are you?

"Come to the window," the voice insisted angrily.

No, Alice challenged, suddenly angry about being bullied *Who or what are you?*

She felt a strange doubt and annoyance that were not her own, followed by a brief flash of rage.

"Boo!" The voice shouted at her as a strange face appeared. Alice shrieked, pushing herself backwards off the cushion, the sound of a book slamming shut reverberating in her ears before the strange presence and voice finally disappeared.

She looked around furtively, barely able to register her

concerned mentor. There was nothing. She knew there was nothing physically there, but something had been in, or trying to get into, her head. There were plenty of questions that this little incident posed, but only one that truly perturbed her – if it *had* managed to make her go to the window, what would it have tried to make her do afterwards?

Despite the spring sunshine, and the gently wafting heat from the radiators, Alice shivered.

"Alice, are you okay?"

"No," she whispered. "I'm not sure I am."

"Excuse me a moment," said Julius. "I will get Stuart."

"Okay," said Alice. Her voice felt small. She stood up and wrapped herself inside her black, cat-paw hoodie, putting up the cat-eared hood in an effort to feel warm and to amuse herself. Robert's expression when she had come out of the library with the hood up, had amused her greatly, since it seemed like he did not know whether to be amused, appalled or slightly endeared. She paced the room, counting her steps, not wanting to think about the face or the sounds. She dug her hands into the pockets and pulled out her phone, quickly opening up her photographs and finding her favourite image, Robert dozing on the sofa with Onion sprawled over his lap. She did not know what Robert had bribed him with, but on days like this, having that image made her feel safe.

She rubbed at her face, pushing her glasses up a bit, and tried to stop biting her lip. She took a deep breath and began to 'sa ta na ma' on her hands, but she would not close her eyes. She stopped the pacing and sat down at the edge of the chair, still rocking herself, as Julius re-entered the room.

"Alice, what happened?" Stuart asked, with a great deal of concern.

Julius handed her a cup of tea, and Alice murmured her thanks, almost feeling like she could burst into tears. She took a sip of the hot drink and as the liquid sent its warmth around her body, she began to feel like an idiot. Again.

"I don't care how it sounds or how stupid you feel,"

Stuart said, reading the expressions on her face. "I want to know what just happened."

"There was something here. I don't know what, don't know why, certainly don't know how, but there was something." She quickly told him about trying to meditate, the voice, the face and the slamming book. "The slamming seemed different though. Like that was something else."

"That was probably the Library intervening," said Stuart, looking worried. "Unusual that it was not aware sooner."

"Maybe the person that bought whatever that was in, didn't know they had it," suggested Alice, staring into her tea.

"A patsy?"

"Yeah," said Alice, nodding. "The Library can judge intent, so obviously the easiest way to circumvent that, is to use someone else. Just slip something into someone's bag."

"Yes, that certainly seems like the only reasonable explanation, given that there was clearly intent behind this little, prank? Attack?" questioned Stuart.

"Test," said Alice, thoughtfully. "I think someone was seeing if it could be done. I don't think it went as they expected though."

"Really?" asked Stuart. He was both bemused and fascinated by Alice's desire to talk things out, as though it allowed her to take the emotion out of a situation and only apply logic to it. Useful as it might be, he hoped she knew it would only ever delay whatever it was she did not want to acknowledge about such events.

"No. I imagine he, she, it, would have expected it to work. That they could bypass the security by using someone else to bring in the hex or whatever, and convince me to go outside, but it was a one-time shot," said Alice, with a broadening, confident smile. "Obviously I need to take steps in trying to protect my mind, but I'll work on that, and the Library will be more vigilant, since she is now aware of a potential exploitative weakness."

"She?" Stuart echoed, eyebrows raised quizzically.

"You don't think the Library feels like a 'she'?" asked Alice, looking at him.

"Can't say that a gender specific pronoun occurred to me," replied Stuart, with a smile. "Now you mention it though, I'm quite sure it will stick."

"If it's okay, I think I'll try and work on your book, rather than trying to meditate any more?" Alice said, after a moment's uncomfortable silence.

Stuart and Julius looked at one another, and the latter nodded his head.

"Thanks. I know it's not going to happen again, but I'm just not ready to just jump back in."

"We understand," said Stuart.

"Thank you," said Alice, feeling subdued. "I'll pop my head in before I leave for the day."

The two men watched as she seemed to shuffle out of the room, seemingly weighted down by shadows. Stuart sighed, pinched the bridge of his nose and readjusted his glasses before looking at Julius. The large man seemed to be in deeper thought than normal.

"I sense a great disturbance in the Force," said Stuart. He knew Julius would not get the reference, but at the same time, he did not know how better else to explain his thoughts. "Do you know what's happening?"

"I need to speak to someone," said Julius, disappearing before Stuart could get out another word.

Stuart let out a long sigh of annoyance. Julius' vanishing act was irritating at the best of times, but in the past year, such occurrences had become far more frequent, and had almost tripled in frequency since he had brought Alice to the Library. Whilst the Head Librarian accepted that the Fallen were higher beings with a job far beyond the understanding of mere mortals, the fact that a once abstract notion was steadily encroaching upon the supposedly neutral institution that he was curator of, was becoming a concern. As was the fact that the Fallen were clearly watching Alice.

***

Lady Jane slammed her fist into the wall and cursed loudly. The building had been long abandoned and since she had set up her watch-post there, not even the graffiti artists, derelicts or rats dared to step on her floor. She had hoped to speed things up a little, but despite the weeks of delicate practice, the plan had failed and the opportunity would not present itself again.

She took a deep breath and centred herself, forcing herself to push all emotions away. She knew they made her careless, which was why she normally did not feed them, but she really hated the Witch. She watched as Alice paced the room in the Library, waiting on her mentor and Angel to come and comfort her. She rolled her eyes, annoyed that every time she thought she had a gauge on Alice's abilities, she just carelessly became stronger. Every time. With no effort at all. She clenched her hand around a star-shaped hira-shuriken, watching the blood pour comfortingly into the chalice by her feet. She did not need the blood at this time other than to soothe her foul temper, but it was pointless to waste it when it would be needed at some point either by her or her master.

She gathered up any and all traces of her visit, pouring ammonia over every surface that she might have touched. There would be no way of getting to Alice whilst she was in the Library and her residence was far more protected than anticipated. If only she could make her Lord accept that it would be far better for all involved if he would simply kill the Witch to open the Veil.

***

"I think we need to have a talk," Stuart said when Julius finally reappeared in his office.

"Yes." Julius sat down in his usual chair and glared at the raven momentarily, before turning back to the Head Librarian. Stuart was slightly taken aback; he had not expected Julius to agree. "What is going on Julius?"

"I am of the Fallen."

Stuart nodded; that much at least, Julius had already shared.

"I gave up my place in Heaven and the garden of the Oldest Gods to help the mortal realm. Most of these were spent watching. Waiting. Reading the signs that were left for those that would care to notice them.

"In becoming Fallen, I pledged my service to the Archangel Raphael; it is he to whom I am supposed to answer; it is his orders I am supposed to follow. He ordered me to come to the Library if you were to ever take up the mantle here. And he told me to watch over a Witch. A Witch that was spoken of in prophecies that were believed to be as accurate as those that foretold of the Three.

"There are many prophecies regarding the mortal realm. Most are incorrect, many cease to be through the ever-changing strands of time and a few are small, innocuous markers that remind those watching that not all should be ignored. The world has been building up to this prophecy, and regardless of whether it truly comes to pass or not, Raphael believes Alice to be this Witch. So does Lucifer, Kronos, Asmodeius and all the other commanders of the legions that reside in Hell. Many creatures have been watching Alice throughout her life."

"Why are the Fallen so concerned with Alice? Surely you can not think that she would side with Demons?" questioned Stuart. He would be hard pressed to name another Witch less likely than Alice to go Dark.

"I do not. But the others do not know her. They know Alice is a very powerful Witch. More powerful than you or she realises. Given that she was raised without the normal Witching education, it was decided that we could guide her should the opportunity arise."

So that is the real reason we have a Witch working in the

Library, thought Stuart, his mind recalling the day that Julius had suggested giving Alice sanctuary. "The Library is supposed to be neutral."

"This Library has evolved. We do not know why, but it has chosen to protect the balance, which means protecting Alice. The Dark made the first move and failed, which is why I was ordered to befriend her."

Stuart closed his eyes and let up a sad sigh. He hoped Alice would never learn of this. "So what is written in this prophecy?"

"I do not know."

"Will I be able to find a copy of it?"

"I do not believe so."

"Does Alice know anything of this?"

"No. Nor can we tell her."

Stuart frowned, not that he had been expecting any other response. "Does this have anything to do with what happened earlier?"

"Perhaps. I have insufficient data. The other side are very good at covering their skins.

"Tracks," Stuart corrected, absent-mindedly. "One cover's one's tracks and saves one's skin."

"No. They cover their real skin with human flesh. It makes it much harder to detect them," said Julius, without emotion.

"Oh," said Stuart, not entirely what he thought about that news. He recalled Alice's question about detecting Demons and wondered if it would be prudent for him to start making his own enquiries.

"The Darkness are truly evil and clever and if they have decided that Alice is needed for them to tear down the Veil, then this will not be their last attempt to claim her. This is why she is here. This is why we are here. Because she will need our help."

Chapter 23

Alice's mood had dipped considerably. Although she made it through her daily routine, when left alone, she hid inside cupboards or under the bed covers and listened to music. She felt tired all the time and she had decided to take a brief respite from working on the '100 Useful Spells…'. The depression said she was being a coward and weak; her inner Witch said it was prudent and wise.

The strange voice had unnerved her. Whilst the explanation they had agreed upon made the most sense, Alice could not help but wonder if the voice had just been in her head, that maybe she had managed to meditate and the creature inside was merely her true self trying to escape. She knew that she needed to look inside herself, but she was not feeling brave enough to discover the truth. Especially, that the truth could be that she was evil.

And so she was hiding. Or, at least, she was trying to. Luckily for Alice, Robert and Onion were not so willing to let her.

Alice had always known cats were special, even without learning that they had been worshipped as gods and were even now considered to be gatekeepers to the Underworld. She was not sure if their role in the mortal world was so easily defined, but she certainly believed that felines knew of things beyond human senses. She also had no idea how the talking worked – seemingly, not all Witches could talk to cats nor could all cats be understood by Witches, although she had to admit that might be purely down to the cat not wanting to talk to anyone. Certainly, in the case of Archimedes only Alice and her grandmother had been able to communicate with him; her parents (both Witches) and her grandfather (not a Witch) could not.

Archimedes had been a formidable ginger, Persian tom with the pedigree of royalty and the air of a bar-room brawler. He had belonged to her grandmother and was the first cat that she had ever come across. Upon learning that a small female witch could understand every word that he was saying, Archimedes occasionally deigned to be something of a friend to Alice. She had never been entirely convinced of his motives, but he had stopped her from eating a number of poisonous plants, fruits and fungi; and from touching curious looking creatures and pebbles. Archimedes had passed away at the ripe old age of 25, two years prior to her grandmother.

She had thought that as a witch, maybe all cats would or could talk to her, but she had actually only had one other cat talk to her besides Archimedes and Onion, and that was the big black queen that had resided in the boarding school barn. That cat informed Alice that her name was Cosmic Creepers, and she had been Alice's only friend.

Alice had tried to fit in; had not used witchcraft, had tried to show an interest in the things the other girls were interested in, but she just could not find any common ground with them. She was more interested in reading than horse riding; was more interested in music, than boys, make-up and alcohol (although admittedly that came towards the end of her boarding school life). She was never bullied, she just did not fit in; she felt lonely and sad, and so she just tried to get on with the work and escape into the world of fiction. Often she would go into the hayloft and sit with Cosmic Creepers, occasionally feeling like she was Wilbur and the cat was her Charlotte.

The day that Cosmic Creepers failed to show, was the saddest day of her life, and she had cried quietly to herself for several days.

From then on, there had always been cats around, but she had never had her own until Onion was left on the doorstep. Her parents had been surprised by his appearance, but they never spoke to her on the subject. Of course, they did not really speak to her about anything, but she knew they were not bad people. They had been – were – doing the best they could based on what little they had been given; which perhaps had not been what was best for any of them.

Regardless, Onion had turned up and did not leave. She did not know who exactly had gifted him to her; there had been a knock at the door one day when her parents had been on holiday, and she had opened it to find a kitten, that looked particularly small and vulnerable in a large cat carrier, a collection of essentials, and a note saying 'Every Witch needs her cat and this cat needs his Witch.'

He was a tiny ball of black and white fluff, with big blue eyes and ears that seemed a little too big, as well as having a little pink nose and long, spindly legs. He was playful and slightly bite-y, and she had fallen in love with him immediately. He had consented to being named 'Onion' and had gradually grown into all of his features until he looked like any other graceful, black tom with the odd little white patch.

Regardless of his personal feelings regarding some of her friends, (although she was quite sure if James turned into a tiger during the full-moon the two would have gotten on), Onion let her know if people could be trusted. Considering just how hard she had instantly fallen for Robert, it had been a great relief that he had gained Onion's approval.

Even though Onion was narcissistic, he was not actually a psychopath; he just had an image to maintain and that involved giving the impression that he cared for nothing and no one. Admittedly, there were a lot of things and people he did not care for – sweetcorn, dogs, the fat Burmese three buildings over – but Onion actually had a great love for Alice and even a begrudging affection for Robert. He also had a little power of his own. It was nothing much really, but it allowed him to open the door every so often and to get into places that he really should not have been able to get into. It unfortunately seemed to have limited charge and range, hence he needed his Opener-of-Tins and Head Slave, Alice.

Although he had witnessed some bad spells before, Onion had never seen Alice in a state of depression quite as dark as this one. He had received a message from The Fallen regarding the incident in the Library, so he knew why she was suddenly trying to push everyone away. Onion, regardless of his orders, knew that it was not a good idea for Alice to isolate herself and he also knew that she would regret it if she did somehow force Robert away. So when Robert knocked on the apartment door a couple of days later, Onion let him in.

Chapter 24

"Hey," said Robert, staring down at the tom sitting in Alice's doorway. He had not expected to see Alice at the door, but he had not been expecting the cat either. He held the bouquet of red, yellow and orange flowers awkwardly in front of him.

"Evening," said Onion, staring unblinkingly. "Are those for me?"

"Not the flowers, no," Robert replied, trying not to blink. He wondered if he could beat the cat but it was not the right time for a staring contest. "But I did get this, just in case I needed to bribe my way in." He pulled a large tin of tuna from his right coat pocket. "If I definitely won't get in trouble, I will give you some of this now. Not all, because I know Alice will kill me if I cause you to be sick, but I'm willing to risk mild physical repercussions for giving you some."

"I am amenable to that proposition," said Onion after a moment's feigned thought, and he walked towards the kitchen thus allowing Robert to enter.

"How is she doing?" Robert asked, laying the flowers upon the small table where Alice had a bowl for her keys. He hung up his coat and scarf, before stowing his shoes neatly beside the door, and put the messenger bag back over his shoulder. Then he picked up the flowers and the canned fish and headed to the kitchen counter.

"What do you know?" asked Onion cautiously, jumping up onto his stool.

"Not enough," said Robert, tipping some of the tuna onto what he knew was Onion's plate. Then he placed the plate onto the little wooden garden table beside the breakfast bar. "She's not been answering my messages, so I went by the Library. Laura mentioned there had been an incident on Thursday, but she didn't know what exactly had happened. And since then, Alice's depression has been particularly bad, to the point that she's been kind of a Romero at work." Robert motioned to the flowers and Onion tilted his head towards the cupboard up and to the right. Robert nodded his thanks as he pulled out a vase and filled it with water. He poured in the plant food and removed the wrappings from around the bouquet of gerberas, roses and chrysanthemums.

"A Romero?" questioned Onion.

"Oh, a shuffling, mindless shell of a zombie, an image popularised by the films of George A. Romero," explained Robert. "It's a term that at least Alice, my room mate and I would use for a zombie that hasn't eaten brains in a quite some time and becomes reduced to a shuffling, mindless shell of a zombie. Because my room mate is a zombie and obviously isn't like that."

Onion looked at him and ate another mouthful of tuna before deciding to speak again. "Something tried to get into her head whilst she was trying to meditate. So, now she's afraid of putting people in danger; or worse, that it's something already inside her." Onion said, between mouthfuls of tuna. It was rude and distastefully common to talk with one's mouth full.

"Figures," said Robert softly, shaking his head sadly. "Anything else?"

"Not really," said Onion, after a moment's careful consideration. "She's managed to make herself wash and dress; she's been drinking a reasonable amount, but she's not been eating. She's been taking care of me okay, but she's not spoken to anyone; literally goes to work and then hides in the bedroom."

"Okay," said Robert, decisively. "It's pepperoni, tomato, pineapple and bacon she likes on pizza, right?"

"Sounds about right," said Onion, eyeing the Vampire

curiously.

"Right, I'm gonna order a pizza, take these flowers in and stay with her 'til she tells me to leave," Robert decided, firmly. "Any objections?"

"Nope," said Onion, secretly impressed with the effort the Vampire was making for his Witch. They both knew Robert would stay regardless of his answer, so he appreciated that Robert was trying to keep him involved. "I will adjourn to the airing cupboard. I'll be there if either of you need me. Not that I don't have better things to do."

"Thank you," said Robert.
Onion nodded his head ever so slightly, his big yellow-green eyes watching the Vampire carefully, as Robert knocked on the door before cautiously entering.

***

Alice's bedroom was completely dark. The curtains were pulled, the lights were off, and the digital clock had been unplugged.

"Go away," said Alice, her voice muffled and sad underneath the thick duvet pulled up around her ears. She was laying on her side, glasses on the cabinet, looking for all the world like she was simply trying to sleep. Except that it was 7:45pm on a Monday evening.

"No," said Robert, simply. Luckily, he could see quite clearly in the dark. He put the flowers onto the chest-of-drawers most likely to be in her eyeline, and took off his jacket, tie and watch. Then he took something out of his bag and placed it on top of the chest that sat at the foot of the bed.

"I don't deserve flowers," she said, hearing the sound of a heavy vase and the slight rustle of foliage. She had always had good hearing.

"I think you do," said Robert. He made sure his phone was turned off, then he flicked a switch on the device he had brought with him.

Pin pricks of light splashed across the room, bright enough to alter the darkness beneath the duvet but not enough to suggest that the light had been turned on. Alice's curiosity got the better of her. She lowered the duvet so that her head was exposed.

"What the..." Alice's voice trailed off and her eyes widened, before filling with tears. Robert had filled her bedroom with stars; the device was a home planetarium.

Robert climbed into the bed and put his arms around her. "You're not getting rid of me that easily, Miss Andrews," he said.

Her cheeks felt warm and her bottom lip trembled as she tried to keep the tears at bay, but they spilled out regardless. Robert did not ask why, did not wipe them away; he just sat beside her and held her close.

Alice felt like she did not know why she was crying, and at the same time, knew exactly why she was. She had not wanted to face any of her emotions, and now Robert, simply by being there, was making her do just that. She did not know how long they sat like that; it felt like no time at all, and forever.

"I might be evil," she whispered, the effort of trying to hold the sobs at bay robbing her of her voice.

"You're not."

"I'm scared of what I might be capable of with these powers."

Robert shut his eyes for a moment and let out a long breath. "Want to know a secret?" He felt her nod against his shoulder. "I worry about what I could do as a full-on Vampire."

"Really?" she whispered. He could hear the surprise in her voice.

"Of course. The gift or curse of being a Vampire comes from a dark place. Whether it stays there, is entirely on the individual, but I worry it might be too much for me to control, just as you do with you powers."

There was a brief silence before Alice said "I could be putting you in danger."

"Anything could do that. Plus, big bad Vampire, remember? I'm not so easy to kill."

"There are worse things than death." Her voice was flat, somehow making the words sound ominous.

"True. And as far as I can see, that includes a life without you." Robert gently lifted her chin and looked into her eyes, wincing at the pain swimming behind the tears. "I heard what happened and I get it, but there ain't no power in the 'verse can stop me being with you. Not even yours." He caught a glint of light around her neck. Curious, he reached over and pulled out a necklace. It was rose-gold with a pendant of two dragonflies beset with amber. "I thought you didn't like it."

"Why did you think that?" said Alice, reaching for the pendant and rubbing it between the two fingers and thumb on her right hand.

"Well, I've never seen you wear it and you were really quiet when I gave it to you."

Alice gave a little laugh. "I was quiet because I was touched and it had been a rough day with my mom telling me I was not supposed to be with a Vampire." She looked down at her little fireflies and smiled tearily. "It's beautiful and it means the world to me, and it's the best birthday present ever. I wear it all the time. Apart from in the shower."

"Ah."

"Plus, I think you tend to be too distracted to see it or something," she said, smirking.

"You may be right," said Robert with a low chuckle, kissing the top of her head again.

There was a sharp rapping at the door. "I will be right back." He returned a few minutes later with two very large pizza boxes, a couple of sodas and some napkins.

"I'm not hungry," Alice said, weakly.

"I beg to differ," said Robert, with a grin. "If you don't want to eat much, fine, but please try to eat something, okay?" They ate the pizza in a comfortable silence under the artificial stars.

When Alice could not eat any more, Robert tidied up, putting the leftovers in the oven. He gave a quick knock on the airing cupboard door to let Onion know she was doing better, and then got back into the bed with Alice. She had not moved or switched on the lights, but at least her face was visible.

"Thank you," she said, snuggling into the crook of his arm as he settled back onto her bed. "For everything."

"You're welcome."

"I don't deserve you."

"That's okay, I don't deserve you either, and I guess as long as we both think that, we'll never stop being good to one another."

"Not just a pretty face, huh?"

"No, but I'm definitely pretty," Robert said, kissing the top of her head.

They sat in silence for a moment and Alice took a deep breath. It was not the easiest thing in the world to do, but she pushed the depression, with all of its insinuating whispers of worthlessness, failure and not deserving to be happy or safe, to one side. She turned her still wet eyes towards him and looked at him, still expecting him to turn away. He did not.

"Will you stay, please?" she whispered.

"Of course."

Chapter 25

It took a few more days for Alice to get back to what was normal for Alice, but she was grateful to everyone around her that she had gotten back there. She took a cake into the Library and apologised to everyone for her recent bad spell. They all told her it was fine, that she did not need to apologise, but upon tasting the cake, said that she could definitely do it more often as long as there was cake at the end. Laura, Kate and Will, each gave her a hug and said they were there if she wanted to talk, and she had nearly started crying again, since the worst part of the depression (for Alice at least) was that it constantly told her that she could not and should not talk to anyone about it. She bought some salmon and prawns to spoil Onion and wondered she could do for Robert. She knew she did not have to do anything, but she wanted and needed to.

"May I have the afternoon off, please?" Alice asked, after tapping politely on the door frame of Dr Anthonys level 2 office.

"I think that would depend entirely on why you want the time off," Stuart replied, smiling at her in amusement.

"Robert has the afternoon free and has suggested we go for a walk in the park. Even though it'll be borderline freezing," Alice said, cheerfully. She also felt that in the good faith of full disclosure to add "And I really don't want to cope with students. I always seemed to get asked all the stupid questions."

Stuart smiled and nodded sympathetically. He was rather glad that he had had the idea of passing that particular task to his younger librarians. "I presume the others are fine with this?"

"They said they were. It does tend to be quiet on Wednesdays." She did think they were maybe giving her a certain degree of special treatment after the recent depressive episode. They were also possibly hoping for 'thank-you' cake. "And I've told them to call me if they do need the designated hands to be on deck."

"I'm sure there will be no need to do that. If the worst comes to worst, I will take over the newbie duties for a day." He looked up at the Witch still lingering in the doorway, surprised that she had not flown off already. "That was me agreeing to let you have the afternoon off."

Alice smiled. "I know, thank you. I was just wondering, er, what do you know of Endora Price?"

"Endora Price? Well, I suppose all things considered it's not surprising that you don't know too much about her."

Alice smiled awkwardly, not wanting to correct him on that point just yet. She looked off to one side slightly, frowning at the raven on a small table. She wondered who had moved it or perhaps she was imagining that it had previously been sat in a nook of the bookcase. The skull it was sitting on looked different too. She shook her head, clearly imagining things.

"Endora Price is widely regarded as one of the more powerful Witches of the recent era. She took on the mantle of Supreme at a very young age; was a member of the High Council as well as ruling over the Grand Coven. She was the leader of The Crown of the Pale Moon, which is unsurprising given that the coven itself was founded several centuries ago by one Mary Alden-Price. What is surprising, is that her daughter did not take up the mantle after her death, given that it's usually passed on through the matriarchal line. She was one of the few that could do some High Magic, and also one of the few Witches that treated everyone with a reasonable amount respect. I had the pleasure of meeting her a couple of times and I must admit that I enjoyed being in her company on those rare occasions."

"Wow," Alice murmured, eyes slightly widening with surprise at the list of accomplishments and the note of admiration with which Dr Anthonys spoke of her grandmother. No wonder the witch had suddenly become so polite. She briefly wondered why her mother had taken her father's surname upon marriage, and why she had not become the leader of the Witches, but that would take several hours of speculation or a phone call that Alice was not entirely sure about making. Especially as she still had not told her parents that she was in a relationship with a Vampire.

"We used to have a couple of books on her somewhere, given that she was a prominent figure in the Witching and supernatural communities but I think those books were requested by another Library in September and have yet to be returned."

Alice wondered if it was a coincidence that the books had left just before she had arrived.

"Given that you've mostly been concerned with Psychics and Vampires of late, I'm quite pleased to see you take at least a modicum of interest in your own kind," Stuart was saying. "May I ask what brought this on?"

"The witch in Modern Magicks was being rude and Sam told her that I knew Endora Price and I didn't know why that would make any difference... now I do."

"Oh," said Stuart, momentarily speechless. Given that Alice had said that it was her grandmother that had been making the amulet and that Endora Price was one of the few Witches with access to the Book of the First Witch, he should have realised sooner. It was surprising how many similarities he could see between the two Witches now. "You're her granddaughter."

"Yes," said Alice, suddenly feeling slightly glum. She felt very conflicted with the inkling of pride, the sudden certainty that she was a familial disappointment, and a nervous concern that it was because of her ancestry that people were so against her being with a Vampire.

He touched the amulet hanging across his lamp. "When you made the pendant for Sam I wondered if you had a strong Witching bloodline, but since then it never occurred to me to ask." He looked at Alice, watching her expressions carefully. "So Andrews is actually your father's name?"

Alice nodded.

"Well, that's definitely unusual, given the weight of the Price name. Of course, that is possibly why they decided to change it," said Stuart, more to himself than to Alice. He looked up at her with renewed curiosity. "It does potentially offer one explanation for your superior powers; you are the conjunction of two extremely respectable bloodlines."

"Do you know every Witch's family tree?" she asked, smiling.

"Goodness, no, but there is a database of sorts within the Library that keeps track of all supernaturals. I don't know how or why, but it is there somewhere and turns up when it deems it necessary to do so. As I say, Price and Andrews just happen to be two of the bigger names within the community. Much like Zurowski, Stonefeather and Kee amongst the Were; de Ravencourt and Vourdalak amongst Vampires."

"And Harvelle-Walker for Psychics?" asked Alice, smiling slightly.

"Yes, and no," Stuart replied. "Yes, in that the Walkers are considered to be the strongest and most proficient Psychics of our time; no, because very few view them as respectable. Sam's heritage is troubled, but I firmly believe that he is a good person."

"Me too," Alice agreed. "Besides, he did manage to pass my gatekeeper."

"I'm sorry?"

"My cat, Onion. I guess maybe it's part of his role as a Familiar. I don't know, but he kinda judges the people in my life, and he let Sam in, so, you know, good person," said Alice, cheerfully.

"Well, there is a lot of useful and intriguing information

on Witches. It might interest you to read up on it at some point."

"I guess so," said Alice, nodding thoughtfully, although she had researched the basics after her birthday.

There were hundreds of different covens of varying degrees of importance all over the world, but the community as a whole was presided over by a Grand Coven and the Supreme. The Supreme Witch was usually of a prestigious line and the most powerful Witch, although the two did not necessarily go hand-in-hand. She knew that Witches ruled through a matriarchy, that they took energy from mysterious sources and converted them into a desired form, and there were rumours that of all the supernaturals, Witches were the ones to have conversed most with the creatures beyond the Veil. However, there were a lot of specifics that she had not looked into, such as her family tree, the First Witch, Myrddin, or the reasons why Witches were held in such negative regard by the others. It had seemed more important to learn about everyone else so that she could help them if they needed it.

"You just don't ever really expect to find out you can read about your immediate family in books when you've kinda been treated like a nobody for so long," Alice added, slightly morosely.

"I do hope no one has made you feel that way here," Stuart said at once, horrified by the idea.

"Oh, oh no," Alice said immediately, looking equally horrified that she could have given that impression. "Everyone here has been wonderful and welcoming, and probably for the first time in forever, I feel like I belong somewhere. Not that everything's been terrible beforehand – university was definitely mostly good – but I've just never really been comfortable before. I am here."

"Good, good," said Stuart, genuinely relieved. "I take it Robert is not waiting on you?"

"Oh no, I don't do being late. He's picking me up after lunch, assuming I get, got, permission, so no, I'm only wasting your time," she replied with a small, teasing smile.

Chapter 26

They had spent the afternoon walking in the crisp air and watery sunlight flitting through the bare but budding branches of Central Park. They wrapped themselves up in big coats and scarves, snuggling together as they walked, their breaths escaping in clouds of white mist. It was proving to be an unseasonably cold April, but at least it was drier than the ones Alice was accustomed to in England.

It was cold and quiet, and since there were no children about, they had sat on the swings, gently rocking beside one another, painfully aware that the equipment had not been built with them in mind. Alice wondered if that was why they were occasionally getting disapproving looks from some of the strangers that passed them by. She decided that it did not matter; just because those people were not in touch with their inner child, did not mean she should feel bad about indulging hers. She was surprised that it seemed to be causing Robert some irritation, but every time she seemed to catch his eye about it, he shrugged it off and changed the subject, or tried to steal the camera. Given it was securely around her neck, there was little chance of him succeeding.

Alice tried to take artistic shots of leaves, lingering ice, brave spiders and him; but she refused to let him borrow the camera to take photographs of her. She had consented to a couple of selfies though, and had even refrained from putting the camera in front of her face. They had come across another photographer, and after a little bit of self-convincing, Alice had asked him to take a couple of pictures of her and Robert.

Assuming they looked as good on the computer as they did on the LED screen, Alice hoped she could maybe even frame one of the shots. She really did not like to look at herself, but she had to admit she did not look so terrible when she was smiling at Robert.

As dusk began its descent, they started walking home and Alice felt slightly sad in a strange way, about leaving the stark and chaotic park for the glass and concrete order of offices and high-end boutiques. It took about twenty minutes to walk towards the foodie area, and they were hit with the warming aroma of cakes, breads and various other delicious baked goods. Alice sighed, wondering if it would be incredibly awful to have a treat before dinner. She supposed she could always buy something for later, although as she swallowed hard for a third time, she realised that she really could at least do with a drink if nothing else.

"Are you feeling alright?" Robert asked, suddenly noticing that Alice's breathing was becoming more and more laboured, and that her energy was dropping far more steeply than he could approve of.

"Yeah, I'm fine," she said, yawning. "Just feeling a little light-headed and tired. I probably just need a drink or sugar or something. I'll be fine. I'm sure at worst it'll be a cold or something – some of us still get knocked down by germs, you know." She yawned again. "Or I might just still be way less fit than I should be."

"Hmm." Robert was less than convinced.

"It's a good excuse to stop for tea and a cinnamon bun at that little bakery at least," she said, suddenly blinking blearily and feeling a little confused. "We are near it, aren't we?"

"It's just 'round the corner," he replied, looking at her in concern. She was looking pale and felt colder than usual.

"I kinda feel like I'm drunk," she giggled. She squinted at him, feeling like he was further away than he should be. "Are you carrying me?"

"Yes."

His tone was short and Alice felt a stab of hurt and surprise to realise that he was losing his temper. She had never seen him cross before. She closed her eyes for a moment, and when she opened them again, she saw they were practically at Mostly Edible Pastries. Her face scrunched up and she pouted. She was beginning to behave like she was a bit drunk – slightly childish, easily amused but easily paranoid, which often led to petulance. "You're angry. Is it me?"

"Of course not," he said, his expression softening slightly as he looked down at her. "Just sit here," he said, practically bundling her into the only free booth in the bakery. "I'll order you a hot chocolate and a cinnamon bun and I'll be back as soon as possible. You'll feel better after a short rest and some sugar."

"Where are you going?"

"I'll be back."

"I don't want to be alone here." Her face creased with a wide-eyed, childish frown. "Are you sure this isn't my fault?"

He kissed her forehead, trying to keep his anger in check. "It's definitely not you. I promise. I will be back."

He went over to the counter to place the order and asked the barista to keep an eye on her, spinning a story about forgotten medication and how he was just going to run back to their apartment to get it. Understandably, the girl in the bakery looked sceptical, and he stood in the doorway whilst she went to ask Alice. The girl pointed at him and Alice smiled; it was obviously enough, because the barista nodded at him. Before the door even finished closing, Robert was out of sight.

It did not take long for Robert to locate the creature feeding off of Alice. In addition to the general recognition that supernaturals had for one another, Vampires had an extra honing ability when it came to finding others of their kind or the humans marked by them. Some humans were marked by an actual bite; others were marked by association so that although he had never bitten Alice, it was still common knowledge that, in their parlance at least, she was his. As such, it was not only incredibly bad-mannered of someone to feed off of Alice, but he or she was doing so with the knowledge that Robert was within his rights to tear his or her throat out if he so chose.

"Stop feeding on her right now!" Robert growled, teeth bared and eyes red. He had never felt so protective and angry before that it caused him to completely release his other side. He grabbed the revenant by the neck with an alabaster-like clawed hand, lifting him forcibly off the ground and slamming him against the wall. "She is off-limits."

There was something that resembled surprise in the creature's eyes, but other than that, the creature remained motionless. It did not protest or argue or attempt to break free, which made Robert even angrier. He had been expecting a fight, needing one with the amount of anger he felt, but he knew he would get nothing from this pitiful being.

"Who or what are you working for?" he asked, glaring at the shell in front of him.

There was no reply but Robert could see there was something lurking behind the dead eyes of the resurrected. "Who are you?" Robert said, slamming his fist into the wall beside the revenant's head. The animated corpse did not flinch, but something was definitely taking notice. "Who are you?" he said again, trying to remember how much agency revenant's had beyond the thrall of their ressurector.

"I said, tell me who you are." Robert demanded, staring deep into the deep eyes, trying to compel the puppet or its master to talk. "Tell. Me. Who. You. ARE!"

The revenant's mouth dropped open, releasing a foul, putrid breath into Robert's face. He snarled and let out a yell of frustration, seeing that the corpse had no tongue, and before he could try to use his mesmer, the puppet master broke their spell.

He plunged his fist deep into the revenant's ribcage and

ripped out what was left of the heart, causing the revenant to disintegrate. He roared and threw his fist into the wall, taking a deep breath as he tried to control his temper.

***

"Damnit!" Lady Jane knocked the small chalice over. At least she had removed the tongue prior to sending her minion out, but that was still far closer than she had anticipated.

"Problems, Lady Jane?" a voice called from the other room.

"An unexpected hitch, my Lord," Lady Jane replied

"Tell me."

"The fledgling tried to mesmer my revenant, and I could feel the pull. Have you come across that in one so young, my Lord?"

"Very rarely," Sargeraxs said, thoughtfully. He had to confess that he had given little thought to the part that the Vampire would play other than being the Witch's paramour. "What exactly what were you trying to accomplish?"

"I had hoped, with her being weakened, that we might gather enough of her energy to finally find her residence; get some fix on her to at least ensure she has the book. But her lapdog broke the connection before I could complete it."

"Hmm. They are quite the couple, it would seem," Sargeraxs murmured, walking in to look at her board. As per usual, he could not fault her thoroughness and dedication, particularly given that she was far more used to killing her target after this much reconnaissance. "We knew this would be... challenging."

"If the Vampire is stronger than expected as well, do you not think it would be better to just kill the Witch?"

Sargeraxs frowned and shot her a look of displeasure. "Surely you're not giving up so easily?"

"Of course not. But I think it is the easiest option."

"Perhaps. But as you well know, it's not that simple. The conditions are far from perfect."

"Then we should wait until the syzygy is upon us and strike then. If we leave her be, she won't expect it."

"If we leave her be, we deny the possibility of her joining us willingly. She is a Witch; her capacity for darkness is great."

"But all things considered…"

"Enough," Sargeraxs snapped. "I admire your initiative but it failed and you can either learn from it or not, but I will hear no more talk of killing the Witch."

Chapter 27

Alice had eaten half of the cinnamon bun and was drinking a second hot chocolate by the time he got back to the bakery.

"Hey," she said, smiling as he came and sat across from her.

"Hey. Feeling better?" he asked gently, thinking that she was looking more like her normal self again.

"Yes," she said, offering him the rest of the bun. He shook his head and she placed the plate back on the table, picking at the cinnamon frosting. "Still a bit tired, but definitely not so ditzy or feeling drunk." She took a sip of her drink and studied him over the rim of her cup. "You fanged out," she said thoughtfully. "I've never seen that before."

"I what?" Robert said with an amused laugh.

"Fanged out," she repeated, her hands wrapped around the oversized hot mug. "You still look a bit … fang-y. Paler. And your eyes are red, like, your irises are blood red." She reached over and rubbed his cheek affectionately. "You feel colder too."

"Fanged out, huh?" he repeated, surprised by the heat in her touch.

"Fanged out," she affirmed. Alice shrugged, a mischievous half-smile on her lips. "It's kinda sexy."

"You think that about a lot of things I do," he teased.

"Not everything though," she replied, thoughtfully.

"Don't think about it too much," he interrupted with a grin. "Are you ready to go?"

"Sure. Would be nice to get next to the fire," she said, linking her arm through his and thanking the barista on the way out. "You're still kinda carrying me, aren't you?"

"Yup." He could feel the weight of her stare. "Why are you looking at me like that?"

"Sorry, 'coz, like, maybe it shouldn't, but I am finding fanged out you very sexy..." She trailed off and looked at him with a bashful smile and a suggestive glint in her eyes.

"It's not supposed to be sexy; it's supposed to be terrifying," Robert admonished, unable to hide the smile of amusement.

"If you were angry at me and had the full fanged out thing going, I probably would be terrified...ish. But you're not. You're angry for me and that sorta makes it even sexier." She was blushing furiously.

"Are you suggesting that I keep the fangs?" he said, opening the apartment door. He had to admit, it would be a far more pleasurable way of expending his energy.

"Yes," she whispered, biting her lip, grateful that he did not make her say it.

"And you seem like such a nice girl," he teased, kissing her gently, aware that his teeth were still sharper than normal.

"I am," she replied. "It's just that sometimes, I aim to misbehave. Especially with you."

***

"If I do this," Robert said, closing the bedroom door in a deliberately slow manner "I'll probably end up 'marking' you, almost like, branding you as mine."

"I'm pretty sure everyone knows that already," Alice said calmly. She knew that Robert did not think of her as an object, so she was unconcerned about others viewing her as his possession.

"This is something more than just a role-play thing, isn't it?" Robert said, looking at her closely. There was a strange serenity to her expression that suggested she had been expecting this moment, and was pleased that it had finally presented itself.

"Oh, it's definitely that too though," Alice said, wickedly. She smiled, before using her eyes to give him a look of gentle encouragement and slight impatience.

Robert let himself "fang out" completely again, feeling the unfamiliar surge of power in releasing his inner demon. It was like another being, an animalistic force driven by very primal desires. He felt strong and powerful and almost without conscience. Every sense was heightened and his skin felt more receptive to her every touch. With the wildly pounding thump of her heartbeat and the slight scent of the blood beneath her flushed skin, Robert was finding it very hard to keep hold of rational thought, but he forced himself to stand still, hands clenched by his sides, as she began to study him.

Alice put her hands on his face. With the colour and blood drained from his skin, his features were sharper, accentuated by the darker shadows in each crevice of his marble-like skin. He felt more solid, seemed stronger and there was a definite magnetic darkness emanating from him. There was a sense of danger that Alice found both sweet and intoxicating, because she knew it would not be there next time.

Her fingers traced over the more defined contours of his face with infuriating delicacy and he could not stop a low growl from escaping in desire and frustration. She parted his lips with her thumb, studying his sharp, prolonged canines for a moment. Then she stared intently into his eyes, almost as if she was searching for something in his wine-coloured irises with their flame-tinged obsidian pupils.

"Have you ever drunk blood before?" she asked, softly, still just standing before him, her hands moving across his shoulders and down his hard torso, never flinching or seemingly reacting in any way. She did love to run her fingers over his chest.

"A few times," he replied, his voice deeper and slightly

hoarser than it had been before. He tried to keep his focus on her dark-flecked brown eyes instead of the pulsing artery in her slightly tanned neck. *Such a delicate neck, so easily snapped, so easily torn, so full of hot, fresh, delicious blood... All I would have to do is squeeze and my claws could tear through so that the blood just gushed through the severed arteries...* The pull of her blood was becoming so strong that he was terrified of losing control and hurting her. Or worse.

"Are you worried about drinking mine?" she asked, very deliberately undoing each button of his checked shirt, one by one, her eyes never leaving his.

"Yes," he whispered, breath catching as her hand brushed against his erection as she undid the last button. He saw her swallow, heard the slight hitch in her own breathing, but she continued as if she was not torturing him with every deliberate touch.

"Is that why you've never tried to bite me before?" she said, still slowly touching him in an almost careless manner.

"Partly," he said, trying hard to stay in control.

"I'm not," she said simply, never removing her gaze. "I know you and I love you, Robert Nathaniel Evans. I am not afraid of you – not one single part. I trust you with my life and I don't believe any part of you would ever hurt me. And I need you to know and be sure of that too."

Alice kissed him then, a kiss of passion, love and complete surrender. He watched, still afraid to move, as she stepped back to place her glasses on the chest-of-drawers and pulled her black jumper dress over her head. She adjusted her rose gold chain so that the amber fireflies were in-line with the valley between her breasts and tucked her dark brown hair behind her ear as she exposed the right side of her neck. She pressed her body against his, pulling his right arm across her breasts and the left across her waist.

"Bite me," she whispered. There was a slight tremble of anticipation in her voice, but no fear.

He hesitated for a moment more, before surrendering to

what he thought of as his dark side. His fangs sliced through her hot, soft skin and at the same time as he tasted her sweet coppery blood, she let out a desperate cry of pain and pleasure. For a moment, he completely lost control, tearing off the rest of their clothes, continuing to drink even as he roughly entered her from behind. She moaned as his claw-like fingernails grabbed at her dark areola and he felt her heart shuddering beneath his touch. She was so beautiful, so innocent, so trusting, and yet so passionate and wanton. Within the haze of bloodlust, need and desire, it was like making love to her for the first time. And he did love her, as completely and as utterly as she loved him. And when he felt her orgasm, he came as well.

He let her catch her breath for a moment, before pushing her back against the wall. He lifted her up and she wrapped her legs around his waist, pulling him in as deeply as she could. He caught the glimpse of satisfied happiness as she stared into his eyes. Moments later, she had closed her eyes again as he kissed her with an urgency he did not know he could feel. Her head rolled back and he kissed along her neck and breasts, holding her close until both of their releases had subsided.

He carried her over to the bed and gently laid her on her side. She frowned sleepily at him, as he covered her with a blanket, his features slowly returning to normal. He waited until she had fallen into a light doze, before throwing on some clothes and entering the kitchen.
Whilst not hungry himself, Robert knew Alice would need a fair amount of food and rest to get her energy levels back to normal. He found the cookbook where she wrote down her recipes and squinted at the ridiculously small, italic writing – it was even worse when she had used a fountain pen. Still, he was pretty sure that even he could not ruin some kind of pasta dish and it was something he could do almost on autopilot as he thought about what had just happened.

He understood now, why she had wanted him to take

her as a Vampire. He had needed it – he had been trying to protect her from his Vampire side when she had known that he had not needed to; it was just another part of him, not a separate entity with its own agenda. Still, as liberating, enlightening and amazing as it had been, he was still concerned that he had been too rough with her, especially given that earlier events had weakened her somewhat. He almost wished he could wake her to check she was okay, but it would be better for her to rest; he would just have to be patient.

Half an hour later, Alice emerged from the bedroom, wearing only underwear and one his shirts. He felt like she never looked more beautiful than when she was all tousled, slightly self-conscious but entirely happy.

"Something smells good," she said, sliding onto one of the stools across from him, grinning as he placed the giant Tigger mug of tea in between her hands. "Thank you."

"Are you OK?"

"Yes," she said. She looked slightly sleepy but she was also grinning like the cat that had had the cream. "Are you?"

"Better than ever," he said, kissing her forehead. He gently brushed her hair aside to look her neck, and frowned. "You're probably going to have quite a bruise there in the morning."

"Meh. I'll just wear turtle-necks and scarves for a while. It aches a bit, but it's not really what you'd call painful, so please don't worry about it," she said. "Is food nearly done? I'm starving."

"Nearly," he said, pulling some bread out of the oven, forgetting to use the oven gloves.

"Show off," teased Alice, sticking her tongue out as he batted her hand away before she hurt herself on it.

"It's been a long day," he said, serving up the pasta in a bowl with the bread on a side-plate, grating some cheddar cheese over the top, before handing her a fork. "Especially for you."

"What happened earlier? You didn't fang out because I had low blood sugar, that's for sure." She blew on the pasta, trying to cool it enough to eat without burning out all of her taste buds.

"Just an overenthusiastic leech-er," Robert said, casually. He knew he should probably tell her the truth but given that she had only just got herself back into normal moods, he did not want this revenant to send her spiralling back into the black. Also he was still processing the fact that it had not been another Vampire but some recently reanimated corpse – necromancy was an extremely uncommon practice.

"And you kicked his ass?"

"Well, he won't be doing it again, that's for sure," he replied. The look she gave him suggested that she suspected there was a bit more to it than that, but she was not going to press. She shrugged and continued to eat with restrained gusto. "After you have finished all of that, and reassured your cat that I'm not going to kill you, you may join me in the shower, if you want to. But *only* after eating and reassuring the cat."

"Yes Sir," she said, with a small, sharp salute. She looked up from the food and called out to him before he entered the bedroom. "Robert?"

"Hmm?" He looked at her questioningly from the doorway.

"I love you."

He smiled. "I love you too."

He emerged to find her curled up on the sofa with Onion being unnaturally accommodating and comforting against her stomach. The cat gave him a disapproving look, but consented to having his head stroked before being covered with the blanket. Much as he wanted to mould himself around her and sleep by her side, Robert left Alice to rest on the sofa while he fell into his own deep slumber on the bed.

Chapter 28

"Aren't you a bit warm wearing a scarf in here?" asked Dr Anthonys, as Alice re-entered the classroom carrying her coat, and taking off her gloves.

"It's not a winter scarf," she laughed. "It's an accessory. It's to add colour and flair to my outfit, or so the fashion mags tell me." And maybe to hide the bite mark from her co-workers. They all knew she was in a relationship, but that did not mean she was comfortable with them judging a hickey on her neck.

"Well, you're going to set it on fire if you're not more careful with it..." He trailed off as he realised his caution was too late.

The corner of the green viscose began to flame and smoulder. Alice immediately batted out the fire and dropped the remainder of the scarf in the bin.

"Dammit, I liked that scarf. Guess I'm still a bit tired from yesterday. Ended up being a long day. Good, but tiring." She rubbed her neck and shoulders roughly for a moment, before rubbing her eyes and covering a yawn.

"What happened to your neck?" asked Stuart, noticing the dark purple patch on the right of her throat.

"I think I just slept on it funny. Guess that's what happens when you crash out on the couch," she replied tilting her head and trying to dislodge some of the stiffness.

"It looks like you've been bitten." He took a closer look at the bruising on her neck. "You've been bitten by a Fledgling Vampire," he said with some surprise, noticing the little, twin pin-prick holes at the centre of the bruise.

"Oh. That," she said, lightly touching the puncture marks. Her neck felt a little tender there, but mainly she did not notice it. She smiled in an off-hand manner and returned to heating up the various tubes and flasks over the Bunsen burner. "Oh, yeah, that happened."

"But how on earth did that happen? I'd have thought you would be immune to a Vampire's mesmerism, being as powerful as you are," Stuart said with some concern.

"Not really sure about all that." She coughed as a cloud of purple smoke billowed from a test tube. She pulled a face and shook her head, as she muttered 'do no harm' over the failed experiment and washed the remnants away in the corner sink. "I think we put too much powdered lilac in that. I'll try reducing it a little. In regards to the bite, well, I just eventually summoned up the courage to ask him to. Headology reasons."

"You what?" Stuart exclaimed, stopping his own experiment to stare at her.

Alice continued to potter along, failing to notice the alarm in the Head Librarian's voice and expression. She shrugged. "I asked him to. I mean, it was gonna have to happen sooner or later really; it must have been on his mind for ages, so I didn't want him to *keep* worrying about it. And *I'd* been meaning to bring it up for ages but I kept wussing out, so since he'd already fanged out, it seemed as good a time as any. Headology, like I said." She paused and grinned mischievously. "Plus, it's really very sexy."

"And what did Robert have to say about that?" asked Stuart, slightly incredulous. *Surely Robert could not have allowed a Vampire to feed on her?* Even if one was an ordinary human, surely one would attempt to stop his or her partner from being seduced?

"*He* said it wasn't supposed to be sexy. Pretty sure he thought it was afterwards," she said with a wicked grin and a hint of smugness. She gave a small laugh, and suddenly realised that her mentor was looking very shocked and puzzled. For a moment, she could not understand why. Then it hit her. She bit her lip and scrunched up her face, trying to hide the sudden laughter behind a thoughtfully posed hand. "I'm beginning to get the impression that I might not have told you that Robert is a Vampire."

"I feel that is something I would have remembered," he replied with slight irritation and great relief.

"Sorry. Erm, well, okay then. My boyfriend is a Vampire; his best friend is a Zombie; *my* best friend is a non-supernatural human; her husband is a Were; my friend Sam is a Psychic, with a capital P, whom I met whilst working in one of the Libraries, emphasise on the capital L. Oh, and my cat can talk. When he wants to. Mostly, he'll just stare at you with an expression of disdain or the evil eye, but that's cats for you. Is that a mark of being a Familiar? I'm pretty sure my cat's one regardless."

"That's quite the mix," said Stuart, in a slightly dazed manner, overwhelmed by the number of different mortals in Alice's small circle of acquaintances.

"You like who you like," said Alice, matter-of-factly. "No point saying you won't mix with certain classes or whatever. I mean, well, it's just daft. Don't get me wrong, I'm definitely not a saint; it's just that if I'm going to dislike someone, it should be for better reasons – like they're mean to animals or give off a bad vibe… or are Yankees fans," she said, unable to hide her distaste for the rival baseball team. "And to be fair, with the latter, I'd be a little flexible if I got a good vibe from you, but you definitely would not be as highly rated as my other friends, as James well knows. Because he *is* a Yankees fan." Just to make sure things were clear, she added "James being the Were married to my best friend Kathie."

"Well, I can't say I'm entirely surprised by your thoughts on the matter, but I must admit, most Witches that I have met tend to be somewhat, how shall we say, snobby?"

"I think that's the politest anyone's put it to me so far," said Alice, with a wry grin.

"Er, quite," Stuart said, tugging at his jumper sleeves with mild discomfort. It was unfair that there were so many stereotypes associated with the various supernaturals and even worse when the majority had arisen from justifiable observations and experiences. "Most Witches show nothing but contempt for non-Witches. Humans generally get a free pass of sorts, which is very gracious of them, considering they are simply humans with supernatural powers."

Alice smirked. "Well, I know you're only a simple human, but *you* don't disapprove of me being with a Vampire, do you?"

"No, not disapproving. A little concerned perhaps, given the general literature regarding the species. By which I do not mean anything you are likely to have read," he said quickly, before she could start referencing a hundred and one different types of literary vampire. "I mean the historical texts that we have in the sub-levels and stories from within the community. Albeit, a pinch of salt must be taken, depending on the source. If you say Robert is a good man; I believe you. I'm quite sure if another Witch was to describe the relationship, you would no doubt be cast as the innocent victim of a vile and manipulative bloodsucker."

"Oh. Well, I take umbrage with description, because he's not vile or manipulative, or even much of a blood sucker. Apparently most Vampires don't need to drink blood that often. Also, he's kind and honest and supportive and amazing, and I'm definitely not that innocent, so yeah, you really shouldn't be concerned," she said. "Onion has fully approved of him. Duty sense at least; I'm quite sure that as a cat he's still kinda plotting to kill Robert, despite Robert being a really good guy. I'll introduce you later if you like, and you can see for yourself. To Robert I mean, not the cat, because honestly, I'm not sure how Onion works in terms of who he can and will speak to. Plus he really hates moving vehicles."

"You have a Familiar?" Stuart asked, surprise making him voice the question even though she had already told him that she believed her cat was a Familiar.

"Possibly. Well, I live with one. But he's a cat, so do you ever really 'have' a cat? I think my grandmother had one as well. Archimedes. Mean old thing. I loved him too," said Alice, affectionately. She waved her hand at one of the empty, unused flasks and glamoured it to look first like Onion and then like Archimedes, before returning its appearance to normal. "Surely its not unusual for a Witch to have a Familiar?"

"Well, no," said Stuart, slightly surprised and mildly amused at Alice showing off with her powers. "It's just less common than it used to be. Something of a revolt on the Familiars' part – lack of respect and appreciation I believe. I do believe I recall something of Endora Price being one of the few modern Witches to "own" one."

Alice sighed and choked on another cloud of purple smoke. She frowned at the experiment, wondering what was going wrong with it. She had greatly reduced the amount of lilac that time and it had still poofed. There was definitely nothing wrong with the amounts that time, but on closer examination of the Bunsen burner, it appeared that the flame had been turned up a lot higher than she had set it. She looked around suspiciously, and headed over to the sink again. "Figures. Are you sure I can't be something other than a Witch? I think I'd feel better about my general existence. Not to mention then I won't be the representative freak of my "species"."

Stuart laughed. "You really need to worry less. Just be yourself and the people worth being around will like you as you are."

"Even if I have purple eyebrows?" she questioned in concern, unable to find a suitably reflective surface.

"You don't have purple eyebrows at the moment," Stuart reassured her. "And I'm sure people would still like you if you did."

"Even you?" Alice teased. She would never have imagined it when she had first started, but she had come to think of Dr Anthonys more as a friend than as an employer.

"You think I don't like you?" Stuart asked.

"I think you like Sam better," said Alice, smiling. She was mostly teasing. "He knows about the dogs."

Stuart paused for a moment and frowned momentarily. "I wonder why he told you. And Sam only really knows because he's Psychic and he started it by bringing a dog here after finding him on the side of the road."

"Well, I don't think he's told anyone else," Alice said carefully, not that she could see any reason for it to be a big secret. "I think he's worried about you. I know Sam acts like he doesn't really care about anyone other than Sam, but it's definitely not the case. You do know that, right?"

"Yes," said Stuart with a kind smile, mildly amused to see a female being protective of Sam, rather than being defensive or disparaging. "I know." He looked over at Alice, who was watching him expectantly. "I take it you want to meet the dogs?"

"Hell yeah," said Alice, looking at him like it was the most stupid question in the world. "You can't be mopey around dogs; they're too chilled and happy. Plus, secret gardens? Of course I'm interested. I love how there's always something new to find out around here."

"I thought you were a cat person?" he remarked, tilting his head towards the door.

Alice grinned, turning off her experiments before following him out of the "classroom" door. "I am; doesn't mean I can't love dogs too. I pretty much like most mammals and reptiles. Have mixed feelings about birds, insects, invertebrates and maybe crustaceans, as I forget exactly what woodlice are, but I hate those creepy little fuckers. Love bees though," she said brightly, following the Head Librarian through several twists and turns of wood-panelled corridors.

"Brace yourself. They are quite excitable," said Stuart, pride and affection in his voice. He opened the door and lead the way into a big and beautiful garden.

It was mostly grass, with four raised marble flower-beds and a stone pathway around the perimeter. There was a bin, six distinctive food bowls and three large silver bowls of water and two cast-iron benches. He managed to shut the door behind them before six furry missiles launched themselves at him. Alice was greeted to several sideways glances before the dogs decided she probably did not need knees either.

"Whoa there boys and girls," she said, laughing and kneeling down to prevent being taken out. "Pleasure to meet you all too." She said hello to each dog in turn, holding his or her face in her hands, rubbing their ears and trying to be as polite, friendly and non-threatening as possible.

"Four boys, two girls. Einstein, Copernicus, Aldous, Barney, Kally and Molly," Stuart said, pointing to a Cairn Terrier, a soft-coated Wheaton, a slightly worn-looking Golden Retriever, two liver-and-white Springer Spaniels and a Jack Russell with foxy looking ears.

"They're gorgeous," said Alice, looking up at him, whilst also trying to give each dog some attention. "Are they all rescue dogs?"

"Strictly speaking, yes. Two were from an actual shelter; the others were strays, just abandoned on the street. Took them to get scanned for microchips etcetera, but as no one claimed them, I took them in. Except for Einstein, who Sam found on a highway. I forget where exactly. Aldous, who has apparently taken a shine to you, was probably in the worst state, but luckily you would never tell."

"He's lovely," Alice said warmly, rubbing at the tummy now on display, as Aldous' tail wagged happily. "They all are, and it's a beautiful garden. It sucks that they had rough beginnings, but I'm glad they have a good home now. They clearly adore you." Aldous scrambled to his paws and tore after the others as Stuart threw a fluorescent yellow tennis ball across the grass.

Alice was looking at the immaculately manicured and well-looked after flower-beds; two filled with roses and two with lilies. Aldous nudged at her hand as she moved towards one of the planters and she softly scratched behind his ears. She recognised the slight silvery shimmer on some of the burgeoning roses and she gently ran her fingers over the velvety, red-and-white petals. It was a hybrid known as the 'Eternally Yours' rose, which although beautiful in its own right, given that there were only roses and lilies, Alice knew there was a far more personal significance in the choice. And clearly for someone more than a friend. She sighed, sat down on one of the benches and frowned as she wondered what Sam was playing at. Aldous seemed to sense her change in mood and promptly jumped up beside her, laying his head in her lap, big brown eyes gazing up at her questioningly.

"What's wrong?" Stuart asked, looking up from the five dogs cheerfully trying to pull his jacket apart as they searched him for treats. He threw the ball again and they tore after it again; Aldous looked up to watch, but otherwise, did not move.

"Nothing," said Alice, quietly, knowing that Dr Anthonys would not believe that for a second. She let out a deep breath. "I, er, this, er, it's a memorial garden."

"Ah," said Stuart, with a sad, gentle smile, as he too wondered exactly what Sam's idea was, whilst being quietly impressed with Alice's perceptiveness. "Yes, it is."

"Whom for? If you don't mind me asking,"

"My wife and daughter."

"I'm sorry," said Alice, knowing it was stupid, but also the only thing one could say to such information. There were no words that could ever really be comforting in the face of a great loss.

"I met my wife at the Natural History Museum in London, during a palaeontology lecture. I wasn't particularly interested in the subject; it was an excuse to meet her. I'd seen her at the British Museum, where she worked, but could never quite work out how to strike up a conversation with her. Silly I suppose, considering I was working at the Library in London, and we had a shared love and respect for heritage and history.

But still, I sat beside her in that lecture, we went for dinner afterwards and we got married six months later. About a year after that, we had our only child, Lily. She would have been a couple of years older than you."

"What happened?" Alice asked, softly. She smiled down at the Golden Retriever that had remained by her side; the other dogs had gone to Dr Anthonys. *And people had the cheek to think animals did not have souls or lives of equal value to humans*, she thought with a shake of her head.

Stuart smiled down at the canines by his feet and on either side, and softly chided them for being silly and reassuring them that he was okay. "Joy was working late at the Museum, taking delivery of a recently discovered artefact; Lily was visiting and was working on her PhD – a thesis on old gods – so went down to the loading bay with her mother. They were attacked and killed, and the artefact, some kind of sacrificial dagger, was stolen. Wrong place at the wrong time. The police never caught the person or recovered the dagger. I couldn't bear to stay in London so they transferred me here."

"I'm so sorry," Alice murmured again, lamely. Losing loved ones was bad enough, in violence and without justice just seemed infinitely more unfair. She wondered why he was touching his side; he certainly seemed unaware that he was doing it.

"It'll be fifteen years this October," he said, quietly. "I've made what peace I can with the situation."

"Did you ever ask Sam to, you know, contact them?"

"Not really. Maybe if I had met Sam earlier, I would have. And he has offered. I said that as long as they weren't angry or in pain, living out some kind of death loop, then I was content to let them rest." He threw the ball, but only Einstein went after it. He spoke to the dogs again and when he threw the ball again, they all started playing. "Anyway, this isn't supposed to be a sad place. Part of the reason I keep the dogs here, is to focus on the happier memories."

"If you ever need a hand with them – dog-sitter or

whatever – then I'd be happy to help out."

"Very kind of you. Maybe that's why Sam wanted you to know; I get the feeling he thinks I need to find a life outside the library." He supposed he should stop trying to find excuses not to call Robia Calendar from the Museum of Modern Art.

"Yeah, are you sure he's a Psychic and not a cupid?" said Alice, with an affectionate smile. "He seems awfully concerned with people connecting to others."

Stuart laughed, thinking of the chaos Sam had caused with his devil-may-care attitude to women. "Sam is definitely not angelic enough to be a cupid. I think it might be because he's so used to passing on bad news or dealing with grief and loss, that it's his way of keeping some balance and sanity."

They both fell silent for a moment, thinking about Sam and wondering what it was like to live with premonitions and visions of the future and knowing that most of it was probably dark because it had a tendency to push harder. Alice began to feel like maybe she should have let him steal a slice of pizza after all.

Stuart was likewise thinking about Sam's most recent visit. "You're doing a very good job here, Alice."

Alice looked up in surprise. "Thank you," she said, pleased and as a natural by-product of being English, a little perplexed. "I love it here. Even without the supernatural side, or dogs, I love it. And in terms of the supernatural side, you're an awesome teacher."

Stuart smiled, also looking slightly uncomfortable, and they both laughed.

"This is very un-English of us." Alice said with a smile. She paused for a moment, looking up at a greying sky that was thick with the threat of rain. Talking about the weather was definitely very English. "Don't you think the rain smells weird here?"

"I'm sorry?" said Stuart, looking up from the whirlwinds of fur that he was teasing at his feet. He mimed throwing the ball, but did not release. They ran part way across the grass before bounding back, trying to jump on him in revenge. He laughed at them and threw the ball.

"The rain smells different here, I think," said Alice, feeling a little homesick. Aldous pushed his nose against her hand and she smiled reassuringly at him. "It's okay, I'm okay," she murmured.

"I think I've probably been here too long," Stuart replied. "I don't doubt that I had similar sentiments when I first arrived though." He managed to grab the ball back and threw it again. "It is remarkable how one notices such things."

"I thought the rain in New York might smell like home. In comparison to Miami. But it doesn't. And you wouldn't even really expect rain to have a smell, would you? Does it even? I suppose it could just be from the things it hits, but I think it has its own smell."

Stuart smiled. "I clearly do not take enough notice of the rain," he said. "I suppose the problem is that one can't tell if rain has a smell when everything smells of wet dog."

Alice laughed. "Yeah, that can be a pretty overpowering scent," she agreed, affectionately rubbing Aldous' head and rubbing his silky, soft ears. "It's just, little things get to me sometimes. I don't think I could ever get used to not thinking of England as home."

"In a strange way, I think I feel the same," Stuart said, glancing up at the grey skies. After a moment, he stood up. "I think I'll put the kettle on," he said, throwing the ball to Alice, trying not to laugh at the sudden panic in her eyes as she fumbled to catch it, either from the suddenness of a projectile in her direction or the five interested fur-balls hurtling towards her. Probably a bit of both, he thought, although he was quite sure that if she really tried, she could have stopped it with a levitation or freezing spell. He just hoped she would stick to using magic on the ball, rather than on the dogs.

Chapter 29

Alice reached over to the side of the bed and grabbed the phone ringing on the bedside table. The sun was up, but as far as Alice was concerned, 9:30 was too early to be getting up on a Saturday.

"Mom? Is everything okay?"

"I'm fine darling, I'm fine. How are you? Is the sun up over there?" Gillian asked, sounding anxious.

"Er, yeah, the sun is up. And I'm fine. Just tired. I was hoping for a lie in," Alice said, pointedly.

"Hmpfh. Is is safe to talk?"

"Why wouldn't it be safe?" asked Alice, feeling incredibly confused.

"Just say the word 'kumquat' if it's not safe and I will get you help," Gillian said.

"What on earth are you on about?" asked Alice, yawning.

"Have you been brainwashed? Do I need to get one of those psychological de-programmers. Maybe I should fly out and talk to the FBI." Gillian continued as though she had not heard her daughter's question.

"FOR THE LOVE OF THE GODS," yelled Alice, unable to take another second of confusion "What are you going on about?"

"There's no need to shout," Gillian replied, a hurt in her voice. "I'm just trying to help."

"I've gathered that much," said Alice, lowering her voice. "But why?"

"I presumed you'd been kidnapped. By a Vampire."

Ah balls. "Why would you think that?" asked Alice, trying to sound nonchalant as she flumped her head against the pillows.

"It's going around all the covens that there's a Witch with a vampire, so obviously the vampire must have kidnapped said Witch and I was worried it was you because of what your grandmother said."

"Maybe the Witch is with a Vampire because she loves him?" suggested Alice, casually.

"Don't be silly dear. Witches and Vampires don't fall in love with one another."

"Why not?"

"Because Witches and Vampires don't get on. Common knowledge."

"Not to me it isn't. Matter of fact, didn't even know Vampires were a real thing until recently," Alice reminded her.

"Yes, that might have been a mistake, come to think of it. Maybe you should come back to England. Given that the Library has clearly expanded your knowledge of the supernatural, maybe you should join our coven."

"No."

"No?" Gillian echoed, surprised.

"That's what I said. No. I like it here. I love my apartment, I love my job, I love Robert. I have friends here. I'm not going back to England, hopefully for a good long while yet, apart from visiting you and the rest of the family. I'm actually happy here, mom. That is what you wanted, right?"

"Of course that's what I want. It's all your father and I have ever wanted – for you to be healthy and happy and safe with a roof over your head," Gillian affirmed.

"Well, I am," Alice replied, firmly.

"So you're not being held captive by a vampire?"

"No mom," Alice replied in a childishly exasperated tone.

"And you're not being mesmered by one?"

"No mom." She yawned again.

"And I don't have to worry about you and Vampires, because you've got nothing to do with them?"

"Er, about that..." Alice began, unable to lie and not really wanting to.

"Even after I told you to stay away from them?!" Gillian exclaimed.

"I was already in love with him by then," said Alice, apologetically.

"Robert? This Robert you mentioned is a Vampire?"

"Sort of. He's not quite dead yet."

"You have to break up. You can't be with a Vampire," Gillian said at once.

"Why not?"

"Well, everyone's talking about how unnatural it is."

"We're not natural," Alice reminded her Witch mother. She bit her tongue regarding the fact that everyone should have better things to talk about than her love life.

"You know what I mean," Gillian said, sternly.

"I do," said Alice. "But I don't care. He doesn't care. So why do you?"

"Because it's wrong."

"No, it's the most right thing in the whole world," Alice said. "If this is an image, reputation thing, fine, disown me if you have to, but I love him and I won't give him up for you or anybody for that matter."

"It's nothing to do with image. It's to do with you being safe. About the world being safe."

"A prophecy?" asked Alice, sceptically. From what little she knew of them, Alice was of the opinion that prophecies should be avoided and ignored.

"Exactly."

"Okay. What does this prophecy say then?" asked Alice. She could tell that the concern in her mother's voice was genuine, and she was prepared to give it the benefit of the doubt.

"Well, I don't know the specifics," Gillian admitted,

reluctantly. "But it's known that a Vampire and a Witch will unite and destroy the world as we know it."

Alice laughed. "You can't seriously believe I would destroy the world do you?"

"No, but a Vampire might make you."

"Why would a Vampire want to destroy the world? Not to mention, I don't think a Vampire could make me do anything."

"You might be surprised at what they can make people do after they've hypnotised them."

"Well, to be fair, I don't think Robert's ever tried to mesmer me," said Alice. "So, if this prophecy is not actually complete bobbins, it's not about me and Robert. We're just two people in love. And I mean that. We really do love one another."

"Are you sure about that?"

"Yes," said Alice. "Why else would a guy as handsome and awesome as him put up with me?"

"You're too hard on yourself," Gillian said.

"Well, that too," said Alice, not entirely convinced. "But I mean, if this truly isn't just a Witch thing, then he must be getting grief from his family and other Vampires, but he's still here."

"Perhaps."

Alice sighed. "Look, I get that you mean well, but you really don't need to worry. I'm happy; I'm not practising black magic; Robert is kind and amazing and a gentleman, and I love him and I hope one day you will see how awesome he is."

"If that's truly how you both feel, I hope so too. But you have to be aware, you might not have a choice."

"What do you mean?"

"If – and I realise it's a big if – the High Council decide that this relationship is at risk of bringing about the fulfilment of an undesired prophecy, then they may forbid you to be together."

"Please be joking," Alice whispered.

"The High Council is there to help protect the

supernatural community, and if they consider you or Robert or your relationship to be a threat to mortal existence, then they will force you apart by whatever means they deem necessary."

"They can't do that. They can't make people not be in love."

"Perhaps not, but they could always take you to the Three," Gillian said, again with a casual tone that suggested this was common knowledge. "Alice, please understand, I am just making you aware of the possibility."

"I appreciate that mom, truly I do, but I am not making any changes to my life right now. Certainly not any that involve me being apart from Robert."

Gillian sighed, accepting that Alice was not going to budge. "Just be careful, please?"

"I always am," Alice said, with a cheeriness she did not feel. "I'll speak to you soon. Love you."

"Love you too. 'Bye," Gillian said, putting down the phone.

Alice sighed, turned over, closed her eyes and smushed her face into the pillow. Then she lifted her head, put the phone back on the side and went back to sleep.

Chapter 30

Alice was uncharacteristically late. Robert had found that Alice would often text to say she was running late if she thought there was even the smallest of chances that she would not be on time, so he was slightly surprised, although not entirely worried, when he had still heard no word from her thirty minutes later than their agreed time.

Although the marking between a Vampire and human was a warning to others, it also helped to reinforce the connection between them. It was a connection that allowed a Vampire to sense when his or her human was in danger and to hone in on where they were, although he preferred to use more traditional methods before resorting to it. He called her cell phone. Then he tried the land-line in the apartment, whereupon Onion informed him that Alice was not at home. He tried her cell one more time before leaving the restaurant and heading to the Library.

The Library had technically closed at 7 pm, but Alice had told him that there was a side door near the south west corner that he could come through if needed; the main doors of the Library would only open after hours to grant sanctuary to those desperately seeking help. Maybe it was the way Alice talked about the building, but Robert found himself announcing his presence at the side door.

"Er, hi. I'm Robert. I've come to get Alice, if she's still here, please?" He pushed against the door, and met no resistance.

It had been a while since Robert had been in the library.

He used to visit regularly, bringing over spare proof copies of the latest best-sellers since he had no further use for them and it was no doubt rare that a library budget stretched as far as it needed to. Since he had been transferred within the publishing firm to a role that required him to meet with potential new writers and follow-through with some of the book launches, he had had less time to collect the unwanted copies laying around. He had ensured that someone else had taken up the task in his stead, so that the library was still well-stocked on the newest releases, but as he entered, he wished he had the time to do it himself.

He was greeted by the familiar wood-based smells, high stone arches and marble pillars, and comforted by the low-lighting from the little green lamps at the reading desks. He could easily see in the dark when necessary, but lighting projected a sense of life and the living, and the general ambience reassured him that Alice was safe in here.

"Hello?" he called out, as he approached the grand staircase. He thought Alice had said her special room was on the first floor, which probably meant that it was on what he would call the second floor. They had come across a few linguistic differences (mobile phone vs. cellular phone, pavement vs side-walk, motorway vs. free-way, herb vs. 'erb; the dropping of the 'aitch' particularly infuriated her, as did pronouncing the letter as 'haitch'; and that was not even touching upon the subject of sports), to which Alice would remain adamant she "was right, wasn't going to change and that he should learn to talk English". Luckily for them both, Robert did not say "'erb" or "haitch", and since Alice got so annoyed when they did use those pronunciations on the television, he did not even dare to tease her by saying either.

Robert heard a sharp rapping at one of the doors along the corridor and immediately headed for it.

"Hello?" Robert said again, not wanting to startle anyone.

"I'm sorry, the library should have been locked up. We're

closed now," Stuart said automatically, knocking a little louder upon the door.

"I'm here for Alice," said Robert, walking down the corridor to where Stuart was knocking. "She didn't show for dinner."

Dr Anthonys replied, looking towards the man walking up to him. He seemed vaguely familiar, which Stuart supposed was not unusual given the number of people that had passed through the Library doors at one time or another. "Well, she's locked herself in her room."

"What, like a sulking teenager or someone incredibly... unlucky?" Robert settled for unlucky, knowing that if he picked a word like 'inept' he was bound to lock his keys in the car or some such nonsense.

Dr Anthonys gave him a look; one that Alice and Sam were incredibly familiar with. "I can see why you two have ended up getting along so well," he said, with an exasperated frown.

"Robert Evans," Robert said, holding out his hand.

"Stuart Anthonys," he replied, shaking Robert's hand firmly. His gut suggested that Alice was right; Vampire or not, he seemed to be a decent man and a good match for her. "I believe she's fallen asleep and the defensive spell she is using will not let me in. At least she trusts me enough not to send me three feet across the room; one of the cleaners thinks the room's possessed or that there's some kind of electrical fault after he tried to open the door."

"What about..." Robert had to think for a moment to remember the name. "Julius? Can't he go in and wake her up?"

"No, Mr Evans," said a voice beside him. "I can not go in there. And the Library will not meddle with her magic, although It could open the door if It wanted."

Robert turned to look at the large man beside him. Alice was right; he was incredibly stealthy given his size. It was unsurprising given his form though. He supposed that Alice had not considered that Julius might not be human, and therefore, had yet to realise that she was working with one of the Fallen. There was also the possibility that Julius had not allowed her to see that he was one of the Fallen and was not quite sure what to make of the fact that *he* was now aware.

"Is she really that powerful?" Robert asked. Since Alice almost never used her magic, he had never judged the strength of her craft.

"It would appear so," said Stuart. "Her abilities are quite remarkable."

"Hm. OK, I best get her then," Robert said, with a careless shrug, reaching for the door handle.

"Are you sure that's wise?" Stuart asked, not entirely sure whether the Library or the Vampire would incur the most damage if he was sent flying as a result of Alice's spell.

"Probably not. She can be quite cranky when her sleep is disturbed, but she can't spend all night here," Robert replied, knocking at the door gently before opening it. He walked across to the desk where Alice was resting her eyes. "You stood me up," he teased, gently rousing her.

Alice sat up with a bleary-eyed start. It took a moment for her to realise where she was and who she was looking at. "I am so sorry. I did set an alarm, but obviously I slept through it."

"I don't know how. The noise from that thing is shocking," Robert said. "Apparently you've been locking yourself in." He nodded his head towards the door.

"Sorry," she said sheepishly.

"We still can't come in," Stuart said, trying to step through the doorway and encountering an invisible barrier.

"Really? Wow, that worked far better than I hoped then," Alice said, with a smile. She scribbled down some notes before she forgot; then she muttered under her breath and used her foot to break the circle of salt she had used to seal the room.

"A salt circle?" Stuart asked in surprise, entering Alice's work space.

"Pretty much. I added a pinch of sage and said no one

was allowed in as I lay the salt down, but essentially, it's just a salt circle."

"But it kept me and Julius out, whilst Robert could enter. How is that possible?"

Alice shrugged. "I guess he doesn't count. Maybe he's just considered a part of me, or maybe love really is the most powerful magic there is? Honestly, I don't know. Besides, it wouldn't occur to me to keep him out, cos I love him."

"I'm not sure if I'm supposed to be honoured or insulted," said Robert, teasingly.

"I'm sure you'll be both," Alice said, with slight irritation. "But you should just be honoured."

"You're such a grump when you're hungry," he said, wrapping his arm around her.

"Yeah, I could probably do with some food. But, well, can I just test something else, please?" she said, suddenly. "Well, a couple of little things."

The three men nodded their assent and Alice tested a couple of variables on her salt circle. First of all, she repaired the gap to see who could leave; then she tried a couple of different specifications to see who she could let in and out. If she left it as a normal circle, everyone could move through; if she specified, then only the individuals in question could move freely. Julius could make the circle keep everyone but Alice out; but Robert and Stuart could not make the salt circle work beyond its original intended purpose, which was unsurprising really, considering they had no magic powers, no one there was demonic or evil, and salt was not considered a Vampire deterrent. And only if she really really tried and concentrated, could she keep Robert away from her.

"You're gonna make yourself sick thinking about it that way," said Robert, grabbing hold of her as she started to sway. Neither of them said anything about the trickle of blood from her nose, although he handed her tissue.

"You have a better idea?" she snapped, wiping the blood away and looking at the stain on the tissue. She did not know why she felt the need to examine it, as though there might be something in or different about her blood; it appeared normal enough. She muttered a fire spell under her breath and burned the tissue over the bin, ashes floating down to cover the day's debris.

"Sure. Your magic is in-tune with your heart and feelings and so on, right? So don't think of it as trying to keep me away from you; think of it as, protecting me from you; I think that'd make it a lot easier for you to stop me crossing," Robert suggested.

"You're probably right...," Alice admitted, somewhat begrudgingly. Magic was her thing; she should be able to work these things out for herself. Her stomach growled and she let out a deep breath, admitting that she was probably not at her best. "But I don't think I want to try right now."

"I think that'd be for the best," Robert said, tightly. He understood Alice wanted to push herself, but there were times when she seemed to forget that there were limits. Given that she had already caused her nose to bleed, and a recurring pattern of enthusiasm followed by dark days had emerged, he was rather anxious that she give herself a break.

"It was interesting though," she said, scribbling more notes. "And yes, OK, I'm done with magic for the day... Weekend... Week?" she amended off of her companions looks. She had to admit that she was feeling utterly drained at this point, but she also knew she had to occasionally keep pushing herself. "And you shouldn't be looking at that," she admonished as Robert flicked through a couple of pages in the book. "It's not safe."

"I can't do magic," Robert said, slightly surprised as Alice's gloved hand slammed the book shut.

"You could do some of that magic. Most of it's designed for non-magical entities to use, plus I reckon you might have managed to, I dunno, absorb a bit from being around me all the time, and from er, my blood."

"She made me do it," Robert said immediately, suddenly

feeling defensive in the presence of Julius and Stuart Anthonys.

"We know," Stuart replied, trying to hide a smile. "Of course, there would have been a lot less confusion had she told us you were a Vampire to begin with."

"It just doesn't occur to me to mention it," said Alice, simply. "Either way, it's not a safe book."

"Sorry. I was just curious, what with creating circles that can keep so much out – it just seemed a bit... excessive," said Robert.

"Pretty sure that's what they want us to think," she said sharply and without hesitation.

"They?" Robert asked, sceptically.

"Demons," Alice clarified. "Or those in league with demonic forces. I know I sound like a conspiracy nut, but it's the only thing that makes sense to me in regards to that book. I don't trust it one bit."

"But there's been no demonic activity in ages," said Robert.

"I know. That's exactly why I want to try and get us more prepared. It doesn't matter when they strike to be honest, that book is still a danger. At least now, when, if, it happens, we all have a better arsenal than we did before. Same principle as a condom; I'd rather have one and not need it, then need it and not have one." She glared at the book, picked it up, and locked it away in the iron cabinet. "Anyway, it's something to do and it might be helpful one day, so, what the hey," she said with a shrug. She turned to Julius and Dr Anthonys. "Would you like to grab some dinner with us? I think we'll only be going to the 'Cauldron at this point, I guess."

"No thank you, although it's kind of you to invite us," Stuart said, trying to hide his smirk at Robert's not-so-carefully hidden expression of relief. "We're behind on our regular routine this evening as it is."

"Sorry, again," said Alice, contritely. "I'll just grab my stuff."

"OK, we'll meet you downstairs," said Robert. "Er, Stuart?" he said, walking alongside the Head Librarian who had started to head to the foyer.

"Yes, Robert?"

"OK, this is possibly going to sound odd, and even worse when I say I'd rather you didn't mention it to Alice, but do you know of anything regarding a female Witch and a male Vampire? A prophecy or something?"

"There is one that has been alluded to on several occasions. I can not find any detailed references or translations of this supposed prophecy, but there is certainly a big concern about one involving a Vampire, a Witch and Demons being brought forth from the Veil."

"I don't think there's anything on this earth that would convince Alice to help Demons. And I certainly have no desire to engage with any, other than those tamed within Vampires and Were," said Robert, feeling that Stuart was at least convinced about the first point.

"There is nothing that I have come across that would identify you and Alice as the ones involved in such a prophecy. I admit, it is unusual to see a Vampire and a Witch together in these times, but I certainly don't see either of you being a cause for concern. It may well be a coincidence; there could be a Witch and a Vampire together in deepest, darkest Peru but social media just hasn't put them on everyone's radar unlike a Witch and a Vampire in New York City."

"I hope you're right," said Robert, rubbing his nape. "I don't want the world destroyed but I don't think it would be so easy to give up being with Alice." He stopped and listened for a moment; she was still too far away even for her hearing to catch his words. "Julius is one of the Fallen, isn't he?"

"Yes," Stuart replied, slightly surprised. As far as Stuart was aware, he, the Guardians, the Library and Sam were the only ones that could tell Julius was a Fallen, outside of the Fallen themselves.

"Why doesn't Alice know?"

"I suspect it is because the Fallen do not wish her to know. As an individual, I don't think Julius would mind her knowing, but the collective obviously wish it to remain secret."

"Is there any reason..." he trailed off, hearing Alice walking briskly across the wooden flooring. Robert supposed there was little point in asking the question; Stuart would be unlikely to know the Fallen's motives beyond the little he had shared. Sadly, it did not alleviate his concerns.

"Are you sure you don't want to get food with us?" asked Alice, as she hurried down the stairs.

"Quite sure, thank you," Stuart replied.

"OK. Well, I will see you Monday then. I will try to get more sleep over the weekend so this doesn't happen again. Apologies again for the disruptions."

Stuart merely shook his head with wry amusement. Since Alice had come to the Library, he had begun to realise quite how often the English would apologise and that he had greatly reduced his own usage over the years. Also, a locked door and salt circle were nothing in comparison to some of the experiments of Novices and inexperienced Witches. He nodded in return to Robert's respectfully nodded goodbye and locked the doors behind the couple.

"So what's the plan?" Alice asked, linking her arm through Robert's.

"One of your herbal teas and takeaway, I imagine. Maybe *Coupling* or *Firefly* or *Black Books*. Something relatively light, in any case."

"I'm not completely fragile you know?" Alice muttered crossly. "Just because I'm a girl."

Robert snorted back his laughter; she was hard work when she was hungry. "I do know. And it's definitely nothing to do with you being a girl. But I also know that sometimes when you've been working hard, it's followed by you going a bit dark, and I don't want that for you. Besides, I'm not taking anything you say to heart until you've eaten."

Alice frowned, and let her out petty annoyances with a

deep breath. She was somewhat unreasonable when she was hungry. "Sorry. I really do love you," she said, kissing him.

"I know."

Chapter 31

Alice was curled up on the sofa with Robert. There was washing-up to be done, but neither of them could be bothered. They were comfortable watching *Altered Carbon* on Netflix, and occasionally throwing popcorn at one another. It was definitely a binge-worthy series and extremely interesting, although Robert did find it amusing and adorable that Alice would look decidedly uncomfortable at some of the nudity. It was a thought that was slightly contradictory to the thoughts that the programme was stirring. He kept looking at her suggestively and although she had resisted his attempts to smoulder her into his arms, (she mainly kept laughing, which was obviously not what he had been going for), he was beginning to feel that he was making progress.

A loud piece of rock music started blaring, alongside the buzzing vibration of Alice's phone going off. She gave Robert a look that suggested he should pass it to her, but he shook his head. She sighed in mock frustration and stretched over him, allowing him a quick kiss before quickly sitting up before he could envelope her in his arms. Whilst Alice was very good at resisting the smoulder, the arms and the kissing she was not so good with. She accepted the call and held the phone to her ear, glaring at her boyfriend. *Behave*, she mouthed at him.

"Evening," said Kathie.

"Hey," said Alice, brightly. "What's up?"

"Nothing much. You?"

"All good here. How are James and Leo?" asked Alice.

"Bit better, although it seems that all of the Were have

been feeling the Turn more of late," Kathie replied. "I think he wants to try maybe going to some special Were retreat with his parents to deal with the full moon."

"Without you?" asked Alice.

"I think so. I think he's worried about hurting me. I mean, to be fair, it's weird how much more intense his Turn has been of late," said Kathie, with a rare note of concern in her voice.

Alice sighed. "I had a look at what I could access on the Were in the Library, but I didn't find anything useful. Half of it didn't even sound accurate to be honest."

"Well, we knew it was a long-shot," said Kathie. "Spose so. Still, I feel like I suck as a friend for not coming up with something useful."

"You do not suck as a friend."

"Not as a friend," whispered Robert with a sly grin, as he was leaning in to kiss her neck and overheard Kathie's reply.

Shh. Fuck off, Alice mouthed at him, biting her lip to stop from smiling.

"What was that?" asked Kathie.

"Just Robert trying to be clever," said Alice, hitting him with a cushion. "How was Vegas?"

"Awesome!" Kathie replied, her tone brightening considerably. "James did really well on the poker tables, so we can afford another little holiday, like maybe a trip to New York to visit a certain someone and her boyfriend that I haven't met yet."

"That would be wicked. I would definitely like that very much," said Alice, who was watching Robert carefully. He was very trying at times.

"Speaking of which..."

"Yes...?" She covered the microphone with her hand "Behave," she hissed at Robert.

"Is Robert a Vampire?"

"Did I not even mention that to you? Jees," said Alice, rubbing at her temple. "Urgh, yeah, Robert is a Vampire."

"I mean, it's not really important, we don't care or anything, but, er..."

"You've heard talk?" Alice finished, glumly. She squeezed Robert's hand as he looked at her in concern. She shook her head, as she was not going to try and tell him about it whilst she was still talking to her best friend.

"Yeah."

"Anything specifically?" asked Alice.

"No."

"I don't get why it's the subject of so much talk then," said Alice, rolling her eyes. "No one ever has anything specific, just these vague whispers of a Witch dating a Vampire. Like it bloody matters. I don't get how it's any more or less important than the fact that I'm a brunette and he has dark blonde hair."

"Apparently witches are kinda racist, so it's a big deal."

"Urgh."

"I know."

"Did James get any kind of grief for being with you?"

"Nope, but apparently none of the others are that bothered. Just Witches. The whole bitchy Witches thing is why James was a bit of a dick to you to begin with," said Kathie.

"Oh. Is that also why it took you so long to tell me he turns into a wolf?" asked Alice. She had been wondering about that for a while, especially as she had never quite managed to ask James about it all. It was not the easiest of topics to broach.

"No, since he knew you were a Witch, we assumed you already knew he was a Were."

"Don't you think I might have mentioned it to you before I tried to set you up, even if I hadn't told you I was a Witch at that point?" said Alice, feeling slightly hurt and insulted by the imagined insinuation. "But, yeah, you would have thought I'd pick up on stuff like that, but actually, it's a fairly recent development."

"Also, this whole Vampire, Witch, thing. I get the feeling there's something a bit more to it than that, but no one's saying what, if they even know what it is. But hey, just wondered."

Does it bother you?"

"The fact that people are talking about me kinda bothers me, but I never hear any of it, really, so meh. Don't care. We're happy, that's all that really matters."

"Of course it is. And yes, you do deserve to be happy." Kathie paused. "Can I ask you something?"

"You may ask. I might not answer," Alice replied, grinning.

"This is true. Especially as it's kinda personal but, er has he bitten you?"

Alice's cheeks coloured slightly. "Yes, but only because I asked. I wasn't hypnotised; it wasn't creepy; it was something I felt that we needed to do."

"Was it as hot as they make it out to be in the films or is it more violent like, I dunno, that hybrid thing from *Blade II*?"

"Erm... er... It was not violent in this particular scenario," she eventually managed to say, the memories setting her cheeks on fire. She definitely could not look at Robert. "I don't know what it's like with other Vampires. You don't hear about throats being ripped out, so I guess they must keep it tidy, if they need to drink blood."

"Just wondered," said Kathie, slightly apologetically.

"I know, it's just, you know, like you said, kinda personal. Anyway, when were you thinking of visiting?"

"Well, depends on room prices and availability, but hopefully August or September. Definitely before the end of the year."

"We've got a book launch to attend sometime in August, but other than that, we haven't really got anything planned, so just let me know when you're ready."

"Will do. Might check on the full moon. Could have a couple of days to myself and James could join after his retreat."

"Whatever works," said Alice, smiling.

"Right, need to sort some food. Talk to you later."

"'Bye for now," said Alice, hanging up and dropping her phone on the floor with a dull thunk. She put her head in Robert's lap and looked up at him, a sad and frustrated expression on her face.

"Everything okay?" asked Robert, pushing some stray hairs away from her face.

"Yeah," she said with a wry smile. "I guess she just wanted to check that you're not a big bad Vampire taking advantage of a poor, mentally fragile Witch."

"As if. Everyone knows that it's Female witches that take advantage of male Vampires. Sorta. Can't say I've ever heard of a male Vampire complaining about it," said Robert. "Genuinely. Everyone except you knows," he amended, with a grin noticing Alice's look of surprise. "If we'd hooked up purely for sex, no one would have thought anything of it. The fact that this is a proper relationship weirds them all out."

Alice sat up and looked at him with concern in her eyes. "Are you getting a lot of, I don't what the right word is really, but, er, criticism, animosity, backlash from other Vampires for being with me?"

Robert thought about lying. "Yes," he replied after a moment's pause.

"Should I try to break up with you?"

"Maybe I should break up with you?" he countered.

"It sounds as though it would be more believable if I did it. Maybe. I don't know, would anyone believe I would dump a guy like you?"

"Of course they would. They would totally expect it to be the Witch that dumps the Vampire. Of course, it's all stupid and honestly, it's never usually an arrangement for one or the other to be dumped. All the same, I'd rather you didn't."

"Seriously?"

"Yes, seriously," said Robert, smiling patiently at her. He hated that she could not see how amazing she was. "I love you."

"I love you too. But I don't want the High Council to force us apart."

"Well, if it comes to it, I really would be willing to give up my immortality for you."

"Don't do that," said Alice at once. "It would surely be easier and better if they just took my powers. I might still be able to do some magic at the Library and I don't think it would be as big a deal as it would for you to have this massive part of you ripped out."

"When you put it that way, we'll definitely try your way first," said Robert, his eyes twinkling. He shrugged and took her hand in his. "I doubt they could do anything, unless there's a magic spell that makes people fall out of love?"

"There isn't," said Alice, squeezing his hand. "Just like there are no real love potions. Any magic that attempts to falsify or manipulate emotions is temporary at best and will certainly make things ten times worse once it wears off."

"We'll be fine," said Robert, pulling her to his shoulder. "I'm quite sure if they were to truly see us together, they'd stop worrying and that's if we're even on their radar in the first place, which I can't really see why we would be." He kissed the top of her head and she gave him a small smile. "I'm telling you, you can not get rid of me that easily." He knew she still did not believe him, but he hoped she would one day. He knew her depression might never go away completely, but he was working on raising her self-esteem.

"I guess I should hoover and wash-up," she said, reluctantly shrugging out of his embrace and starting to stand. Robert grabbed her wrist and pulled her back down onto the sofa, twisting her around so that she was pinned down against the cushions. "I am willing to vacuum and wash-up," he said.

"In exchange for?" asked Alice, smiling, eyes glinting wickedly to match the lust and mischievousness in the most wonderful pair of blue irises she had ever seen. Sometimes, she found it very hard to stay mopey when he looked at her like that.

"You taking advantage of me," said Robert, kissing her.

"I guess I could do that," she said, putting her arms around his neck and kissing him back.

Chapter 32

For a few months, life just pottered along. They went to work, they met for dinner and Robert eventually moved in, which mainly just meant they ate in more often and there was a little less travelling to do.

Onion had reluctantly adapted to the fact there was now another male in the apartment and that trying to kill, bite or claw Robert for no good reason was just going to lead to him spending the night in an alley. Realistically, Onion knew he was not being replaced and Alice was not paying any less attention to him than she had before Robert had entered her life, but he was a cat and sometimes that meant he had to act like a bit of a bastard. He was secretly pleased Alice was happy, and was a little smug about the fact he had helped make that happen. Plus, he also had to admit that Robert was pretty good to him – spoke to him as Alice would, sometimes bribed him with extra treats, and still trusted that he was looking out for her.

As Robert had recently been promoted and the greater responsibilities had in part been down to his involvement with a new book, it had once again been strongly suggested that he attend the book launch that was going to take place at a fancy town house in the Hamptons. When the event had first been mentioned, it had seemed like a good idea; a new experience if nothing else, since Alice had never been to a black tie event. When the day actually arrived, neither of them much felt like it, albeit for different reasons. Alice was not comfortable in large social situations and for some reason, Robert just wanted to keep her away from the book and everything connected with it.

"Urgh," Alice groaned, reluctantly opening her eyes. She hit the snooze button and flumped her face back into the pillow, as she always did on mornings where she really did not feel like getting out of bed.

"We could just both call in sick."

"You always suggest that on mornings like this," she said, her voice muffled by the pillow, not moving as she tried to drum up the energy to get out of bed. She gave a warm sigh of pleasure as he lightly massaged her shoulders.

"And how many times have you actually done that?"

"None." She sighed again as he worked at the horrible knot in her right shoulder.

"There you go then. It wouldn't be so awful. Just spend the day at home, we could even make clothing optional." He rolled her onto her back and kissed her, and she wrapped her arms around his neck.

She laughed. "You, sir, are incorrigible."

"I love it when you talk dirty using intelligent words." She laughed even more and pulled him down for another kiss. "I love you, even if you are a scruffy-looking nerf-herder."

"Who you calling scruffy-looking?" he said, playing with the buttons on her shirt. Even now, after several months together, when his fingers grazed her areola she gasped. Her breath was beginning to catch, and the almost sleepy way in which she stretched, seemed unintentionally inviting. She was definitely wavering.

The snoozed alarm went off again with a noise too horrendous to ignore and she sighed and rolled out from under his touch, kissing him lightly on the cheek. "You've got your big important dinner book-launch today. Can't just turn up there after not being at work."

"I don't care. We can skip that too. I'd rather watch *Star Wars* and eat pizza and then ravage you all night."

"Hmm, ravage. I like it when you use your sexy words,"

she said, grinning.

"Come back to bed; we can start early," he said, raising his eyebrows suggestively.

"No," she said, gently but firmly. "You know in terms of your job, this is kind of a big deal. And honestly, I kinda want to continuing working on that book at the Library."

"I'd rather you worked on me," he muttered under his breath.

She rolled her eyes, stuck her tongue out and threw her shirt at him before stepping into the bathroom.

***

They pulled up to the Library and she kissed him good-bye.

"We could still just go home," he said.

"Is something wrong?" she asked, her hand lingering on the door handle, looking at him.

Robert sighed. "Not really. I just feel like this would be a better day if we stayed in bed."

Alice was studying his face carefully, her brow beginning to furrow. "If you really feel like something's wrong, if you really want to just sack all this off for today, I will."

Given that he had no explanation, he felt guilty seeing the worry he was causing her. He tried to brush it off. "Nah, it's probably just cos I hate this book, and the people around it."

She did not quite look convinced, but she tried to find a silver lining for him. "Well, then, try to think of this dinner as a super expensive, at no cost to us, celebratory dinner that this is the last thing you have to do with this book. I can even check contracts and things for you if you like to ensure you never even have to work with the author again, assuming he is actually good enough to release another book."

"I don't know what I did to deserve a girlfriend as awesome as you, but I'm glad I did it."

"Me too," she said, kissing him again. "I'll see you later then."

"OK. See you later." He watched as she ran up the Library steps, glad that she loved her job so much and wondered why it was he suddenly hated his.

He really could not explain why it was he hated the book so much. It dealt with some horrible themes, had some horrible characters and some overly graphic scenes, but it was nothing new and certainly not out of the ordinary for the genre. Perhaps his mind would have been more at ease if he had just let Alice read the book instead of trying to "protect" her from it. She had asked once or twice to read it, but he had refused to give it to her. She had asked why, but he had been unable to properly convey why which had lead to an argument of sorts, or the closest they had come to one so far.

If he thought about it now, his concerns were akin to how she described her "contamination issues"; it was like there was something wrong with that book and he did not want it anywhere near her in case it infected her somehow. Sometimes, when he was forced to look over extracts for press releases and upcoming book readings, he thought that the female lead seemed too much like Alice, and that truly disturbed him, even without the horrific occurrences that befell the character.

He did not know why the book had changed so much – did not understand why the firm had allowed such drastic rewrites to go ahead, given that it had become a perversion of the original manuscript. He sighed, wishing that he did not give so much time and thought to it. Alice was probably right. He should just look at the book launch as a celebration that he could finally wash his hands of the project, and as much as he wished he did not have to expose her to the damn thing, if he was celebrating anything, he wanted to be with her. Not to mention that if there was anything actually wrong at the launch, Alice was more than capable of dealing with it.

Chapter 33

Robert leaned back in the slightly broken, black leather executive chair and stared at the ceiling. Much like his cubicle before, his office was fairly lacking in personal touches. He did have a potted plant and two large framed, black-and-white landscape photographs that Alice had taken. He was lacking a window and the chair tilted a little too far backwards for him to see the photographs, so he stared at the white squares of ceiling. Whatever was bothering him about *The Devil Possesses* and the launch party was not shifting. Being stuck in the office doing stuff he did not want to be doing did not help matters. He had not wanted the promotion any more than he had wanted to be back on the launch project. He had suggested that they give the position to Bruce, since Bruce had more experience and Robert wanted to stay in a more hands-on position, but his superiors refused to take no for an answer.

As he counted the squares of ceiling tiles, he began to consider a change in employment. Given that he was going to have a lot of time to try a lot of different things, he had not actually imagined leaving the publishing house until it got to the point where his lack of apparent ageing would be a problem. Not that he had any clue what he would do; again, he had imagined it was something he would figure out in his down time, the decade or so spent hiding from the world until he could re-emerge with a new identity.

He also had to consider what Alice would want too. He was certain that she would not want to leave New York and the Library for some time yet, especially as she had not been there all that long and felt very happy, comfortable and safe in her life, and they had not really discussed the whole 'siring' thing since that first morning-after conversation.

Robert sighed. There was also the possibility that everything would go back to relative normality once the book was released. *Alice is right; grown-up thinking sucks.* The fact that the book troubled him perturbed him in and of itself. Whilst he was all for gut-instinct and following hunches, he was happy to leave the ideas of premonitions and superstitions to the professionals; being plagued by a "bad feeling" was not supposed to be something that happened to him. Especially towards something as ridiculously trivial as a badly written horror novel.

He did believe in signs and spirits, curses and hexes, and he could not entirely rule out the idea that pixies, goblins and fairies existed either given that *'There are more things in heaven and earth, Horatio, Than are dreamt of in your philosophy'*. However, a cursed horror novel seemed like a stretch. It made no sense, nor did the idea that Houseman was possessed. And the idea that it was somehow connected to him and Alice made even less sense.

He opened the desk drawer and looked at the photograph Alice had printed off from their afternoon in Central Park. Every time he looked at it, it made him smile. It was more than just seeing how happy they made each other; it was the way it invoked the memory of the entire day. It was a reminder of the day he knew he had to ask her to marry him. And he kept the photo hidden away, in much the same way as he had never encouraged her to come by the publishing house – because of *The Devil Possesses,* and the strange feeling of needing to keep Alice protected from it as much as possible.

However, there was no way to keep her distanced from it any longer. He had tried to remain tactfully non-committal about attending the big party, but he had eventually caved to professional and peer pressure. Patrick, Jeff and Bruce had all been eager to attend, but had constantly said "it would be weird" for them to go and him not to, when he was the one who had brokered the original deal. They saw it as both a business opportunity, by way of mingling with the company big-wigs, and as a social event, where they could show off to their partners and certainly in this case, treat them to something special. It was mostly for them, that Robert had agreed to attend. With Alice.

He locked the drawer and ventured into the main office. As soon as he returned with his coffee, the teasing about Alice began again. Robert tried to brush it all off good-naturedly and tried to share in the celebratory air – although the book had not yet been officially released, pre-sales suggested that *The Devil Possesses* was going to be the biggest selling book of the year, which was a massive achievement for a relatively small publishing firm – but he just did not feel it. Again, he could not help but feel that a year ago, he would have been reacting to this all very differently.

He grabbed a few manuscripts off each of his workmates' desks and gave a small sigh before returning to his office. Bruce had given him a look of concern but he shrugged it off, claiming he had a headache. He put everything on his desk, and spent another five minutes staring at the ceiling before trying to get back into reading the latest submissions.

"We can get through today," he whispered, touching the jeweller's receipt like a talisman. "We can get through today."

Chapter 34

Alice was already at home, getting ready by the time he got back to the apartment.

"Your hair looks nice," Robert said, noticing how glossy and wavy her dark hair looked.

"I should hope so," she said, smiling. "It cost enough to get done."

"You're always worth every penny," he said as she kissed him on the cheek. The bathrobe she was wearing slipped slightly and he momentarily perked up.

"No," she chided softly, covering herself again and pulling the belt tighter. "There's no way we have time if the car is coming at 6:30."

"I can try to be quick. Or we could be fashionably late... Or not go."

She frowned at him and he tried to give her a look to convince her he was just joking.

"I'm not thrilled about going either, but we said we would. Mostly for your team, remember?"

"Indeed, they are all are dying to meet you. They might be disappointed to find out that you're just an ordinary, super-powered Witch and not a bloke."

Alice laughed. "Really? Why?"

"Because they're the ones that made me sign-up for that dating website, in the hopes of having a laugh when I went to meet a beautiful woman and ended up meeting a catfish. I lost a wager."

"Ah, I did think it was weird that you'd be on a dating

website," said Alice, with a small smile.

"Why does everyone keep saying that?"

"Seriously?" asked Alice, her amusement increasing when he nodded. "Well, honey, that is because you are a gorgeous, sexy, confident, intelligent, reasonably sociable, well-dressed man and you constantly have admirers throwing themselves at you." She kissed him. "Like that bobble-headed skanky ho in the grocery store."

"Oh," said Robert. "Wait, what was that?"

"Huh?" said Alice, feigning innocence.

"That example at the end there? Something about the grocery store?"

"I thought you smiled at me in a grocery store, but the er, blonde in front of me threw herself at you, so, yeah, you know."

"I was smiling at you, but that's definitely not what you just said." He grabbed her wrist and pulled her to him. "Tell the truth, or I will start tickling you."

"I'm not that ticklish," said Alice, sticking her tongue out.

"I'll do other things instead then," he whispered in her ear, letting his fingers slide softly down her back.

"Do your worst," Alice retorted, although she gasped and her body arched against him. "You're only hurting yourself."

He had to concede that she had a point. He decided to change tack again. "Please tell me what you said?"

Alice sighed and hung her head in shame. "Fine. I called her a bobble-headed skanky ho."

Robert laughed. "Wow. To think I could have been referring to them as bobble-headed skanky ho's instead of bubble-blondes all this time. Shame on you, Andrews, for holding out on me." He kissed her. "You know it's adorable when you get jealous."

"I hate it when you say that."

"You're even cuter when you're trying to be angry," Robert said, kissing her neck.

Alice rolled her eyes and pushed him away. "Stop being incorrigible."

"Oh, twice in one day. A new personal best."

"I need to finish getting ready. You need to start getting ready. Go have a cold shower or something," she said, shaking her head and slipping back into the bedroom. "I don't know if wine counts as Dutch courage or whatever, but you can always try what I assume is an expensive bottle of wine; certainly looks it," she called from the bedroom.

He noticed the wooden box on the counter and looked briefly at the card before he slid it open. "A 2007 Barolo Monprivato. They're really expecting big things for this book if they're sending out $200 bottles of wine. Do you want some?"

"Might as well try it, I guess. If you're sure it won't be wasted on my unadventurous and unsophisticated palette."

Robert had a feeling it probably would be but he kept that opinion to himself and smiled. Alice was many things but a connoisseur of fine dining she was not. He uncorked the bottle, took out two standard wineglasses from the back of the cupboard and after letting it breathe for a few moments, poured a little of the expensive red into Onion's spare drink saucer.

"Does this seem safe to you?" he asked Onion, who was prowling around the box.

"Safe?" the cat questioned, eyeing up the box and wondering if he could fit comfortably in it.

"Yeah. Does it seem cursed or poisoned or something?"

The cat looked at Robert as though he was insane, but delicately sniffed at the liquid. It was his job as a guardian Familiar after all to look out for such things and given the fruity nose on this particular vintage, he would not be doing his due diligence if he did not at least taste it for poisons. Then he lapped it up and carefully considered the palate before delivering a verdict. "Seems to be an excellently aromatic red, with notes of oak and red fruit, which would no doubt benefit from proper aeration in a wide, crystal wineglass. You can certainly leave it with me if you think it poses a threat."

"I don't think so," Robert said with a grin. He poured out two generous glasses, swirled them both and then tested one. It was an extremely pleasant wine and he thought even Alice might enjoy the taste, despite her general ambivalence for the drink. He would occasionally argue that if they bought a nice wine, she would probably enjoy it more than the cheaper brands they had tried, but he could hardly disagree with Alice's preferred spending choices of games, technology and Lego. It was not necessarily that they could not afford both, but Alice was cautious about spending too much money. "I'm going mad," he muttered.

"Next thing you know, you'll be talking to cats and even worse, they'll start talking back," said Alice, swanning into the kitchen to grab one of the glasses of wine. She was still only wearing the robe.

"For goodness sake woman, put some proper clothes on," Robert said, practically growling with desire.
She laughed unapologetically, loving the fact that she could tease him so easily. "Apparently, getting ready for a black tie event is a lengthy process, and I'm trying to distract you from the potentially long and boring night."

"You're distracting me alright," he said, grabbing her for a long, hard kiss as she reached for her glass.

"Take a cold shower then," she said sweetly, twisting her face away and sipping the wine. Her face brightened with surprise. "Oh, this is actually rather nice. Kinda fruity and not so bitter and alcohol-y."

"Wine critics are despairing at that description right now," said Robert. "Even Onion is hanging his head in shame." They both looked at the cat, who was obstinately not hanging his head but was also giving off an air of minor despair in his mistress' critique.

"Go shower," Alice said, sticking her tongue out at Robert and pushing him towards the bathroom.

"That's what you're planning on wearing?" he asked,

noticing the clothes laid out on the bed. Specifically a flash of green silk and glossy black nylon. "You want me to go to a black tie event, knowing that you are wearing *that* lingerie and stockings?" As their relationship had developed, Alice had bought a few nice lingerie sets and he particularly liked the way that shade of green set off her eyes while the set as whole seemed to make her especially playful.

"Yes," she replied impatiently, rolling her eyes. "I told you, if you're that reluctant to go to this thing that everyone, including me, has bullied you into going to, I am going to try and give you at least one reason to be glad you went. Now go shower," she said.

He grabbed her wrist and pulled her close. "I am the luckiest guy ever," he said, kissing her.

"I'm pretty lucky too," she said, kissing him back. "Now, …"

"Go shower. I know, I'm going, I'm going."

Robert emerged from the shower a short while later and dressed himself in the custom-made black suit. He did up the crisp white shirt sleeves with the silver cuff links Alice had given to him as a gift for his promotion and walked into the kitchen.

"Would you zip me up please?" she asked. Her lips looked incredibly sumptuous stained with the wine that had bled into her lip gloss. She turned away and gently gathered her hair to one side.

"Of course," he said, slowly zipping up the gold bodice of her dress, deliberately pushing the zip against her spine so that she could feel the delicate pressure.

"That's not playing fair," she said, shivering as his cool breath gently teased the back of her neck.

"You started it," he replied, kissing her neck from behind.

"I suppose I did," she admitted, briefly melting against

him. She did so love it when he kissed her throat.

"Can you do bow ties?" he asked her.

"Never tried. I don't want you to wear a bow tie, I feel they're best left to the Eleventh Doctor. Along with tweed and a Fez." Alice sashayed into the bedroom and came out with his best Italian black silk tie. "I like this better," she said, tying a perfect Windsor knot. "Much sexier."

"But technically incorrect for the occasion," Robert admonished, checking the neckwear in the mirror. He tugged lightly on the lapels of the tuxedo jacket and straightened up the cuffs.

She smiled at him, feeling confident and relaxed under the effects of the rather potent wine. "Do you really think anyone is going to care? I'm quite sure when you tell them your slightly intoxicated girlfriend insisted, no one's going to argue."

He certainly could not disagree with that. Most of the men he knew were well aware that it was far safer for them not to argue with the women in their lives.

"Besides, I like being able to pull you to me with it, like this," Alice said, demonstrating and kissing him. "Can't do that with a bow tie."

"Hard to argue with that reasoning," he said, smiling at her, amused by the fact Tipsy Alice was already starting to come out and play.

She rested against the side of the chair and slipped on a pair of elegant black pumps. "I tried to get some heels, but I felt like I was trying to walking in stilts whilst someone was squashing my toes in a vice." There was no reply. "What is it?" she asked with sudden concern, standing up and turning to face him.

Alice was wearing a long dark dress, made up of a gold bodice and high waisted long black skirt; her hair cascaded over her shoulders in dark brown, glossy waves, her fringe angled and straightened to overlap the left corner of her black spectacle-frames. She had made a rare effort with her make-up, with the deep red lip gloss, Cleopatra-like eye-liner and deep green eye-shadow; he knew she did not like to bother with it much, but she had managed to do an outstanding job of looking quite natural and elegant.

"Nothing. You look stunning," Robert said, admiringly. "Like a 1940s movie starlet stunning."

"Thanks," Alice said, giving an unsure smile as she pushed her glasses up self-consciously. "Honestly, I still feel really stupid, hence I've probably had too much of that wine already. But you, you look even sexier than James Bond," she said, using the black silk tie to pull him towards her again and kissing him. "You can change the tie if you want. I mean, if it is strict black-tie as opposed to black-tie as code for formal," she said, adding as she was hit with an inexplicable wave or paranoia "Or maybe we could just stay home."

"We'll be fine," he said reassuringly, actually believing it in that moment as he kissed her. "I suddenly have the extremely primitive and macho urge to just show you off. And I'm totally fine with the tie, because it will give me even more reason to point out the fact that I am there with the most beautiful girl in the world, let alone the room."

She looked at him with that embarrassed yet pleased smile, that said she appreciated the compliment but thought he was being silly. "OK, then," she said "I guess we're doing this."

"Are you going to wear gloves?" he asked suddenly.

"The dress came with some, but I hadn't planned on it, to be honest. I'd have to take them off to eat, after all, and I only have a small bag which I didn't think they'd fit into."

"Would you mind wearing them?"

"Okay," she said, gliding into the bedroom and returning with the gloves. She picked up the small gold clutch bag from the kitchen counter and finished her glass of wine, quickly moving all remnants out of Onion's reach. He gave her a look of disappointment, and she stroked his ears. "We should go down. I'm sure the car will be here any minute now."

"Okay," Robert said, grabbing Alice's keys from the little frame by the door. *We'll be fine*, he thought to himself again as he locked the door behind them, his confidence beginning to fade.

Chapter 35

"'*Last night I dreamed I went to Manderley again*,'" Alice murmured as the car took them up the long, winding driveway, up to the grey brick mansion in the Hamptons.

It was an impressive building, designed to be perfectly symmetrical and echoing the Gothic style of old England; it reminded Alice of a scaled down version of Margam Castle, as there were fewer turrets and tall though the windows were, they certainly suggested that the ceilings were not quite as high as castle standards. It was a beautiful house, despite the burning torches, the flaming clear skies and the intentionally overgrown trees that were lending it an air of calculated menace. It had been a couple of days since it had last rained, but as yet, the heat remained dry, and the evening air was warm and comforting as opposed to oppressive and suffocating.

There were already a number of expensive cars parked outside, ranging from top end sports cars to high-end luxury town cars, and several groups of extravagantly dressed people were making their way into the house. Alice began to wonder if she perhaps looked more like she was attending a high school prom than a book launch with a guest list that mostly included the wealthy and elite of New York and literary circles. It was silly. She should not even care. She was here to support Robert and celebrate the fact that he no longer had to work on a book he despised.

Alice shivered slightly and pulled on the black silk gloves. Although Robert had not mentioned them again, she was sure that the main reason he wanted her to wear the gloves, was so that Damien Houseman's hands did not make direct contact with hers. She was not sure if Robert was overreacting, but she nonetheless respected his instincts, and as they walked up the steps to the iron studded oak door, she could not deny the unsettled feeling that washed over her. *Look like th'innocent flower, but be the serpent under't;* Alice felt that this was a good house being used to disguise something darker. Admittedly, it could all be in her head, but she was trying to trust her own instincts and they told her something dark was trying to insinuate itself into the house.

She marvelled at the interior beauty as she ascended the red carpet lain grand staircase, admiring the light fixtures, flowers and artwork adorning the warm-coloured walls. Clearly it was a house designed to imitate old architecture, since it was much more modern, warmer and there was far less exposed brickwork than Alice was used to seeing in castle-like abodes. Admittedly, she was no expert, but it certainly did not feel like a house that was thousands of years old – maybe a hundred or so – and she was mainly trying to concentrate on design details in order to avoid interacting with the other guests.

However, there was no escape once they entered the upstairs ballroom, especially when the noise level died to an awed hush. The string quartet continue to play, but the conversation levels stalled momentarily. Alice bit her lip and tried to keep the panic at bay as she tightened her grip slightly on Robert's arm.

"Are they staring? I feel like they're staring. And if they are staring, what are they staring at?" she whispered, feeling like she wanted to die. *It's funny how the Earth never actually opens up and swallows you when you want it to.*

"You. Because you're the most beautiful woman in the world. Or they're being really judgemental about the tie," he whispered back, squeezing her hand and making her smile.

"Thank you. For always being my hero," she said quietly,

kissing his cheek.

A middle-aged man with greying black hair, a sharp black suit and red smoking jacket, started making his way towards them. "Robert. Good of you to make it," said Damien Houseman, with a beaming smile. "And who is this enchanting creature?"

"This is my girlfriend Alice," Robert replied. To the casual listener, Robert sounded perfectly amiable; to Alice, he sounded stiff and hostile. "Alice, this is Damien Houseman, the author of *The Devil Possesses*."

"Nice to meet you," she said, politely.

"Soon to be "best-selling author", I hope," Damien Houseman said in a jovial manner. He turned his attention to Alice. "Charmed to make your acquaintance," he said, taking her gloved hand and kissing it. He did not let go of her hand right away and Alice pulled away as politely as possible. "Could I interest you in some wine?" He waved a hand, and a waiter appeared at his side with a silver tray of elegant glasses filled with decadent wines.

"Thank you," she said, taking a glass of red from the proffered tray, as did Robert. She swirled it confidently, and held it up to the light. Then she sniffed it delicately. "Barolo Monprivato," she said, taking a long, slow sip. "Two thousand and... seven?"

"It is indeed," Houseman replied. He looked at her again, clearly assessing and judging her, seemingly impressed.

"I thought I recognised it," Alice said, attempting to ignore the scrutinising gaze that lingered decidedly longer than was comfortable in certain areas. She tried to keep control of the conversation by continuing to discuss the wine before the subject could change. "Such a complex aroma isn't? And it's almost like there are notes of oak amongst the crisp raspberry and rose petal, wouldn't you agree?"

"Quite," he replied, looking remarkably taken with her. She could feel Robert's gaze on her, but reassuring as that was, she was also afraid to look at him in case he made her laugh. She was having enough trouble keeping a straight face as it was. *The giggle-loop is trying to get me*, Alice thought, which definitely did not make the not-laughing any easier. She had to get somewhere quiet and collect herself. Houseman looked as if he was going to try and engage them in further conversation, so she firmly cut him off before he could begin. "I'm ever so sorry, but please excuse me, as I believe one of Robert's colleagues is trying to flag us down. No doubt we shall see you later in the evening, if you can fit us in amongst your admirers."

"I'm sure I can make time for you," Houseman said, suggestively. He was looking at her with a curiously awestruck expression. "Until later."

Alice smiled wanly in return, and walked away, leaving Robert to follow her. He held up the index finger on his right hand as he caught Patrick's eye and when Alice felt sure Houseman was no longer watching them, she dragged him out on the balcony. As soon as they looked at each other, they burst out laughing.

"'Notes of oak'," Robert said, laughing. "I can't believe you spouted a wine critique that was provided by your cat."

Alice laughed too. "I also checked the internet," she said. "And Onion is is very sophisticated when he's allowed to be… And it really is quite a nice wine." She stuck her tongue out at him childishly and smiled.

He laughed a bit more and pulled her in for a kiss. "It does seem quite palatable," he said, pulling at her lips with his teeth.

"I think some things taste better with you too," she said, smiling sweetly. "It's a stunning view at least," she said, looking out at a still, clear lake, flanked by tall trees. It was a near perfect mirror of the fiery sky and the deep foliage, with only the merest ebb of the large water's natural tide causing occasional flaws. Insect and bird activity was winding down, and the heady haze of a glorious summer's night hung ripe with the promise of a clear view of the night's heavens. The ambient light pollution would be low enough to see a million more stars than was possible in the city, and it was at least one thing to feel optimistic about now that they were there. She sighed, feeling a moment of blissful contentment standing there in Robert's strong embrace. She kissed him again. "If we were the only ones here, this could be perfect," she murmured quietly.

"Anyone would think you were anti-social," Robert teased.

"I am," Alice said, with a small laugh. She took a deep breath, stealing shy glances into his deep blue eyes. She loved that he could still make the butterflies dance in her stomach, like they were meeting for the first time all over again.

"Well, once we get past the first thirty minutes or so, which will be all of the handshakes and introductions, we can just try and stay with the team, and that should be a bit less overwhelming," Robert said, trying to be the sensible one and ignore Alice's mischievous and tempting smiles. "You won't have to pretend you know about wine with them."

"I don't know why I did that," said Alice, with a slight frown. "Well, I do. Partly I want to make sure I don't show you up by being inelegant about the food and drink, but mostly I didn't want to talk about myself," she said. She knew there was a little more to it than that; there was something about Houseman that made her want to hide who she really was. She looked back at the house and her cheeks reddened as she wondered how many of the rooms above were unoccupied bedrooms. She raided an eye brow suggestively and threw her gaze up towards a bedroom window.

"I'm not sure there's any way you could show me up," said Robert, as she tiptoed up to brush her lips against his, and pulled lightly on his lips with her teeth. "Although, you need to stop trying to get me into trouble."

"Sorry. I can't help it. You look sexy, I feel kinda sexy and the wine's made my head feel the nice kind of fuzzy."

"I know, but, well, behave," Robert said with great reluctance, trying to keep his hands from wandering away from her waist. Tipsy Alice was always frustratingly playful at the most inappropriate of moments. "I thought I was supposed to be the badly-behaved sex-pest in this relationship?"

"You are. Most of the time." She let out a petulant sigh, knowing he was right and giving herself a mental shake. "OK, so what about when I have to admit that I haven't read the book?"

"There will be plenty of people in the room that won't have read it, for whatever reason."

"I'm sure Mr. Houseman will want my opinion of it, so what do I say when I am inevitably asked?"

"Whatever you want," he said, wrapping his arms around her waist again. "I'm not concerned about what anyone in that room thinks. It's really not important. You are the only one that matters, and I still can't explain it, but I really don't want you to read it. Not this version in any case. Weird paranoia aside, I don't think it's worth reading."

"He does seem, off, somehow," she said thoughtfully. "It's weird, because I don't want to look at him, because he kinda creeps me out a bit; but at the same time, if I try to look at him, it's almost like my gaze slips off him. It's not right."

They stood in silence for a moment, both reflecting on their own feelings of unease.

"We'll try and make our excuses to leave after not long after dinner," Robert said.

"Really? That would be good," Alice said, with obvious relief.

They kissed one last time and reluctantly went back into the bustling ballroom, navigating their way through various meetings with people from Robert's building. Alice smiled politely, murmured 'thank you' at the compliments, and nodded as Robert's boss and other high-ups in the publishing world spoke of what a catch it was for Robert to have signed Houseman given the imminent success of this debut novel. She was proud of Robert and it was good to hear that he was being valued at the company, but since she knew how much he hated the book and how he had tried to distance himself from it, there was a note of discordance to it all.

Eventually, they made it to a large dresser flanked by two standing candelabra and covered in opulent, fragrant red flowers – mostly roses and orchids – where Robert's team (Patrick, Bruce and Jeff) and their respective partners (Sally, Christopher and Susan) had managed to create their own little bubble.

"So Alice is real after all," said Bruce, as Robert made all of the introductions, everyone smiling and nodding to one another, a few handshakes and polite hugs with air kisses.

"Could still be a man though," teased Jeff. He smiled reassuringly at Alice. "Don't worry – I know you're not."

"And yet she'd still be the most beautiful woman in here," Robert said, wrapping his arms around her, partly to comfort her and partly because he felt weirdly possessive.

"No wonder you didn't notice the blonde from the sixth floor," said Patrick. "She couldn't hold a candle against Alice."

"That's very sweet of you to say," said Alice, reddening slightly. Nice as it was to be complimented and reassuring as it was to know that her presentation was acceptable, she was nonetheless unused to so much attention. She began to search the room, curious to see if she could spot anyone that might be the blonde in question. "And is she here?"

"Oh yes," said Susan. "The whorish looking creature in the shimmery-white Jessica Rabbit dress and the red 'So Kate' Louboutins. I'm sorry," she said off her husband's look, "but every woman in here is thinking it, even if every man isn't."

"She looks toxic," said Alice, unable to see anything beautiful about the woman other than her impeccable appearance, which nonetheless bordered on being inappropriately revealing. She superficially looked quite stunning in her long white dress, Veronica Lake-styled blonde hair contrasted with the red shoes, shiny red lipstick and little red clutch purse, but it was only surface. There was something cold and cruel about her, that went beyond the expression of tightly controlled anger in her sharply defined features, and Alice felt her spider-sense tingling. That sense of cold rage seemed distantly familiar, and Alice looked away uncomfortably before the blonde started staring back.

"Absolute poison," Christopher agreed, draining his champagne flute. "And she's positively seething right now." He grinned smugly; it was always nice to see the prideful take a tumble of sorts.

"Oh?" Alice asked politely. Something bothered her about the woman, and it was nothing to do with jealousy. That said, Alice was definitely willing to stab this woman with her own heels if she got too close to Robert.

"Well, look at her," Christopher elaborated. "She came here expecting to be the most attractive woman in the room, the woman that every man would be secretly wishing they had, and for a good hour, she was. And now she's not and that bothers her."

"Robert wouldn't find that attractive, would you?" she asked, looking up at him.

"Nope, never have really, although they seem to be attracted to me," Robert said, looking briefly in the woman's direction.

"Well, they're not blind," said Susan and Christopher, shrugging as their partners frowned at them.

Alice pretended to be shocked, but she was unable to hide her amusement, especially as Robert did not know whether to look modestly flattered or not. She decided to play nicely for a little while. "True. He is a very, very handsome man," she said, pulling him by his tie for a brief kiss.

"Well, of course Robert wouldn't," said Christopher, with a smile. "For one thing, anyone can see the two of you are madly in love with one another, and for a second, he walked in with the woman who is now the most attractive female in the room."

Alice blushed, and shrugged. "I'm only beautiful because he makes me believe it," she said, smiling up at Robert.

"I want to hate you so much," said Susan, with a smile. "But I can't. We," (she indicated herself and Sally) "said that when you walked in and everyone stopped to stare. All of our men whispering about how beautiful you are, and not only could we not disagree, we can't even hate you for it because it's obvious that you don't really want the attention and only have eyes for the man you walked in with."

"The last bit's true at least."

"I really should be throwing up in my handbag right now," said Christopher "But you're too adorable."

"That's a lovely dress, Alice. Isn't it a Keveza? Where on earth did you get it?" asked Sally.

"Oh, yes, it is," said Alice, looking down at the beautiful gown she did not feel she deserved. "I got it as a thank-you gift from a photographer that was working on a *Vogue* shoot in London. I can't even remember how I ended up there to be honest. And I don't recall doing anything much, but Nikki wanted me to pick a dress, and she said that if she could have one photo of me in it, then I could keep it. I felt so ugly being around all these professional models, that I really almost declined. But it was probably my one and only chance to own something that beautiful and expensive, so after much internal debate, I agreed. I'm a bit rubbish with fashion to be honest, so I only know it's a Romona Keveza because that's the collection Nikki was shooting. It's mainly just been sat in a gift box that looks equally expensive, waiting for a day to be worn. Plus, I'm really glad this was stashed in the closet because I hate shopping for dresses and shoes."

"You what?" said Jeff and Patrick in unified disbelief.
Alice laughed. "Genuinely, I hate shopping for dresses and shoes."

"Can we trade?" Jeff quickly asked Robert. "Three days of shopping trips, until Susan settled on that beige-y one."

"It's gold," said Susan, aghast. "Just because the silk is somewhat matte as opposed to being glittery, it does not make this dress any less gold."

"Three days? Three weeks for Sally's," said Patrick, shaking his head in accompanying exasperation.

"I needed a specific shade of red to go with these cute shoes I found," said Sally, pointing her foot into the middle of the group. "Just 'cos you have it easy with wearing a black suit to these things."

"Admit it though," said Christopher, grabbing another couple of champagne flutes from a passing waiter. He passed one to Alice, and tried to make sure the jesting did not turn into an actual argument. "You loved having an excuse to buy a new outfit and dress up."

"Well, of course," said Sally. "Why else would we bother to come to these things? Although, I have to say, this is by far and away the best one yet. This place is gorgeous; the hors d'oeuvres and the wine have been divine, so I can't wait to see what's being laid on for dinner."

"How long did I take to find an outfit?" Christopher asked Bruce.

"Not sure. Three hours maybe, wasn't it? But not shopping, just going through what we already had in the wardrobe, because we'd spent enough getting these suits made for your brother's wedding last year. We spent most of that time trying to agree on the exact shade of black shoe to wear with our tuxes," said Bruce.

Sally and Susan seemed to think that made perfect sense; Alice and the others looked quizzically at one another as if they could not quite believe that kind of thing happened.

"Seriously, can we swap?" said Jeff, deciding Alice was the most sensible woman he had ever met.

"Hell no," said Robert, casually. "I wouldn't inflict this powerful ugly creature on my worst enemy."
Susan, Sally and Jeff looked at Robert in horror, whilst Alice nearly spat out her mouthful of champagne from laughing.

"You are such a dick," she said, hitting him. She turned to the others, and quickly reassured them. "It's a quote from *Firefly*, which is one of my favourite TV shows. He's not actually insulting me. I think."

"Ah yes, just wanted to see if you paid as much attention to my outfit habits as these two do to their better halves," Christopher grinned as he indicated Patrick and Jeff.

"Hell on earth those shopping trips," muttered Jeff. "And of course, once she'd picked the dress, we then had to go buy another tie so that we kinda matched. Well, we would have, if this wasn't black-tie," he amended when Susan glared at him.

"To be fair, colour coordination is important," said Alice, trying to ensure that Sally and Susan were not being too put-upon. "And your wives look very beautiful in their dresses – the colours really work well, and the cuts are extremely flattering. And I love the shade of your lipstick? Balm? Gloss? Susan."

"Thank you, it's a lipstick shade called Espresso Obsession" said Susan, delighted. "Have to say, Alice, I think you're a tad unlucky, this being your first book launch. None of them have ever been this lavish and they probably won't be again. And some of the designer stuff here is astonishing. $6000 shoes and $12000 dresses floating about like they're small change, which they probably are to most of these people." Something caught Susan's eyes and she excitedly pointed it out to Sally. "Ooh, Sally, have you seen that woman's handbag? Looks like a Fendi, don't you think?"

Christopher caught Alice's eye and grabbed her arm. Partly out of genuine interest in the seating plan, and partly because he could see that Alice was about one sentence away from being dragged into a conversation that she would no doubt drown in, he decided to rescue her, knowing that Robert and the others had already drifted onto a different topic, that Alice looked equally uninterested in – football.

"Sorry ladies, Alice needs to come with me; we're going to insist that the eight of us are seated together, because I rather feel like we won't be," Christopher said with a charming smile, as he lead her away to look at the seating plan displayed on a stand at the dining room entrance.

"Thank you," she said, quietly.

"You're welcome. You looked like your eyes were one step away from being Krispy Kreme'd."

Alice laughed. "Yeah, I'm not good with fashion or whatever sport it is the guys were talking about."

"Football. Specifically NFL. Not that I follow it much myself. I prefer basketball. Although I hear you crazy English call soccer, football."

Alice narrowed her eyes slightly and let out a very long and deliberate breath. "I'm not getting into another linguistic debate about how Americans are wrong," Alice said firmly, after a moment's measured silence.

Christopher chuckled and then peered at the seating plan, moving his finger along the layout to keep track of everyone's names. "Ha! I knew he would try to move you," Christopher said, tapping at the plan triumphantly. Whilst Robert, Christopher and the rest of the group were seated together about halfway down the long-table, Alice was at the top of the table to the left of the author.

"Who?" Alice said, deciding to play dumb. She did not like the fact that she was not seated with Robert either, but unlike Christopher, she did not believe it was a last minute decision.

"Houseman. You on one side, poison blonde on the other no doubt. Jane something? I know Bruce has told me and she was in the news when the tragedy happened, but I can't for the life of me remember if that's it right now. Strange really, I intensely dislike the man now but when I met him a year ago, he made me think of my favourite school teacher. And I could imagine *that* man wanting you sat next to him in order to have a lively debate about literature and film, and Robert would probably be on the other side of you, but this guy now... I feel like he's just trying to sleep with you. And I know I shouldn't speak ill of him really, considering the awful business with his family, but I swear either the loss of his family sent him off the deep end or money really does change people." There was a small display of *The Devil Possesses* on a table to the other side of the dining room archway. "Here, look," he said, showing her the author's photograph in the book. "It's like a different person."

"They look the same to me," Alice said, not sure she should admit that she agreed that they were different people. The man in the book jacket had as approachability that suggested you could have intelligent conversations about writing and other people's novels; the man present this evening was like an actor trying to play the man in the photograph and not quite succeeding.

"Oh, physically, yes, but at the same time, if you're someone that's studied people, it's like looking at a man and his evil twin. I don't know what your story is, but I know you can see it too. It's the same with toxic blonde – perfectly attractive just to see her, but if you start to look properly, you can see how ugly she is."

"Yes, that's quite a good way to describe it," Alice agreed, glancing back into the main ballroom. Toxic blonde and Damien Houseman were not in her eyeline. *By the pricking of my thumbs* she thought, still unable to shake off that ominous feeling.

As members of the catering staff entered the dining area, Christopher managed to catch the attention of the maître de.

"Good fellow," said Christopher, trying to replicate Alice's English accent. At least she thought that was what he was trying to do. "There seems to be a mistake with the seating plan. This lovely creature here has somehow been separated from the rest of our party. We're all here," he said, pointing to the seating plan, "and she's all the way up there."

"I'm sorry sir, but the seating plan was finalised yesterday."

"Surely you could swap my poor innocent sister to a seat down here, and just scooch everyone else along? Would that be at all possible, please Albert?" Christopher asked, squinting at the gold name tag.

"I would greatly appreciate it," Alice said quietly. Alice had good genes, and coupled with the glasses that made her big brown eyes even bigger, she looked younger and more innocent than she really was. It was not something she knowingly took advantage of, but she certainly played it up now.

Christopher lowered his voice conspiratorially, but asked quite seriously "Would you want your sister sat next to that man? On her own?"

"No, I wouldn't," Albert replied, firmly and without hesitation. He happened to have a sister several years younger than himself, and a shadow of discomfort crossed his eyes as he momentarily considered the notion of Barbara being alone with the host. "I'll make sure you get seated next to Robert and Christopher, is it?" he queried, looking at where Christopher was pointing to on the seating chart.

"Yes, please. Thank you so much, Albert," she replied with genuine relief.

"Happy to help," Albert replied with a quick smile. "It's a good thing your brother thought to check the seating plan before dinner began."

"He has his moments," she said, brightly. "Thank you again."

They watched Albert deftly switch a few names around and returned to the rest of the group. Alice immediately took Robert's hand. Robert looked at her with some concern and she shook her head slightly, since it was not something she wanted to bring up in front of the others.

"I was right you know," Christopher declared dramatically. "He'd had her moved to the top of the table, trying to separate her from the rest of the herd, probably to intimidate and terrify her before killing her with a straight razor."

"That is creepily specific," she said, eyes wide. She did not correct Christopher on the fact that the seating plan had been finalised the previous night and the flicker of fear she felt was nothing to do with straight razors; she was quite sure there was some other reason why she had been deliberately removed from Robert's side. And Christopher had at least dropped the dubious accent.

"It's a scene in the book," Robert said, quietly.

"Oh."

"Haven't you read it?" Jeff asked her. "I got the impression from Robert that it would be right up your street."

"Oh, I'm not one for horror novels. Horror movies, yes, but not novels. My imagination is too over-active for that. I can barely play through *Alien: Isolation*, because I get so wrapped up in it," Alice replied, disguising the uneasy lie with truths. "I'll spend like half-an-hour hiding in a locker."

"Which is hilarious, by the way," Robert commented, deftly stepping aside as she went to hit him again.

"It's an amazingly immersive game, isn't it?" said Patrick, catching her remark.

Alice brightened and nodded.

Meanwhile, Jeff made an expression of understanding and said "It's OK. Susan and Sally haven't read it either. I don't think I've seen Susan pick up a book that wasn't a romance of some description."

"But it's OK. My little sister and I got it fixed," Christopher was saying, looking pointedly at Alice for confirmation.

"Yeah, erm, we're related now, just in case it comes up," said Alice.

"I've always liked the idea of a sister," said Bruce, thoughtfully.

"Well, now you kinda have. As *my* sister, she's practically yours too."

"Poor Susan and Jeff, not being part of the family," said Bruce.

"Family don't end with blood," said Alice, quickly. Although she did not necessarily appropriate it for the immediate situation, it was nonetheless a statement she believed in.

"True enough," said Christopher.

Sally and Susan excused themselves, and Alice politely declined the invitation to join them as they re-applied their make-up. For one thing, she did not have any make-up with her, and secondly, she was feeling as though the room was a little stuffy. It was a weird feeling, considering how large it was and that it was probably only filled with three-quarters of the number it could comfortably accommodate. The terrace doors were wide-open, allowing a gentle summer's breeze to help with air flow, but she supposed it was the candles, incense and various expensive scents that were getting to her.

Alice put her hand on Robert's arm. "I'm gonna go sit outside for a bit. It's a bit much in here; I want to look at the water," Alice said, quietly.

"Do you want me to come with you?" asked Robert, turning away from the other men momentarily.

Always, she thought. "No, it's fine. You should talk to people, I just need a little space. It's not like I'll be far away, if I fell in the lake or something."

"Okay," he said, kissing her cheek. "If you're sure."
Neither of them felt sure about separating, but neither of them had any explanation for it.

Chapter 36

Although there were several waiters and waitresses weaving amongst the groups of people with silver trays of champagne and wine, there was also a bar at the east end of the ballroom. Alice declined several offers of drinks, and eventually managed to get a glass of water and ice, and duck out on to the balcony again. No one else was there, and she breathed a sigh of relief as she sat down on one of six small marble benches. She could still hear the buzz of conversations and floating beneath it, the melodic tones of the string-quartet. She tilted her head, eyes narrowing slightly as she tried to identify what they were playing, eventually deciding that from what little she could hear, it was a part of Vivaldi's *Four Seasons*.

She closed her eyes for a moment and visualised that there was a volume mixer for the world, and she mentally turned the voices off and turned up the music, the gentle rustle of leaves and the low lapping of the water. For a few minutes, she enjoyed the solitude and the cool night air and the colours of a sky that was fading from the last embers of sunset, into the yellow and purple haze of dusk. Stars were beginning to twinkle and the moon was already a bright satellite against the darkening sky. She closed her eyes, and breathed deeply and calmly, just enjoying the moment. There was a natural perfume in the air, maybe honeysuckle and jasmine, that was marred by a more mammalian scent. She opened her eyes, looking for some sign of a cat or a dog. There was always something reassuring about the presence of a cat.

Strange that they would have hemlock and snakeroot in

these planters, she thought, suddenly noticing the two similar collections of small white flowers, spouting out of the top of gargoyle-shaped grey pots on either side of the benches. It was probably the hemlock that was undercutting the fragrance of the trees. *I guess if we get desperate for an excuse to leave, I could always poison myself.* She chided herself for being so bleak, tapped her mantra out on her hands nine times, and let out a deep breath, trying to capture the moment before poisons had ruined it. She looked up at the brightest of the stars and smiled, thinking about how if she had a house with such a long driveway, she would stud it with lavender for the bees she would keep.

Her calm was broken by a man stepping out onto the balcony. He nodded at her, and proceeded to try and light a cigarette. Alice smirked to herself as his lighter failed to produce a flame. He tried a couple of times and she thought she caught some recognisable words muttered under his breath, but he still could not produce a flame.

"I don't suppose you have a light?" he asked, turning to look at her. He was handsome, maybe a little younger than she was, spoilt, arrogant and wealthy; she could tell from the unsubtle way in which he would flick his wrist ever so slightly to reveal his expensive timepiece.

"I don't smoke," she replied bluntly. She could make her own flames, but since she had already gone to the effort of destroying his, she was not about to divulge that particular skill. "Maybe you'd have more luck at the other side of the house; no wind off the lake there."

"I'm sure I'll manage. They say these things will kill you in any case." He looked at her again, with more scrutiny in his unremarkable blue eyes and decided to sit down. "So which coven do you belong to?"

"I'm sorry?"

"Which coven do you belong to? I haven't seen you around Wesker's – The Pale Moon I mean – so I assume you belong to one of the others."

"I don't belong to one," Alice replied, guardedly.

"What about your parents or grandparents?"

"It's not really been discussed." Alice's responses remained clipped and polite, as she tried to shift slightly away from him. She did not intend to broadcast the fact that technically her family could own the Crown of the Pale Moon, and certainly did not feel it was any of his business.

"Odd," he continued, looking her up and down. "You don't look like a squib."

"Squib?" said Alice, slightly confused. "A Witch that can't do magic?" she ventured.

"Yeah," he replied, with some slight disdain. He blinked laconically, looking down his nose at the notion of a non-powerful Witch.

"No. I'm not." Alice looked at the man curiously and marvelled that he had no idea how ironic his attitude was. She was trying to assess whether he was a particularly useless witch or whether her ability to detect that he was a witch was overpowered by the arrogant ass-hole vibe he was projecting.

"There is definitely something weird about you," he said looking at her again, deciding that powerful or not she would be entertaining for a short while at least.

"I appreciate the compliment," said Alice, knowing full well that it was not intended as one.

He frowned at her, clearly puzzled. "You've not had to associate with that Vampire, have you? Sometimes being around the lesser forms can disturb our energies. Apparently he's connected with the book though, so what can we do?" He seemed disappointed and perturbed by her lack of disgust. He looked at her with slimy eyes and decided to try a different tack. "Are you here alone?"

"My boyfriend is inside. I just wanted a moment's peace and quiet." Alice replied, futilely hoping he would go away. The man did not take the hint.

"Which coven does he belong to?"

"He's not a Witch," said Alice, grinning to herself. It

amused her to keep it a secret that the Vampire was her boyfriend. As the stranger's eyes suddenly took on a predatory glint, she realised that she needed to stop smiling so much when she thought of Robert; other men seemed to be completely misreading it. She did not know if that was down to stupidity or arrogance, but so few seemed to realise it was because she was in love with the guy she had just mentioned.

"I'm here with my girlfriend. She's not a Witch, but she *is* a super model and she wants to be an actress. There's already talk of them turning this book into a film, so she begged me to bring her. I know she'll make it up to me, so I used my father's invite to bring her here."

"Lucky her," said Alice, dryly. Unfortunately, the witch did not detect her sarcasm.

"She doesn't have to be the only one," he said, putting a hand on her leg and flashing her what he thought was an irresistible smile.

"Please, don't touch me," said Alice, jumping up at once. *Dammit, always with the politeness;* it did tend to mitigate a lot of the warning in her tone.

"Oh come on, I know you want me," said the male witch, trying to grab her arm.

"No, I really don't," said Alice, disgusted and beginning to get angry.

"Come on. I can be quick. It doesn't count when they're not even Witches."

"You are seriously damaging my calm," Alice said warningly, unwittingly backing into the wall. *Eejit,* she thought, cursing her stupidity as he pushed up against her. "You have about ten seconds to leave me alone before I give you reason to regret this."

"A little thing like you can't..." he started, pushing up against her and trying to lean in for a kiss.

Given that he was only an inch or two taller than her and certainly a good deal slimmer, he was clearly trying to belittle and insult her gender further.

Alice promptly kneed him in the groin as hard as she could. The man crumpled to the floor, curling up into a ball of pain. He swore and glared at her in disbelief.

"Yes, I can," said Alice matter-of-factly, rolling her eyes. "Just be glad it was me as opposed to my boyfriend. Although, all things considered, I might still be okay with him ripping your throat out."

She was about to storm back into the ballroom but suddenly caught the faintest of mutterings coming from his lips. "Trust me," she added, bending down so that he could see exactly what kind of Witch he was dealing with "you will regret it, if you continue trying to curse me. Because let me be quite clear, you will fail."

Something in her eyes made him stop his incantation, but he still shook his head and muttered that she was a bitch. She let that slide, although she decided she was at least going to press her foot threateningly against his testicles.

"And you might want to keep this quiet, unless you would like the embarrassment of being taken out by a "little girl", the very real likelihood of my boyfriend kicking your ass and a general blacklisting in social circles. Do we have an accord?"

He looked at her blankly, still doubled over on the ground.
Alice let out an exasperated breath and rolled her eyes. "Do you understand me?"

"Yes," the man muttered crossly.

"Enjoy the rest of your evening, and try not to grope anyone else, unless you'd like a repeat performance."

She muttered crossly to herself about the audacity and arrogance of some "men", not really paying attention as she went back into the ballroom. She walked straight into Damien Houseman.

Balls.

"I'm so sorry," she said, apologetically.

"Not a problem. Happens to us all. And to be quite

frank, I'm glad to have run into you, Alice," said Houseman, beamiously.

Alice smiled politely, whilst dying internally. "How charming of you to say so, Mr Houseman. Are you enjoying your book launch?"

"Please, you must call me Damien. And yes, it's quite something to be the centre of attention as a result of some words." The false modesty was ill-fitting.

"Words are important," Alice said, carefully. "You shouldn't be quite so dismissive of composing something that might have great meaning to someone else."

"I take it you are an admirer of the written word?" asked Houseman. "Do you find they have a great effect upon you?"

"Sometimes," she said, smiling. Even when she was uncomfortable with the person in front of her, it was hard to keep the brightness in talking of the things she loved from bubbling to the surface. "It all depends on context and composition and I guess, just the general connection one can get from reading or listening. Much like music, it can be evocative in a long-lasting way or a fleeting moment of escapism. Either way, the capacity to have an impact is there."

"Have you ever thought about writing yourself? You have quite the way with words."

Alice coloured slightly; she supposed deep down she still had secret desires of being an author, not that she would admit it to anyone other than Robert or Onion. "Not really. I've come to realise that words can be more powerful than I first realised, and consequently, they are perhaps better off in someone else's hands."

"How delightfully enigmatic you are," said Houseman, looking at her curiously. "I'm almost afraid to ask what your thoughts on my book are."

"I must confess that I have yet to read it," said Alice, apologetically, trying to look him in the eye as she said it.

His reaction surprised her, not that there was any big emotion there. It was just that Alice could have sworn that there had been something strange in his eyes; like there was momentarily another person who expressed relief and the dominant personality who looked briefly enraged. She was not sure if it would even have counted as a micro-expression, but she would have sworn both emotions were there. She suddenly wished Sam was there.

"That would be my fault," said Robert, appearing at her elbow. "I meant to bring a copy home but kept forgetting." He could feel Alice's relief.

"Well, I will have to make sure you do not leave without a signed copy this evening," Houseman said, with a smile that did not reach his eyes.

"Thank you," said Alice, as warmly as she could muster. She put her arm through Robert's and put her other hand on his arm. She was trying harder than normal to hide her true thoughts and emotions, but she felt as if her resolve was failing. At least as far as onlookers were concerned, it seemed to be working, and should her shield slip, there was always the sure-fire fallback of catering to ego. "I'm sure I'll thoroughly enjoy it. I hear it's already poised for the top of the bestsellers list."

"We shall see, we shall see," said Houseman. "Perhaps you would join me for a drink on the balcony?" He grabbed two glasses of the red wine and passed one to Alice.

Alice did not particularly want any more wine, especially as she felt like her evening was currently in a tarnished state, but it seemed far too impolite for her to refuse. She murmured her thanks and took a small sip as she desperately thought of a plausible excuse to not be alone with Houseman.

"Ah, unfortunately the reason I had to come over, was to politely steal my girlfriend away from you, as Peter wants to introduce Alice to his wife. Apparently, Rose has been liaising with Mrs. Jenkins regarding the historical New York display that they're putting on at the NY Library."

"Has she really?" asked Alice, feeling some genuine

relief at the excuse to move on and to perhaps have a conversation that she might actually feel she could contribute to. "We got all the stands in for that last week. Lots of shifting things around, digging out old letters and coins and photographs, it's quite interesting."

Houseman smiled politely although something about his gaze suggested that he did not share in Alice's view. "Later, then. Or maybe we'll get a chance at dinner," Houseman said magnanimously, with a smile that did not reach his eyes.

"Of course," said Alice, feigning hopefulness. She smiled at Houseman as Robert led her towards his immediate boss, Peter Caffrey, and his wife, Rose.

"Thank you," she whispered.

"I've heard talk that you've been beating people up on the balcony," he teased quietly.

"Liar," she said in an equally hushed tone. She smiled at him. "You heard *me* deal with unwanted attention, which is not entirely the same thing."

"Sure you don't want me to use fisticuffs upon that witch?"

His words made her smile brighten and for what seemed liked the millionth time, she thanked the gods for him. "It's tempting, but no. I think it's handled, and if it's not, I want to punch him myself for suggesting that you are a 'lesser being'."

Robert shrugged, too used to the attitude to get upset by it. "That's most Witches for you. As long as you know I'd have been there the second it seemed like you couldn't or didn't feel comfortable handling it."

"I know," she said, kissing him quickly. "Somewhat unrelated, there's snakeroot and hemlock on the balcony. Don't people know they're poisonous?"

"I think they're probably just here for tonight, because someone probably used the plants in the book. It's just one more way in which they're trying to emulate the whole macabre, *Exorcist, Rosemary's Baby,* evil and opulence theme."

"Mr Houseman seemed quite, actually, I don't quite

know how to explain it..." She cut her sentence short as the elegant couple that were maybe ten years more senior than them, turned to face them.

"Ah, so this is the charming young new librarian I've been hearing so much," said Rose Caffrey brightly, her blue eyes sparkling as she clasped Alice's hand.

"Pleasure to meet you," Alice said, politely.

The Caffreys were extremely pleasant and much more down-to-earth than Alice was expecting, and she and Rose ended up having quite a good conversation about the upcoming library display.

"You never mentioned whether they were using your photographs or not," Robert said, suddenly.

"Oh?" queried Rose, looking at Alice expectantly.

"Oh," echoed Alice, with surprise. "Er, yes, they are. Quite a few actually. Mostly blown-up for the back-drops. Traffic jams, the Statue of Liberty, the usual suspects for shots although using my photographs is cheaper than buying access to stock images and the like. Some of the photos are smaller and framed to go alongside old photographs that had been found within the library, which kinda shows you not only the evolution of the city but the quality of camera imagery too."

"We have quite the display to go up," said Rose, proudly. "I've already told Peter he has to visit, assuming we can't convince Stuart to have a little charity gala or fund-raising evening for its opening. Of course, it would be nothing on this scale, but I'm sure the library could use the money. In fact, I'm amazed it's still open and running."

Alice and Robert exchanged a secret smile as they both assumed magic had a lot to do with it.

"Oh, darling, perhaps you could get one of your New York based authors to do a reading, maybe auction off having them creating a character, alongside other donations. Is that Nikki Heat man still doing those?" asked Rose, not waiting for her husband's response as she turned to Alice, her blue eyes sparkling with enthusiasm. "I have a friend who could donate some gorgeous flowers and Charlie Mills at the marina owes me a favour. We could get a celebrity to do a horse-drawn carriage through the park. Oh, this is wonderful. You will have to help me to convince Stuart that this is a wonderful idea."

Alice smiled. "I don't think Dr Anthonys would mind too much. It's all the books that are the problem."

Rose and Peter laughed.

"Oh, oh. You didn't happen to take that series of photographs of the frozen statues in Central Park, did you?" Rose asked, suddenly.

Alice nodded.

"Oh, how wonderful. I love those. I wonder, if perhaps you would meet me for lunch and we could discuss me buying a set from you? And we would definitely have to put some of your photographs in the auction."

"I'd be happy to get a set printed for you," said Alice, surprised and slightly embarrassed.

"No, no," interrupted Peter. "From what I hear, you have quite the eye and you should do this properly. Never turn down the chance to get paid for something you did well."

"Well, it would be a pleasure to meet up with you again," Alice said finally, still feeling very flustered.

"I have to be in the library on Wednesday afternoon. Perhaps we could meet for lunch beforehand?"

"Er, yes, of course, that should be doable," Alice replied, looking at Robert before answering Rose, suddenly feeling very overwhelmed in a weirdly positive manner.

Robert smiled and squeezed her arm reassuringly and proudly.

The first bell rang for dinner, and they quickly exchanged details before politely parting ways to rejoin the people they were most likely to be seated with at the dining table.

Chapter 37

Partly at Christopher's insistence and partly because she wanted to talk to Robert, Alice held back a moment from entering the dining room with the rest of the group. There would be at least two more bells before the doors closed in any case.

"What?" asked Alice, smiling nervously as Robert beamed at her.

"I'm just proud of and pleased for you. I think it'll be great for you to work with Rose on a fundraiser for the Library and it's brilliant news about your photographs. I kinda wish you'd told me about that before though. I'd have taken you out to celebrate, or at least swung by Mario's and that fancy chocolate shop you like so much."

Alice shrugged apologetically. "I genuinely hadn't thought about it, and I guess it didn't really seem like a big deal."

"It's brilliant and you should feel proud of it. As it says in one of your favourite books 'All your life, other people will try to take your accomplishments away from you. Don't you take it away from yourself.'"

"Yeah, I guess," said Alice, smiling uncertainly.

A second bell rang, and Alice shot a nervous look towards the dining room, hoping that no one had discovered the seating changes and switched them back.

"Why was someone separated and straight-razored?" Alice asked, suddenly.

Robert's brow furrowed and his head tilted slightly as he

tried to recall the relevant scene in the book. "Er, if I remember correctly, it was because they needed a body as a host for a demonic force. Or maybe they were just a nuisance, or it got a bit rape-y and murder-y. One of those. It wasn't something in the original, so it could be in this book or some other horror novel, because I swear to you, this new version is so generic I can not distinguish it from anything else."

"Fun," she said, drily.

"I'm sure no one wants to straight-razor you," Robert said, looking at her curiously. "Well, maybe the witch you beat up."

Alice laughed. "I kneed him in the balls; it's hardly "beating up"."

"I don't know, sounds like you were pretty harsh," he teased.

"Well, he shouldn't have been such a jackass then," Alice replied, sticking her tongue out briefly at him, and shaking her head in mock disbelief. "Nor should he have insulted the man I love."

Robert smiled and kissed her, but the shadow had already fallen back into her eyes. There were a few stragglers, but mostly the ballroom was clear apart from a few waiters, musicians and photographers. "Want to dance?"

"I can probably handle swaying," Alice replied, putting her left hand on his shoulder and allowing him to take hold of her right in his. If she had not happened to catch a glimpse of Houseman and Toxic blonde out of the corner of her eye, she might have been convinced to try and have a 'Once Upon a Dream' moment, but it was not to be. "No, I'm sure no one wants to kill me," said Alice simply. "But someone did want me separated from you; was just wondering if the book might shed some light as to why."

"Are you sure it's not just Houseman being creepily, but understandably, enamoured with you and wanting to steal you away?"

"No one could steal me away from you. Even if they

kidnapped me, I'd still be yours."

"I'm just teasing," Robert said, suddenly worried by the seriousness of her tone.

"I know. I know. I... It's just that... I don't know, I don't. There's just so much that is off about all this."

"I know. Like we agreed before, we'll try and leave as soon as possible after dinner." He tried to squeeze her hand reassuringly. In all honesty, he wanted to grab her and run, but like Alice, he had no definite reason why, and given the number of people there that considered this night to be at least partly of his making, it meant he would need a phenomenal excuse to leave before the meal. Given the theme, it was likely to be top-shelf quality catering as well and it had been quite some time since Robert had last had that kind of meal. The third dinner bell rang.

"Oh, one more thing before we go in there. Am I being dense again, somehow?" asked Alice, quietly.

"You mean Christopher?" he asked, with a crooked smile.
She nodded.

"No, you're not. He's definitely gay." Robert chuckled as she punched him in the arm. "No, he's not supernatural. He just sees people for what they really are. He works in child services, so he's become quite adept at spotting monsters."

"Ah," she said, looking slightly sad as they walked into the dining room. She looked down the table and spotted the supermodel and her unfortunate choice of a man. Alice gave a little wave at him before pointedly kissing Robert and refrained from laughing out loud as her action suddenly elicited several small frowns of disgust from other nearby individuals. That seemed to be a good way to tell other Witches apart from the rest of the crowd, particularly if she could not tell otherwise. Then, she looked at Christopher carefully.

"He's just told you about my job, hasn't he," said Christopher, as they joined him standing behind their allocated chairs. "All the good souls get that expression when they first hear. And since this is supposed to be a party, of sorts," he said, as everyone sat down "I will give you the basic run-down, which is yes, it's tough; yes, there are times when I want to beat the shit out of some of the parents and/or abusers; yes, it often breaks my heart. But, it's rewarding and you sometimes get lucky enough to really change some lives, and I can sleep at night with a clear conscience knowing that I'm doing my bit."

"They're lucky to have you in their corner," Alice said, kissing him lightly on the cheek.

Christopher coloured slightly. He was not quite sure why the innocent gesture and admiration from this relative stranger made him feel so touched.

"I honestly don't think I've ever seen him embarrassed before," said Jeff, bemused.

"Me neither," said Bruce, staring across at the slow burning blush creeping across his husband's cheeks. "I didn't think it was even possible for him to get embarrassed. The man has no shame."

"You can talk. It's not embarrassment. I'm just touched that my little sister would think so highly of me," Christopher said. "Why couldn't you have just told her that I tried my best to hit on you the first time we met?" he asked, looking at Robert.

Bruce pretended to look shocked. "How could you?!"

Christopher grinned and blew him a kiss across the table. "Like you didn't." He knew very well that Bruce had at least thought about it.

"You didn't?" said Susan, not quite believing that they could have thought Robert was gay.

"Of course I did. Look at those shoulders and the impeccable style. Of course, I tried to get my finely manicured claws into this big piece of yum."

Alice burst out laughing, and repeated the phrase quietly, trying to commit it to memory. *'Big piece of yum'? Priceless* she thought, still giggling.

"You do realise that I am going to be teased mercilessly for that description, probably for the rest of my life," said Robert, giving Christopher a look that suggested Christopher had committed a grave betrayal.

"More than I would have thought, it would seem," replied Christopher, catching sight of the mischievous glint in Alice's eye, as she continued to smirk.

"She's not as nice as she looks you know – she's a bona fide terror."

"Yes, but you love me anyway," she said.

"Only because you're super hot. I'm kidding. To a degree," said Robert. "You are super hot though."

"Many a gay man has tried their luck with our Robert here," said Bruce. "As well as many a lady…"

"…or skank," finished Susan, catching sight of the woman they were now, by unspoken agreement, referring to as toxic blonde, who was indeed sat opposite to where Alice was supposed to have been.

"And none have succeeded, until the fair Alice captured his heart," concluded Christopher.

"Don't worry, it doesn't happen any more," said Robert, just in case Alice was beginning to feel insecure, and his work-friends laughed.

"Oh yes it does," said Bruce, greatly amused by Robert's obliviousness. "There were at least three people in the past week."

"What? No there wasn't," said Robert. "There definitely wasn't," he assured Alice.

"There was," said Jeff. "Even *I* noticed. There was the waiter at lunch yesterday, and the UPS woman, and some blonde in the coffee shop."

"Not to mention toxic blonde has continually been trying to catch your eye for the last ten months or whatever it is," Patrick chimed in.

Robert looked at them in disbelief, but they all nodded, their faces open with honesty. "Really?" he asked, genuinely surprised.

"Really," said Bruce, with a laugh. "Just goes to show you that true love is blind or at least makes you oblivious. And, in all fairness, I'm sure there's more than a few men that have still tried to hit on Alice, despite her clear adoration for you."

"I wouldn't go that far," Alice said, smiling at Robert with shining eyes. "He's tolerable I guess."

"I do love this girl," said Christopher, bringing her in for a hug. "Look, even with me he's bristling."

"I am not," said Robert, rolling his eyes. "I'm hardly going to feel jealous of her gay, much older brother."

Alice felt like she could practically hear them all going 'aww' at the pair of them. She squeezed Robert's hand. "Please excuse me," she said to the group. "Back in a minute."

She got up from the table and went to ask Albert for directions to the bathrooms, whilst also wanting to thank him again. She hoped that if she gave Robert a minute's space, they might stop teasing him and move onto other topics by the time she got back. She caught Houseman's eye as she passed, and gave him a polite nod and smile, trying to quell the sense of unease that he evoked in her.

Chapter 38

Damien Houseman was actually relieved that Alice was seated several seats away from his body, however the Demon occupying his body was incredibly annoyed. The evening had been meticulously planned in order to isolate the Witch and bring her powers to him, and thus far, he had been thwarted by seemingly innocent coincidences.

Lord Sargeraxs had had many different names throughout the millennia, although this was the one that he felt sounded best. He did detest having to place himself inside a pathetic meat sack, but unfortunately, he had no other choice. As long as the Veil remained as it was, his true form could not exist in the mortal realm.

The majority of mortals had long forgotten the words of ancient prophecies and had largely fallen out of favour with the few that remembered, however such predictions were always of interest to the creatures beyond the Veil. The prophecy of the Witch and the Vampire had always been of interest to Sargeraxs, not least because it spoke of his escape. He had waited patiently for the Witch to rise, wondering if it was just another false divination, as the millennia crawled past and the divide between Witches and Vampires grew. Still, he watched the Witches, taking special interest in the strongest bloodlines and the direct descendants of the First Witches, and kept his minions adapting to the ever-changing landscape of the human world.

He had made contact with several Witches, all of whom had ultimately proved worthless beyond that of his own amusement, and it was not until the last quarter of the so-called twentieth century, had a new birth truly piqued his interest. Unfortunately, he was not the only one to have noticed, and many of his attempts to entice the child had ended in failure. Then, she had suddenly disappeared from view until her thirtieth birthday suddenly propelled her onto the magical stage without her knowledge.

Given how quiet the supernatural world and his minions had been, he presumed that the Witch had been unaware that energy had been gathering around her, drawn to the powerful reservoir of magic that had been largely untouched. He had sent his most loyal assassin, Lady Jane, to spy on her, an assignment he knew that the half-demon resented, especially when for nearly four years, the task had been greatly underwhelming. The past twelve months had proven to be most interesting. Several members of the Fallen had come out of hiding; the Library had opened its doors to her, helping her to unlock the powers within; and a Vampire had taken to courting her.

He ordered Lady Jane to find him a suitable vessel – one that might be primed to make contact with the key to his infernal prison – and promptly took over the body of Damien Houseman, keeping the consciousness of the author locked within, partly for necessity, but mostly for amusement. There was almost nothing better than inflicting pain on a mortal's loved ones, when they were powerless to stop it.

He had orchestrated the book launch, ensuring that greedy publishers would be more than willing to upgrade the event after garnering such immense media interest upon Lady Jane's slaughter of the family. It had been both a marketing ploy and a way to appease his prized pet's frustrations, as well as disposing of certain annoyances. Houseman had struggled violently to try and save his family; now he was broken in a corner of his own mind, tethered where Sargeraxs had imprisoned him. It had also put an end to the tediousness of being the "family man", freeing him to indulge in his own appetites without having to concern himself of the potential repercussions and affecting his plan to entrap the Witch.

He had worried that the Witch would ultimately prove not to be worth the trouble, especially as attempts to meet her sooner had failed; upon seeing her, he had no doubts. She was exquisite; her power was unequalled. The last Witch to have any significant power had sought out the Severed Hand, several centuries ago. That Witch had not been strong enough on his own accord to manipulate the Veil, thus the added powers from the Severed Hand were bestowed merely for their own amusement. But Alice had a natural power that was stunning, and even more impressively, it was still growing. It was indeed the sort of power that prophecies spoke of; the kind of power that could bend and snap the Veil and let those beyond into the earthly realm.

It was therefore unfortunate and disappointing to Sargeraxs that she appeared to be drawn to the Light. However, she was a Witch, and that meant there was always the potential to corrupt her and make her even stronger. Few Witches had ever really tried to resist Lord Sargeraxs' promises of power and extravagance; but they, along with many other more willing subjects, had succumbed in the end. Despite being "good" and "in love", and possibly even protected (none of his minions dared get too close to the Library to find out for sure), Sargeraxs was confident that Alice would ultimately prove to be like any other Witch.

Alice's appearance, her admiration of the house and her wine knowledge showed that she at least had one trait in common with her fellow Witches; she had a taste for the finer things the mortal realm could offer and that was something he could certainly cater to. Indeed, he had tried to plan it so that there were several bread crumbs to help Alice find her way to him, only they had been innocuously swept up before reaching his intended target.

First of all, there had been the book. There had never been any guarantee that she would read the book prior to the launch, but he had been reasonably convinced Robert would have given her a copy. It was unfortunate that *The Devil Possesses* had not reached her, since it been rewritten to show all that Alice could have if she chose to join him and all she would lose if she was foolish enough to resist. Whilst the book alone would never have brought the Witch to him – not if she was as powerful as it was rumoured – he had hoped that the seeds of darkness would have at least been sown, seeds that should have ensured that Alice would not mind being separated from Robert when it came to dinner.

Unfortunately, the second annoyance was that someone had altered his carefully laid out dining plan. He had assumed no one would have noticed that Alice was placed at the top of the table instead of with her beau, until everyone was seated. At that point, either dark desires or politeness would have ensured that Alice was seated beside him, giving him ample opportunity to spark further growth, or maybe even bring her darkness to full fruition.

The obvious devotion between the Witch and the Vampire as they had entered the ballroom had been a surprise. Like the supernatural community at large, Sargeraxs had expected their relationship to be, at best, a fling. The Witches certainly believed it was a one-sided affair; that the Vampire was in love, most likely drawn to her powers, whilst the Witch was stringing him along for the sexual benefits of his increased strength and stamina. It was hard to believe that any Witch could ever consider a Vampire as an equal, let alone a Witch of Alice's potential magnitude, but it appeared that in this respect, Alice greatly differed from her peers.

Her feelings for the Vampire were so unexpectedly strong, that he had momentarily believed she must have been under the Vampire's mesmerism. A second look clearly showed that Alice's powers were far too great, and it tempered his annoyance regarding the book; such hypnotisms were like parlour tricks and would have little to no effect upon her. It served as a reminder that this was a delicate operation that needed to be treated with a great deal of skill; it might be more of a challenge than he had originally thought, but he was confident of his inevitable victory. And to crush such affection so completely would be all the more satisfying.

However, since he could hardly whisper in her ear whilst she was at the opposite end of the table, he angrily dismissed the notion that Alice would be his before the end of the night. The additional complication of being unable to engage her in conversation for more than a few minutes at a time also made it difficult to administer his particular poisons in her ear. If he was not being interrupted by some grovelling insect heaping praises upon his narcissistic prose; it was the annoying persistence with which her friends and lover would provide her with a reason to move on.

He leant over and spoke quietly to the blonde seated at his side.

"Is the conjuring prepared? It seems that we will require its services after all," he murmured.

"It is ready my lord. All it needs is the marker."

"Good. Ensure that she gets the correct food, and put another Barolo in the car," he snapped, his temper fraying momentarily as he caught sight of the Witch kissing the Vampire.

"Of course, my lord."

He watched as Jane confidently headed towards the kitchens, knowing that his assistant would not fail. He felt the twitching of his human body, and decided that perhaps he should "reward" his pet for her patience. He knew that she wanted to be out maiming and killing for the cause, but he did not wish to underestimate the Witch by putting anyone other than his best soldier on the line. He watched as Alice left the table and looked a bit longer than necessary after catching Jane out of the corner of his eye. Jane was, after all, so much more fun when riled up. He just hope she was professional enough not to stab the Witch whilst in the rest-rooms.

***

The Toxic Blonde had been born with the name, Jane Wrexham, although as time had passed, she was more commonly known as Lady Jane. Despite her petite and demure appearance, she was ruthless, narcissistic and cruel, all qualities that served to make her the Severed Hand's top assassin. For several months now, she had been tasked solely with following the Vampire and the Witch. In the beginning, she had not known why they were of interest to the Severed Hand, and she certainly did not understand why a soldier of her calibre was being tasked with such a menial assignment. But her loyalty was unwavering, and if the Severed Hand said 'jump', she did; as high as she could. As she had continued to watch them, she had seen the Witch's powers grow and began to realise the importance of her task, although it remained boring and nauseating.

Part demon and part human, Lady Jane was able to step with relative ease through the Veil, a gift few possessed and even fewer used. She embraced the Darkness and the added powers it would bestow upon her, relishing in her unrestricted sins. As long as it did not interfere with the Severed Hand's plans, she was free to do as she wished, unfettered by conscience, morals or rules. In fact, the sins she committed were often met with praise and reward from her Dark Lords, who basked in the death, misery and despair she would leave in her wake and she saw no reason to regret her indulgences or argue against her masters' wishes. However, there were times when she felt irritated when it seemed that her talents were going to waste and being unappreciated. She liked to be admired, would bask in the carnal desire she could arouse in male and female creatures, taking a special source of pride from wrecking relationships by fucking men (or women) and discarding them without further thought.

Although she smiled and acted her part accordingly,

beneath her calm and demure mask, Lady Jane was seething. She did not normally feel anything towards earthly creatures – at best, they would serve their purposes and then she would dispose of them appropriately – but she had come to hate the Witch. She was jealous of Alice's natural power and the ease with which she had garnered the attention of her master, Lord Sargeraxs. Lady Jane had worked hard to get herself noticed by the elite in the ranks of the Severed Hand and had worked even harder to stay there. Thus, it infuriated her that such an unremarkable human Witch could have such appeal. Of course she knew in part, her masters were infatuated by their desire to destroy something beautiful; that they sought to seduce, corrupt and poison in order to prove to the world that there was no such thing as Good. It was a source of egotistical pride, particularly with unwilling female Witches that were supposedly in love, to take those Witches and destroy them.

And not only did the Witch bore and infuriate her with her determination to be "good", the fact that the Vampire ignored her presence, made her want to scream. Lady Jane did not want the Vampire as such, but she despised being ignored when she was making the effort to entrap someone. No one had ever resisted Lady Jane when she wanted them. But Robert Evans had never given her a second-glance and all in favour of that plain, nerdy, brunette Witch who was only moderately of value because of the immense power she was squandering. A Witch who could have been dark and deadly; inspiring devotion and terror; a beautiful, destructive goddess with demon overlords bending over to fulfil her every whim, because she would have power absolute over the Veil… instead she remained pathetic and ordinary, living in a little apartment with a Vampire and a cat.

Even now, when so many others were undressing her with their eyes, the Vampire had barely looked at her. Clearly she had come up in conversation, as she had caught them looking in her direction, but beyond that, nothing. She was also frustratingly aware that the only reason all the other men in the room continued to steal glances at her, was because they could at least imagine they had a chance; it was quite obvious that they did not have one with Alice.

Lady Jane tried to calm herself; one did not become the best assassin on either side of the Veil by giving into foolish emotions. She let out a deep breath, fixed an interested smile on her face, and continued the charade of a literary groupie and public liaison from Achronos's sixth floor.

She took her seat beside "Damien Houseman", and tried to hide the look of surprise as a portly gentleman in some political office took the seat opposite her. Lady Jane had not been relishing a night of playing nice with the Witch, however, it was necessary for the plan. There was the possibility that a dark Alice would prove to be a worthy mistress or at least a playmate, but unlike Sargeraxs, she was not convinced that Alice could be tempted. Persuasive though he was, Lady Jane was better at reading peoples' true natures, and she knew Alice was not naturally inclined to be evil. Alice also believed in her love for Robert, and although it would prove to be her undoing, it would initially give her a reason to fight.

In truth, Lady Jane was secretly pleased about that. She did not want to share her position of being the desired female in her dark society, nor did she want to bow to the greater powers of Alice Andrews, if she would willing control the Veil for the Severed Hand. Lady Jane wanted to see Alice Andrews stripped of her powers and destroyed, and she wanted to relish every second of pain and desperation. She wanted Alice broken, bleeding and reeling in the darkest depths of despair, and then she would strip the last vigil of Alice's hope by fucking Robert Evans right in front of her, before cutting out her heart.

Lady Jane could tell that her lord was displeased that yet another element of his plan had gone awry, but there was no way in which they could have foreseen someone switching Alice's seating placement. There were moments, such as this, when Lady Jane felt that Sargeraxs allowed the unfamiliarity of being inside a human vessel to make him reckless. This was also one of the rare occasions when she did not mind – she would much rather they tried to trap and destroy the Witch, than endure another night like this. Sargeraxs' preferred method was seduction and he was used to it working quickly; Lady Jane knew that if he was to seduce the Witch, it would take many more nights like these.

"Is the conjuring prepared? It seems that it will be necessary after all," Sargeraxs said in a low voice of barely contained anger, leaning in towards her.

"It is ready my lord," she replied, aroused by the rage and desire in his eyes. "All it needs is the marker."

"Good. Ensure that she gets the correct food, and put another Barolo in the car," her lord and master snapped.

"Of course my lord," she replied quietly, using her head to execute a small bow, before rising from the table.

Lady Jane called down to the driver to ensure that there was another bottle of wine, chocolates and a copy of the book in the car for when Alice and Robert left, and ensured that one of their followers was in charge of plating and delivering Alice's food. As she was about to return to her seat at the right-hand side of Lord Sargeraxs, she noticed Alice making her way to the restrooms, and followed at suitable distance, trying to ignore the ridiculous stab of jealousy as she caught him watching the Witch.

Lady Jane entered the bathroom after hearing the click of the stall lock and stood in front of the mirror, admiring herself. She waited for the flush, and then sprayed her perfume onto Alice as the cubicle door opened. The Witch coughed in surprise and tried to hide her annoyance, her face screwing up in slight disgust as she clearly did not like the scent. Lady Jane caught the merest glimpse of a challenge in Alice's eyes, the kind of look that suggest if you attacked what she loved, Alice was more than willing to tear your fucking throat out. But it was gone in an instant replaced by the strange programming that was so very particular to English people.

"Sorry," Lady Jane said. "It used to come in a differently shaped bottle, so now I always make such a mess with this thing."

"It's fine," said Alice, shrugging and shaking her head slightly, with a look that suggested that it was not fine at all.

The English were a curious nationality in that they seemed to detest the notion of being impolite, quite often apologising when the blame was squarely on the other individual; on one occasion, Lady Jane had seen an Englishman apologise to a lamp-post after walking into it.

She waited until Alice had left, reapplied her make-up, shifted her dress slightly and returned to the dining hall.

"It's done, my lord" she said quietly to Sargeraxs, whilst sliding provocatively back into her seat. She was well aware of the effect that needlessly thrusting her chest out was having on several male diners. The corners of her mouth curled wickedly. "She doesn't suspect a thing."

"Very good. I expect to see you in my chambers when this ridiculous evening is done with."

"As you wish, my lord," Lady Jane replied, practically purring with anticipation, desire and self-satisfaction. It was not entirely without its rewards for Lord Sargeraxs to give into the desires of the flesh. Lady Jane smiled; not only would she be rewarded with a long overdue satisfaction of her own urges, but if all went according to Lord Sargeraxs' plan, the day of Alice's downfall would be tomorrow.

Chapter 39

As the dinner progressed, Robert was sure that they would not need to find an excuse to leave early, since Alice was looking somewhat green. She was beginning to blink and squint like she did when she was drunk, but she was not laughing or going off on rapid tangents as was the norm. To be honest, Robert was surprised that she had not become drunk, considering someone always seemed to be pressing another glass of wine into her hands, but she had kept herself on the cusp of intoxication, that little ledge where she was tipsy, but not saying she was drunk every two minutes. He thought she seemed subdued and he wondered if it was the depression, not liking the food or something more sinister. Although nothing had been overtly out of the ordinary or sinister, he had still been unable to shake the sense of unease that seemed to be following him when it came to *The Devil Possesses* and everything associated with it. He took her hand from her lap and held it tight, eliciting a small smile from her.

They had reached the end of the meal, with only coffee and brandy to follow. Alice was not sure what was wrong, especially as she had barely touched her food. A seven-course menu seemed excessive, and although there were bits of it that were truly delicious (such as the sea scallops with cedar reduction, and the pork done three ways), it was too much for her – she liked simple foods, like sandwiches or bean-sprout chow mien or a tomato gosht and boiled rice. Not sturgeon mousse with rhubarb and black truffle cream, and venison with fois gras and a bed of wheatberry risotto. To be honest, she thought maybe there was something wrong with the food, other than its decadence and the meat being undercooked in her eyes, but she could not say what. *They did have poison on the balcony* she reminded herself. She had to admit that she was becoming increasingly paranoid about the evening and even though it might have all been in her head, she could not stop the panic rising in her chest.

"I think I need some air," Alice whispered, looking at Robert with big and frightened eyes. She could feel something was wrong on an unearthly level, but could not say so in their present company. Her head was beginning to hurt and she supposed it was down to drinking too much, since no one else seemed to be experiencing any ill-effects. She took a sip of water, thinking it tasted slightly acrid.

"We're going home," he said quietly.

She could feel the same tense anger that he had tried to hide that day at the park. "Are you sure?" she asked, almost ready to cry with relief.

"Yes. Neither of us really wanted to be here, we tried to make the best of it, but if you're feeling bad now, we're going home."

"That would be even better." She stood up slowly and felt her vision blacken like she was about to faint. She squeezed her eyes shut for a moment, holding onto Robert's shoulder. When she was sure she would not faint, she moved her hands to the back of his chair as he stood up. She knew she should probably sit back down again, but she was worried that she would not get back up again.

"Are you okay?" Christopher asked. He had been asking on and off for the duration of the meal, partly because he knew about Alice's depression (he had noticed her tapping her fingers and the deliberate breathing) and partly because Alice had not been looking particularly well since they had started eating.

"You look like you want to throw up," Susan said, sympathetically. "Do you think it could be food poisoning?"

She and Sally looked at the remnants of their Death by Chocolate and the accompanying gold, flecked vanilla cream as if food poisoning was contagious or late-acting.

"Maybe. Probably not though." Alice reassured them, them with a weak smile. "I... I, er, wasn't feeling that great when we left the apartment. I guess it's getting to me now. Probably just a bad, summer cold." It felt like the smells were trying to suffocate her, like an entity trying to snake down her throat. It made her think of *The Little Mermaid,* when Ursula took Ariel's voice.

"Sorry guys, but I'm gonna get her home," Robert said firmly, his unusually stern countenance brokering no argument.

"Is she allergic to anything?" asked Christopher, worried.

"I don't know, to be honest. It's never come up. Besides, if you've never had a thing before, how would you know you were allergic to it?" Robert said, logically. All the dishes had been far beyond the means of the small mid-table group, given that most of the plates would have fetched in excess of a few hundred dollars each. "I'm just going to let Damien know we're leaving."

"Alright," Christopher said. He put his hand at the small of Alice's back, steadying her as Robert went over to talk to the guest of honour.

Even if she was ill, Alice would not forgive him if he was not at least polite about their departure. *Manners maketh man, after all,* Robert thought dryly.

"Excuse me for interrupting," Robert said, giving a cursory glance to the dinner guests that Houseman was in conversation with. "Our apologies, Damien, but Alice and I need to leave; she's feeling extremely unwell."

"Do you know what's wrong?" Houseman asked, looking down to where Alice seemed to be holding the chair for dear life. He hid the traces of a smile, behind a pondering finger.

"We think maybe she's having an allergic reaction to something she ate."

"I'm so sorry," the host said immediately, a look of supposed distress at the thought that he might have somehow been the cause. "Of course, dear boy, you must take care of your good lady. We have some rooms upstairs if you think she might recover after a lie down?"

"We appreciate the offer," said Robert, not even contemplating it "but I think we'd best get home."

"Of course. There will be a car waiting for you downstairs."

"Thank you," Robert was too busy glancing down at Alice to notice the look that passed between Houseman and the blonde. "I hope you enjoy the rest of the evening and good luck with the book. Good evening," he said, smiling tightly at the author.

***

Robert said good-bye to his team and reassured them that he would let them know when they got home. They all looked at Alice in concern, wishing her a speedy recovery; hoping that whatever it was, it would not be too bad. Alice smiled faintly and nodded, not trusting herself to speak, afraid of what might happen if she opened her mouth for some reason. She was not afraid of vomiting; more that she would say something that could not be undone, and the fact that her thoughts seemed to make no sense to her made her feel even worse. Then Robert all but swept her up into his arms and they exited the party.

Robert carried Alice to the front door and then forced her to stand up, so that he could look at her eyes. They seemed to be better than they had been a few minutes earlier, but there was still fear in them.

"What's wrong?" he asked softly, as they waited for the car to be brought around.

"I don't know. It's like being drunk in a bad way. How

I'd imagine a bad trip would feel like," she said in a whisper. "I don't know what it is, but I don't like it and I don't want to stay here. I feel a bit better now, being outside."

"You do look it, I guess." There was more colour in her cheeks, her eyes looked slightly less glazed and she managed to walk over to the car in a reasonably steady fashion.

They climbed into the back of the luxury sedan, noticing the bottle of wine, glasses and chocolates.

"Thank you," Alice said to the driver. "I'm not feeling so well, so I'm going to put the screen up. I don't want you to see that."

"Quite alright, madam," said the well-groomed, suited driver, looking at her via the rear-view mirror.

"Thanks," she said with a weak smile, pressing the button that brought up the black partition window, hiding them from the view of the man in the black hat.

Robert opened the window and Alice stuck her head out into the cool night air for a moment, breathing deeply. He noticed goosebumps forming on her exposed skin and gently pulled her back before closing it again.

She reached over and poured some wine.

"I'm not sure you should be having any more wine if you think you might be sick," he said, taking one of the glasses from her.

"I don't feel so bad now," she said, with a small half-smile. "I don't understand it," she continued, with a shrug. "Maybe it was just the heat and the overly rich food and that sense of evil I felt when I went near Houseman and that blonde woman, because I feel almost okay again. Besides, we're going home now, which means you don't have to think about *The Devil Possesses* ever again. Which is why we should have a celebratory drink while we still have access to the good stuff." Alice felt him looking at her and she smiled reassuringly.

He frowned but could not deny that she was looking a lot better than she had. Her cheeks were flushed and there were faint shadows under her eyes, but her pupils seemed brighter and more alert. Perhaps there had been something wrong with the house and that the increasing distance between them and it, meant that whatever was trying to take sway of her was now out of reach. "Sometimes, you're very hard to argue with," he said, mirroring her actions by drinking, unable to stop watching her without incredible scrutiny.

"It's one of many talents," she said, smiling suggestively. She lifted her skirt so that his hands could roam if they wished and sat astride him. "And I feel I deserve to have some fun with the sexiest man I have seen all night," she said, kissing his face and neck delicately. "I'm quite sure you deserve it too."

"That certainly doesn't sound so bad," he said carefully, searching her eyes before kissing her hungrily. She loosened his tie and undid his top button. He still felt hesitant, but it was hard to resist when she was kissing him like that, and was sliding his hands up so that his fingers brushed against warm skin and cool nylon. Much as he was being turned on, he could not help freezing slightly when she undid his trousers. "Alice..."

"Why not?" she said, pulling on his earlobe with her teeth. She began stroking his cock with firm and confident strokes. "Doesn't it feel good?"

He gasped as she lightly grazed the tip with her fingernails. "Of course, but..."

"Then just let me do this," she interrupted, looking deep into his eyes for a moment. "Please? I swear, I know what I'm doing, and I want to do this." Something in her eyes was desperately begging him to do as she requested and concerned though he was, he could not say no. "Please? Promise me you'll do as I ask," she whispered.

He closed his eyes for a moment and hoped that he was not going to regret his decision. He looked deep into her eyes, ensuring that she was definitely aware. She nodded slightly.

"I promise," he said, and he saw a flicker of relief flash in her eyes. He began to kiss her back, kissing the curve of her neck and caressing her breasts as best he could through the gold bodice of her dress. He undid the zip and pulled it down just enough to expose the upper half of her breasts, and she moaned in pleasure. The stroking stopped and a moment later she seemed to impale herself upon his willing cock, crying out with an almost heart-breaking sound that he had not heard before.

"Bite me," she begged.

Again, Robert could not prevent the momentary freeze, but he had made a promise to her and he would keep it. He kissed her lips and breasts again before plunging his fangs into her throat, and the same cry fell from her lips as she continued to ride him.

For a moment, he drank deeply, licking at the droplets of blood that escaped from his kiss. He tasted it as expertly as he could, finding only her sweet coppery blood infused with the rich Barolo. He was surprised at how the wine seemed to saturate her bloodstream; it seemed to have displaced the underlying hint of black tea that was usually there. He thought that maybe that was strange, but it was also incredibly intoxicating, and for the first time in the evening, Robert began to feel drunk too.

"I'm right here, baby," he whispered. Concerned as he was, he could not deny how good this felt. How good she felt. "Oh, Alice," he gasped, sinking his teeth into her again. She began to ride him, harder and faster, trying to take him in deeper, desperately trying to bring about his release so that she could find her own.

As he called out her name again and shuddered against her, she let out an anguished, frustrated cry, her back arching against his supporting hands, head thrown back with the force of an uncontrollable orgasm. There were tears on her face as she all but collapsed against him.

He tried to wipe the tears away, but they kept falling. Unsure what else to do, he cradled her in his arms and whispered reassuringly in her ear.

***

"Sir. Madam. We should be arriving at your brownstone in about ten minutes," the driver said, over the car's communications system.

Robert leant over and pressed a button to talk. "OK. Thanks," he said. "Nearly home now," he said to her softly.

Alice slowly climbed off him, allowing him to tidy himself up a bit before she grabbed his hand. "Don't let go," she whispered desperately. "Please don't let go."

"I won't," he said, even though he was suddenly unsure that she was talking to him.

The car stopped moving and a moment later the door was opened. They climbed out, and Robert put his jacket around her shoulders before picking her up.

"Would you like some help, sir?" the driver asked politely, albeit somewhat tentatively.

"No, I've got her," said Robert. Supernatural strength aside, he did not want anyone else touching Alice. "Thank you. Have a good evening."

"You too sir. I hope madam feels better in the morning. Good night," he said, getting back into the car and driving off into the night, as Robert hurried into the apartment.

The driver hit the call button on the in-car phone, not relishing the news he would have to deliver. It did not matter if one was a coward or the most hardened mercenary on the planet, Lady Jane and Lord Sargeraxs had the ability to make a grown-man's balls shrivel and turn his blood to ice.

"Yes?"

"They're home, sir," the driver said.

"What?"

"The Witch seems quite ill, but she and the Vampire are both lucid and alive."

There was some cursing and muttering as the message was relayed.

"How did they fuck this up?"

The driver gulped nervously, and braced himself as he spoke up. "Permission to speak freely, sir?"

"Yes?"

"No one's fucked up, sir. I could see it in the mirror. She's just stronger than y..., er, anticipated."

There was a long pause and he swallowed hard.

"Right. Go home, Wrenfield. We'll expect you bright and early in the morning. We'll have other guests to return home."

"Yes, sir. Thank you, sir."

He hung up the phone and let out a sigh of relief, knowing that he had probably only escaped the repercussions of failure because they had at least considered the possibility. Wrenfield knew he was lucky; most people who delivered bad news to Lady Jane did not live to do it again.

***

"Does she seem OK to you?" he asked Onion, after laying her on the bed and reassuring her that he would not be gone for long. He had even left the bedroom door open.

"She looks exhausted and inebriated," the cat replied. "And something is obviously troubling her, but I can't see, smell or sense anything wrong with her. Is this related to your paranoia regarding the wine earlier?"

"Maybe. I don't know," said Robert, frustrated, pacing between the sofa and the kitchen counter so that she could see him, if she looked up. "One minute she can barely stand, the next...well, we won't go into that. I'm almost positive that something's wrong, but I can't find it, not even in her blood and I'm sure if there was anything there... And if you're not finding anything either... Maybe I am just being paranoid. Maybe this is just a really bad drinking experience. It's not like I've seen her drunk very often, so maybe she's just reacting badly to it now."

"I think we'll just have to wait until the morning," said

Onion, looking at his mistress and wondering if paranoia was contagious when he too felt a stab of concern.

"I guess so." Robert placed a pitcher of water, a glass and a large bowl on Alice's bedside table, gently pushing aside her copy of *Dracula* and the firefly necklace that she usually wore. There was also Alice's favourite photograph from their afternoon in the park, and he was reminded again of how it was the smallest and simplest things that gave her the most happiness. He was suddenly struck by the stark contrast between the confident happy woman in the frame, and the scared girl that was laying on the bed watching him intently, as though she were afraid of blinking only to find he was gone. He had seen a variance of that look before when the depression was particularly dark, but this was a step beyond that and he really hoped that it was just a disagreement with the evening's food and drink.

He took off her shoes, before stripping himself of the cummerbund, jacket and tie. He climbed onto the bed and wrapped his arms around her.

"Shh, it's alright. I've got you and I'm not letting go," Robert whispered, stroking Alice's hair as she nestled into him, curling up into a small ball. He did not notice the angry spark that flew from the black tourmaline in his triquetra cuff links; he just kept whispering and cradling her, until he fell into his own troubled sleep.

Chapter 40

It was grey and blue and green. It was like being underwater. There were the partial remains of either a shipwreck or a submersible. He moved closer, finally reaching the object and looked through the algae-clad windows, desperately trying to see inside. Red sparks and black stones started whizzing past his head like a rain of meteorites and a hand suddenly slammed against the glass. As the clawing hand was dragged down, it cleared away some of the algae and he saw a figure choking within the writhing seaweed. Her desperate eyes clamped on to him and Alice pleaded, even as the seaweed rammed itself into her throat. *"Help me!"* she screamed. Her desperate fingers slammed against the window again.

He awoke in shock as Alice's morning alarm went off. He could not remember what he had been dreaming, but he could not shake off the feeling of unease it had left him with.

"Urgh," Alice groaned, reluctantly opening her eyes. She grabbed her phone from off the side of the bed and hit the snooze button but otherwise, she did not move. "I hate mornings."

"You could just call in sick," Robert said cautiously, thinking her voice sounded slightly strange.

"You suggested that yesterday," she said dryly, remaining on her side.

"Yep. And you went in anyway. Besides, last night was super weird and honestly, I'm kinda worried about you." He rolled her onto her back, and winced at the almost black bruising surrounding two small puncture marks on her neck.

"I'm fine," she muttered, irritated by his glance. "It's not like this is the first time you've done that."

"I know, and to be honest, I'm really not that concerned about your neck. It's just everything else that took place during and after the party."

"I just drank and ate too much," she said flatly, blinking tiredly. Her eyes were a little blood-shot, but she kept shutting them before he could get a good look. "I'm fine now."

"Are you sure that's all it was?"

"Urgh, I'm fine," she said again, crossly.

It was sudden but he did not believe her this time. He placed a cool hand on her forehead and was almost shocked by the heat radiating from her skin. "Actually, I don't think you are."

Alice sighed impatiently and tried to shrug it all off, still avoiding his eyes. "OK, fine, I feel a bit rubbish but that's my fault for letting myself drink enough to warrant a hangover. And no, I am not calling in sick when this is entirely self-induced."

The alarm went off again and she hit the stop button on her phone, checked that the alarm was switched back on for the following day and shambled into the bathroom, without any signs of affection or comments on the fact that they were both still in last night's clothes. She quickly showered, dressed and went to sort out the cat without saying another word.

"Are you okay?" Onion asked her. He could feel his fur prickling as he went towards her and could not quite understand why. It was more like knowing Alice too well than it was his task as a protector. Neither his feline senses or the Familiar ones were detecting a problem.

"I'm fine," she said, placing the fresh food bowl down on his mat. She did not touch him.

Grumpy bastard that he was, Onion did not like this. He expected his morning head massage and hug. Even when Alice was cross with him or suffering one of her darkest days, she always spoke to him and showered him with affection first thing in the morning. If nothing else, it was a part of her routine and if she could help it, she rarely deviated. Even if she was hungover, as she had claimed to Robert, Onion knew Alice would give him love purely out of habit.

Instead, she sorted out her tea and breakfast in uncharacteristic silence, ate and drank mechanically, and said "See you later", leaving for work an hour earlier than she normally would.

"OK, what did I do?" Robert asked Onion, as he came out of the bedroom and stared at the closed door. Alice had never left the apartment without kissing him goodbye.

"I don't think it's you," the cat said, also looking at the door.

"That's what I was afraid of." Robert went into the bedroom for a minute and came back holding Alice's mobile phone. "She's left her phone and her iPod. She never goes out alone without music." He looked at the locked screen, and then to the cat. "Do you know her pass-code is?"

"Don't you?" Onion returned, smug with his little piece of knowledge.

"No. She's always here and I've never needed to use her phone before. She might have told you for emergency purposes though." Robert tried to keep his tone even, but Onion could still detect his growing panic.

"Her birthday, your birthday, my birthday," Onion said finally, concern beginning to override his need to be one up on the Vampire male. "Why?"

"I need to call Dr Anthonys. I think Alice needs help."

***

It took longer than usual for Alice to get to work. It was akin to her darkest depression, where everything was done on autopilot (if it could be done at all) and she felt like she was a lost soul looking through an unfeeling meat suit, barely able to see, hear or care. But it was worse. Somehow, whatever this was, it was worse. She trudged up the steps to the library and pulled on the antique bronze door handles.

The Library doors would not open.

"Hey, what gives," she muttered. "It's me. Come on, let me in. I feel cold today."

She pulled on the handles again and rattled the doors in frustration.

"Julius, why won't it let me in?" she asked as the big man appeared from one of the side doors. She moved to go inside but he stepped outside and began to usher her away from the building.

"It would let you in, if you were alone. Come."

"What do you mean?" said Alice, a note of distress in her voice. She felt ill and confused and it was so dark and cold. *Why is it so cold?* "I am alone. Well, apart from germs and a hangover, maybe."

He lead her across the street and through a small doorway, up the stairs into what seemed like a small chapel. Dr Anthonys was already there, with a doctor, a priest and several Guardians. She suddenly realised that there was an old hospital bed to one side of the room, an iron bed with restraints. Something inside her panicked and she was going to bolt, her hands flying up, ready to defend herself with magic.

"What's...Ow," she said, turning around. The injection had not hurt that much but it had certainly surprised her. Alice shook her head, trying to make sense of it all, but it was all beginning to fade. "What..." The words faltered and she fell into Julius' arms.

Julius handed the syringe back to Dr Caulson, picked Alice up and strapped her to the bed. Austin wheeled it into the middle of the room and they quickly drew a salt circle around her. No one looked happy about it.

"It's the right thing to do," said Stuart quietly, placing a hand on Julius' arm.

"Yes," said Julius, looking at the Witch on the bed, surprised by the emotions attacking him. "But this does not feel good."

"No," Stuart agreed, feeling equally worried and upset as he looked at Alice. "No it doesn't."

***

Although, Stuart was anxious to begin, he had promised Robert that he would wait before starting the ritual. Having to keep her restrained and drugged was something he had never imagined doing to anyone, let alone Alice. But she was far too powerful for them not to take such precautions, particularly if the demon was able to find a way to tap into her powers.

Realistically, he knew it was a testament to both Robert and Alice that they were in this position; were they not the remarkable individuals and couple that they were, it would have been impossible for them to gain an advantage over the presence invading Alice's body. As it was, Robert's phone call meant they were prepared by the time Alice had arrived, whilst her formidable powers meant that she had been able to alert the Library.

The Library had not kept Alice out; Alice had told the Library not to let her in.

Chapter 41

Long before Stuart had taken up the mantle of Head Librarian at the New York Library, arrangements had been made to use the chapel should the Library refuse admittance to anyone on the grounds of evil intent. Although no one thought Alice was evil, seeing her arrive at least made them sure that the chapel was indeed necessary.

As a precaution, Stuart had called in the assistance of a Witch and medical doctor, Dr Philippa-Marie Caulson, and a Catholic priest, Father Bernardo. In terms of the work that he did for the Library, Father Bernardo's religious doctrine did not matter; it was the power of his Faith that made him an effective exorcist.

Although no longer used as a place of worship, the room still carried an air of divinity. There was paraphernalia from most of the modern, practised religions, as well as iconography for some that had been long abandoned. They were there to help create a sense of love and inclusiveness, so that anyone who was suffering could find something to focus on that would help bring them hope and strengthen their faith.

The bottom-half of the walls were covered in oak-panelling; the top was painted in olive green. Old pews were propped up at the sides and sacred candles burnt in sconces of iron or silver. There were also four burners holding sage smudge sticks, and an iron poker lay next to Father Bernardo's bible on the generally disused lectern. There was a small font of holy water beside the lectern and a mini-fridge stocked with various fresh herbs, spices and barks, as well as bottled water.

A pentacle had been drawn in the middle of the floor and the hospital bed had been wheeled over it. The bed was made of cast iron and blessed calf leather, and a thin mattress had been covered with a cotton sheet and two thick pillows had been tied to the head of the bed. As comfortable as they had tried to make it, the bed nonetheless looked like a prop from a movie about an evil insane asylum or haunted hospital.

As soon as they closed the salt circle around her, everything about Alice changed. Her body stiffened and flinched as tiny little cuts started appearing upon her skin. Stuart gave a quick glance to the Guardians and Austin reappeared a moment later with a small silver mirror. Whilst most mirrors would reveal a supernatural entity that humans could not see, this particular mirror had been crafted to show the true form of any supernatural entity that attempted to hide or deceive. Stuart angled the glass so that Alice was in view and was shocked at the appearance of wispy black tendrils weaving around her body, reaching through the exposed openings of her body, forcing her skin to turn an unnatural grey pallor as it seeped into her veins.

"What is that? It's not like any demon I've ever seen," Father Bernardo commented, catching a glimpse in the mirror. Although his knowledge of demons was far from extensive, he had nonetheless encountered them before. Five exorcisms thus far, the last of which had been in the very room in which they were now standing.

"It's not a demon… more like a pet or demonic essence, but I am hoping that many of the same rules apply," Stuart said, watching Alice's reflection closely.

"I will… do my best," Father Bernardo said, not entirely sure he would be much help. Although every possession was slightly different, they ultimately followed the same pattern; most demons were named and they wanted to take complete control of a host, particularly if the demon had not been invited; their agenda was to corrupt human souls in order to anger the One True God; and they mostly targeted the innocent or vulnerable, which did not seem to be the case with Alice. At best, Father Bernardo thought this creature was like a computer virus that had attacked and found that the host had put herself into safe mode before it could do too much damage.

The other stranger to the room, was Dr Philippa-Marie Caulson, a Witch and medical doctor. As a surgeon, the tiny chapel was a world removed from her operating theatre and office in the city's largest, private hospital. Like most Witches, she believed that she was better than the other earthly forms, but she did respect the office of the Head Librarian, and as such, she was willing to aid Stuart when he had "urgently requested" her assistance.

Although she had never seen a possession, what disturbed her was amount of barely restrained power in the Witch laying on the bed. *And to think it's being wasted on a Witch that chooses to be with a Vampire*, she thought with a modicum of disgust. She had asked Stuart why he had not reached out to her coven for help, and he had, with seeming reluctance, told her that Alice did not belong to one. All things considered, Caulson knew this would all greatly interest her coven master, Alcina Wesker, who could possibly extend an invitation. If Alice survived the exorcism.

Robert burst through the door. Stuart was not quite quick enough to drop the mirror and Robert fanged out with a growl at the sight of the strange creature attacking his girlfriend.

"OK, calm down, Robert," Stuart said keeping his voice low and steady. "We still have time to save her."

"What the hell is that thing?" Robert asked, anguish on his face. He took a deep breath and managed to retract his fangs. "How did it get her?" He wanted to ask why they had restrained her, but he already knew the answer; it was necessary. Perhaps he did not understand how powerful everyone thought she was.

"It's a demonic wraith of some sort," Stuart answered,

gently pushing Robert back through the door and closing it behind them. "A mid-level creature that was deliberately summoned and commanded to target her."

"Why would anyone do that to her?"

"I don't know. Maybe it's not really after her at all; perhaps whoever conjured it thought they could use Alice to deceive the Library."

"Could she? I didn't think anything could get past the Library, especially if there was even a suggestion of the demonic about it."

"Well, given what happened to Alice previously, things sometimes slip through. Maybe they felt their next patsy needed to be someone that worked at the Library, and they chose Alice. Luckily, we won't have to find out, because somehow, she managed to warn the Library."

"That's my girl," Robert whispered, swallowing hard, trying to catch a glimpse of her through the small pane of glass in the door.

"Now, honestly, I would not have you in this room while we try to exorcise and destroy this thing, as there is a chance that in casting it out, it will try to latch onto one of us. However, Alice says she is never stronger than when you're with her, so I feel I must allow it." He looked the Fledgling in the eye. "This won't be easy, and it may well be painful, but we have to get rid of that thing before it burrows into her like some kind of parasite which may well kill her if we tried to remove it."

"I get it," said Robert testily.

Stuart sighed. He was not convinced that Robert truly understood just how much pain they might inflict upon Alice in trying to dispel the wraith, or that there was a chance that she may well die from the strain of fighting it, but he could see that Robert was not concerned with listening to the disclaimer.

They re-entered the chapel, and Robert put his coat on the chair that had been placed beside the bed. He sat down next to her in the middle of the pentacle. Small red sparks flickered at Robert's wrist, but Robert was more concerned about Alice. He took her hand and kissed it, wishing there was something he could do.

"And at least that's one less thing to worry about," Stuart said, noticing the sparks. "I was concerned that in expelling the wraith, it might try to latch onto another vessel. Given where you are sitting, you would be the obvious choice."

"But?" asked Robert, not taking his eyes off Alice.

"But it would seem you are already protected. Did Alice happen to make those cuff links?"

"She gave them to me, but she didn't say she'd made them. But of course she wouldn't." Robert kissed her hand. "Thank you," he whispered "Now come back to me."

Chapter 42

Alice felt like she was inside some kind of optical illusion; one moment she was inside some kind of chapel; the next, she was drowning in a washed-out sea, grey and dank and smothered in black clouds and charcoal seaweed. One place smelt of sage and fire; the other of sulphur and blood. She felt like she was choking; her skin prickled and crawled, as wispy tendrils brushed across her and caused a multiple pin-pricks of pain as it tried to stab its way inside her body.

To begin with, it felt like a bad dream or a depressive episode with a layer of hallucinations. Her limbs felt heavy, her skin felt unclean and she felt unbelievably tired. Not that sleeping would normally help all that much, but it did at least make the time pass. However this was slowly becomingly far far worse.

At first, the wraith had tried to bribe her with greater powers; it suggested that she could be sitting at the right hand of a demonic overlord. It tried to seduce her with images of wealth and luxury, of disturbing sexual gratification at the scaled and taloned hands of this demon king; but from within her revulsion and disbelief, she had laughed. Despite her protests, the wraith continued to tempt her, at least until it realised that they were both trapped.

Then it had started bombarding her with images of Robert being killed in numerous violent and disturbing ways. In some ways it made her angry and more determined not to let it happen, but the idea that she could cause that kind of pain, or that demons would do that to the ones she loved just because of her, also made her feel weak and useless. And it was not just the images; it was the accompanying smells and sounds. Hearing all the screams, the accusations... Smelling the blood and the stench of decay... Seeing them reach for her with rotting hands, half-formed faces leering at her as maggots fell out of eye sockets and blackened mouths.

She tried her best to ignore it and focus on what was real. She could feel the others trying to help and fail. The other witch was making things worse; the exorcist, although well-meaning, was having no effect on the wraith, because the wraith had no concept other than its singular purpose of delivering Alice to its creator. Could sense the worry and concern, but she could also feel him, and she wondered if she could actually get back to consciousness. It probably would not last, but it would be something. Meditation in reverse almost. She gathered her thoughts into a tiny ball and pushed that ball through to something she knew would be on the other side.

***

"Alice?" Robert said, looking at her with some confusion, noticing that her eyes were suddenly open and more alert. He had not expected to see her for a couple of days – he had been preparing himself to look into those eyes and see something empty and dark; or something alien and pervasive that had insinuated itself into her body – but this was definitely his Alice. Tired, scared and worried but still her.

"Hey," she said groggily, turning her head to smile crookedly at him. Her hope felt renewed; the wraith had no chance whilst Robert was with her.

"Is it gone?" he asked, hopefully.

"No. It's just briefly subdued or something," she murmured, unable to really care. "I don't know. Can you remove the restraints please? I need the bathroom."

Robert looked at the other occupants of the room. They seemed equally stunned.

"Seriously, for the moment, I'm okay, apart from needing to use the bathroom." She coughed and winced in pain. "Not so okay then, but mentally clear for a bit. If you seal the room, it'll be fine; it's not going anywhere. But seriously, hurry it up."

With a fair amount of trepidation, Stuart broke the salt circles and helped Robert remove the restraints. Together, they walked Alice to the small toilet and gave her a moment to relieve herself.

She stood in front of the mirror, still unable to see what was truly afflicting her. She could feel something writhing and rolling across her skin, scratching like sandpaper, making her feel gritty and greasy. She banged her hand in frustration against the cold reflective glass and quickly wiped away angry, tired tears. "Show yourself," she demanded, suddenly remembering Dr. Anthony's book and the spectral sight spell. She drew the symbol on the mirror and murmured the incantation, willing it to work more fervently than anything she had ever tried to cast before. "Show yourself wraith," she demanded again, her eyes widening with shock and despair as a strange cloudy-black eel-like manifestation appeared, oozing and snaking its way in and around her body like a perverse snake. She felt it bristle with anger and hatred, and she bit back a scream as spikes suddenly pierced her, inside and out. She took a deep breath and braced herself, not wanting Robert to see how much pain she was really in.

"Thank you," Alice said. She was feeling so stiff and knotted up that she felt like she needed to be put on a medieval rack. At the same time, even the slightest stretch sent waves of pain across the surface of her body, as if her skin was tearing with each movement.

"How is this even possible?" Stuart asked, guiding her back onto the hospital bed.

Alice looked at him blankly.

"Let's just say, that the common notion of demonic possession is not far off from the real thing. By all accounts, you should not be moving of your own volition," Stuart explained. They had all expected her soul and consciousness to be displaced until the demon was removed, only to be revealed when the demon wanted to torment them with her pain.

"I don't know," said Alice, remembering not to shrug. "I mean, it's not a proper demon, which probably helps."

"It isn't?"

"It's a nekrofolis wraith, I think. I'm sure they were mentioned in one of the books, underground."

"Oh," said Stuart, looking over to Austin. The Guardian promptly disappeared to give the information to the Library and discover the book.

"I think it's kinda confused too. It wasn't expecting to get trapped. It's trying to get a message to whomever summoned it because I'm being stubborn and not going with it."

"That figures," said Robert.

Alice smiled weakly, and looked down at her ragged and broken appearance. She assumed she was in some state of shock, because to look at some of the gashes in her skin, she should be screaming her head off in pain. "There is a stronger salt circle combination written down in my version of the 100 Spells. Julius should be able to get it. And there's a binding that you can use on me, so that when I request a bathroom break, you don't have to be so worried, not that I plan on letting this thing get into my powers."

"It doesn't want anything from the Library?" asked Stuart.

"Nope."

"Are you sure?" he asked again.

Alice shrugged, and wished she had not. She also wished that she was not required to talk, but she supposed the questions were unavoidable. "Pretty sure."

"What does it want then?" Stuart asked.

"Me. This thing wants to take me to its demon overlord."

"They want you to break the Veil," said Stuart, slowly.

He supposed he should not have been surprised, but it was very easy to deny a thing right up until it was actually happening. Sometimes, even while it was happening.

"I would've thought there would be more powerful and willing Witches than me up to that task," said Alice, unable to stop the shrugging or the yawning, despite the pain they caused. "All I know is that it wants me." She closed her eyes for a moment and swallowed. She coughed painfully. "Pentacle is fine, you can leave that, 'coz better safe than sorry, but I think the wraith can only attack me. Could inflict pain, but it can't "possess" you. Can I eat that, please?" she asked, spotting a sandwich on the nearby table.

"Of course," Stuart said at once, grateful to have such a normal request to respond to.

Robert passed her the sandwich and a bottle of water. He would have offered to do it for her, but she looked determined to try and do things herself.

She ate and drank quickly, whilst talking, not knowing how long she would be in control. "This is gonna get rough, so if you feel like you don't trust what I'm suggesting, okay, but I don't plan on letting this thing win. You can apply the binding to bandages, otherwise white ribbon wrapped around my wrists, okay?"

"Okay," said Robert, swallowing hard. He did not like the sound of that.

"Right." Alice nodded slightly and bit the left part of her lower lip. "I guess you better strap me up again," she said, laying back on the hospital bed. "And if it's okay, I'd like to talk to Robert for a moment without you all crowding us," she said pointedly to the hovering doctor, priest and assorted Library employees.

"Yes, of course," said Stuart. "Sorry." He stepped back, and the others followed him into one of the corners of the chapel, unable to stop looking back at the strange couple in the middle of the room.

"Hey you," Alice said, softly. She still had one free hand

and she used it to stroke his face. She did not like the fact that he looked so tired and hurt because of her.

"Hey," said Robert, placing his hand over hers. "Something other than the obvious wrong?"

"Not as such. Can you get rid of the other Witch though? I'm not sure I trust her. Medically, I guess she's probably sound, but her spells are all wrong for this."

"And the exorcist?"

"He can stay if he wants, especially if it makes anyone else feel better, but honestly, it makes no difference. I'm not sure why the exorcism hasn't worked already. Maybe this wraith is somehow bound to me through something I ate or drank; if so, then hopefully this will all be resolved in a couple of days."

"And if it isn't?" Robert asked quietly. He reluctantly took her hand from his face and strapped it down.

"Then I'll need Sam," said Alice, wincing in pain as she felt the wraith trying to scratch away again. "I love you," she said, before her eyes rolled back into her head. Her body convulsed like something was trying to burst from her chest.

"I love you too," he said, holding her hand and desperately wishing there was more that he could do.

Chapter 43

"Remarkable," said Dr Caulson, watching in fascination as the Witch succumbed to a different level of perception, her body moving in accordance to a physical assault that no one else could see without the aid of a mirror.

"This is a most unusual possession, Stuart," said Father Bernardo, worried and impressed by the young woman on the bed.

"She's an unusual individual," Stuart Anthonys replied, glancing over at the couple in the middle of the room. "They both are."

"I'm not sure there's much call for our services," the Father added.

"Not at the moment in any case," said Robert, quietly coming over and standing next to the priest. His eyes never left Alice. "Sorry, I don't mean to be rude."

"No, it's perfectly understandable given the circumstances," said Father Bernardo. "And we can go if you feel it's best."

"I think it might be. Alice feels that nothing will work for the next couple of days at the very least. I guess if it's not gone by then, we'll probably need the medical help, but at the moment, it's safer for you both if you don't stay."

"I am perfectly capable of handling a wraith," said Dr Caulson, looking at Robert with great disdain.

"No, you're not," said Robert, briefly looking at the Witch with undisguised disbelief at her arrogance.

"How dare you..." the doctor began.

"Please, Philippa, this is not the time or place for class resentments," Stuart quickly interjected. "Robert is perfectly correct. That is a nekrofolis wraith. It is hell-spawned, not a weak, lingering shadow of a former demon. We have tried for several hours to exorcise this thing and it's not shifting."

"Alice thinks it's bound specifically to her somehow. She's kinda been acting a little off since last night, so it may be related to something she ate," said Robert, quietly.

"It's certainly possible," Stuart said, after a moments consideration.

"It can take up to seventy-two hours for something to completely pass through the digestive process, so yes, I suppose it might be worth trying again in a couple of days. Would you like me to take care of those bindings that she requested?" Philippa-Marie asked, too busy looking in her handbag to notice Robert's firm shake of the head.

"No thank you," Stuart said, watching Robert closely. "The specific formula to which Miss Andrews refers is in a Library tome that would be best fulfilled by the Head Librarian or a Guardian."

"As you wish," said Dr. Caulson, with a slightly derisive sniff. "I will leave the cooler with bandages, silver nitrate, iodine and co-codomol, should they be necessary. If things get worse, and she can not eat or drink, let me know and I will sort out an intravenous drip. This is clearly a Witch we do not want to lose. You have my number, Stuart."

"Thank you, I will call if it becomes necessary."
Dr. Caulson nodded to him and Father Bernardo before leaving. She took one last look at Alice and strode out without another glance at the Vampire. Robert certainly did not care.

"Care to explain, Mr. Evans?" Stuart was giving him a look of displeasure.

"Alice has...reservations," Robert said, trying to being diplomatic. "Well, benefit of the doubt, Alice says the spells the doctor thinks should be helping, are actually having the opposite effect. And no offence meant to your friend, but I would trust Alice over anyone else any day of the week."

"I see," said Stuart, frowning slightly. "Well, I don't believe that she would intentionally aid demonic forces, but I am certainly more inclined to trust Alice's judgement on this matter."

"And Miss Andrews' thoughts on having an exorcist?" asked Father Bernardo, his eyes crinkling with a certain dry amusement. He already knew that his own experience was not helping to expel the creature, it was simply a matter of being a comfort to the young woman if it made her feel better.

"Appreciated, but unnecessary," said Robert.
Stuart looked to the bed again. If it were not for the occasional tremor, he could almost believe Alice was dead she seemed so pale and still. "So she genuinely thinks there is nothing we can do to help her?"

"Not yet. She mentioned that if the exorcisms don't work, we might need Sam," said Robert.

"I'll call him at once. It'll take him some time to get here, I'm sure. He might well have more insight, not that spirit possessions are the same as demonic," Stuart said, thoughtfully. "Well, in light of Alice's advisements, I suggest most of us try to attend to our everyday duties. I presume that you will be staying here and I will leave a couple of the Guardians with you, just in case. If you need anything, do not hesitate to call. I will be back in a couple of hours with Alice's bindings, as well as more food and water. Father, shall we walk out together?"

"Certainly." The priest turned to the vampire. "Mr. Evans, I know you and Miss Andrews might not believe in it, but I shall keep you both in my prayers and ask God to guide you both through this ordeal."

"Thank you," said Robert kindly, before returning to his seat by Alice's side.

Chapter 44

Alice awoke, still feeling a bit tired and drained. She turned onto her side and was disappointed to find that Robert was not next to her. She liked being able to look into those beautiful blue eyes and run her fingertips across his face and lips before kissing him, but he could not always stay in bed, waiting for her to get up. She yawned, stretching like a cat beneath the thin white sheets, trying to ignore the gentle warmth of the morning sun streaming through the large double doors leading onto the balcony, tempting her with the desire for more sleep. *A morning back massage would be heaven right now* she thought, imagining the delicious thrill of his hands on her shoulders.

    A window was open and she could hear the faintest of breezes in the treetops wafting in the sweet morning fragrance of lavender and honeysuckle. She thought she could even hear the low, gentle buzzing of bumble and honey bees and she smiled contentedly. The idyllic little moment was broken by the sound of gentle footfall, the perfume of flowers replaced with the smell of fresh coffee and toasted bagels. Alice pushed herself up onto one elbow and smiled at the man standing only in boxers, with the breakfast tray in the doorway. Her heart almost wanted to skip a beat; it was not his body that made Robert so attractive but it certainly did not hurt that it was damn-near perfect.

    "Morning, sleepy-head," he said, his eyes smiling at hers.

    "'Morning." said Alice, watching carefully as he walked around the bed and placed the tray next to her.

He sat down on the side of the bed and his eyes closed as he leaned in to kiss her. Before their lips touched, she placed a finger on his lips, and his eyes opened in surprise.

"What's wrong?"

"I'm not in the habit of kissing strangers," she said, studying the blue eyes in front of her carefully.

"Strangers?" he echoed. "We've been together for nearly nine months and we're strangers?"

"I've been with Robert for nearly nine months. I have no idea who you are."

The man's blue eyes crinkled, head slightly tilted as he looked at her with confusion. "Of course, I'm..."

"No, you're not," Alice interrupted crossly, her eyes narrowing dangerously. "I don't know who or what you are, but it's no good trying to convince me that you're Robert. Because you're not. So if you want to open some sort of weird discourse by manipulating my perceptions, fine, go ahead. But unless you want me to figure out how to rain holy hell upon you, change your face and stop pretending to be Robert."

"But I am..."

"NO YOU'RE NOT," screamed Alice, and the scene crumbled around her, flaking away like old paint into some kind of dark abyss.

The thing that looked like Robert flinched, standing in surprise as the illusion fell apart, but his visage did not change.

"Get out," she said, clenching her fists tightly. She imagined her powers as a ball of energy, gathering it together like a green fel-bolt before hurtling it at the thing in front of her. It gave a cry of surprise and disappeared. Alice let out a sigh of relief and felt a sudden stab of pain in her head. She winced, scrunching her eyes shut, trying to escape the feeling of dizziness. Then the world went black.

***

Robert let go of her hand as they started to ball into tight little fists. The bed began to shudder and shake, and then suddenly stopped. Alice's body went limp. He grabbed her hand again and searched for a pulse. It was still there and he breathed a sigh of relief.

Her eyelids fluttered slightly and he gently reached to stroke her cheek. She gave him a brief, tired smile.

"I knew you were still here somewhere," she whispered, still within the slumbering pull that would send her back to sleep if given a chance. The lure of sleep was more than tempting but as she resisted, the pain began to creep in like the deceptive drizzle that was a precursor to a torrential downpour. Sleep was no longer an option.

"Of course I'm here. I'm not going anywhere."

"I know. Apparently neither am I," she joked, coughing weakly. Her chest felt tight and heavy as if she were getting a cold and she almost laughed. A cold would be the least of her problems. "Any tea, please?"

"Is that wise?" asked Robert. He did not know why but it seemed like she should be requesting something strange and healthy and full of strange herbs and magic, not her everyday beverage.

"Is it wise to deny me tea?" she said trying to project a sense of threat to him.

"It's not so bad when you're hands are tied," he teased, kissing her gently.

"And it's not even the good way," she whispered, eyes twinkling.

"Not the time," Robert said, unable to hide a smile.

"We need to work on that. You're never interested when I am," she whispered.

"I was interested, but it was hardly the right time or place."

"We could have made it work. Been one of those crazy couples that sneaks off to the bathroom or a bedroom or a cupboard."

"It's okay to be scared."

"Why would I be scared? There's a wraith in my body and demon talking to me in my head. Surely that just makes it a....?"

"Saturday," finished Robert.

"Already? Well, this looks set to be the best weekend ever."

"Alice..."

"I don't know how else to deal, okay? I couldn't tell you I thought something was wrong and I can't tell you I'm scared now, okay? Although, it's kinda different..."

"Okay, okay, okay. I'm sorry, I'm sorry," he interrupted her, smoothing her hair down and kissing her head. "It's hard to sit here and not be able to do anything to help."

"Tea would help a lot," Alice said with a faint grin, wincing and trying not to cry out as he raised the head of the bed and released one of her hands. "Besides, you keep me sane and alive and here. You give me a reason to live. I love you and I'm not letting some demon take that away."

"I love you too. And I will be right here. With tea and whatever else you want," he said, holding up a mug. He blew on it gently and slowly helped her sip from it.

"Thank you."

"Sandwich? Chicken and bacon."

"Yes please." She took a bite. "I mostly feel okay you know. Tired, a little confused, majorly skanky, and I guess I should try and walk and use the bathroom while I still can. Ooo, bandages and ribbons. Pretty. I like," Alice said, looking at her wrists as she watched Robert unclasp her other hand. She was slightly perturbed by the red stains, having always thought if such 'accessories' were needed, it would have been as a result of her own hand and the ongoing depression. She leaned on Robert, her legs feeling shaky and weak.

"Everyone else okay?" she asked, exiting the restroom.

"Tired. Most of them are gone now. Mainly just me and a couple of the Guardians. Stuart and Julius check-in regularly too."

"You should get some sleep." She sat down on the bed and continued to eat and drink, unaided, now that she was untied.

"I get a few minutes here and there. I've never needed as much as you anyway," he teased gently.

Alice smiled weakly. "Not sure any one does," she joked. She nibbled at the sandwich, finding it hard to swallow. She tried to ignore her pain and concentrated on drinking the tea.

"Any new ideas?" Robert asked, walking over to the fridge and pulling out a sport's drink. He unscrewed the cap and passed it to her.

She smiled apologetically and sipped at the glucose and electrolyte laden liquid. "Not yet. What about from the Library?"

"I don't think anything's been found. We all know you're probably right and that we have the tools already. We just don't have the right conditions to use them."

Alice sighed unhappily and then perked up slightly. "It, He, the demon, tried to convince me he was you. That was stupid," said Alice, her eyes twinkling.

"Was it?" Robert asked, bemused. He could not help but smile at how pleased she looked with herself.

"Of course. There's only one you after all." She smiled and caressed his face. "And even if the body's the same, I can tell the difference. It's like how you can dream of someone and they look completely different, but you know who they are."

"I'll take your word for it. I don't often remember my dreams."

"Well, I can't remember mine at the moment, although to be honest, I'm not entirely sure I'm getting any real sleep. It's all very, very weird. I don't know if anyone else has lived through this kind of experience but I can see why no one would think too highly of them if they wrote it down. It's so hard to explain in any coherent, relatable terms."

"So, there's a demon and a wraith trying to possess you?" Robert asked, wondering if encouraging her to talk was a good thing or not.

"No. I think the demon is using the wraith to talk to me. Not sure why he's wasting his time on me; I won't make any deals or be possessed or destroy the Veil or whatever it is they might want from me."

"Not even slightly tempted?" Robert teased.

"Nope," Alice replied. "Things are pretty darn perfect the way they are, or were three days ago… kinda, well, you know what I mean." Her hand shook as she passed the drink to him and lay back down. She fumbled with the different straps and Robert took over, leaving one hand free in case she had longer than she thought.

"Somehow, I almost always know what you mean," said Robert forcing a smile, as he sat back down. "And we'll get back there."

"I know." Her breathing began to get rapid and ragged again. "It's back," she managed to gasp, before losing consciousness again.

Robert groaned in frustration and kissed her hand before tying it down. He reached out of the salt circle for the bowl of warm water and gently ran the towel across her face, wishing he could do more than wipe the feverish sweat from her brow.

Chapter 45

Lord Sargeraxs blinked his stolen eyes. It took a moment to register the fact that not only was he back in Damien Houseman's penthouse hotel suite, but he was also several feet away from where he had started his mind-walking.

"My lord, are you okay?" asked Lady Jane, rushing to his side.

"I want that Witch," he hissed crossly to himself. He turned to Lady Jane, eyeing her sternly. "Tell me again your thoughts on the Witch."

Lady Jane frowned and tried to hide the unfamiliar stab of fear. "Alice Andrews. Witch. Born in England to..."

"Not statistics and facts. I want your opinions, your assessment. Your knowledge from following her," he demanded, unceremoniously getting to his feet; if the body was in pain, Sargeraxs was ignoring it.

Lady Jane licked her lips and spoke slowly, trying to recall her observations beyond her personal dislike and distaste for the Witch. "She has great power. Could be the most powerful Witch in existence but squanders it by almost never using it. She's erratic, allows her emotions to get the better of her which creates pockets of chaos since she does not fully control her gifts. She loves the Vampire – believes it to be absolute which will be her downfall in the end. Caring too much about others tends to make the otherwise strong, weak. Allows herself to be pulled down by depression, wants to be "good"."

"Intelligent? Strong? Defiant?" Sargeraxs questioned,

watching her closely.

Lady Jane did not like this strange feeling of being the one interrogated. "Moderate intelligence. No physical or mental strength to speak of. Prefers to avoid conflict, even when she is within her rights to raise her voice to offenders. Will be resistant at first, but will be broken event..."

He grabbed her by the throat and slammed her against the wall. "Wrong," he shouted angrily. He looked into the frightened eyes of his prized acolyte. Rarely had he lost his temper with her and she was right to be afraid now. "Are you jealous of her?"

Lady Jane swallowed hard, and tried to muster some defiance. "Jealous of that Witch? Don't insult..."

"Do not lie to me!" he roared, hellfire blazing in his eyes as he slammed her against the wall again. "You say you are above your human emotions and yet the pettiest of all may well be our undoing. For months we have been watching her, waiting, setting up this launch to lure her into our trap and bait her with all that her heart could desire, and you have messed it up by being jealous and unwilling to see what she is truly capable of. She will destroy this wraith and with it, all that we worked for."

"It will not happen again."

"No, it will not." He threw her down, and watched as she scrambled to her feet, swallowed hard, eyes downcast, contemplating her failure. "Have you found them yet?"

"No, my lord. They are somewhere near the Library, but that is all we can ascertain. Either the Library itself or the Fallen are shielding it from our eyes. Of course, there is nothing that can be done about the wraith, but they are preventing us from finding the bodies."

"Go to the Council. Tell them to prepare themselves for the wraith to fail. It will kill or be killed; I suggest they come up with contingencies for both scenarios, while I continue to work in this realm both on Alice and other sources."

He went back to the cushions and the chalice of blood, not

looking up as the door to his side quietly closed.

Sargeraxs seethed quietly in the lavish hotel room. He walked over to the silver chalice and picked it up by the two ornate serpent-like handles. The serpents' eyes glowed with hellfire gems, deep ruby coloured stones with swirling black ash within the depths, whilst the middle of each side of the bowl was adorned with three small black diamonds. The rest of the bowl was etched with a border of runes and sigils, sandwiching a mural of Dionysian activities. The top fangs of the beasts were perched on the rim of the broad goblet, the bodies arched and curved to make the handles, whilst their tails twisted and intertwined around the stem. The base was decorated with monstrous, but very real, tiny skulls, that had been encased with pewter when the chalice was forged. It was currently filled with a very ancient, very potent spell that was akin to dream-walking, since it allowed Sargeraxs to enter an unused level of consciousness within Alice's mind, where he would be able to persuade her to join with him. Assuming he could maintain a presence there without her forcing him out.

He placed the chalice carefully upon the large white side cabinet. He supposed he was fortunate that it remained unbroken and unspilled. Getting the right blood and the right blend of herbs was trickier than it had been when he was last in the mortal realm and he could already foresee needing a lot more than originally anticipated. He made a note to send someone to get the blood of a virgin Witch, the flowers of the Kynara Superba, Redwood bark and black mamba venom.

Switching on the laptop and opening up the musical files Lady Jane had provided for him, Lord Sargeraxs poured himself a large glass of an expensive and exquisite Cabernet Sauvignon as he listened to various classical works by Wagner and Holst. There was no point in expending more time and energy on the Witch today. He had underestimated her and paid a small price that he was not willing to pay a second time.

The wraith should have brought her to him almost immediately. That it had not, was a concern; that she had bound herself and it, was both remarkable and unimagined. Such action had forced him to mind-walk and thus he had encountered several new problems, that had also been inconceivable. For one, he had not been able to sculpt the landscape as he would have liked. Alice had conjured some strange, idyllic bedroom with a very homely air; he had wanted a grand four-poster bed, large and lavish, strewn with exotic scents and flowers, surrounding her with jewels and gold and a feeling of absolute power. Secondly, he had taken on the physical form of the Vampire and instead of it causing her to fall into his arms at once, she had taken one look into his eyes and refused to engage in any physical contact.

It puzzled him. Sargeraxs knew that it was the right form to take – on previous occasions, he had either taken the form of his prey's lover or of their "dream partner" – since Robert was apparently Alice's idea of the "perfect guy" and yet, she had not believed it to be Robert. She had defied him, argued with him and intriguingly, had become angry with him. It was astonishing, and in her anger, she had done what he had not thought possible – forced him to leave.

It infuriated him and made him want her more. He felt angry and curious, intrigued as to what else she might be capable of, as he was forced to consider that she was more intelligent and powerful than the Severed Hand had been expecting. He had assumed that she would be as weak as all the other mortals he had watched over the centuries and that was a mistake. Just because the masses appeared to be stupid, did not mean an individual was.

He knew that the wraith was showing her all that could be, depending on whether she chose to accept or reject his offer. She claimed not to want sex, power and wealth, and had determined that the threats were idle and unsubstantiated, and he had the sneaking suspicion that she knew that they would remain so. He thought about having one of her friends or parents, maybe even one of the annoying animals that she seemed so fond of, kidnapped and tortured as leverage, but he found himself erring on the side of caution. Perhaps the Fallen were somehow behind all of this, in which case, there were powerful depths that Alice might be able to tap into that would destroy any and all chance of Hell's minions escaping back to the playground of Earth.

There were other ways to gain her trust and convince her to abandon those that she thought she loved. Given that Alice's innocent beauty would deteriorate as she continued to fight, Lady Jane might have better luck seducing the Vampire in the coming days. Even if Robert continued to spurn his assassin's advances, Sargeraxs was sure he could make the Witch believe in his infidelity. After all, Witches did not trust other supernaturals; and women as insecure as Alice did not believe they could compete for a man's attention against Lady Jane.

Disappointing as it was to find that Alice was not as easily enticed as they had imagined, at least he had finally made contact with her. It had not gone to plan, but each visit would give him more insight into her darkest thoughts and secret desires, and gradually she would accept and embrace them. Even if the wraith perished sooner than expected, a doorway between his mind and hers had been opened.

His musings were interrupted by a growl of his host body. As much as Lord Sargeraxs enjoyed indulging in gluttony, there were times when he forgot that this human vessel actually needed to be fed and watered. If he was going to make the body last as long as they had planned, he had to try and take care of it. He used the telephone to order an expensive dinner of duck and fois gras tartlets, the best steak, dauphinoise potatoes and seasonal vegetables, a lavish selection of delicate pastries and miniature cakes, luxury chocolates and another two bottles of wine. He poured himself a glass of still, mineral water that claimed to have been sourced from an Arctic iceberg and sat back down on the couch.

Reluctantly, Lord Sargeraxs had to contemplate a scenario where Alice continued to refuse him and the offers of the Severed Hand. Other than the infuriating knowledge of his own failure, the annoyance of having to rely on the Ritual of Blood, was timing. With the scent of escape closer than it had ever been, the denizens of Hell were growing impatient, and the Ritual required very specific conditions. They would need to uncover the Dark Alter; wait for the perigee syzygy; gather the necessary components for the sacrifices and potions; all of which would most likely prove simple in comparison to actually capturing the Witch and bleeding her dry.

Still, if that was what it took, then that was what they would do. One way or another, Alice Andrews would open the Veil and Earth would belong to Demons once more.

Chapter 46

Alice awoke, still feeling tired and drained. She turned onto her side and was disappointed to find that Robert was not next to her. She liked being able to look into those beautiful blue eyes and run her fingertips across his face and lips, before kissing him, but still, he could not always stay in bed, waiting for her to get up. She yawned, stretching like a cat beneath the thin white sheets, trying to ignore the gentle warmth of the morning sun streaming through the large double doors leading onto the balcony, tempting her with the desire for more sleep. *A morning back massage would be heaven right now* she thought, imagining the delicious thrill of his hands on her shoulders.

A window was open, and she could hear the faintest of breezes in the treetops wafting in the sweet morning fragrance of lavender and honeysuckle. She thought she could even hear the low, gentle buzzing of bumble and honey bees, and she smiled contentedly. The idyllic little moment was broken by the sound of gentle footfall, the perfume of flowers replaced with the smell of fresh coffee and toasted bagels. Alice pushed herself up onto one elbow, and looked at the handsome man standing in the doorway, dressed in a loosely-tied dressing gown and boxers, holding a breakfast tray of bagels and tea.

"Morning, sleepy-head," he said.

"'Morning." said Alice, watching as he walked around the bed and placed the tray on the covers next to her. She pulled the blanket up close under her arms, unimpressed that she was naked underneath the duvet. She never slept naked, could not for some reason, so she visualised her typical nightwear, a pair of pants (underwear, not trousers) and one of Robert's checked shirts. He had tried buying a man's checked shirt for her, which she had immediately swapped for one of his old ones. Maybe it was weird and silly but it made her feel close to him, made her feel safe, made her feel like he was always there even when he could not physically be there.

The man sat down next to her and tried to reach for her hand, but she pulled away.

"Thank you for not using his form," she said. She took the tea, finding that there was comfort in the small actions somehow.

"You didn't leave me much choice," he replied, watching her with equal caution. "Surely it would be much easier if I did look like him?"

"I fail to see how," said Alice, blowing onto the hot liquid before taking a large sip. "This isn't going to be easy, full stop."

"But it could be."

"It won't. I don't plan on going gently into that good night," said Alice, calmly.

"We don't want to kill you, Alice, although if you persist in fighting us, it is a probable outcome. The human mind and body can only endure so much."

"I can endure enough," said Alice, confidently.

"I guess we shall have to wait and see."

Alice stared at him over the rim of her tea, wondering why he did not drink the coffee, given she would not. "What do you want?"

"We want you to open the Veil," the handsome stranger said.

"No," said Alice.

"Why not?" he asked, surprised to find himself genuinely curious.

"For one thing, as imperfect as this world is, I have no wish to hurry its destruction. For another, I don't have that kind of power."

"We think you do. And we're not the only ones. The Fallen are also watching you," said the man with a smile.

Alice's confidence faltered a bit. The truth had a funny way of doing that, particularly when the repercussions were far from encouraging.

"It's almost amusing to see such a powerful being be so naive about what she's capable of and of those around her," the demon mused, smirking.

"It's not naivete," she said, immediately regretting it. She had not wanted the demon to know quite how little she thought about herself to have never considered that the great forces in the world would ever look to her.

"No. You're quite right. It's not. My mistake," the green-eyed man said.

"Yeah, it's nice that you're making so many," Alice retorted with a grin.

"A childish ploy, Alice, very childish," he said.

"Perhaps, but it's true, and as you can see, the truth hurts."

"Why does knowing that the Fallen are watching you, make you so uncomfortable?" he asked, rubbing the dark hair at the back of his head.

"It's disappointing, when someone is your friend and they knowingly withhold important information," said Alice, staring at the steam rising out of the mug.

"I can understand that, I suppose," her companion replied. "Of course, we don't really do "friends" and I kill anything that makes that kind of mistake."

"Simple, I suppose," said Alice, carefully.

"You should have more faith in yourself. You are an exceptional Witch; the Fallen should have told you that, instead of letting you believe you were unworthy of the attention. If you wanted, you could make the whole world bend to your will, that's how remarkable you are."

"Even if that's true, it's not what I want," Alice said simply.

"We can give you what you want," he said.

"I don't think you can."

"Just give us your powers and you can have your quiet little life," he said.

"Strike one," said Alice.

"What?"

She shrugged and smiled, sitting back against the pillows. They were nice pillows; it did almost seem real, except that the two most important creatures in her life were absent.

"Alternatively, just give into your dark side and we'll let you keep your lover and friends as pets."

"Strike two," said Alice. She eyed the bagel suspiciously and then decided to try it anyway. She could feel the hunger in the pit of her stomach and wondered when she had last eaten. "What are you?"

"A demon," he said. "I think you already knew that."

"But you're not the thing attacking me, that's different."

"As you deduced, the wraith is a messenger of sorts. It was supposed to bring you to me," said the demon.

"What went wrong?" asked Alice.

"You are stronger than we anticipated. We should have learned from the little trick at the Library – and in a sense, we did – it just wasn't enough. So, since the wraith is unable to bring you on its own, I'm trying something else."

"Oh." It was beyond her wiring to believe she was that strong.

"Yes, so it would seem," he said cryptically.

"Does that anger you?"

He eyed her curiously, bemused and entertained. "It's infuriating. It's also very exciting, intoxicating, arousing even. I think you even amuse me slightly."

"That won't last."

"I'm quite confident that you won't last long enough for me to get bored."

"Oh, you won't get bored," said Alice, feeling a modicum more confident and defiant in this world. "You won't stay amused, either."

"Is that so?" asked the demon with scepticism and amusement.

"Yes. As I said before, I plan on enduring long enough which means you will lose patience and get angry," said Alice.

"Why not just stay here and ease your own suffering? And I don't just mean the physical pain you're trying to block out at this very moment; I've seen the scars on your arms," the stranger said, in a low, coaxing tone.

Alice pulled up the shirt sleeve and ran her fingers over several raised white scars. "Simple answer, because I don't and can't believe this is real. Therefore I have to go back and save the world or whatever it is I'll be doing."

The demon let out a sigh of annoyance. "What if we just kill the vampire?" he suggested with a dark smile, unbridled glee at the thought shining in his eyes.

"Strike three," said Alice, calmly setting the breakfast tray down on the small pine cabinet by the side of the bed. "But, I will tell you one thing. You won't kill Robert, because neither of us is quite sure what I'm capable of. For all we know, in my anger and grief, I might be able to seal up the Veil or obliterate your very existence. Or maybe I would use up all my magic trying and if I died, then my magic would scatter on the winds so that it might never be balled up in one person again." She let out a long breath and smiled sweetly at him, watching as his face took on a look of confusion. "Same time tomorrow?" she said, before fel-bolting him out of her mind again.

She got up from the bed, the wooden flooring cool under her feet. She pushed past the white net curtains and opened the balcony doors, briefly glimpsing blue skies, lush gardens and bee hives, before it all vanished.

***

Alice's eyes fluttered open, and she squinted and sniffed. She wanted to rub her nose and push her glasses up, but she could not move. She also realised that she was not wearing glasses, but there was not much to see staring up at a ceiling of white paint and wooden beams. She turned her head and felt tears running down her face. A groan escaped her lips, as well as a cry of pain, and she felt Robert's hand tighten around hers.

"Everything hurts," she murmured.

"I know," he said.

"Can you let me sit up for a bit? And I'd like my eyes back please."

He put the glasses on her face, brushing her cheeks gently and adjusted the bed.

"Thanks. Do we have any tea?" she asked, trying to ignore the pain and the desire to retreat from it all.

"If you stick around long enough, I'm sure we can get you some," Robert replied, softly. He kept his voice low; she looked fragile enough that loud noises might cause her to crumble.

"I'll try. I don't like being away from you."

"I'm right here."

"I know. And I feel you, sort of, but you're not there. Wherever it is I keep going." Her eyes closed for a moment and Robert shook her shoulder as roughly as he dared. They fluttered open again. "Fallen," she whispered, feeling Julius' presence behind her. "Should have said…"

A look of concern crossed Julius' face as he placed a cup of tea on the small table within Robert's reach. Robert picked up the mug, blew on the golden liquid gently before sipping it. He passed her the cup, hoping he had cooled it to the right temperature for her.

"I love you but don't steal my tea," said Alice, with a faint smile. She sipped slowly, her throat both soothed and burned by the liquid. "Are you taking care of Onion?"

"Clive's been going 'round."

"Thank him for me. Are you taking care of you?"

"Of course," said Robert, trying to grin disarmingly.

"Liar," said Alice, drinking a little more, as she noticed that he was still wearing the white dress shirt and tuxedo suit from the launch. "I need you to..." She tried to swallow and wet her lips again. Her teeth felt awful. "I need you to be stronger. Promise?"

"I promise."

"Also, you need a shower. Yes, I'm well aware I do too, but I can't get to one."

"I think I have more important things to worry about."

"Well, I'd feel better if you went home, had a shower and a proper meal. And a shave," she added, running her hand across his stubbled chin. She pulled a face. "It looks sexy, but it feels scratchy." She laughed weakly and squirmed away as he leant into rub his face against hers. She pushed feebly against him and he smiled, kissing her forehead instead. "I'll be okay if you let me steal your jacket. It kinda makes me feel like you're there when you can't be." She dozed momentarily and suddenly jolted awake again. "I need you to pretend things are normal and I need you to go spend some time with Onion for me."

"Try to eat this, will you, please?"

"Oreoes? Really?" she said, with a faint grin. "I'm not a child." She stuck her tongue out, and he pressed the biscuit gently against her lips. She took a small nibble, unable to taste anything but blood. "And no deflecting, you have to be good."

"Would you?"

"At some point. If you begged me to," said Alice, trying to ignore the lead weights upon her eyelids. "It's hard to know whether the contamination thing or my love for you would win out. But I definitely think showering is a good idea."

"Gee thanks," said Robert, smiling. He loved her for trying to be so normal, but would have been equally relieved if she was falling to pieces, as long as she was present and with him. "We've got a saline drip too, when you stay still long enough for it to work. You need to try and keep still, if you can."

"Can you see it?" she whispered, not entirely sure she

had much control over her movements.

"Only in the mirror," he replied.

"What about when you fang out?"

"No."

"Just wondered," she said, feeling the darkness pulling her back inside. She winced, squinting like a bright light was in her eyes, and she pushed against it. She knew she would not be able to resist for much longer, but while she could, she would not go back.

"I can't believe you're trying to approach this as though it's some kind of experiment."

"It helps me cope," Alice said, with a weak smile. "Please will you read to me when you get back? It must get tiresome trying to talk to me, and hearing your voice is comforting."

"Anything in particular?" he asked.

"*Dracula* I suppose, even though you make me feel bad about the ending now," she teased.

"As if. In your mind, we're Mina and Jonathan. The vampire aspect doesn't come in to it."

"Very true," said Alice, her eyes beginning to lose the battle of staying open. "We are the characters that I think should be together."

"Well, I shall start when I visit after work tomorrow," Robert promised, reluctant though he was to even entertain the idea of going about a normal day.

"Thank you," she said, relieved. She yawned and coughed again, feeling her grip slipping. "I'm sorry. Teeth feel bad. Need... go... so much pain..." She coughed, feeling blood and bile in her mouth. "Remake salt circle. Safer. Please?" He offered her the tea again and she drank what she could. "Need you... Onion and you... need to tell him... love..." She screamed, and as a huge tear appeared in her already shredded jumper, Alice passed out again.

"Alice? Alice?" Robert said desperately, even though he knew she had already been snatched away from him. He lowered the bed back down and placed the mug on the side, before slumping back into his chair. He rubbed his right eyebrow three times and buried his head in his hands for a moment. Then he picked up a bowl and gently washed the fresh wound on her side. He whispered reassuringly to her, talked about random things, knowing that she could not hear them and that they could do nothing for the immense pain that she was feeling. He felt worse knowing that he was adding to it, that the iodine and silver nitrate antiseptics and dressings would be stinging like hell before they helped her feel better. He also tried to make a mental note to bring Alice's toothbrush and toothpaste when he came back. It seemed like such a stupid and mundane concern, but if it would make her feel even a little better, then he would make the effort.

Robert hated that she was right, hated that she had asked for things that meant he had to leave her side, hated even more, that she would know if he did not do them.

"I love you," he whispered. "Don't give up on me or yourself." He picked up his suit jacket and laid it over her. He kissed her forehead. "I will be back," he promised.

***

While Robert had been talking to Alice, Stuart had been stood in the corner trying to get a hold of Sam. On the third attempt of this current try, his Psychic friend finally picked up.

"Sam?"

"Hey Doc. Sorry about not returning your calls. Things are going a bit crazy. I'm on my way though," said Sam, his voice sounding slightly fuzzy and faint against the noise of what sounded like whirring motors.

"You are? That's something of a relief," Stuart said.

"Don't get too excited. I only left an hour ago and it's going to take me a few days to get there. How's she doing?"

"She's in a lot of pain. Seems quite lucid when she's conscious. She can't get rid of it entirely, but she can push it out for small periods. Is this what you saw before?"

"No, I don't think so. The thing I've just dealt with in Roswell decided to have some fun by telling me that my friend was dying and that the Witch would be on their side soon. I know they lie but I got the sense that this wasn't completely untrue."

"No, not completely. She's restrained, bound and sealed. Mostly of her own volition."

Sam gave a low whistle. "She really is amazing. Has she managed to find out its name yet?"

"It's not a demon."

"What?"

"It's not a demon. It's a nekrofolis wraith."

"A death wraith? I thought they were borrowers and that they only had a short existence. Job done and gone, kinda thing."

"What little I can find on them says as much. However, Alice is clearly not prepared to let it do its job, so it's still here. There's no literature of people fighting them because there's been relatively little demonic activity in over two hundred years. And what little there has been, has been towards humans, not supernaturals, which means that if there is anything, it would take forever to trawl through all the records, if we can even read them."

"Fuck me," said Sam absently.

"Sam," said Stuart disapprovingly.

"Sorry. And you can't exorcise it?"

"No. Alice thinks it's bound physically to her, but we don't know how. We can't see anything."

"What about Julius?"

"I've not asked. I'm not sure I want to know that answer."

Sam was quiet for a moment. He could sense Stuart's anger and disappointment, and shared it but there was nothing any of them could do or say to make the Fallen do anything beyond the scope of their own orders and rules. "Any idea who's behind it?"

"Plenty of theories, but nothing definite. And all things considered, we're not even positive as to when this thing latched onto her," said Stuart, looking over at the troubled couple.

"Can they find her? Physically I mean. The demons and their agents?"

"No. We're on hallowed ground and protected from prying eyes by The Fallen. It was set up as a sanctuary long before my time and since Alice essentially got herself here, it's presumably deemed appropriate."

"They'll still be watching Robert. Maybe you as well," said Sam.

"What do you propose?"

"Try to act like everything is normal."

"You don't think that will just give them a chance to follow us?" Stuart asked.

"Even if they could, they won't be able to enter. But at least it gives the impression that no one's that worried about her; might even create some doubts to Alice and Robert's relationship. Might just be that their forces are more spread than they wanted them to be. I don't know. My gut just says you should try to play it as though everything's fine."

"I'm not sure Robert's going to take too kindly to the idea," said Stuart, looking at the Vampire tenderly doing what he could for Alice.

"Convince him," said Sam, sharply.

"In all honesty, I'm more afraid for Alice if he leaves her side. Even if he leaves for a minute or two, she appears more agitated."

"She'll be using him as anchor, which might make things more complicated." He paused for a moment. "I'll get there as soon as I can. Just make sure she stays alive."

There was suddenly three sharp beeps as the call failed.

Chapter 47

It was unseasonably cool for the time of the year and as Robert and Stuart stood in the doorway, they each secretly wondered if it was somehow Alice's doing. Robert took a deep breath and sighed despondently; as horrible as it made him feel, it was pleasant to be out of the stifling chapel that was filled with heat, the unpleasant odours of blood and sweat and the heartbreaking sight and sounds of Alice's pain.

Although they were stood in full view of various passers by, anyone who looked at them would not be able to see Robert and Stuart; instead, they would see two unremarkable, average men, in conversation as they smoked their cigarettes. It was part of the Fallen's defences, a camouflage to blind evil eyes from those that needed the most protection. Even if Lady Jane herself was to look directly at them, she would not see them.

"I spoke to Sam. He's on his way, but it's a long drive from New Mexico and there's an equally long story as to why he can't fly. Anyway, he thinks whoever is doing this is probably watching you."

"Alice thinks so too," said Robert, his voice tired and flat.

"I realise that this is not what you want to hear, but it might be best to keep up appearances, especially if they both want things to appear normal."

"Who is Sam? I'm sure Alice has mentioned him before, but it never seems to stick."

"Sam's a Psychic. He's been a friend of the Library for several years now; he and Alice seemed to strike up an immediate friendship, not long before she met you. I'm sure he'll find whatever it is that's preventing us from expelling the wraith," Stuart said.

"I hope so. I didn't know it could hurt so much to be so helpless."

"Go home Robert," Stuart said gently. "I'll sit with her for a couple of hours. The Guardians will watch her the rest of the time. I realise they are not the friendliest bunch but I assure you, they are very fond of Alice, especially Austin, so she will not feel alone."

"It feels wrong."

"I know, but it isn't. If nothing else, Alice told you to look after her cat, and I believe that is something quite important to her. It's as much a message of love as she can send to him, as it is for her to give you a break."

Robert took one last look up at the building and reluctantly accepted that there was nothing more he could do for the moment, and allowed Stuart to lead him over to the curb and hail a cab.

***

Robert shuffled into the apartment. It was strange how cold and empty a place could feel when it had not been properly lived in for even a couple of days. He flicked on the lights, washed his hands and put some pasta on the boil. He knocked on the airing cupboard door before opening it, but Onion was not inside.

"Better not be on the bed," Robert said sternly, entering the bedroom with false normalcy.

"Technically, I'm not," said Onion, who was laying on a blanket on top of the bed. "She sent you home then." He smirked, comforted by the knowledge that things were not so dire. He hoped.

"Yup. Are you okay?"

"Not so bad."

"It's okay to miss her," Robert said, bending to stroke

behind Onion's ears as he had seen Alice do on numerous occasions. The cat recoiled, nose wrinkled in disgust, and Robert looked down at the three-day-old clothing, smudged and stained with blood (hers), sweat (his) and tears (theirs). It was unusual for Vampires to sweat, but he supposed things were not very normal at the moment. "Yeah, I guess Alice was right. Let me shower first."

"How is she?" asked Onion, his bravado gone as his gaze flicked to Robert's eyes.

"I don't really know," said Robert sadly. He cleared his throat and pushed open the en suite door, feeling a strange warmth and comfort as he stood beneath Alice's stars. "I'll give you the rundown in a few minutes."

He took a bit longer in the shower than he had planned, getting distracted by memories and opening Alice's shampoo just to remind himself of how her hair usually smelt. It was silly – he knew she was going to be okay, but it felt like it had been a long time and he knew it would not be over just because they would get rid of the wraith. He brushed his teeth, shaved and collected Alice's toiletries in the little bag she kept on the side. He made a mental note to gather up her dress and his suit to take to the dry cleaners, and rummaged through his side of the closet, looking for jeans and his blue-checked shirt, which he eventually found on Alice's side. He smiled, shaking his head with mild annoyance, and went back into the kitchen.

He drained the pasta, threw some sauce into the pan, along with some pancetta and parmesan, and took out a beer from the fridge. He also put a small amount of tuna out for Onion and tipped his own dinner onto a plate. He grabbed a fork and sat on the stool, realising that it was the first time he had been in the apartment on his own.

"How is she?" asked Onion, quietly jumping up beside the Vampire.

"Hanging in there. She's stronger than she gives herself

credit for."

"Of course," said Onion. "Most people are." He ate the tuna, watching Robert picking listlessly at the pasta. "But what's actually going on? Did we miss something?"

"No, I think if it could have been found, we would have. Especially as I'm pretty sure Alice tried to get us to find it." He thought briefly of the car ride home and Alice's insistence that she was okay to be bitten. His thoughts travelled along a long road or what ifs and should haves, and he was grateful that the cat allowed him a moment to gather himself. Robert took a deep breath and shook himself. "It's a nekrofolis wraith."

Onion's eyes widened. "Seriously?"

"Yup."

"No demonic activity towards supernaturals in centuries and they start with this?" He frowned, annoyed that no one from the Fallen had mentioned any of this to him. He knew there was little that he could do, but given that he was Alice's keeper, he had a right to be told.

"I guess so."

"Who is it?" asked Onion, adding off Robert's look "Demons are like terrorists. They tend to try and take credit for things like this. Or at least boast to the wrong person."

"Don't know. I've half been expecting Alice to suggest we let her go to find out, but I don't care what she says or threatens, that will be over my dead body. Like properly, no rising again, dead body."

"Reckless as she can be if she thinks it might help others, I don't think she would go that far," said Onion, carefully. The two males looked at each other, as if they were not quite convinced.

Robert shook his head decisively. "Doesn't matter. It won't be happening. We've got her sealed in multiple salt circles; the Guardians are watching over her, as apparently are the Fallen. Presumably beyond just Julius. And I'm not sure how she'd get anywhere given her current pain levels and her appearance. Someone would either suggest she see a priest or a doctor... even though she's seen both and they couldn't do anything." His mind wandered into the tiny chapel, seeing Alice strapped to that bed, covered in scratches and cuts and bruises, soaked in sweat and tears; sometimes thrashing about as though she was physically fighting something, sometimes staring unnaturally into some other space where he could not reach her; occasionally there with him and rarely, seeming to be at rest. She looked like something in *The Exorcist*, only less grey and more human.

"Who told her?"

"Huh?" said Robert, snapping back from his thoughts. He looked at the cat quizzically.

"About The Fallen?"

"Oh. The demon in her head," said Robert. "Working theory is that because the wraith could not get her to the demon who conjured it, the demon is using it as a conduit to communicate with her."

As far as cats could, Onion frowned. He was no expert, but he would have thought that between the involved parties, they could get rid of even an old creature of hell energy. "What's stopping the exorcism then?"

"Not sure. I guess it can't be the food or the drink, certainly nothing she's wearing, but it's physically attached somehow and none of us can see how. So we're waiting on Sam."

Onion bit back a laugh at the displeasure with which Robert said the name. They were all the same when they got a bit jealous. "Yeah, a Psychic should be able to see it."

Robert rubbed Onion's ears affectionately and was rewarded with a rare purr. "She loves you, you know?"

"I know. Of course she loves me. Why wouldn't she?" Onion replied, smugly. "Kathie's been ringing. That's something you'll probably need to deal with."

"It's probably too late to ring now. I'll try in the morning. Add it to my to-do list."

He put the laundry on, put the dry-cleaning by the door

and stuck a note by the phone, fighting the urge to go back to the tiny little chapel where Alice was spending another night. He lay down in the bed, again struck by how alien it was without her. He set his alarm for an hour earlier than normal, and picked up the photograph, doing that weird and pointless thing of running his fingers over her image. He sighed, put it back on the dresser and eventually fell into an uneasy sleep, where his dreams were plagued with people he could not save.

Chapter 48

Alice awoke, feeling tired and drained. She turned onto her side and was disappointed to find that Robert was not next to her. She liked being able to look into those beautiful blue eyes and run her fingertips across his face and lips, before kissing him, but still, he could not always stay in bed, waiting for her to get up. She yawned, stretching like a cat beneath the thin white sheets, trying to ignore the gentle warmth of the morning sun streaming through the large double doors leading onto the balcony, tempting her with the desire for more sleep. *A morning back massage would be heaven right now* she thought, imagining the delicious thrill of his hands on her shoulders.

A window was open and she could hear the faintest of breezes in the treetops wafting in the sweet morning fragrance of lavender and honeysuckle. She thought she could even hear the low, gentle buzzing of bumble and honey bees and she smiled contentedly. The idyllic little moment was broken by the sound of gentle footfall, the perfume of flowers replaced with the smell of fresh coffee and toasted bagels. Alice pushed herself up onto one elbow, and looked at the handsome man standing in the doorway, dressed in a loosely-tied dressing gown and boxers, holding a breakfast tray of fish fingers, custard and tea.

"Morning, sleepy-head," he said.

"'Morning." said Alice, watching as he walked around the bed and placed the tray next to her. She pulled the covers up close around her waist as she sat up. She rubbed her lower left arm absent-mindedly, finding comfort in the soft cotton of

Robert's olive, checked shirt. He had once tried buying a man's checked shirt just for her and she had immediately swapped it for one of his old ones. Maybe it was weird and silly but it made her feel close to him, made her feel safe, made her feel like he was always there even when he could not actually physically be there. She almost thought she could hear him, his voice a rumble in the distance, like a thunder storm several miles away.

"I don't want fish fingers and custard," she muttered, crossly.

"Pardon?" said the demon-man, looking at her curiously, as he sat upon the edge of the bed.

"Huh?" said Alice, confused. She looked at the tea and bagels on the tray. "Sorry, finding it a bit hard to concentrate. Feel bad today." She reached for the tea and drew in the warmth through her hands.

"Your body is probably going into shock. Wraiths are quite toxic and the human body – any body really – is not supposed to endure them for so long."

"I want Robert," she said. "And no, not you looking like him. I want Robert, and you can't give him to me. So please, no lies about that right now."

"As you wish," said the demon, dismissively, watching Alice closely. Once again, he was facing things that no one had ever imagined encountering with a mind-walk.

"Why is it so hot in here?" Alice asked suddenly.

"What are you doing?" asked the demon, suddenly able to feel a great heat emanating from the bed. He stood up and walked over to the window.

"I'm not doing anything," said Alice with a crazy smile. "I think it's your wraith. Maybe it finds *me* toxic."

The image of the demon-man flicked a couple of times before solidifying again. "They've changed something. I can't tell what, but it's making things harder for the wraith and that's making you more ill as a consequence. You really aren't looking well on the outside." He looked at her, a red glow in the centre of his green eyes. "I can make it all stop. Make everything better again," he said in a soft, gently enticing voice.

"I'll live," said Alice, before she fainted.

***

Robert had slept for as long as he was able to in their bed, but as soon as he had dressed and fed Onion, he had gone to Alice's side. He nodded to the three Guardians on watch, letting them know they could take a break if they wished, and a moment later they disappeared. Alice appeared to be sleeping, and he tidied up as quietly as he could. He remade the salt circle as Alice had directed in her book, re-applied the bindings on her wrists, washed her face and pulled the blanket up to her chin. He pulled out his own copy of *Dracula*, but the words looked slightly out of focus and he realised he was too tired to start reading to her. Instead, he tried to get as comfortable as he could and dozed in the chair next to her. He awoke suddenly, startled to see her eyes open as she thrashed about feverishly on the bed, muttering as she did so.

"I don't want fish fingers and custard," said Alice, confused and surprised.

"Alice? Alice? Hey, sweetie, stay with me, please?" Robert said, sitting upright and taking her hand.

"I just want Robert."

"I'm right here," he said, squeezing her hand as tightly as he dared.

"Why is it so hot?" she whimpered.

"It's not..." He gave up, realising that she was speaking to someone or something else and he had no explanation for why she would suddenly be feeling hot. He noticed that sparks were flashing rapidly from his cufflinks, something he had not seen since the first day in the chapel. He frowned, but was too concerned about Alice's violent movements to pay much attention.

"I'm not doing anything. I think it's your wraith. Maybe it finds *me* toxic," Alice said, with a crazy little laugh.

"Alice? Who are you talking to?" Robert asked, quietly, wondering if his question could somehow lead her to a name. He did not much care whether it was to the host or the demon itself, so long as he had someone to blame and demand that they remove the wraith immediately.

She went quiet and still, her breathing shallow but steady.

Robert placed his fingers on her neck, feeling her pulse slowly return to normal. He let out a long low breath and sank into the chair, momentarily putting his head in his hands as he waited for his own panic to subside. He placed his hand back on Alice's forehead, noting that it seemed cold even to his touch. There were a few extra blankets in the corner and he tucked another around her after bathing and dressing the latest cuts and bruises. He sat there grasping her hand in both of his as he waited for Stuart to arrive, as he usually did at precisely 8:30am.

"Are you sure I have to go in to work?" Robert asked after informing Stuart of the early morning events.

"Yes. There's nothing you can do for her, other than adhere to her wishes. I'll call Dr Caulson. Perhaps Alice has caught a chill or fever? I would imagine this much strain on her body must be affecting her immune system."

"Well, for the record, I want to reiterate that I do not want to be leaving her side," said Robert, reluctantly kissing Alice goodbye and stepping out of the circle.

"Duly noted."

"I'm surprised no one's recording this. I'm glad they're not, but it's the kind of thing Alice would think of," Robert said.

"Recording these things, well, possessions in general let's say, tends not to help much. Whilst there are similarities, possessions vary from person to person and the truly useful information would be gleaned from the inside, not out. And I have no doubt that Alice is trying her best to gather that kind of data," Stuart said, with a wry shake of his head. He did not think it was necessary to tell Robert that Alice had asked them to try and make some visual recordings, especially when he felt quite uneasy taking such photographs. He understood that people had to cope in their own way, but he did wish Alice would rest and think about taking more care of herself once in a while.

"It helps her cope. I think it makes her feel better about letting it happen in the first place."

"Letting?" Stuart questioned sharply. That seemed like an unfair assessment of the situation.

Robert's expression and hand gesture suggested that the word was not his choice. "That's how her brain works. She'll imagine there's some way she should have expected it and stopped it."

Stuart frowned as he absent-mindedly cleaned his glasses. He placed the thin-wire frames back on his head and pushed them up his nose. "That girl puts too much pressure on herself."

"Do you think it's the bindings? Do you think remaking them changed something?" Robert asked. "It's the only thing I can think of that might have had an effect."

"I guess if they're putting more pressure on the wraith, then it might also affect Alice. Her body seems to mostly be reacting to the wraith as if it were a virus. As I said, I'll put in a call to Dr Caulson and hopefully things will be more settled when you come by after work."

***

Alice blinked slowly. She pulled the sunglasses down slightly, looking over the top of the frames at the gently rippling lake, disturbed by a lone mallard. Lavender and sage permeated the air, and the low buzzing of bees and twitter of bird song lazily drifted to her ears. She pushed the glasses back up her nose and reached for the cocktail resting beside her sun-lounger. She eyed the mongrel dog sitting by the lake, watching it carefully.

"Good evening," he said, taking the lounger beside her. He was dressed in a tight black t-shirt, blue jeans and grey trainers. His hair seemed darker and his eyes looked more green. He was certainly handsome and not dissimilar to her general type. She presumed he would taller than her, given that was one quality she actively looked for in a guy.

"'Evening," she replied, politely.

"You seem better than earlier," he remarked, eyeing her with some caution.

"I guess so. I don't really remember earlier," she replied, feeling a sense of confusion.

"Nor should you. We wouldn't want you getting ideas now, would we?" He smiled, an expression of false charm and deception. "Fancied a change I see."

"Didn't realise that I was the one controlling it," said Alice looking around at her surroundings once more. She felt like maybe it was somewhere she had been recently.

"Most of the choices here are yours. I try to influence of course, but it's ultimately down to you. This little fantasy is of your making. I assure you, this is not what I would create. I must say I admire your talents. Most people recreate their surroundings or somewhere they felt safe, but you've pictured a house you visited once. It's remarkable. You should be proud of yourself."

"I'd be prouder if I could get rid of you both and go home," Alice said, glaring at him.

"Why, Alice. You hurt my feelings," he said, a smug smirk accompanying the wicked arch of his dark brown eyebrows. He made a small laughing noise as she merely glared at him and he shrugged his broad shoulders. "Well, as you are aware, you can send me away, but until you get rid of the wraith, you can't stop me from coming back."

"Lucky me," said Alice, wryly.

"You are not like the others I've dealt with," he remarked, looking at her and weighing her up in this different light.

"Yeah, I get that a lot," said Alice carefully, feigning boredom. Admittedly, it was not the conversation she wanted to have, but she had to try and be smart. If that was possible, given that things were inside her head. At the same time, if the demon could just read her mind then why was there all of this? It was like the undead thing or time travel – it started to hurt if you thought too much about it. "I wouldn't have thought you'd have had many mind conversations."

"No, not so many. They are rarely needed. Sometimes we use dream-walking to help shape things, but I can see that we would have been hard pressed to present you with the right options," the demon answered, carelessly looking at his fingers, frowning as if mildly disgusted by them.

"There are no right options here except to leave me alone," Alice said, pointedly.

"What kind of demon would I be to give up so easily?"

"A sensible one."

He laughed, looking at her with another appraising gaze. "You have a lot more spirit than you let on."

"I fight when it's necessary," Alice replied, shortly. "Usually, it isn't."

"This could all be yours," the demon said, waving his hand towards the house and the lake. "I'm willing to let you keep your Vampire and you can both live in this big, beautiful house and remain in a blissful little bubble away from it all."

"Where's my cat though?" she asked. "I refuse to live anywhere without a cat."

The demon grimaced slightly and the dog barked. "We prefer hounds."

"I prefer cats." She tried to picture Archimedes, since she felt like she needed a bad tempered fighter on her side, and will him into being like she had the fel-bolts, but there was a persistent stinging that kept distracting her. "Are you afraid of them?"

"I'm afraid of nothing," replied the demon. Certainly he was not afraid of anything Alice might do in the mindscape.

"That's not quite true now, is it?" said Alice, with a smirk. "Is it because of Mafdet? Deity of justice and executions? Or a growing popular trope that they are guardians of the underworld, able to send the souls of the dead or unworthy back to whence they came?"

"No, but I admire your imagination. We get dogs; the Fallen get cats. When the animals wish to cooperate of course."

"Why are you telling me this?" Alice asked, suspicious.

"You asked," replied the demon with a casual smile. "Your curiosity amuses me and if perchance you do manage to escape all of this, you won't remember anything you think you've learned." He took a sip from his own cocktail. "Besides, the Fallen could have told you all about this, had they been so inclined to share with you."

"And what do you belong to? The Friars of Ascension? The Chattering Order of Saint Beryl? The Sons of Lucifer? Or are you a lone wolf, an agent of Hell working only for himself?"

"What an active imagination you have," the demon said with a dismissive laugh. "Although again, I must admire your style."

"I didn't come up with those names – they're in different books and TV shows. I guess we're subconsciously worried about you taking the world from us, and consciously afraid to admit that it's happening. Still I'm not too worried about you and your Shadow Syndicate."

"What makes you say that?" he asked, curiously amused and irritated to see that she genuinely was unconcerned.

"Well, for one thing, you're clearly pretty desperate if you need my help. And also, if you were that good, there would be whispers. Maybe you have a really bad moniker, that could also be it. Changing the band name can do wonders for a brand."

"We're good enough that we don't need whispers," the demon boasted.

"Whatever." Alice shrugged, trying to turn her attention back to the book. She could feel his eyes on her, disappointed and annoyed that she had seemingly given up and lost interest so easily.

"You don't believe me."

She sighed, as though it were a chore to be continuing a discussion she had assumed was over. She closed the kindle case again and looked at him. "Nope. It's against nature. Almost everything in this world is about ego and being able to show you're better than someone else. Of course you're more likely to get away with things if you tell no one, but where's the fun in that? There's a reason there's no such thing as the perfect murder. Because people who think they've gotten away with the perfect crime want others to know. They certainly don't want anyone else taking the credit for it. Even if I managed to commit the perfect crime, the one thing that will fuck it up, is the fact that I would need the world to know I had done it, that I outsmarted them all, which kinda nulls the perfect aspect of it, and also why I'm not worried."

"There are plenty that are."

"So you say. I've been warned against groups and no one's mentioned you." That was a lie since no one had really warned Alice about anything, bar things like 'don't drink and drive'.

"I assure you, there are plenty of reasons why you should be worried about what I can do. You might think you know the groups, the factions, the reasons behind man's atrocities, but you don't, because it's all a front for the Severed Hand. We are the whispers in the darkest recesses of your Library, working with an infamy that borders on legend, like Moriarty, too evil to be considered a reality. That is what I control; that is what you are up against when you are brought to kneel before me." There was a sudden darkness to his presence, a gathering of energy that momentarily made him seem larger and more imposing, and a slight chill began to cut into the scene.

Alice smirked to herself, trying to keep her triumph at bay. "Well, it certainly won't be voluntarily. Surely this is just a tiresome conversation at this point anyway. Neither of us plans on changing our minds and neither of us is giving up."

"And your proposal is?"

"I don't have one," said Alice. "I just figure this will get boring, like Sherlock and Moriarty, waiting for the other to make a mistake, to reach the inevitable checkmate. Or concede a draw, which face it, is not happening, ergo, mistake or patience."

"How disappointing," the demon remarked, lazily twirling the stick in his drink.

"Are you real?" she asked quietly, suddenly hit by a strange wave of unreality and fear.

"You doubt it now?"

"Yes. It's all too circular. It's boring, overly complicated. It's like arguing with one's self. And if that's the case, I'd rather stop it now."

"Then how do I prove to you I'm real?" asked the demon, conjuring himself a new drink and a decadent piece of glassware filled with deliciously plump, chocolate covered strawberries.

"Again. It's the *Shutter Island* crazy person argument all over again."

"Well, I have no idea what that means; we'll get rid of the dog shall we? And it was not the food. Not the food alone."

"Perfume..." she muttered, not quite able to get to the whole memory, as the wraith scratched away at her again.

"That was another... breadcrumb. Don't want to spoil the fun by telling you what it actually is." The demon smirked.

"No. You're not stupid enough to make that mistake. My friend will find it though and then I will destroy your wraith."

"If your body does not fail you by then," countered the demon, reminding her of her fragile form.

"I'm sure it will last. What would happen if I got turned into a Vampire?" she asked, suddenly wondering if Robert might try to save her that way, if it truly seemed that she was dying.

"What?" asked the demon, smiling carelessly to cover-up that there was yet another scenario he had failed to consider.

"If Robert was to turn me, what would happen?" she asked again, more insistently.

"It wouldn't make any difference to us," lied the demon, with a careless shrug. "Where is your knight in shining armour?"

"He's with me," Alice said confidently.

"Oh, is he?" taunted the demon. Lady Jane already informed him that the Vampire had been seen at work.

"Of course," said Alice. "Where else would he be?"

"At work? With another woman? Men are so fickle after all. Get a bit grotesque after being possessed for a while and people tend to leave."

"Good thing he's a Vampire and not just a man then," said Alice, sharply.

The demon laughed and looked at her in disbelief. "That, my dear, is incredibly naive."

"I trust him."

"Not everyone is a strong as you. They can be seduced far more easily."

"That's because they want to be. I don't. Apart from this," Alice said crossly, waving her hand at the imaginary scenery "I'm very happy thank you."

"Are you sure *he* is?" the demon continued to press. "Are you so certain he would not be better suited to a woman with more confidence in her beauty and talents? I hear there's an attractive blonde that works at his office who is very interested in him."

"Of course other woman are interested in him, but just because they try to seduce him, doesn't mean they'll succeed." She was not worried, not really, but it did not help that the demon was stirring up all of her insecurities.

"Do you not worry it's different when they work together? So close all the time?"

"I think you should leave now," said Alice, quietly, suddenly finding the charade was getting a little too close to the bone.

"Yes," said the demon, looking at her closely. "Perhaps I should. Enjoy the rest of your evening."

Alice watched as he faded out and picked up the kindle. She looked over at the water, noticing that the glass in her frames had changed. Maybe in this world, she had reactive lenses. It was a lot cooler and darker than it had been too, and the stars were beginning to come out, but there was no moon. It was beautiful and still, a brief and welcome respite from everything. She lay back in the lounger, looking up at the stars and hummed to herself for a moment, hit by a memory of Miami University and the friends she had had there. She still felt sad to think of Tyler; she wished she had been a better friend instead of allowing the miles and years to pile up between them, and it still made her heart heavy to think that if she ever made it to Fenway, she would not be able to meet up with him. She sighed and returned to her reading.

Chapter IV

Jonathan Harker's Journal (continued)

I awoke in my own bed. If it be that I had not dreamt, the Count must have carried me here. I tried to satisfy myself on the subject, but could not arrive at any unquestionable result...

"*To be sure there were certain small evidences, such as that my clothes were folded and laid by in a manner which was not my habit. My watch was still unwound, and I am rigorously accustomed to wind it the last thing before going to bed, and many such details...*" Robert read. He paused. "F. Y. I., I don't like having to do voices. I'm pretty sure I don't live up to your expectations for them, but I'm trying all the same. We've also moved a kettle in, and a new drip should be arriving this evening. Onion is…

"They're definitely watching you," Alice croaked, suddenly.

"Wait a sec. Let me get you some water; then I'll make tea," he said, kissing her forehead. He held the bottle and tipped it gently into her slightly parted lips.

"They're watching you," Alice repeated, after licking her cracked lips and attempting to clear her throat.

"We thought they might be," Robert said, waiting on the kettle to click off with the boil.

"Not a thought. They are." She paused for a moment. "Is Sam here?" she asked hopefully, trying to sit up.

"Not yet," said Robert, watching as her face lit up and darkened again. "He's on his way though."

"Oh," said Alice, disappointed, the brief glimmer of hope drowning again. "This is all my fault..." she murmured. "Everyone's watching because a Witch fell in love with a Vampire. It's not fair. Why is nothing ever fair?"

"Shh, shh. It'll be okay," said Robert.

"Sorry, just really tired. When it's not the demon, I get the wraith showing me lots of lovely images. Apart from the brief moments when I can make it to you, or my brain temporarily switches off." She sighed, listening to the kettle rumble and click. "The demon's trying to make me believe you're being unfaithful because you went to work. He thinks he's causing doubts, but he isn't."

Robert laughed softly. "I guess you're better at lying in there than in the real world then."

"I guess so," she said, coughing. "Let me up, please?"

"Sure," he said, gently undoing the restraints. He helped her sit up as gently as he could, noting that every breath seemed to be causing something to hurt. "You want some painkillers?"

"No," she said rubbing her wrists carefully. "But I might have to take some anyway."

He handed her a couple of co-codomol and she tried to swallow them with the remainder of the water. It took a few attempts, and the bitter, chalky tablet taste mingled with the blood and bile on her tongue. He helped her to the bathroom and gave her a few minutes to herself.

She stared at the reflection in the mirror, barely recognising the face staring back her. Her hair was stringy, wild and greasy; her lips were cracked; her eyes were dull and ringed with deep black shadows; her skin felt dry and dirty, and looked bloodless and grey; the acne had flared up and there were a couple of small cuts. Her hands looked old; the fingernails grimy and a bit too long, if they were not broken and jagged. Her clothes were soaked in sweat and blood, torn as if she had been mauled by some huge clawed creature. At least, that was what she could make out through the gaps of swirling tendrils, the choking waves of black that were currently floating around her as if in some kind of standby mode.

"Well, you certainly have yourself a powerful ugly creature now," she joked sadly, as she exited the restroom. As sure as she was, she could not help but feel Robert was definitely too handsome to be with someone like her now.

"Okay, so you're not looking your best, but you'll never be ugly to me," said Robert. He did not tell her that he was trying to focus on her aura as opposed to her physical form. She would use it as proof that she as ugly, when it was because if he saw how small, grey and hurt she was, he was blinded by heart-break and rage. Her aura was a little subdued and murky, but it was still the brightest light in his universe.

"Promise me, as soon as we get home, you will burn these clothes and leave me in the shower for a day," said Alice.

"I can promise a variation on that request," said Robert, with a smile. "You wanna try and walk around a bit?"

Alice nodded and they started to circle around the chapel. She lifted a hand weakly at the Guardians and smiled at Austin and Phoenix (it had taken a long time, but another Guardian had given her a name). "If I had enough skin left, I swear it would be crawling at this point. I feel distressed by this personal grime."

"I'm doing my best with the wet-wipes and the wash cloth."

"I appreciate that. I think maybe I keep blacking out just because I can't deal with this level of contamination," she joked half-heartedly.

"It could be a factor. Doesn't matter. As long as you're surviving."

"It's so tiring," she said, tears in her eyes.

"You're doing great," Robert assured her.

"You look better today. Smell more like you too. How's Onion?" Alice asked, missing her favourite ball of fluff.

"He's okay. He didn't say it, of course, but he does love and miss you too." He paused for a moment and glanced down at her. "Are you feeling better? You seemed really out of it this morning."

"I don't remember," said Alice. It was too hard to think. "I like your voices though."

"Well, I'm reading you *Dracula*. Someone else is reading you *Rebecca* when I'm gone – audiobook of some description."

"Thank you."

"When I get sick, I expect to be treated at least as well as this."

"Do you ever get sick?" asked Alice, smiling as best she could.

"There's probably something, but yeah, it's rare," Robert admitted. He felt a momentarily flash of relief that in being a Vampire, he would hopefully never have to put Alice in these shoes; he did not doubt for a second that her experience was the worse, but the thought of her feeling this same kind of helplessness and desperation because of him was painful.

"How was work?" she asked, knowing that it would not matter if she heard and remembered the answer or not.

"Okay I guess. TV was on a lot with people wanting to hear about the book launch and Houseman doing the talk show circuit for further promotion. Bruce and the others all asked after you, so I said you were still feeling a little fragile. Didn't notice anything out of the ordinary though. Although there is one thing I have to tell you, that you won't be thrilled about..."

"Oh?" she ventured weakly.

"There may be several magazines carrying photographs of the launch and let's just say at least one shot of you is included. In like, all of them."

"Urgh, really?" said Alice, momentarily feeling normal with the automatic reaction. "Good thing I almost never look like that and no one will recognise me. If needs be, I'll glamour myself."

"You can do that?" asked Robert.

"Oh sure, that's easy stuff," said Alice with a shrug. "I could be a red-head tomorrow if I fancied."

"Hmm. Interesting," Robert said, letting her see the teasing glint in his eye. He smiled gently at her. "Anyway, I've got a meeting with one of the photographers tomorrow; she's a friend of a friend of Christopher's and she seems to think that there's a few we should have copies of."

"That's nice, I guess."

"I think so. And at least they should be nice, candid shots as opposed to us looking like we're at prom."

"I never went to prom. Partly because we don't really have those in England, or certainly didn't, and I have no doubt that I probably wouldn't've gone anyway, because I never feel pretty and I wouldn't've had anyone to go with."

"You didn't miss much. It's mainly a lot of awkward teenagers in an awkward social situation, with ridiculous social pressures mainly caused by film and television."

"I so don't miss high school."

"Me neither."

"University was pretty good. Not quite what I'd dreamed of, but still better."

"Ah, speaking of university, Kathie's been calling."

"You can't let her come!" said Alice, suddenly panicked,

clutching his arm. Her breathing became rapid and shallow and Robert held her steady, trying not to panic himself.

"It's okay. I've told her you've got the flu and that it would be better to hold off for a couple of weeks."

"Well, if she turns up anyway, don't let her come here," Alice pleaded, trying to take deep breaths and calm herself. Kathie was not protected and Alice did not think she had enough strength to keep her safe. She almost felt dizzy the panic attack had been so violent and unexpected. "There's too much talking..." she muttered. She started heading back to the bed and wrinkled her nose. "This poor thing is so gross. If I wasn't so afraid that something might go wrong, I would let the bindings go and clean everything."

"I'm pretty sure she will not come here until after the full moon at least now," said Robert, handing her the tea. "And this thing has probably dealt with a lot worse than you."

"One hour... then go home. You can read until then, please."

Robert looked at her and decided to forego whatever he had thought about saying. He picked up the copy of *Dracula* and began reading again, taking her hand in his. "*But these things are no proof, for they may have been evidences that my mind was not as usual, and, from some cause or another, I had certainly been much upset...*"

Chapter 49

Alice had no idea what time it was. It kinda felt like a Monday afternoon, but she was also pretty sure it was actually later in the week. She kept drifting in and out of consciousness, drifting in and out of reality, drifting in and out of several different dreams or realms or something. She knew the wraith was a real entity, although what it was showing her was not; she knew that the chapel, and the people in it, were real; but it sometimes felt like she existed more fully when she was talking to the demon. Particularly when Robert was at work or at home. She hated that he left; hated it even more knowing that she made him; hated that she could not just ask him to stay. But it was not fair. There was nothing he could do for her at the moment, and it was only causing them both pain for him to stay by her side.

She also did not know how to tell him how horrible it was. Of course he could see the cuts and the bruises, saw how her body would shake and convulse and arch in abnormal ways, knew that she was freaking out a little, a lot, from being covered in dirt and grime and sweat, wearing clothes that were several days old, but she could not tell him all the horrible things that the wraith would show her. Things that repulsed her, made her want to be sick, made her want to scream. A barrage of sex and violence and despair that she could not always force away. Knowing that she had her own constantly rejected darkness did not help matters; it would be easy enough to say yes, to let the pain stop and be dominated by the demon.

Alice wanted an easy life, but she just could not get past the fact that she believed in doing the right thing for the right reasons. Given that she did not see any value in her own life, Alice was not going to let the demon take her pain at the expense of the rest of the world.

She tried to think of all the things she would do when she finally got back to her real life. A really long shower would be the first thing, obviously, and a change of clothes. Then a decent night's sleep in Robert's arms, scrambled eggs and bagels for breakfast with her giant mug of hot tea. Then, even though it was August, she wanted to sit in front of the fire, with Robert and Onion and watch old movies, either noirs (*To Have and Have Not*, *The Blue Dahlia* or *The Thin Man*) or the kids films that she grew up on (*Return to Oz*, *The Dark Crystal* or *The Princess Bride*). And eat Turtles ice cream just because she could. And listen to lots and lots of music played very very loudly. If she was up to it, she wanted to go for a walk and sit by the lake. She missed being outside, walking through the park, even just going to the subway was looking like a treat. She missed the feel and smell of English rain, missed crushing lavender between her fingers and staring at the stars with Robert.

The rain splashed against the windows, droplets bouncing against the paving stones, and pouring out of the mouths of the gargoyles mounted on the top rafters of the house. She tried to look past the weak reflection of the conservatory and out towards the lake, where the wind was whipping up waves. The sky was grey, darkening with the coming night and rolling storm clouds. She thought she could hear voices, almost felt like she should try and make something to eat, but could not quite be bothered. Instead, she picked up the kindle and tucked her feet up under her. There was a cup of tea next to her on the little wicker and glass table, and she warmed her hands around it for a moment.

If the pattern held, there was not a lot of time before her unwanted head guest reappeared. She felt lost. Obsessive.

Almost like those first few bad days she had had after meeting Robert, when she had been doodling little hearts and 'I love R. E.' everywhere. At the core of it, she was scared. No matter where her consciousness went, it seemed like there was a reason to be afraid.

She took a deep breath, drank some tea and tried to read. There were a couple of voices in the background but honestly, she could not find the strength to care. She stared at the rain until she dozed off. For a moment, she thought she heard something else, maybe even saw a glimmer of two people talking in a fancy hotel room, a face, blonde hair, darkness and curtains and chalices, but it did not seem important. None of it seemed important.

13th September. - Called at the Berkeley and Van Helsing, as usual, up to time. The carriage ordered from the hotel was waiting. The Professor took his bag, which he always brings with him now.
Let all be put down exactly...

"*...Van Helsing and I arrived at Hillingham at eight o'clock. It was a lovely morning; the bright sunshine and all the fresh feeling of early autumn seemed like the completion of nature's annual work...*"

Alice felt the sun stream through the window, and blinked blearily as her ears caught the faint male American voice reading aloud. She could not help but smile and follow the words back to reality, the scary, dark, painful reality that was at least less bleak because it had Robert.

"*...The leaves were turning to all kinds of beautiful colours, but had not yet begun to fall from the trees. When we entered we met Mrs. Westenra coming out of the morning-room.*"

"Hey," Alice said, unable to open her eyes. "I think there's glue on my eyelids."

"Just a moment," Robert said, grabbing one of the wipes from the packet on the table, and gently cleaning her face.

He put the spectacles gently behind her ears and kissed her fingertips. "Hey."

"Still here then," she said, with a smile. Her heart swelled knowing that he was always there when she was awake. It was beginning to get harder to fight against any of it when he was not there.

"Still here. Until ten; and then I go home, like a good boy."

Alice coughed, and winced. "I need to get up. I need to see the outside. Is it raining?"

"I can help you up. I'm afraid that I can't take you outside, and there are no windows. I guess exorcisms and windows don't really mix well."

"Lame," she said, as he helped her up. "Demon left me alone today."

"I guess that's good?"

"No idea. I never remember much. I try, but it's a lot like dreams in that sometimes I'm just left with impressions rather than specifics."

"That's okay, you know. No one's expecting you to be able to write textbooks on demonic possessions; we just want this to end."

Alice sighed. "I know. I just feel stupid for letting this happen." Robert smirked to himself; he really did know her too well. "It's not your fault."

"It kinda is."

"How? How is this your fault?"

"It's my fault because I didn't believe in my powers and I didn't bother to protect myself," she mumbled glumly.

"How could you possibly have predicted this?" Robert snapped, crossly.

"I shouldn't need to. I'm supposed to be all about being prepared. I have protections on tons of things, notebooks, safes, my boyfriend, my friends and my cat. But not me."

Robert sighed, letting his anger out in one deep breath. Whatever he was angry about or with, it was not Alice. "There is nothing I can say that is going to make this alright for you, so can we wait to fight about this when you're better?"

"What's the point?" said Alice morosely. "I messed up. They'll get my powers one way or another. Maybe I should just give in already – maybe I can at least bargain for swift deaths."

"Oh, for goodness sake," said Robert. He grabbed her, putting his hands on each cheek and forcing her to look at him. He could feel the weeping cuts on her cheek, the scabs rough under his hands and slightly damp from tears, and hoped that he was not adding too much to the pain. He wondered if she was even feeling it any more, given that Dr Caulson had started giving her morphine. "Normally, I can just sit with you and let you ride out the darkness, but this is not 'normally'. You need to claw out of this or at least not give in. I need you to promise me that much."

"I don't want to," said Alice petulantly. "Not allowed to break promises."

"I know. And this pains me to say, but I don't care about that right now. What I care about is you coming back and us going home. I just want you back."

Alice swallowed and failed to blink back tears. "Okay," she said, doing her best to hug him, although her arms felt like lead.

He picked her up and carried her back to the bed. "You going to try and eat anything?"

"No thank you. I'll just have some water or something."

"Are we okay?" Robert asked, pulling a new bottle of water from the mini-fridge.

"Of course? Why wouldn't we be?" she asked, looking confused, taking some water. "I think I need tea. Can I go outside? I'm hungry."

"I'll put the kettle on for you," said Robert, patiently. "And you know we can't risk letting you outside."

"We could make a massive salt circle around the whole building," said Alice, suddenly feeling desperately trapped and claustrophobic.

"Theoretically. But I can't imagine it would be that successful, given the footfall past this place," said Robert, hating that there was nothing he could do to aid such a simple request or the panic in her eyes.

"Spose. Thank you," she said, as he placed a sandwich (just in case) and a cup of tea next to her. The panic dissipated and she closed her eyes for a moment. "Sometimes, it feels like there's a cloud in my eyes. I wish it was raining."

"It's pretty grey out," Robert offered.

"I feel like the rain is our weather," Alice continued.

"Because of one kiss?" asked Robert, bemused. Unless the shower counted, in which case, maybe it was given that there had been a lot more than one kiss in the en suite.

"Has it only been one? That makes me sad," said Alice. "I listen to songs and they make me want to dance in the rain with you, and kiss, and maybe other stuff. You know, if we were somewhere alone."

"We'll work on it," said Robert, gently, putting a hand against her forehead. She did not feel feverish. Maybe the morphine was making her seem scattered. Or the wraith. Or the lack of real sleep, food and drink. "What would you like to dance to?"

"I don't know. I can't dance. Like I said before, I can sway. Although not sure I can even do that right now."

"I don't think it matters," he said gently, scrolling through his phone. There was not a lot on it, seeing as Alice usually took control of the music, playing it through her iPod docks or the PC, and she cared a lot more about it than he did. He did find that he still had the playlist he had made for her birthday, but that did not have the song he had in mind. He went online and found 'You Can Do Magic' by America, a song that Alice loved and that he had come to think of as his song for her. He did not know why it seemed important right now, but he supposed he just wanted an excuse to hold her for a little while and remind her why she should not give up.

"Want to dance now?" Robert asked.

"Is it raining?" asked Alice, looking bemused and slightly scared. She really did not want to admit to that she was afraid of the amount of pain it might cause, even though she was fairly certain it could not be any worse than taking her little walks.

"I don't know. But I want to dance with you."

"I don't have the energy."

"You don't need to," he said holding out his hand. "I've got you. We'll place you on my feet and I will move us both. And it's only for another two minutes."

Part of Alice wanted to be mad and stubborn, but it was also sweet and it would definitely be better to use her energy to dance with him than fight. She gave a crooked smile, a small shake of her head and took his hand. "Thank you," she whispered, placing her head against his chest. She hummed along and looked up him for a moment. So much strength tempered by such kindness. Her gaze dropped back down to the floor; it was too much effort to keep her head up. "I am so lucky to have you."

"Yeah, you are," he said, kissing her head gently as the song ended. "Come on, let's get back to *Dracula*. They won't kill that vampire if we don't keep going,"

She laughed softly. "I am not adverse to more dancing if it's like that."

"I'm sure we can give it a try some other time," said Robert, carrying her to the bed.

"What's wrong?" Alice asked, as he gently laid her down.

"Just..." He trailed off and sighed, not wanting to voice doubts or acknowledge that her death was actually a very real possibility. "Do you want me to call your parents?"

"Oh." She lapsed into silence, thinking intently. If she did not make it, she might regret not having them there, but on the other hand, she had promised not to give up, so there was no reason that she would not survive once Sam got rid of the binding agent. "No," Alice replied, finally. "It's bad enough that you have to deal with this. I don't want them to see it too."

"Are you sure?"

"Yes."

"Okay," Robert replied, kissing her forehead. "Sam should be here soon, so you might want to keep your energy up." He unwrapped the sandwich and although she pulled a face, she took it from him.

"Sometimes, it is *so* annoying when you're right," said Alice, taking small nibbles at it.

"You know you don't have to keep pretending you're fine."

"I'm used to it," said Alice, wearily. "Sometimes it's almost easier to wear the mask of "I'm fine" than it is to be honest. It's like everything – tired, fed-up and numb. I feel like I'm here and I know that the drugs are helping to keep the pain away, but they also make me feel like I'm not in my body. I don't really know how else to be. I'm sure I'll get through, like I always do." She shook her head and handed him back the remains of the sandwich.

He wordlessly strapped her down again, noting that he had to go up a notch for them to fit. As frustrating and horrible as it was, the leather straps were for Alice's protection as well as his and the others. The way her body would convulse and writhe, contorted by the wraith's attacks would probably have snapped several bones, including her back and neck, had she not been restrained. He sat back down and flipped open the book where the small white ribbon marked his place. He looked at Alice, who was watching him intently, and he squeezed her hand one last time before he began to read.

***

"Have you found them yet?" Sargeraxs asked, deciding to abandon the night's sojourn into the strange little realm that was Alice's mind. Not only was it proving difficult to get in there, it also seemed slightly madder than anything he had seen before. Such a barrage of emotions and images that appeared completely nonsensical to him. He wondered if they were pushing her sanity to its limits or whether that was simply how Alice's psyche was choosing to cope. His host body was also feeling the strain of these trips; not only was Houseman's mind shattered, but the physical form was also suffering. A day off would be prudent, especially when there were so many other souls that were far easier to corrupt.

"We believe they must be in a Fallen safe-house," replied Lady Jane. "I have followed the Vampire as closely as I dare, but I always lose him before he gets to her."

"Circumstances being as they are, that is not entirely surprising. Pass me the chalice for the wraith; we must ensure that it proceeds with some finesse." The failings of this physical form reminded him of what Alice had said about preserving hers.

"My lord?"

"The Witch suggested that the Vampire might turn her. We must ensure that if the wraith were to kill her, it would do so before a siring could take place."

"Could that be done? He is still a fledgling after all," Lady Jane said. Like the rest of the Severed Hand's inner circle, she had not considered that the relationship would last long enough that it could become eternal. None of them had considered the possibility that a Vampire would choose to turn a Witch. Of course it was unlikely that the relationship would last to a point where that problem would arise, but certainly their demonic interference during Alice and Robert's early passions might cause unexpected consequences.

"I am sure they would find a way. It is not something I wish to risk given that we must break her if she will not bend. Her blood is key; it may not work if it is tainted with the Vampire curse."

Lady Jane handed him a gold chalice filled with blood and herbs, waiting next to the phone and the door to ensure disruptions would be kept to a minimum, while he communed with the wraith. She was surprised when he walked into the main suite after a few moments.

"Come, Lady Jane. I believe you have earned yourself a night off, particularly as this body will not be able to enjoy the earthly pleasures for much longer. Let us find some easier prey to play with."

"As you wish, my lord," said Lady Jane, feeling a tingle of anticipation and pleasure. She would have to be careful; after all, it would not do to leave anyone with the impression that her antics could be linked to the best-selling author of *The Devil Possesses*, but there were plenty of ways for the wider world to take the punishments in place of the Witch she wished to ruin.

Chapter 50

Alice opened her eyes. She pulled the sunglasses down slightly, looking over the top of the frames at the gently rippling lake, disturbed by a lone mallard. Lavender and sage permeated the air, and the low buzzing of bees and twitter of bird song lazily drifted to her ears. She pushed the glasses back up her nose and reached for the cocktail resting beside her sun-lounger. She eyed the mongrel dog sitting by the lake, watching it carefully.

"Good evening," he said, taking the lounger beside her.

"'Evening," she replied, politely.

"I'm surprised that you feel you need glasses here," said the demon.

"I've been wearing them for too long, I suppose."

"You seem to enjoy making life difficult for yourself."

"Life's not supposed to be easy. And no, I don't enjoy the feeling of things being too difficult and I don't like feeling the way I do. I just don't believe that an easy fix won't come without a cost."

"And if I could assure you that the cost would be borne by someone who, perhaps, deserved it?"

"Makes no difference. I refuse to sell my soul for parlour tricks. Besides, I can hardly be the good guy if I allow bad things to happen to others for my own gain. I have Robert, I don't need to try and impress anyone else. More importantly, I'm actually quite happy wearing glasses."

"Takes all sorts I suppose."

"Yes. It does," Alice said crossly, giving him a dirty look.

"At least you've cheered up. Yesterday's settings were

rather dreary."

"You weren't here yesterday."

"I was unfortunately busy in the real world and you seemed a bit out of it when I tried to call. There was a large blue box and space ships and so many other things that made no sense to me. And you wanted a moose and a squirrel, because you believed they would be of help."

Alice laughed, but refused to clarify.

"It's nice that you notice when I'm not around. Perhaps you're beginning to have a change of heart after all," the demon teased.

"No," said Alice, simply. "Would be nice if you were here to say you were going to leave me alone."

"Why would I do that?" he said, sipping a drink that suddenly appeared in his head. "You should try it; champagne, whiskey and a dash of cayenne pepper."

Alice shook her head. "I'll stick with the pina coladas, thank you." *And getting caught in the rain*, she thought, also thinking about dancing with Robert.

"Well, you can never tell when you might catch a person at their weakest. Also, it's fun. It's fun to check on your progress, or lack thereof; fun to see if you can cope with the pain. And I adore seeing you fight against the wraith. We're giving you very generous options and yet you refuse to see the potential in them."

She jumped, surprised to see the flashing images of the wraith's message that they would kill Robert slowly and painfully in front of her if she refused to submit. She blocked it out. "Go to hell," Alice hissed furiously.

"Sadly, I'm sure I'll be back there soon enough. You really have proven to be more troublesome than expected. Don't worry though, there's always a plan B."

"Who are you?" Alice asked, looking at him closely.

"A demon of no importance," he lied easily.

"Liar."

"It is remarkable how quick you are to throw that

accusation out. Do you have trust issues?"

"No, I just seem to have a good sense of when I'm being lied to. Not to mention, common sense is usually a decent indicator in cases like this."

"Indulge me," said the demon. Irritated though he was by her stubbornness, he was intrigued with the constant challenges. It was rare that any thing could challenge him without dire consequences. "How does common sense suggest that I am not as I say?"

Alice pushed up her glasses, and rubbed her nose for a moment. "Alright. *If* I'm as big a deal as you say I am, then this task wouldn't be left to just any demon, it would have to be someone important. Maybe the most important demon, because of egotism. How could the leader of the Bleeding Lip not be the one to conquer and seduce the mortal realm's most powerful Witch? Surely it would take such a being to match her powers?"

"Perhaps," the demon acceded, an amused smirk on his face.

"Also, if it was so important, how could you possibly trust some insignificant henchman to get the job done? Especially when you had your best on it and they failed you."

"They underestimated you. Not a mistake she will make again."

Alice continued as if she had not heard him, but she was trying to commit such little details as 'she' to memory. "Although, I suppose, you could actually have just gotten lucky. Maybe some better demons got in first and you managed to piggyback the signal, so that it seems like you're all big and important, but actually, you're telling the truth and you powers are paltry."

"These fictions are becoming less amusing, Miss Andrews," said the demon, a spark of anger in his eyes betraying his easy smile and nonchalant voice.

Alice decided to press on. "Oh, so that *is* what happened. The Fractured Fist piggybacked the Devils of Darkness' attempts to capture me." She noticed the look of surprise on his face as she casually dropped in a real group within her purposefully incorrect names for his own faction. "Oh yes, I've heard whispers about the Devils of Darkness. So presumably this is their scheme and as a minion of the Decapitated Foot, you got a lucky tip and snuck in first."

"The Severed Hand work for me!" he roared angrily. "You will quit this incessant prattling about forces you do not understand. Devils of Darkness indeed," he sneered in disgust. "To call them amateurs would be to give them too much credit. They do not have the skill nor the patience to carry out a plan of this magnitude. And yes, mistakes were made, but I assure you, when we come for you next time, there will be none."

Alice looked him in the eye, a faint glimmer of pity in her cold stare. "Coming after me again is the biggest mistake you could ever make."

"Meow," said Archimedes, jumping up on Alice's lap, grinning wickedly at the demon. The ginger tom was bigger, more scarred and about a hundred times meaner than he had been in life, but he still exuded charisma and cunning. Alice smiled and gave him a cuddle that he would never normally have allowed.

"Clever," said the demon, eyeing the cat warily.

"I'm learning," said Alice. "You're looking somewhat red. And something seems to be wrong with your hand."

"Allergies," said the demon dryly, a curious look on his face as he looked down at his left hand, which had become scaly and red, with two fattened fingers and a thumb, studded with thick black claws, sharp and dangerous.

Alice swallowed hard, recognising the hand from the visions that the wraith had shown her. A hand that had been wrapped around her throat, and had alternately trailed down her body to touch it in ways she had been distinctly uncomfortable with, or had sliced her open with those dagger-like talons.

"See something you like?" he asked as he noted her

discomfort, waving his malformed hand, smirking arrogantly. He licked his lips lasciviously with a forked tongue and Alice felt decidedly unclean under his gaze, a feeling that was vaguely familiar.

"At least it proves my point, that you are not of "no importance" in this scheme, or the visions wouldn't line up with this as they are doing. Sure you don't want to tell me your name?"

"Quite sure."

"Even though I will supposedly forget everything from in here?"

"I believe I have underestimated you enough. I certainly wouldn't want to give you extra ammunition or the chance to summon me back before I was properly prepared."

"Spoilsport," muttered Alice, not that she had really believed the demon would be careless enough to let his own name slip. She watched him out of the corner of her eye, wondering what it was about Archimedes that was making the demon so uncomfortable. Was it something to do with Familiars as a whole, Archimedes himself or the fact that she had managed to will a cat into this space? She supposed he might just not like cats. "Your host body must be quite busy," she said, suddenly.

"What makes you think that?"

"You've been spending less time here. Mostly evenings now too."

"Are you sure about that?"

"Sure enough," said Alice. "And how is it your assistant can watch Robert and be with you?"

The demon could not hide his surprise. "There are certain creatures on this earth that can, in theory at least, be corporeal in all realms. They are very very rare, and rarer still are the ones that can actually harness and use the skill. My assistant happens to be one of those few, allowing her to travel differently to the rest of you." He chuckled to himself. It was a harsh and menacing sound. "You really are very tenacious and clever, Miss Andrews. You really would be so much better suited working with me, instead of against me."

"No thank you," said Alice.

"I'll even call off my pet, so that you need not worry your pretty little head about Mr Evans' well-being or fidelity." He reached out and put his hand on hers before she could pull it away. She was hit with an image of Robert with a vaguely familiar blonde woman, laughing over drinks and dinner, and she was trying to pull him towards her hotel room by his tie, and pushing him onto a bed.

"As I told you yesterday, I'm not worried about that," said Alice, her face hardening, eyes narrowing slightly. She calmly lifted his hand off of her arm and refused to acknowledge the burning pain it seemed to have inflicted or the image he had projected. The tie thing was for her to do with Robert and even though she knew it was not real, something about seeing that bitch do it still hurt. Archimedes made that strange yowling, snarling growl that angry and frightened cats make, glaring dangerously at the demon.

The dog had already disappeared. The lake churned angrily, as leaves began to fall off the violently shaking branches. Alice's hair began to fly wildly in the wind, but other than that small detail, Alice and Archimedes seemed unperturbed by the sudden tempest.

"Really? Because it seems to be something of a nerve you have regarding Mr. Evans," the demon mocked.

"Yes. And I'd have thought you would have learned to stop poking at it," said Alice stiffly.

"But it's so much fun," said the demon. "You might not say much, but you still give a lot away when you're angry. Your powers, for instance. You seem far more willing to push them when you're angry."

Alice contemplated that for a moment, but merely concluded that she still needed more control when dealing with strong emotions. She sighed and calmed the weather; if it was all in her head, there was not much point since she probably was not doing any damage to him. The dog had not returned. "I'm not sure that's much of a revelation."

"Perhaps not, but it's always good to have notes on one's opponent," he said, that little look of surprise and admiration flitting across his face again.

It was probably nothing; if he had tangled with other Witches, Alice was sure they could have manipulated the landscape just as she was doing. "I do not consider the fate of the known world to be a game."

"At the end of it all, everything is a game of chess; it merely depends whether you're in charge of the board or a pawn upon it."

"Maybe that's why I don't play chess. I rather believe that all souls have a value."

"But not equal value. You're only human after all. As objective as you may try to be, can you really deny that the life of one Robert Evans is not worth more to you than the rest of the world combined?"

"No," said Alice, quietly. "I can not." She swallowed, knowing that even though it was just a lie wherever her consciousness was right now, a lie this big felt bad. "But then again, if he is sleeping with your assistant as you would so firmly have me believe, then I guess, I shouldn't hold it in such high regard."

"Indeed," said the demon, grinning broadly. "Of course, you could always just even the score and then we could see whether you'd actually trade the world for him. Or you could trade it for anything really. Anything that you could imagine," said the demon, leaning towards her eagerly. "Perhaps we should try?" Before she could pull away, he put his hand on hers as he had done earlier, pressing down more firmly this time, and her vision was slammed with images of her writhing and moaning under his touch, both in this and what she supposed was his true form. "Sleep with me."

"No," Alice replied firmly, assaulted by more images, the details increasing with every nano-second that she could not pull her hand free. Sights, sounds, sensations that she had only ever truly experienced with Robert, being usurped by this monster and his disturbing appetites.

"Really, Alice, this is becoming tiresome," the demon said, beginning to sound angry. "I will admit, it has been an amusing, almost welcome challenge after so many millennia of easy prey, but I grow weary of all this "flirting". End your suffering; give into your desire and join me..."

The visions suddenly stopped, as did the burning pain in her hand and she heard the yowling battle-cry of Archimedes as he launched himself at the demon's throat. She saw the claw marks and the blood running down his neck and hands as he struggled with the cat. When he threw the cat to the floor, Alice's temper snapped and she stood up, facing him with more anger than she had ever felt before.

"I SAID NO!" she screamed, suddenly exploding a small pulse of green flames outwards from her body.

He reeled back, his clothing on fire but he was still there. Pain was beginning to etch its way across his face, overtaking the shock and surprise.

"If you go after Robert, hurt one of my cats or touch me like that again," said Alice, coldly, shaking with anger "Then I swear by my pretty floral bonnet, I will end you."

"I believe you'll try," the demon retorted, face contorting with pain as he continued to burn.

"You should believe that I will," said Alice, firmly. Then, she let him go. She could hear strange thumping sounds as she picked up Archimedes who appeared to be unharmed. "Thank you," she said, nuzzling into his neck. She took two steps towards the house and the world went black.

Chapter 51

"Grab the fire blanket!" shouted Robert, as the bed suddenly erupted into flames. "Quickly, before..." Even as he shouted commands, the flames disappeared almost as quickly as they had appeared. There was a shimmer of heated air and a high-pitched screeching sound, and then nothing. "What the..."

He tentatively reached out for Alice, noticing the strange burn that had appeared on her hand. It had appeared just as he had arrived; then a few minutes ago, it had started deepening, and the room had suddenly grown incredibly hot. The mark had suddenly seemed to glow and then a moment later, there was fire. Now, other than the strange mark looking an angrier red, there was no sign that anything had happened at all.

"Did that...?" he started.

Austin nodded.

"Right. Okay, well, unless the Library says otherwise, we don't tell anyone that happened, okay?"

Austin looked at his brothers. A moment later, he tilted his head slightly as if listening to something just out of comfortable hearing. Then he nodded an assent.

"Thank you," said Robert. He did not need the others worrying unnecessarily, reporting it to whomever and making more of it than it was. They certainly did not need to know that she was able to do magic despite being bound. Admittedly, it was a binding done by a non-witch and not one of High Magic, but it was still something that would alarm the others and certainly put a stop to her short periods of freedom if they knew.

There was no evidence; there was no damage to the room, to the bed or Alice and were it not for the fact that the three Guardians had seen it too, Robert could easily have dismissed it as a dream.

He sat back down, and gently bathed the strange handprint-like burn. It faded slightly under the holy water and silver nitrate and he wrapped new bandages around her hand and wrists, tying the ribbons a little tighter in case it had an effect.

Alice did not move throughout his administrations. She was still alive; he could hear each wheezing breath that accompanied the laboured rise and fall of her rib cage; he could hear her heart beat, alternately too fast and then too slow; could still see the light that shone within her, which was still the brightest he had ever seen despite the wraith and what it was doing to her. But he also felt that she was not there.

Twenty minutes later, Stuart returned with Dr Caulson.

"Have there been any changes?" he asked, glancing towards the bed before looking at Robert.

"Sort of," said Robert. He felt the eyes of the Guardians boring into him curiously. "Not quite sure how to describe it really, but I feel like, maybe she's switched off, or something." He thought for a moment. "I don't know if it's somehow related to what looks like a burn on her right hand."

"The one that appeared not long after you got here?" Stuart asked.

"That's the one. It got worse about twenty minutes ago." Robert carefully undid the dressing and held up Alice's hand.

Stuart and Dr Caulson looked at bright red mark in concern and fascination.

"What on earth has caused that?" asked Dr Caulson, peering as closely as she dared. She was not going to cross that salt-circle.

"No idea," said Robert. "It looks kinda like a hand print, well, if the hand was doing a Vulcan salute, I guess." He decided to rub a small amount of salve and cut off a new piece of gauze to cover the burn before wrapping it again.

"Maybe the demon only has three digits?" suggested Dr Caulson. "If you consider that there have been some physical effects from whatever is going on in Alice's head, and the only other entities involved are the wraith and the demon, then perhaps it's the demon."

"Makes as much sense as anything," said Stuart, after a few minutes contemplation. "Particularly if they keep having conversations in there."

"He should keep his hands to himself," Robert muttered, his anger flaring protectively and jealously. He wordlessly stepped in and out of the circle to conduct the various tests that Dr Caulson wanted to run. He attached the blood pressure cuff, took a pin-prick of blood from her finger to place on the glass slide, and then returned his attention to the cuff and read out the readings to her. "That's lower than yesterday, isn't it?"

"It's the kind of reading I would expect from a coma patient," Dr. Caulson said, with some concern. "How does her heart and her breathing sound?"

Robert listened for a moment. "Fainter than they should be, but present and steady."

"I don't think there's anything more we can do. It's a shame that I can't use an EEG. I understand that the magic might interfere, but it would certainly be helpful, especially now, to have a comparison. We shall just have to continue as we have been doing. Although the numbers are low, the fact that she has stabilised is promising, far better than all the rapid changes that her body has been straining with." She packed the instruments back into her bag. "I will drop this off again tomorrow, just in case I can not be here when your Psychic arrives. I've tried to keep my day as clear as possible, but there are some surgeries that can not be postponed."

"Of course. Quite understandable. Thank you," Stuart said. "Shall I walk you out?"

"You always were a gentleman, Stuart," Philippa-Marie

replied, smiling. "But no, thank you. You attend to your ward, I need to hurry back to the hospital." She shot a contemptuous glare at the vampire, briefly tried to memorise what she could about the Witch's state and headed out of the door. As soon as she got into her cab, she called Wesker.

Robert watched the doctor leave out of the corner of his eye, still unable to completely trust her. Whilst he believed Stuart's assessment that the doctor had not deliberately intended to cause problems on that first exorcism attempt, he nonetheless felt that she had an ulterior motive.

"Any news from Sam?" Robert asked, laying Alice's hand in his.

"He thinks he'll be here about this time tomorrow," said Stuart, hovering at Robert's shoulder. Dr Anthonys' worry for Alice grew each day that she lay bound upon the bed; somehow in this moment when she seemed to be most at rest, it felt like she was the most lost. There was a greyness to her pallor that had not been there before and he thought that he understood what Robert meant about her not being there. "Are you staying here much longer?"

"Couple of hours most likely. Have to make sure everything is prepared either for bringing her home or having a bag ready if we go to the hospital or something, and she wants or needs Onion here when Sam arrives, so..." He trailed off and shrugged. He still had no idea what she had planned.

Stuart nodded sympathetically, not that Robert was looking at him. He glanced over at the Guardians, who indicated a need to return to the Library. He nodded at them, and much like Julius would, they disappeared.

"The Guardians have departed, but the relief should be here in an hour or so. I can stay with you if you want the company."

"No, thank you. It's nice to get some alone time; sometimes it just feels weird knowing they're listening to you get a bit mushy and emotional."

"I quite understand. I will see you in the morning then."

Robert nodded and when he heard the door click shut, he pulled up some music on his phone and let it play as he begged Alice to find her way back.

***

"My lord!" said Lady Jane, relieved to see Houseman's eyes flutter open with the demon behind them. She had been surprised to see the body fly across the room again; even more so when it had momentarily been engulfed in flames. She had thrown a damp towel over him as quickly as she could, feeling the intense heat radiating from the green flames. Her panic had grown when he had not immediately returned, wondering what game he was playing at to remain in the blaze, particularly as he knew that the host body was failing more quickly than they had originally planned for.

"How much damage did she do?" Sargeraxs asked immediately. He felt no physical pain in this realm; he siphoned it off for Houseman to experience. He was more perturbed by the fact that he had been held there long enough for any damage to be done at all. He knew she had done it deliberately, but did she realise quite how powerful a feat that was? He suspected not.

"It's superficial, mostly," Lady Jane replied. "Just the clothes. The scratches on your neck might require some medical attention."

"She conjured a Familiar," he said, standing up and shedding the remainder of his burnt clothing. He studied his host body in the mirror. The cat had done more damage than he would have imagined, and the added effort of dealing with Alice was beginning to take its toll. And that had been before she had set him alight. "How much longer?"

Lady Jane frowned; as useful as it was to learn from the interactions with the Witch, she could not help but feel it would have all been far better to have abandoned the plan at once, instead of pursuing it to a fruitless conclusion. Given that the Witch had lasted this long, they were clearly just waiting for the wraith to die, for Lord Sargeraxs to return to Hell, and for her to return to babysitting duties whilst the Severed Hand devised a new plan.

"My preferred set-up for disposing of this host would require you to maintain the body for another ten days. There is a contingency if it should fail before that though, my lord."

"I'll make it last," he said.

He looked at Lady Jane, who was hovering cautiously behind him. His eyes met hers in the mirror, seeing the questions she dared not ask. "She's exquisite. Her powers continue to grow and I almost believe she could actually do some serious damage to us if she were given the chance. And you are quite right about her feelings for the Vampire. They will most likely be her undoing, but they must be handled delicately; I should have remembered that she must be handled like a courtship and not a tryst. I pushed when I should have let her come to me," he murmured to himself. He refocused his attention. "Keep an eye on the Vampire, but be careful about how close you get to him. I am not sure she so easily forgets the happenings of the mind-scape where he is involved."

"As you wish, my lord." Lady Jane brought over the small medical kit and began to sew several small stitches. "The majority of these scratches should be covered, if we continue to utilise the college-professor look. I suggest we tell a variation of the truth should anyone comment upon it; namely that a cat turned out to be less friendly than expected."

"I bow to your superior knowledge of the human world, as always," he said. Although he had yet to convince the Witch to take his hand, he was greatly pleased with the progress made on her affections. And her growing powers only made her a more desirable asset. He would have to ensure that the other factions were aware of the fact that she was his prey and that to make a move on her would have dire consequences.

"Any news?"

"No, my lord. The youngest of the Walker line is expected to arrive tomorrow; the Vampire remains by her side when he is not at work or going to the apartment to sleep and it all appears to be business as normal at the Library. Word is that the Witch is off with influenza, so none of the others are expecting her return for a few weeks. By all accounts, the Witch is weakening but continuing to fight despite considerable physical damage."

Sargeraxs listened carefully, but as his pet had already noted, it was nothing that they did not already know or expect. He pulled out a smart and expensive suit and dressed quickly, frowning at the claw marks that were not quite covered by the shirt. He hated cats and that she had had the audacity to use such a Familiar against him infuriated him. He recognised that cat as Endora Price's, recognised it for the thorn in his side that had waylaid attempts to entrap the Witch as a child. That these details were so unconscious to Alice was an added sting.

He offered his arm to Lady Jane, who had re-emerged from the other bedroom in an elegant but revealing dress. He could tell from the shade of her lipstick that she planned to take no prisoners in her night's revelries, and he smiled coldly. If she had even a quarter of the power that the Witch possessed, then the world would already be broken.

Chapter 52

Robert paced his office, anxiously looking at his watch, the clock on the computer and any other time-telling device that caught his eye-line. He hated having to pretend that everything was fine and he especially hated being away from Alice when she needed him. Or maybe he needed to be with her in order to feel useful in some way, even though he knew it was a vanity on his part. Regardless of why he felt the need to be there, he wanted to be there, wanted her to know that whatever was happening with her, he would be right there with her.

It did not help that he knew Sam was due to arrive some time during the day nor that he was afraid that the worst could happen. No one wanted to talk about it, but Alice's body was understandably weak. She asked for food and tea, but she could barely eat or drink any of it. If the convulsions in her body did not dislodge the IV drip, then the wraith would knock it out, and no one wanted to risk sedating her because they had no idea what effect that would have on the wraith and its ability to manipulate her body. She had lost a lot of blood, despite the majority of her wounds being superficial and he knew that the lack of windows was making her more than a little crazy.

It also did not help that Damian Houseman's face was constantly in his, with people sending him various links to the latest interviews, podcasts and reviews, the TV tuned to the latest daytime talk show that Houseman was on. It was strange, but they had cut to a side-stage view and he was sure the blonde from the office had been in the background, even though they had been standing in the elevator together not two hours earlier. The sight of Houseman merely angered Robert further, as he recalled his misgivings about the book and the event and how everything had gone to shit since that night. It had to be a coincidence but he could not shake that niggling feeling that if he had listened to his gut and insisted that they stay home and watch some crappy horror movie, then the love of his life would not be fighting for hers.

So many what ifs floated inside his head… as if he had any more idea what could have happened than Alice could have. He supposed that when he heard of the prophecy and the notion of a Vampire and a Witch tearing the Veil asunder, he had imagined that the pair would have been commanding some dark cult with a dark alter and dark rituals, wanting to bring about an Apocalypse for whatever reasons they might; he had not imagined that it could pertain to them without them being willing participants and if he gave it too much thought, he was concerned as to what the demons would try to do next.

Despite the fact that very few people had been informed of Alice's situation, the supernatural world still seemed to know. He had noticed more of them hovering near the Library, and he was suddenly fielding calls from concerned parties and trying to convince people not to come and visit. He knew Alice did not want anyone to see her in her current state and that despite her robust bindings in the chapel, she was worried she would not be able to keep everyone safe. He tried to allay their fears, whilst desperately wrestling with the unwelcome idea that what if this would be their only chance to say goodbye to her? He was also concerned with the notion of trying to save her himself, whether it was possible whilst wondering if that would be something she wanted.

He was perfectly willing to take the risk of punishment for Siring Alice without permission, but he was not sure if he was able. For one thing, he did not yet possess all of the powers of a true Vampire and secondly, he was not sure if a

Siring could take place if the person was possessed by another demonic force. He did not much like the idea of someone else being her Sire, but he would rather that than lose her completely. Still, to make that call was to give up and he could not lose faith in her and her insistence that once Sam found whatever was binding the wraith, they would defeat it and go home.

    He opened the desk drawer and took out the photograph from that day at the park, and his heart broke seeing how different Alice now was in comparison to that day. The jeweller's receipt sat to the side and he angrily slammed the drawer shut and furiously punched the metal cabinet to his side, feeling no satisfaction in the dull ache it produced or the crumpled dent that was a poor substitute for a demon's face.

Chapter 53

As far as Alice could tell, her day had been an ever-changing mess of the spaces she had grown accustomed to. Sometimes she was alone; sometimes the demon reared his arrogant head; sometimes she was in the chapel. The wraith had started attacking with renewed vigour, filling her senses with pain and decay; whilst the remainder of her time had been blissfully blank. But this was something new. Although technically, this was still the strange in-between where her consciousness met the demon's, the settings were a far cry from the quiet, homely bedroom, garden and conservatory.

"May I have this dance?" he asked. The demon-man was wearing a black suit, white shirt and black tie, with a purple and green mosaic Jolly-Jester mask that covered the top half of his face. His eyes seemed darker, the irises blood-red, the pupils tinged with a yellow glow.

She looked down at the midnight blue gown she was wearing. It was a beautiful dress, with a smattering of beading that caught the light so that it looked like she was wearing stars. The sweetheart neckline of the extremely tight corset bodice was beautiful and Alice felt both sexy and exposed, as it pushed up her breasts but revealed the blemished skin of her back and shoulders. She tried to imagine that her dark hair was a little bit longer and tried to arrange it so that most of the acne scars were covered. The matching navy satin gloves covered the white scars on her arms. There were a lot of large mirrors, gilded in gold and ornamenting the ivory walls, and she momentarily stared at her reflection.

Her mask was tied behind her head with a thick black ribbon, holding the black and blue Colombina over her eyes. A black filigree butterfly adorned the right side of the mask and was studded with blue gems that matched the colour of her dress. It really was quite a gorgeous costume, although she did not feel that way about the person wearing it; Alice only ever believed she was beautiful when she was with Robert.

Alice did not answer but she took the proffered red-gloved hand and allowed him to lead her down the stairs into a beautiful ballroom. Elegant chandeliers hung from the forty-foot high ceiling like fat, golden egg-sacs from the spider webs of gilded Rococo stucco that resembled numerous entwining vines with leaves and butterflies. Towering windows were partially hidden by heavy, velvet curtains neatly tied back with elegant cords of shining threads. Several of the doors were partially open to allow the merest breeze to creep in, preventing the air from becoming too heavy with perfume and candle heat. Baroque chairs sat between tables burdened with opulent flowers, fruits and pitchers of water. A small orchestra was seated upon the stage opposite the grand staircase, the musicians wearing light filigree Colombina eye-masks that were somehow as eerie as the solid porcelain, glass and leather masks of the guests.

There were hundreds of other guests, most of whom were dancing upon the dark, hardwood floor. They were dressed in an array of beautiful, dark-coloured costumes with masks that bordered on the grotesque and hideous. Lavish suits and stunning dresses in shades of reds, blacks and greens; masks of burnt gold, greys, blacks and ivory, twisted into plague doctors, phantoms, panthers and birds; and others that made her think of the splicers in BioShock, the creepy Fireys from *Labyrinth* and the Clockwork people from *Doctor Who*. There was something alluring, beautiful, tragic and disturbing about them, and goosebumps began to cover Alice's flesh.

"I've always wanted to attend a masquerade," Alice said, softly.

"Had I known, it could have been arranged. If nothing else, it might have given me a chance to get you alone."

"To what end? You can not seduce me," said Alice, noting that the formal settings were bringing out her 'very proper English' side.

"I have barely been given the chance to try," said the demon, matching her formal speech pattern.

Alice looked at him closely, but he did not appear to be mocking her. "You seemed to be giving it a good try yesterday," she countered pointedly.

"Admittedly, that did not go to plan. I "jumped the gun" as they say," he said, trying to keep his annoyance at bay. "But I felt we were making progress."

Alice sighed wearily. "Look, I grant that there is a certain appeal to the darkness and attractiveness of this form you are currently in." She glared as his smile took on a hint of smugness. "But it's meaningless. It has no weight, because, it's, well, it's nothing."

"Because you're in love," the demon said, mockingly.

"Yes," said Alice firmly, knowing that the demon still did not understand.

"I have taken many a Witch that claimed to be "in love"," the demon said, leading her around the ballroom in time with the other dancers.

"So you've said. But when you've tried with the others, did you simply take their loved one's appearance and get the job done?" asked Alice.

"Mostly," said the demon with a smirk.

"But not with me."

"No. Not with you," the demon acceded. "I think it's the first time anyone has ever sent me away for assuming the form of their loved one."

"Because I knew you weren't Robert. I am well and truly in love with him and I'm not just saying it. I believe it with every fibre of my being and that certainty, is unbreakable. I believe in him; I believe in my love for him; and I absolutely believe that true love is the strongest force in any realm of existence," Alice said earnestly. "I get that you can't understand it, but you should accept it."

The demon remained unconvinced and Alice shook her head, sighing in resignation.

"If this love is so strong, how comes you're still here, trapped in your head, body being destroyed by a paltry minion?"

"My Psychic is taking his time getting here," said Alice shrugging.

"You think a Psychic can break you free from this?" asked the demon, spinning her out and back in again. He tried to pull her closer but she firmly maintained an appropriate distance, shooting him a look of displeasure.

"I know there's something binding the wraith to me, you admitted as much, but I don't know what. However, my friend should be able to see it."

"I guess your patience won out after all," said the demon, nonchalantly.

"You don't seem surprised," said Alice, a little disappointed in his lack of reaction.

"I have more confidence in you, than you do." He twirled her around, leading her in the same dance that all the others were performing. "I'll just make sure that I do a better job next time."

"Please just leave me alone," Alice said quietly, unable to stop her shoulders from dropping. She looked up at him, almost pleadingly. "I don't want this. I don't like conflict."

"Then give me your powers," said the demon, simply. "One little word and everything will appear to be exactly as you wish it to be."

"I can't do that."

"I know," said the demon. "But you have what we need and as you won't give it to me willingly, we will take it from you."

"Then you'll have to kill me."

"Yes. I suppose I will," said the demon, shrugging his shoulders. "Disappointing, but whatever it takes."

"I suppose this all makes sense then," said Alice, looking around at the beautiful setting and the elegant dancers.

"It does?"

"Yes. The end, the grand finale, the reveal. I feel like there's always a revelation in a ballroom or dance scene. In my mind at least, it's tied up with horror movies, like *Phantom of the Opera* or the *Masque of the Red Death*. I don't know. Either way, this is the calm before the storm, the last dance before the declaration of war," Alice shrugged and smiled. "Or maybe it's just one of those weird, hidden fancies in my mind, some long-forgotten imagining of horror, dancing, desire and death."

The demon smiled patiently, almost like a parent that does not quite understand what a child is babbling at them. "If only I had known. I could have given all of this to you at the book launch. Darkness and desire, even death. It might even have been easier to make you believe you were with Robert when you were actually with me."

"Not bloody likely" Alice said, with a brightening smile. She shook her head; there were only so many times she could say it. "Anyway, he'll be here soon." It was only a small pendant, but she could suddenly feel the fireflies against her chest like a hand over her heart.

"It's not possible."

"Everything's possible when you're in love," said Alice, smiling. Sometimes, to make something real, all that mattered was one's belief. "Can't you feel it?"

"I can feel you dying," he said, glancing around with barely disguised unease.

"I'm human. I've been dying since the day I was born," Alice replied. A loud thumping bass had begun to get slower and louder and they both knew that it was her heartbeat.

"What are you up to?" the demon demanded, his temper beginning to show with the pervading sense that something was amiss.

"Same thing as the day this started. To get rid of this stupid evil creature that persists in trying to burrow its way into my mind, and get back to my life," Alice replied calmly. "Why have you made a mistake that we should be taking advantage of?"

"There have been no more mistakes." He looked around again, missing his step although he recovered quickly and gracefully. There was certainly something wrong with his current connection to her, and he was beginning to feel the mind-scape bend to accommodate another presence. "No. How can your Vampire be here?"

"Same way you are. But different. Less blood, less violence. More English," Alice said with a laugh.

The ballroom seemed to brighten as Alice suddenly smiled broadly and the slightly subdued glow started to shine. The tempo and volume of the music rose, the dancers seemed energised and the colours became more vibrant.

Much as he disliked admitting that he was wrong, he appeared to be continually underestimating the ability of the Vampire to influence Alice's emotions and powers. Even though he had been expecting Alice to defeat the wraith, he had not anticipated having to forfeit his prey so soon. And certainly not as a result of the Vampire mind-walking. He felt the shift in atmosphere and the first cracks of this world buckling under the strain of another visitor; it was most certainly time to leave.

"Winning a battle is not the same as winning the war," the demon hissed in her ear.

"Of course not," said Alice, feeling more beautiful, powerful and confident than ever. "But it's a damn good place to start." She smiled as he shot her a look of anger and hatred before he disappeared and she began to look for Robert.

Chapter 54

Sam burst through the chapel door and immediately stopped dead in his tracks as he saw the state of the people inside. He let out a long breath and looked at each of the sad and tired faces. Even Julius looked strained. He looked over at Alice and understood the range of desperate emotions. Her skin looked almost grey in the small patches that were not covered in blood or dirt, her eyes were turning black and her body was convulsing like she was having a seizure. It was worse than any possession or spiritual hijacking that he had come across.

"Shit. I'm so sorry you guys. I should have been here sooner, but traffic and…"

"Something is stopping us from getting rid of the wraith," said Stuart, interrupting him.

"Are you sure? How can this just be a wraith?" said Sam, surprised. "This is…"

"Not the time Sam," Stuart interrupted again. He was watching the wraith in the mirror and was concerned with how agitated it was becoming. He was also beginning to feel that Alice was running out of time; that if she could not be freed soon, her body would simply give out from the strain.

"No, sorry. What do you need?"

"We need to find whatever's binding the wraith to Alice. There is something physically attached to her and we can't see it. There are just too many cuts and bruises and we don't know what we're looking for," Stuart said.

"On it. Like you said, there's a lot going on here, so it might take a little while," said Sam. "Just…"

"There's something else," said Robert, cutting him off. He might not know what Alice wanted doing, but he was sure it was something she wanted before the wraith was removed.

"What?" asked Sam, looking at the worried Vampire. He seemed taller than he had in the brief vision he had had upon meeting Alice. He reluctantly admitted that Robert was probably more handsome than him, and it was no wonder that he had been unable to turn Alice's head, not that he had actually been trying.

"I don't know exactly. She demanded that I bring the cat; she said you'd bring flowers or herbs, something, and that you would know what to do," said Robert.

"Oh?" Sam looked confused for a moment. "Oh. Er. What? Really? Okay then, I guess…" Sam muttered, the pieces clicking together. "I'm not sure what or why, but er… Alice wants you to go there."

"Huh?" Robert grunted.

"She wants you to go wherever it is; in her mind. She wants you to go in her head, the mind-scape or something," said Sam, trying to explain as best he could. Considering that he had only just come across dream-walking as Alice intended it, meant that it was not an easy task.

"Is that even possible?" asked Robert, surprised.

"Alice obviously thinks so. I mean, there are some… Eh, we can deal with that later," said Sam, slinging his bag onto the floor. "I've never done this before but I guess, we brew the tea and Onion helps guide you into Alice's mind, kinda how the demon is using the wraith. I assume we're trying this at least?"

"Guess so," said Robert.

"She has a book," said Onion, jumping up on the pulpit and looking at them all imperiously. "It should tell you what to do, assuming you can read her writing. There should be a notebook in her bag." He nodded his head to the corner where Alice's shoulder bag had sat for the past week.

Sam walked over and unzipped the tweed-and-red cat bag. "This is her Craft book?" asked Sam dubiously, pulling out a star-covered a5 spiral-bound pad.

"The rough draft," said Onion, rolling his eyes. "She has a proper copy in her safe. Bound and protected. This is where she works things out until it's perfected."

"So how will we know the right things to be using?" asked Robert, recognising the book from the salt-circle incident.

"I'm sure she'll have highlighted it somehow," said Onion, snippily. He was hardly going to do everything for them.

"Well, I can't read it if I can't open it," said Sam, unable to prise the covers apart.

"Oh, right. Robert can open it for you," said Onion. *Did these humans know nothing?* No wonder Alice was generally so disparaging about the males of her species. "She tends to only let a few people access these things. Bit paranoid like that – afraid for herself and of putting people in danger. Which will only get worse now, I suppose."

Sam passed the book over to Robert, who opened it like he would any other book.

"And the Library is okay with this?" Stuart asked, shaking his head and not really expecting a satisfying answer.

"I think we have to accept that Alice has a very unique relationship with the Library. It knows that she would rather die than bring harm to it or anyone inside," said Sam.

"What am I looking for exactly?" asked Robert, flicking through pages of Alice's tiny italic writing. The first couple of pages had a lot of little hearts with his initials in, and he smiled, running his fingers over them. The book had been almost completely filled with notes on different supernatural subjects, interspersed with doodles, little scraps of paper and post-its. There were lots of crossings out, printed capital letters and question marks, and he could see why Alice had a different tome for her Craft book.

"Something regarding tea, African Dream Root, cats?" suggested Sam.

Robert flicked through the pages, wondering how normal people could ever read Alice's writing. He supposed, the short answer was that they did not. He ran a finger down a page, squinted slightly, noticing some of the words he was looking for. Clearly he was getting closer. He turned another couple of pages and found a sketch of a bed and a list of things in a thought bubble that had been boxed by several strong lines.

"Okay, I think that what we need is one teaspoon ground African Dream Root, one teaspoon cinnamon, one teaspoon ginger, one teaspoon honey, one pinch lions dagger and a pinch of calea za-ca-tech-ichi?" He sounded out the plant name as best he could.

"I think I have all those. I picked up a ridiculous number of dream walking slash mildly hallucino... er, also not important right now. I will mulch that together whilst the kettle boils." Sam rummaged through his canvas bag, pulling out a variety of dead plants, and began grinding them together in a black marble mortar and pestle.

"And I have to drink it?" said Robert, wrinkling his nose in disgust at the dried up stalks and leaves. It was bad enough accidentally biting into a bay leaf after all.

"Really? Alice is dealing with that and you're being a wimp about some tea?" asked Sam, squeezing in some honey. He did not always carry it in his bag but it was fairly common for use in herbal teas and he had been expecting to brew something.

"I'm not being a wimp. I just think it's ... gross," said Robert looking at the gloopy, almost black paste that Sam was trying to deposit into a mug.

"I'd drink it, but she doesn't want me going in her head," said Sam, pulling a face as the boiling water sent a billowing wave of dream tea into his face. It was not a good smell, somewhere between hot tarmac and farmland dung and garbage left in the heat. He started stirring and passed it to Robert who continued the action, the look of revulsion on the

Vampire's face deepening. "Although, I will admit, I am glad I don't have to drink this."

"Thanks," said Robert. He spooned up the strange black liquid and kept stirring. The paste did not seem to be mixing particularly well.

"You alright sleeping in that chair? This thing should kick in pretty quickly."

"It's fine."

"Okay, and we need Onion to sit here so that he acts as a buffer between you. Please," he said, addressing the Familiar.

"One moment," said Stuart, reaching into his pocket. He pulled out the protection charm. "May I?" he said, looking at Onion with the cord open.

"Yes, thank you," said Onion. He did not like the idea of a collar, but he certainly appreciated the value of being protected. It was unlikely that the wraith would try to attack him, given that he was – by demonic standards – too small and unimportant, but desperate creatures could attempt desperate measures. He jumped down and onto the bed, his fur bristling, red sparks flashing as the wraith moved against him, unable to touch him.

"Is that necessary?" said Robert, feeling concern for the black tom regardless of the protective charm.

"I'd rather he be there than not. Familiars can manipulate the mind-scape a bit more easily and Onion could drag you out if necessary. If things got really bad, we wouldn't lose you both. It shouldn't come to that, but I imagine when we find this anchor point, it's gonna get damn scary in there."

"Got it." Robert pulled a face, braced himself and drank the dream-tea. He gagged and coughed in revulsion, fighting to keep the mixture inside. He took a look at Alice and forced the gloop down his throat. He coughed again, unable to be entirely stoic about it. "Oh dear gods, that tastes awful. If I ever have to do this again, someone glamour the taste first." He placed one hand on Onion's back and took Alice's hand in the other.

"Just relax, and let the sleep pull you under," said Sam

in a low, calm voice. "Just concentrate on your breathing; in and out, in and out, in and out. You should be able to feel Alice reaching for you, so just allow yourself to find her. In and out, in and out." Sam kept repeating the words until Robert's head drooped down against his shoulder. He turned to Stuart. "Please keep an eye on him. Julius, if you could keep an eye on me, I'd appreciate that."

"Of course," Stuart replied.

Julius nodded.

"Just so you know, and don't freak out, my eyes will go white, there may or may not be some levitation. All totally normal and should not take too long," said Sam, trying to reassure himself as much as the others. Truly invoking his Sight was a cold, dark and hideous place too; whether he was experiencing a memory, a vision or a spectral walk to discover a paranormal answer to a supernatural problem such as this. Sam walked to the other side of the bed and took Alice's hand. "Hang on in there kid."

He took a deep breath and channelled his spirit self, using his spectral sight to locate the anchor point on Alice's body. "Can you lift her head please?" he asked Julius.

Finally he saw something black glowing at the back of her neck, black smoke billowing out and through. Sam picked up the pure silver scalpel Dr Caulson had left earlier and very carefully began to cut the small sliver of darkness from her skin. Alice did not flinch but the wraith started snarling and snapping at him, trying to tear at him with monstrous teeth. Sam ignored it, protected by the amulet around his neck. He picked up the pair of sterile tweezers and gently eased the shard of black glass out of Alice's body. The shadow around her shifted slightly and the wraith writhed and whirled angrily, lashing and biting at Alice since it could attack no one else.

Sam dropped the shard into a small bowl of salted holy water, gave a deep shudder and returned to the normal world. Stuart, Julius, Onion and the Guardians looked at him expectantly.

"The exorcism should work now."

Chapter 55

A man dressed in a white shirt, red-and-black brocade waistcoat and a black suit was trying to make his way through the dancers. An ivory Venetian Phantom mask obscured half of his face, an elegant black opera cloak flowed down to his ankles, and a silver sword lay sheathed in the scabbard at his belt. He was far from being the only man dressed in attire that resembled the Opera House ghost, but he was the only one Alice could see. She ran into his arms and he spun her around, kissing her passionately.

"I've missed you," Alice whispered, feeling as if her heart would burst to know that Robert was truly with her again. Not a dream, not an illusion, not a memory; truly him.

"You've seen me every day," Robert said, also feeling like he finally had Alice back even though he knew this was not the reality in which they physically existed.

"I know. But it always felt fleeting and unreal. I actually feel like I'm with you now, not as if I'm going to float off or fade away into nothingness."

He kissed her and held her tighter still; if this dance required them to swap partners, he was having none of it.

"What have you been reading me?" asked Alice.

"*Dracula* and *Rebecca*. I told you that a couple of days ago. Why?" asked Robert, not entirely surprised by the sudden interrogation; it was so very Alice to go in random conversational directions. The thought of normal Alice interaction gave him a simple joy that he had taken for granted.

"There's a costume ball in *Rebecca* but it's nothing like this. This is far more Gothic and extravagant," said Alice, eyeing him carefully through her mask. She briefly glanced over his shoulder and realised that there were a few men in Phantom masks or dressed as the Red Death or as a triumphant Don Juan.

"I may have accidentally left the soundtrack of *Phantom of the Opera* playing instead of someone reading the book," said Robert, as the musicians began to play a piece that greatly resembled something from the musical.

Alice laughed, her eyes sparkling. "You've been singing the Phantom's bit though. And if I spot Gerald Butler, I'll know you went for the film version."

"I would never," Robert said with mock indignation.

"You have though, otherwise the demon would be the Phantom and you would be Raoul, Vicomte de Changy."

"You might just think Christine should be with the Phantom," Robert suggested, a mischievous smirk playing upon his lips.

"Hmm, that's possible I guess, but I'm not sure that the allure of dangerous and mysterious would outweigh the fact the Phantom was a murderer," said Alice, quite seriously. "Especially as I think the attraction is mainly created by the musical. The novel and probably the old movies were intended to be horrors. A monster inside and out, albeit one that might have been nicer had anyone shown poor Erik any kindness in the beginning. At least you can argue that Dracula killed for survival."

"I can see this becoming one of *those* topics. Like *Dracula* and all the adapt..."

"Don't even. I've warned you before – this is not a subject with which to tease me, cos one day, it will end in blood."

Robert laughed and spun her around, admiring the grand ballroom. He could feel the occasional draft as fellow dancers swept by, as well as the heat from the low-burning candles and Alice's breath soft against his skin.

"So this is what it's like being in your head?" he teased, gently.

"Sorta. It's not usually this relaxed or elaborate."

"It feels so real."

"It is, kind of. It's like a dream, but more. Maybe a bit like V. R. with physical effects. I have no idea how to explain it."

"And why did I have to drink some horrible dream slime to be here?" he asked, twirling her out and in again.

"Because I need you," Alice whispered. "It's going to get crazy and painful and when the demon realises that I actually am going to destroy his wraith, he's going to try a lot of things to make me fail, and honestly, if I'm here alone, I just might. 'Cos I am really, really tired."

"'I need you' is all you had to say," said Robert, looking into her troubled brown eyes. "You look like a beautiful Disney princess."

Alice could not help the broad, shy smile from lighting up her face. "And you are my hero," said Alice, kissing him.

"How long do we have?" Robert asked, strangely aware that he was somewhere he really should not be.

"Just until Sam finds the source." She melted against the touch of his hand against her neck, his fingers brushing away wisps of hair, before leaning in for a kiss.

"Scared?" he asked gently, as he pulled away.

"Terrified," Alice admitted. "I think I've been hiding it quite well, but yes, I am, and I have been, scared. Scared of being trapped in here, of losing my mind, of giving up, and of the pain I have to return to."

"You don't have to go through any of it alone. You've got me, and Onion, and a lot of others who care about you," Robert said, holding her close.

"Are you scared?" asked Alice.

"Only of losing you. Everything else will be fine," Robert replied, confidently. He moved his right hand up from her waist to the upper middle of her back, and gently lowered her backward into a graceful dip, before he pulled her up again.

"So, does real Alice know how to dance like this?"

"No idea, but probably not," said Alice with a laugh. "This is all from watching movies, so yeah, I think I could follow if I was being lead properly, but who could say. I guess if I'm really bad, I'll just stand on your toes again."

"You want to try? My parents hold a masquerade every Halloween."

"Seriously?"

"Yeah, Halloween brings out the crazy in some people. Honestly, my parents at Halloween makes me think of *Carpe Jugulum*."

Alice laughed. "I'm almost sold on that. Definitely different costumes though."

"Well, I shall ask you again, properly, when we're back in the real world."

"It would be easy to just hide in here," said Alice, biting her lip, the fear beginning to settle in as the beating bass began to get louder.

"It would. But even if we could fool ourselves for some of the time, we'd also know it wasn't real a lot of the time. And we appear to be surrounded by a lot of demons," said Robert, suddenly noticing that the grotesque faces were no longer masks. Real teeth were snarling; real eyes of blazing orange, yellow and red were glaring at them; and real talons were pointed menacingly in their direction.

Alice lifted her head from against his chest and looked around the room. The beauty was slowly disintegrating into the monstrous and beastly. *The end is nigh*.

"Eh, I think the one actual demon has gone. These are possibly my metaphorical ones manifested as party-goers," Alice said shrugging, swallowing hard.

"I'd expect nothing less from you," said Robert, kissing her.

"Or they're a parting gift from the demon," Alice said, closing her eyes momentarily and willing a sword of some description to be hanging from a sash around her waist.

"Couldn't you just envision, I don't know, a machine gun or something?" asked Robert, as he watched a scabbard appear on her side.

"That would spoil the immersion. It might also be a bit too much; this is beginning to fall apart as it is, and something too out of place might make this shatter too quickly," Alice said, watching carefully. "Besides, we might not need to fight those things. This is just in case. We should try to make it outside."

"Have you ever used a sword before?" he asked.

"Have you?" she returned.

"Of course I have. I'm a Vampire."

Alice looked at him.

"… I'm a Vampire with very old parents of wealth and means. I've been forced to take all sorts of training in all sorts of things, including fencing," he amended.

"I had to ask," said Alice, with a smile. "No, but I figure, if I stick the pointy end in them, I'll be getting at least part of it right." She was watching the guests that were now demons out of the corner of her eye, noticing that they were closing in. "And I've watched a lot of films with swords and lightsabers in them." She pulled the sword from its sheath and gripped it lightly.

"Is that Elvish written on your blade?" asked Robert, unsheathing his own sword. It looked a little like Frostmourne.

"Ancient Greek," Alice said. "Jealous?"

"Not as long as this does the job," he replied.

"We just need to get outside before…" Alice's thoughts and words were interrupted by the sudden shock of the room shaking as if a giant earthquake had hit. The windows and mirrors shattered, and the chandeliers shook violently. Various items crashed and clattered to the ground; others smashed. A number of the seemingly female guest shrieked and screamed, but no one actually moved. There was no running, no terror, and Alice seemed to be the only one fighting the urge to duck or raise an arm above her to protect her head from potential falling debris. "Before this room – before my mind – collapses."

The room shook again.

Robert stood at her back, and the demons started to lunge.

Chapter 56

It was hardly an epic sword battle given that they were the only ones with swords, but it was nonetheless hard going to slash and hack their way to the balcony. What the demons lacked in weapons, they made up for in numbers, biting and scratching whenever they could to prevent Alice and Robert from escaping.

"Eww," said Alice, as blood sprayed and splashed across her face. It was slightly cooler than she had been expecting; more viscous and pungent too. She ripped the mask off, not that it helped much, and Robert did the same. "I can't see." She allowed her glasses to slip down her nose slightly, alternately peering over the top of the frames and through the blood splattered lenses. She slashed wildly, knowing that she would not hit Robert and at worse would do slightly more damage to herself than she was enduring from the grasping talons.

"It's okay, I'll take point," said Robert, gently manoeuvring so that she was now facing towards the back as he slashed a path to the broken windows.

Shrieks and screams pierced the air, limbs and heads were flying along with viscera in different shades of red and green. Robert was kicking the bodies away as best he could before they dropped, ensuring that the way was a little easier to navigate for Alice. Glass and bone crunched under foot, and fires were beginning to break out where the candles had fallen from the sconces and onto unmoving bodies, curtains and other flammable furnishings. Cracks had begun to appear in the walls, the ceiling and the floor, but there was not much further for them to go. Robert kicked a demon through the window and knocked out the most jagged looking shards with his elbow. Then he grabbed Alice's arm and pulled her outside, just as the chandeliers began to smash upon the floor, trapping some of the remaining demons.

"Now what?" asked Robert, looking between the lake several feet away from the third storey balcony and the fiery chaos behind them.

"You wake up," said Alice, simply, slicing off another hand that tried to pull her back inside.

"No. You first."

"We don't have time for this," said Alice, noticing how much slower her heartbeat was getting. She jammed the sword through the nearest demon and walked over to Robert. "Just wake up already!" she said, and promptly pushed him off the balcony.

She watched as he flailed in the air for a moment, a look of surprise on his face. Then he was gone. Alice took a deep breath, climbed up on to the stone railings, and closed her eyes before allowing herself to fall backwards into the gaping chasm between her and the grass below.

***

Alice felt overwhelmed as she crashed back into reality. Although she had had moments of clarity before, the presence of the wraith had made it seem like it was blanketed beneath a haze or behind a piece of dirty glass. Now, it was like breaking through the surface of a lake after being underwater for a bit too long, desperately gulping in air, assaulted by colours and smells and sounds and a lot of pain.

Robert was grabbing her by the hand, asking if she was okay, looking worried and relieved as he frantically tried to undo all the restraints; Sam, Julius, Stuart, Austin and the other Guardians were all chanting; Onion was yowling and snarling. The wraith was hovering above her, trapped in some kind of green light that was flickering and wavering as the chanters were losing their concentration. It was overwhelming chaos and not quite what Alice wanted upon her actual return. Alice's body was telling her to go to sleep, to black out to escape and deal with the pain, but the wraith was writhing above her and no one else seemed able to do anything other than momentarily contain it.

She suddenly sat up and pointed at the wraith, her eyes blazing angrily. She slowly closed her fist and the wraith began to squirm, eyes popping as if it were being choked to death. Everything hurt but there was no one else to destroy it and she refused to give it a chance to go back into her.

"Demon to woodlouse." The words might have come out as a whisper but they could not have carried more weight if they had been a screamed battle cry. Scared but furious, Alice was shaking with the determination that that thing would become her most hated little creature. It writhed and shrieked but the wraith stood no chance against her. With a sickening pop, the nekrofolis wraith became a woodlouse and Robert crushed it angrily underfoot. It was no more. "Useful after all," she said with a drained smile, before losing consciousness.

Chapter 57

Alice opened her eyes, tired and unable to see clearly, but she felt too drained to try and find her glasses. She thought she recognised the bedroom; it seemed warm, safe and comforting. The last time she had been in here, it had had a decidedly more male smell; now it was heady with the incense of lavender and sage, although there was a familiar scent of shampoo and deodorant. She shifted slightly, trying to prop herself into a slightly upright position. She stifled the cry of pain that moving caused, but was too tired to really think about what and why things were hurting.

"Hey," she said in a cracked voice, but with a smile as bright as she could manage. She could not see him clearly but she knew he was there and that was almost enough.

"Hey," he said, gently. He sounded incredibly relieved.

"Why are you all the way over there?" she asked, unable to stop herself from squinting in his general direction. She assumed he was sitting in his old computer chair, when he should have been on his old bed with her.

"Upon pain of death, was I to get in that bed with you," Robert said, perching on the edge of the mattress and taking her hand. "Actually, I forget the exact words used, but it amounted to the same kind of threat. I've been sleeping on the floor, next to you."

Her eyes glistened and her heart felt like it could burst; she really did love him so much. He helped her take a sip of water, and she swallowed painfully, wetting her broken lips. She took another sip before speaking. "Well, who are you more afraid of – them or me?"

"Definitely you...ish," he said smiling. "I just need to let them know you seem to be over the worst of it now."

"OK. But when I wake up, you better be next to me on this bed," she said, settling back down into the pillows and immediately falling asleep.

***

The following day was spent drifting in and out of consciousness and he held her next to him as much as possible, altering his body temperature so that he did not have to let go. Sometimes she would thrash about, her body hot and feverish; other times she would curl up and shiver with an icy chill. Her brow would constantly furrow and she would sometimes struggle against his embrace, and he did whatever she needed to let her know she was safe, until the nightmare finally gave way to restful sleep.

There was a gentle knock at the door, before it opened. "Come get some food," said Sam, sticking his head around the door. He looked at the harried Vampire and the sleeping Witch, glad that Alice was in a more restful state than the last time he had come in.

"I'm not hungry," Robert replied.

"She'll stick another spatula in your shoulder if you don't eat something; you know she'll be more concerned about you than herself when she wakes up," said Sam, knowing the Vampire was lying at least a little. "Besides, do you really think you won't be back in here to be the first thing she sees? She's safe and she's strong, and if she demanded that you take care of yourself while a wraith was attacking her, she would definitely demand you do it while she's recuperating on a bed... And don't make me tell on you. Besides, whatever Clive's cooking up smells really good."

Robert looked at Sam with a frown and glanced down

at Onion, who was curled up at the foot of the bed. Onion blinked slowly with a look that suggested he agreed with the Psychic. Robert sighed, rolled his eyes in annoyance, before slowly and carefully extricating himself from around Alice. She whimpered and moaned, her eyelids flickering as her brow furrowed. Robert paused but as she settled again, he allowed himself to be ushered into the kitchen, where Clive was serving up some Cajun jambalaya.

"I will admit, I do miss your cooking," said Robert, as he and Sam sat down at the table. Clive placed a bowl in front of each of them and they looked at him with suspicious eyes.

"There are no brains in it, at the moment," the chef said, holding up a Tupperware pot of brain bits. "Like I'd waste it on you guys."

"One sec," said Robert, spoon poised to taste. "How spicy is this?"

"At the moment, not very. Why?"

"Onion likes good food and your food is good," said Robert. He could not believe he was spoiling the cat on Alice's behalf. "Seriously, the cat is a connoisseur and I think he'd appreciate it." Sam and Clive looked at him. "Yeah, I never expected to be saying that either. To be fair, he is not your average cat."

"O-Kay," said Clive, putting a ladle aside for the cat. All things considered, it was not the weirdest request ever. He added his brain nuggets and a lot of extra chillies, stirred it and gave it five more minutes on the stove so that the meat was warmed through, before he took his own portion to the table. "How's she doing?"

"Okay I think. Getting there," Robert replied, cautiously. "She seems to be actually sleeping now, as opposed to just falling unconscious. The cuts seem to be healing up really well, although I'm pretty sure there will be some scars. Can't say other than that."

"Sam?" asked Clive. Although he had never met the Psychic prior to the previous day, the fact that Sam had landed on his doorstep with Alice, Robert and Onion was enough to mean that he was good people.

"As far as I can tell, she's recovering. There's nothing otherworldly involved now; it's all on how her psyche deals with it. I mean, I can help her if she asks for it, but nothing doing until then. This is outstanding, by the way," said Sam, waving his spoon towards his jambalaya appreciatively.

"Thanks," said Clive. "I gotta ask, how much of all I'm hearing is true?"

"What are you hearing?" asked Robert, forcing himself to eat. It was exceptionally good, but it just seemed wrong to enjoy food when Alice could not.

"Short version, that the Witch vanquished a wraith that was trying to take her to a demon that wanted to make her his Veil-destroying pet."

"Kinda, then," said Robert, smiling slightly. He was incredibly proud and impressed with Alice's powers and strength. He just wished something could have been done sooner. "She turned a wraith into a woodlouse which I then stomped on."

"Woodlouse?" asked Clive.

"Yeah, she really really doesn't like those things. She probably figured no one would feel sorry about killing a woodlouse." Robert quickly recapped the whole experience.

"I didn't know that was a valid method of getting rid of spirits, wraiths or demons," said Clive, bemused. It was certainly an impressive, if highly unusual feat.

"I'm not sure anyone does," said Sam, shaking his head in amazement. It was certainly nothing he or his great grandmother had heard of. "It was quick thinking on Alice's part. I don't think you could actually do that to a demon, unless you could force the demon into a woodlouse first, but for wraiths it's obviously a thing. Don't think it would work on a spirit either, not that you should need to get that creative to get a spirit to depart."

"Consider me corrected," said Clive good-naturedly.

"I have a question though," said Sam, looking uncomfortable. He was pretty sure he already knew the answer but this was definitely something that he wanted confirmed. "Was Alice still bound when she turned that wraith?"

Robert looked at his food. "I'd undone the straps," he mumbled, not particularly wanting to lie to his friends or Alice's.

"Not what I meant," said Sam, pressing gently, even though the Vampire's evasive reply was answer enough.

"I know," Robert said, running a hand through his hair. He glanced around, as if to ensure that they were alone and mentally checking whether they had warded Clive's house as well as the apartment, so that nothing that had not been invited inside could see or hear them. "And I know I can trust you guys, but it is weird how this stuff is getting out, and I don't really want anyone knowing that yes, Alice still had the binding ribbons on her when she transmorphed the wraith. And that at one point, she kinda set the bed on fire. Just for a moment, but still."

"I'll be damned," said Clive, impressed.

"No one else knows?" asked Sam, his brow furrowed. Whilst he did not know the specifics of the book Alice was working on, he knew that her sole purpose was to provide tools to non-supernatural humans to battle supernatural threats – including the ability to bind a Witch. He was not worried about Alice going Dark, but he was concerned that she had broken magic that should have kept her powers contained.

"Onion probably noticed. I don't know that anyone else did. Austin, two other Guardians and the Library know about the fire. No one else. I don't think Alice is aware of either event to be honest."

"Caulson obviously didn't. Quite sure there would be more chatter about Alice if she had," said Sam. The mention of green fire stirred some deep rooted memory that he could not reach.

"I took them off before she entered the room, although

to be fair, it's not like the bindings were made by someone well practised in magic, so maybe if another Witch had made them, nothing would have happened," said Robert. None of them were particularly convinced. "You think she's the one who's been talking?"

"Makes sense. She's the only one who isn't a friend of Alice's or part of the Library, and she's a member of the Pale Moon; you can bet they've been after as many details as possible. A Witch I met on the way up said there were a lot of covens interested in recruiting Alice, and none more so than the Pale Moon."

"I'm sure she'll be thrilled," said Clive drily, remembering her lack of enthusiasm when discussing covens one evening. "So, I guess that makes you the Witch and the Vampire then."

"What?" said Robert, surprised. Clive had not mentioned anything to him before about hearing more specific chatter.

"The Witch and the Vampire that everyone's been talking about. I mean, obviously you were the two in regards to the whole relationship, but I guess given everything, it also puts you inline for the whole vague prophecy honour too," said Clive. "Female Witch, Vampire husband. Presumably you're going to destroy the rest of us now."

"Oh sure. World domination has always been at the top of my list. Not to mention Alice's." Robert rolled his eyes. "Can you imagine? Honestly, it's just stupid."

"Sure, to us it is. But not everyone knows you. All they know is that there is a Vampire in a relationship with an extremely powerful Witch. As far as they're concerned, that's part of the prophecy come to pass. The next bit is bound to follow," said Clive, deciding that another drink was needed. He looked to his guests and Robert shook his head.

"So, this is a genuine, across the board, supernatural concern? Not just the Vamps and Witches? Have you been hearing this too?" Robert asked, turning to Sam.

"Variations of. From dead people mostly. But the truth of it is that one in a hundred prophecies is actually accurate, and there are two types; the ones that can be prevented and the ones that can't. That a Witch and a Vampire are in a relationship is happening; demonic apocalypse, might not. No one seems to know the exact wording of this supposed prophecy so who can possibly know?"

"Can't you? Know I mean?"

"Sorta," said Sam, nodding his thanks as the Zombie passed him another beer. "The future is always in motion. Most of the time, things change. A few don't. I do know there is a lot more to this prophecy than the two aspects people seem to be focussing on." He took a long drink and pondered again how something so small could have life-changing impact. "Everyone assumed that the Witch would be or would go Dark. Hopefully Alice has proven that's not the case."

"Let's hope," said Robert drily, pushing the empty bowl away from him, anxious to get back to Alice. He did not like to speculate on the prophecy and the impact it was beginning to have on his life. His idea of the perfect life might not be quite as sheltered and secluded as Alice's, but it was certainly one that did not involve being the subject of attention and gossip. "Anyway, I'm gonna relieve Onion and try to get a bit more sleep."

***

He woke up to find her looking at him. Her face was pale, accentuated by dark shadows, but her eyes were brighter than they had been for the past three days. The afternoon sun was streaming through the gap in the curtains.

"Hey," she said, touching his face.

"Hey. I've missed you."

"I'm back. Are you OK?"

"I am now," he said, tenderly stroking her hair.

"Is everyone else?"

"Yes. Your friend Sam's been using Clive's couch; Stuart has been checking in every day, as has Julius. Kathie's been asking if she can speak to you, but I told her you're not quite up to it yet."

"Good," said Alice. She was not ready to face the wider world just yet. Her stomach rumbled and for the first time in what seemed like months (although she knew it was only days), she actually wanted food. "Please may I have some soup or something?"

"Of course. Anything you want," Robert said, throwing the covers off his side of the bed. "I'm pretty sure Clive has some vegetables I can blend up."

Alice smiled weakly. "You can let Sam and Onion in to see me, if they want to."

"Onion's already here. He's been sleeping on the dresser the last few nights." Robert decided to pick the cat up and plonk him onto the bed, having the feeling that the stubborn fur-ball wanted to be next to her but was being too cat to admit it. Onion had been sleeping at the bottom of the bed, but the struggling Alice had been doing in her sleep had caused him to retreat to the dresser. He also handed Alice her glasses, before helping her to sit up. "I'll be back in a minute."

"Not always such a horror, are you puddin'," she said softly, resting her hand on Onion's side, as he curled up on her lap, carefully avoiding the spots where he thought they had applied bandages and plasters. Although a lot of the physical damage had healed up, there were still certain wounds that would take a long time yet. "Hey Sam," she said, as the door opened again.

"Hey. If you wanted me to visit this much, you could have called." Sam pulled the door to, before perching on the side of the bed and taking her bandaged hand.

"Next time, maybe," she joked. "Who called you this time?"

"No one. Well, the Doc did, but I was already on my way.

A source gave me a message."

"Are you doing OK?" Alice asked, looking at him in concern.

"Yes. Although you should hardly be worrying about me," Sam replied with a smile. "Or any of us, really. You need to focus on yourself a bit more."

"Just cos it latched itself on to me doesn't mean that you weren't all hurt in some way." She shrugged, feeling pain strike like lightning throughout her body. "Besides, I always worry about my friends."

"Well, try not to, because everyone is fine; well, no one else got hurt, and yeah, we'll all treat you like you're made of glass for the next week or so, but mostly, we're all just relieved you're getting back to "normal"."

She tried to punch him for actually air quoting "normal", but did not have the strength since her body still felt like it was full of lead and he grinned at her.

"You're not looking your best, but I am really glad to see you."

"Thanks. I've missed you too," she said. "And thank you for coming to help me."

"Of course. I told you that I would. I'm just so sorry that I couldn't get here any sooner."

"I know you got here as soon as you could. So. What was it?" she asked.

"Tiny sliver of some kind of black glass," Sam replied, knowing that she was asking about the anchor that had bound the wraith to her. "It pretty much dissolved in the salt water though, so can't say much more than that."

"Bugger, that's not very helpful."

Sam laughed, unable to hide his amusement at Alice's reaction. "Not really. And I know you have a million more questions, but now is not the time. You need to rest," Sam said gently.

"But I need answers. I need to know the hows and whys and the ways to stop it happening again..." said Alice, tears forming in her eyes, her voice cracking slightly.

"I know," Sam said gently, "but not now. All I'm gonna say for now is that you are completely demon free. Nothing was left behind. Believe me, the big guns were called in to double check that." He did not know the exact details, but Stuart had informed him that several members of the Fallen had been to see her as she slept.

"It had something to with the book launch, I'm almost sure of it. That woman... and that horrible perfume..." Her breath started to catch and her eyes began to dart around wildly. She could not keep the rising panic at bay, as the memories of the dinner party began to merge into ones of the wraith and the visions it showed her, and she flinched away from Sam's hand.

"It's OK. Shh, just leave it for another day," said Sam, concern in his eyes. "The rest of them will kill me if I let you keep on with this. I know you feel like you need all this info to help you process, but you don't. Just rest for a few more days first, okay?"

"You lot are too violent, that's the problem," she said with reluctant resignation. In all honesty, she knew she was not ready for that conversation yet and she definitely did not want to relive the experience.

"We'll talk about this another time, when Stuart and Julius are around too, if we need to."

"We do. There's no way that pretending this didn't happen is healthy. Besides, other people will be talking, cos they always do," Alice said.

"Don't worry about it. All you're to do is rest, okay?"

"Fine," said Alice, unable to stifle a big yawn. She closed her eyes for a moment, shook her head and then looked at Sam again. "Seriously, thanks for coming Sam. I'm glad you're here."

"I told you, any time." He gave her a quick and gentle hug.

"And if you're going to the Library, reassure them that

they definitely did the right thing. Mostly."

"Will do," promised Sam, shaking his head in amused disbelief. "Now get some more sleep or whatever. I'll tell Robert to hold off on the soup, okay?"

"Okay, I might," she yawned again "just do that."
Her head drooped slightly and her hand rested listlessly on Onion, as Sam slowly and quietly shut the door behind him.

"She really is doing a lot better now," Sam said as he entered the kitchen. His nose wrinkled in disgust and he quickly hid the expression before Robert could see it.

"She fell asleep?" Robert asked, looking up from the large pan he was stirring on the stove.

"Yeah."

"I guess she still needs it. And at least it gives us time to make a better soup," he said, looking at the disgusting, hot, grey mulch he had managed to create.

***

"You do know that Sam is just a friend, right?" Alice said, as Robert entered the room with a large cup full of soup. He looked slightly taken aback, not realising that his feelings were quite so obvious to her. "That smells good."

"I know," said Robert slightly defensively, placing the mug on the small table beside the bed. "That I don't need to be jealous. And that it smells good."
Alice smiled and shook her head wryly. "In fact, you should be thanking him, because I only went on that dating website cos he kinda told me I should."

"I'm not, like, properly, jealous..."

"There's no need to be any jealous. You're the one I love."

"I know. I love you too. It's just what happened. I'm a bit overprotective at the moment."

"My hero," she said, trying to pull him in for a kiss. She did not have the strength, so Robert leaned in and gave her peck on the lips. "And I mean that. I'm here because of you." She knew he did not feel that he had done anything.

"Well, eat your soup," said Robert, deciding not to argue with her. Just because he did not feel like her hero, did not mean that Alice did not believe that he was. "And try and get some more sleep."

"I almost feel like I'm fed-up of sleeping," she said, slowly sipping at the mug of soup. "Clive had roasted pumpkins?"

"You kinda dozed off for an hour. I had time to... well, I got Clive to make soup." Robert was not entirely sure what he had made, but it certainly had not been soup. Maybe just 'grey'. Alice smiled. "Where is he? I need to thank him for letting us stay here and for being a good friend."

"He knows. And he has been to check on you; you've just been asleep each time."

"How rude of me," Alice said, looking mournful.

"I'll maybe let you get out of bed after the next sleep and you can shuffle out to thank him then."

"Why are we here instead of at home?"

"Because you couldn't stand and Dr Caulson said that your wounds would heal better if you could soak in some special herbal bath. I don't quite know what was in it, but it has been working and Sam and Onion said it was fine. It smelt a lot better than the dream tea I had to drink. It probably would have tasted better too."

"Yeah, I did think that all the cuts and scratches were looking far better than they had any right to be," Alice said, pulling up a shirt sleeve and examining her arms. The original scars did not look any different, but there would be new ones soon enough and there was the strange looking burn on her hand. Something about it made her very uncomfortable and she tried to pull the shirt sleeve down further to cover it. "Thank you for being there. And I'll see if I can fix the taste of it when I'm able to."

"You need to fix your handwriting so that people can read it," he teased, smiling at her indignant pout.

"Most of the time, I write for myself, not others," Alice replied. "I wonder if I could put some kind of spell on my writing so that if you had permission to read it, then it would appear "more legible"." She pulled a face as she air-quoted the last two words.

"Perhaps, but you're still on bed-rest and no magic, remember?"

"But if we go home, I'll need to make an amulet and put wards on the door, maybe start growing some angelica or betony, devise some kind of weaponry that can be used against demons…"

"Hey, calm down, shh, it's okay," said Robert, reaching for her hand. He tried not to be hurt as she unconsciously flinched, although she did not pull away. He knew it was going to take her some time to get used to everything being okay again. Physically, she was healing well, but even though she was spending more time awake, she would not yet speak of what happened. All he could do was wait. "Sam, Julius and Stuart have already put protective wards in the building and our apartment, and I will get you whatever seeds and shrubs you want for us to plant. Everything else has to wait until you're better."

"I am better," Alice replied stubbornly.

"I'll consider you better when Julius stops bringing twig water for you to drink."

Alice could not stop the broad grin spreading across her face.

"What?" asked Robert, bemused.

"I was beginning to think I was the only one who felt that way about those herbal teas."

"They all taste like twigs in hot water to me, even though I have a much more sophisticated palette than you." He kissed her cheek again. "They do work though."

"Yup. Got to give them that much," she said with a yawn. She put the empty mug on the side, and snuggled back into him, before falling asleep again.

Chapter 58

It was a lot like getting over having the flu, although it seemed to take less time to get back on her feet. She had promised to take it easy until her friends deemed her energy levels "normal", and she did not like to go back on her word. When she had had enough of sitting in the apartment, Sam took her to the library, where she would sit in one of the higher reading rooms, curled up on some cushions in the bay window seats, speeding her way through *The Hobbit, Lord of the Rings, Rebecca*, the *Robert Hunter* series and various Stephen King novels. It was fine, but it was also annoying when the whole thing seemed like a mystery that needed solving. *Why her? Why now?*

Not that that was the worst after-effect of the possession. She had spent about two weeks in bed, spending about 75% of her time sleeping and trying not to dream. Then there had been another week of not doing magic and resting up, which had been fine, and she was not particularly bothered by the multiple new scars on her body. The scabs had been irritating and she had been far more conscious about her clothing to ensure that the materials did not catch or reveal too much, but overall, they had not caused her much concern. It was the psychological wounding that was the worst.

She felt constantly unclean and fearful; if a wisp of material or spider-web or even a cat happened to brush against her unexpectedly, it took every fibre of her being to not blow it up with a fire spell. She was also finding it very hard to be in crowded places and she could barely look at or talk to any of her friends. It was not simply that she thought they might see how tainted she was now, but that she could not always keep the vivid images of what the wraith had threatened at bay. Since she had left her bed, she had hardly been able to touch Robert, almost afraid that if she did, she would cause him to blister and bleed in agonising pain before disintegrating in front of her. And she had been unable to express why.

Kathie had rung, being relatively kind, supportive and sympathetic to Alice, whilst also making it known that she was unhappy about being left out of it and unable to help; Robert, on the other hand, was treated to a "full-on bollocking" as Kathie felt less inclined to be gentle with him. Phone calls from both sets of parents had also been fielded, but Alice still felt too drained to deal with all of the worms such cans presented.

Alice had also eventually read *The Devil Possesses*. A copy, wrapped up in brown paper and tied with string, had been left in her cubbyhole in the staff room. The Library had not been too pleased and kept forcing the book out of her hands, until Alice quietly asked Julius to take it into her reading room, with all its wards and protections. It had been a perturbing read to say the least. She appreciated the Library trying to protect her, but she did not think it would have had (nor had it) any effect on her. It was quite a weak attempt at an influencing and although the description of the book's "heroine" was not of her, there was no mistaking the fact it was supposed to be her. *No wonder Robert didn't want me to read it.* It also explained Houseman's weird behaviour and it supported her theory that the wraith was tied up with the book launch somehow.

"Here," Alice said, placing the stapled papers on Dr Anthonys desk. "I think I covered everything without being needlessly graphic."

"You've written a report about being possessed?" he said, briefly scanning the pages.

"I thought it might help."

"Did it?"

"It might do," said Alice, not quite meeting his eyes. "At least if it happens again, someone will know they aren't alone in experiencing it."

Stuart sighed, not sure if it was his place to say anything. "You are not alone Alice. You have people that care a great deal about you."

"I know. May I sit here for a while?" Alice asked, looking at the fire.

"Of course," said Stuart, watching her with almost fatherly concern.

"Thank you," Alice said, taking a seat in one of the big plush armchairs. She stared into the flames, feeling a strange pull, a connection, something akin to understanding as she watched the smoke and the heat and the colours. "Why do you have the fire on?"

"The temperature doesn't change down here. It's always cold unless the fire is on. I'm not sure it's ever gone out, to be honest," he said.

There was a knock at the door frame and Robert cautiously entered once Stuart waved him inside. He looked at the room with a look of approving admiration, understanding how Alice could find potential refuge in the Head Librarian's office. There was a comforting warmth and a sense of security, and Robert was quite sure that no one would find their way down there without a great deal of practise or help from the Library. He gave Stuart a nod of gratitude and took the seat beside his broken-looking Witch.

"You okay?"

"Sure," said Alice, wondering if the flames were really following her fingers, and if she could really see a tinge of green in their orange light.

"Please talk to me," Robert said. He did not really expect her to, but he had to keep trying. Judging by the pieces of paper he had collected, she was at least starting to process her possession. But writing a scientific observation of her experience was a long way from talking about what she had actually felt and experienced.

"Nothing to talk about," Alice said, wriggling her fingers, drawing the infinity symbol over and over again, almost like she was playing with a sparkler.

"There is. You know there is," Robert said patiently, as they both tried to ignore her flinching at his touch. He took her hand in his. "I read your report."

"What?" Alice looked up at him in shock. "I... it wasn't for you to read." She withdrew her hand and pulled the sleeves of her hoodie down over them, and went back to staring at the fire.

"Well you left a copy in the printer. Rupert at least thinks its a short story or something, from the cover page – I don't think he read it." Robert nodded at Stuart as the Head Librarian carefully excused himself. "I'm sorry."

"Whatever." Alice shrugged, trying to ignore everything.

"No, not whatever. You need to talk about this. No one's expecting you to be okay, but you need to talk to me, at least a little. Why do you keep flinching? Am I hurting you? Are you still in pain?"

"No, it's... not... it's not... I... There's no physical pain," Alice stammered. "And it's not you....Damnit, you have no idea," she said, bursting into tears. How was she supposed to say that she wanted to kiss him; that she wanted and needed his touch, but that every time she closed her eyes, she could see flashes of maggots, jagged flesh and the myriad tortures inflicted to desecrate his perfect body and soul?

"Then tell me," he said, taking her hand again.

"You don't want to know," Alice said, trying to focus on the fire, wishing that he would stop asking.

"Probably not," Robert replied honestly, gently touching her face and forcing her to look at him. "But tell me anyway – you've been trying to deal with this by yourself for too long."

"You read it – isn't that enough?" she said, angrily averting her gaze.

"No," said Robert, firmly. "It isn't. It sounds horrific and terrifying and painful, but we both know you left so much out of it. And those things you haven't talked about are the ones that make you flinch and cry, and I know I can't fix it, but maybe I can help, if you would just let me..."

Alice sniffed, desperately trying to hold back further tears, her heart breaking... She shut her eyes tightly and with absolute resignation whispered "Because sometimes I see the things they showed me and I can hear it and smell it and feel it and it's not fair that they're trying to ruin something good. And I know it's not real, that it was never real, that I would smite them all before they could do such things, but it's still what I see. You touch me, and I see you... and I also see how they left you after torturing you and killing you and just... just doing horrible horrible things. Everyone I love, but most of all, you... and I couldn't stop it. Of course I couldn't stop it – it was my fault. Everyone dead because of me..."

"It wasn't real. And it's not your fault. None of it is your fault. They don't need a reason for doing horrible things – they just want you to blame yourself to add to your torment. No one that loves you would ever blame you."

She went silent for a moment, and let out a small sigh before looking up at him. "Am I being selfish, staying with you when I could be putting you and the world in danger?"

"No," Robert replied immediately. "Because I'm not letting you go. Maybe it makes *us* selfish, but that blame isn't yours alone. Besides, I don't think it matters. Maybe us being together is some kind of indicator for them, but you have their attention regardless; they won't stop just because we're not together. It just gives them more ammunition."

Alice sniffed slightly, and considered his words carefully. He was probably right, which was a small comfort. "I don't want this. I don't want to be afraid of that happening again. Or worse. I don't even want to think about it now in case somehow it triggers something I can't control."

"We're in this together. And you're much stronger than

you give yourself credit for. And honestly, I think even if your powers were to get a little out of control, you're not going to do any real damage. You're too conscious of others for that. You try to do what's right and you have so much love, and all of that makes you strong – it's what makes you stronger as a Witch. And I love you for all of it."

"I love you too," she said, stroking his face. Tears fell from her eyes. "And I'm so sorry. I want so badly just for things to be normal again, but I can't…"

"It's okay. It'll be okay. Whenever you're ready, you know that," he said, gently. "Just sit here with me, okay?"

"Okay," she said.

"I've booked a holiday for us," Robert continued, his voice low and comforting as he kept his arm around her. "We need to get away and we haven't really done the whole vacation thing of just the two of us escaping from our lives. Clive will come and feed Onion, so for two weeks, we can just leave all of this behind."

"Where are we going?" she asked, curious.

"I'm going to keep it a surprise, because it'll infuriate you," he teased, kissing her head.

"I hate you," she said, smiling.

"I know," he said with a grin. "Don't worry, I'll give you a list of things to pack."

Epilogue

Flying to Nairobi had been somewhat stressful and the small flight to the Masai Mara was terrifying, but as soon as Alice was hanging out of the windows to take photographs of all the nearby animals, she decided it was definitely worth it. They had a quick clean-up and lunch at the camp, before going out on a short game drive to see whatever the Mara would offer up.

For the next twelve days, they would leave early in the morning (at about 0550) in a specially designed jeep with a heavy duty canopy at the back that Robert could hide under when necessary, while Alice spent her time desperate to get "the perfect shot" and enjoying every second out in the Masai Mara. Depending on which reserve they visited, depended on whether they went back to camp for lunch or parked up in a shaded spot for a couple of hours, so that they could make the most of their time finding different animals for Alice to photograph. And there plenty of those amidst the trees, long grasses and dusty ravines. Leopards, hyenas, cheetahs, zebras, hippopotamuses, crocodiles, baboons, gazelle, vultures, warthogs, kingfishers and eagles, and of course, wildebeest.

With it being the end of September, they had arrived at the time of the Great Migration, an annual event which includes the crossing of the River Mara, where millions of wildebeest attempt to swim across the crocodile infested water to reach lush new grass as they follow the rain clouds to the next food source. From a photographers point of view, Alice was somewhat disappointed not to see any crocodiles taking out any members of the herd (or fighting with hippos), but from the nature-loving side, she was a little relieved that the animals she saw made it across. They also saw elephants, giraffes, lions, rhinos with an armed guard, water buffalo, monkeys, fire ants and a whole assortment of other mammals, birds, insects and occasionally, reptiles. Alice was loving every minute of it, especially as she did not have to think about anything. It was blissful to live in each and every moment, to chase the shot and nothing else, surrounded by fresh air, warmth and the comforting presence of the man she loved.

They would return to camp after the blazingly colourful sunsets and relax for an hour or so after a delicious meal, before getting possibly the best night's sleep either of them had ever experienced. As far as Alice was concerned, she had never been so happy and at peace in all of her life. The thought of going home and the idea that the memories she had not needed to deal with might come back with a vengeance, felt like an added incentive to not return. But she knew that they could not stay there forever and she did miss Onion.

"This has been the most amazing experience ever," she said, grabbing a blanket and sitting on the wicker chair next to Robert. It was their last night and she wanted to enjoy being out under the stars and next to the fire for as long as she could keep her eyes open. It was too dark to see now, but their tent overlooked a small creek and they had often seen wildebeests and zebras grazing on the plains across the water. "Thank you so much for this."

"I think it would make a good honeymoon destination," said Robert, casually. He twirled the velvet box in one of the many pockets of his cargo pants.

"I'm not sure," she said thoughtfully.
He looked at her in surprise.

"Don't get me wrong," she said quickly, grabbing his hand and smiling. "I have loved every second and I definitely want to come back. I just think maybe it's a bit too... tiring for a honeymoon."

"You're incorrigible," he teased, although he had to

admit she had a point. Happy and contented as they were when they got back to the tent, she had not been able to keep eyes open long enough to engage in any nocturnal activities. "However, I think it would be less tiring if you weren't so afraid of missing your shot – whatever that might be – so that we could have actually slept in once in a while."

She stuck her tongue out at him, and smiled before sighing, contented yet wistful. "I kinda don't want to go back. Travelling across these wide open spaces, blue skies, warm sun on my face, breeze in my hair, camera round my neck and my hand in yours, coming upon so many amazing animals. Even when it rains, it's been magical. I've never felt so content. I'd like to think those moments are what Heaven feels like." She could feel the weight of his gaze, and she blushed. "Maybe that's a bit OTT, but it is how I feel."

"I'm just thinking about how lucky I am and how beautiful you've looked out here," Robert said. He might not have been as enthusiastic as Alice about all the driving about and essentially seeing the same animals several times, but to see Alice so completely and purely happy more than made up for his own moments of boredom. He also had to agree, there was something magical about the place and if this was a vision of what Heaven could be with Alice, then he would take it.

"Because it's hard not to be happy – I like the fresh air, I love seeing these animals in their natural environment; the food and accommodation have been amazing; and I've done all this with the one guy I love most in the entire universe. Even I can't not look beautiful out here. It's been perfect," Alice said, earnestly, eyes shining.

"Hope this doesn't ruin things then," he said.

She looked at him, bemused, her eyes widening and smile becoming even brighter as he knelt down on one knee and presented a small, black box. Hands trembling slightly, she opened it and looked at the white gold band set with two small diamonds either side of a beautiful, dark blue star sapphire. It was simple, elegant, and made of stars; her idea of the perfect engagement ring. "It's beautiful," she said.

He chuckled softly. *She was so smart, and yet...* "Alice Elizabeth Andrews, will you marry me?"

"Yes! Of course yes," she said "Like you even need to..."

"Yeah, but I did," he said, grinning. He placed the ring on her finger and kissed her, feeling almost as happy as she looked. He almost could not look at her because her joy was so blindingly bright. From out of nowhere, the rain began to fall. He looked up at the clear night sky, so pure and devoid of ambient light that he could see the Milky Way. But he was still getting drenched. "Really?" he said, giving her a long hard kiss before pulling her into the tent.

"Sorry, guess I'm just that happy," she said, laughing. "But at least a cold rain wakes you up a bit. And besides," she said, standing on tiptoes to help him to pull the wet jumper over his head "it *is* a very effective method of getting you to take your clothes off."

Printed in Great Britain
by Amazon